The Experts Praise
Deranged
by Jacob Stone

"*Deranged* is a dark and different serial killer novel that will haunt the reader long after the book is closed and back on the shelf. Author Jacob Stone transfixes us with dread, and something more. He has the rare capacity to startle. Read if you dare."
—John Lutz

"*Deranged* is a fascinating and exciting blend of misdirection, topsy-turvy, and violence."
—Reed Farrel Coleman

"Gutsy and written with such casual grace, as if the author were sitting across the bar from me, telling me the story, *Deranged* just might be one of the most compelling, thrilling and truth be told, at times look-away-from-page-frightening serial killer novels I've read in a long, long time."
—Vincent Zandri

"Los Angeles has seldom seen such grisly fun. It's James Ellroy meets Alfred Hitchcock in a bloody, yet bizarrely humorous romp on the psychotic side of the street."
—Paul Levine

"This series comes out of the gate swinging with the first offering, *Deranged*. Morris Brick's determination and grit make him a great hero for a thriller series. The surprise twists really kept me engaged. I hope to see Brick have a long shelf life."
—Outofthegutteronline.com

Also by Jacob Stone

Deranged
Crazed

Malicious

A Morris Brick Thriller

Jacob Stone

LYRICAL UNDERGROUND
Kensington Publishing Corp.
www.kensingtonbooks.com

First Electronic Edition: March 2018
eISBN-13: 978-1-5161-0182-5
eISBN-10: 1-5161-0182-0

First Print Edition: March 2018
ISBN-13: 978-1-5161-0185-6
ISBN-10: 1-5161-0185-5

Printed in the United States of America

for David Kanell

Chapter 1

The killer sat naked in front of the mirror and put in the cosmetic contact lenses to change his eyes from brown to blue. Nine months ago, he'd shaved his head, and since then used a razor each week to keep up his bald appearance. He now carefully attached a hairpiece to his scalp that made him look as if he had neatly trimmed sandy-brown hair. It was an expensive hairpiece, and the killer was pleased with the way it altered his appearance. After taking a moment to admire the hairpiece, he glued on a matching goatee. Earlier that morning he had shaved off his eyebrows, and he now glued on fake ones that were the same color as the hairpiece and goatee. He had other fake eyebrows that matched his natural hair color. Later when he removed his disguise, he would use those until his eyebrows grew back.

He put his face through a series of exaggerated contortions. According to his reflection, his fake hair held in place and looked natural. His entire adult life the killer had dressed casually. Chinos, either a button-down plaid shirt with sleeves rolled up to his elbows or a polo shirt, and always running shoes. He couldn't remember the last time he wore a suit. But when he left later today he would complete his disguise with an elegant Versace pin-stripe, button-down tan shirt, a muted yellow tie, and a pair of calfskin Italian loafers that also matched the color of his fake hair. Finally, he would slip on fake glasses and a $14,000 Hublot watch that he had bought specifically for this occasion.

The killer got up and wandered over to the kitchen area, and used his Nespresso machine to brew a single serving of caramel-flavored coffee. Right now his target was in a Pilates class. He had plenty of time before he'd have to leave. As he sipped his coffee, he was amazed at how calm he felt. He had spent a year of planning and preparing—really two when you considered that he was forced to throw away a year's worth of plans because of that meddlesome Morris Brick. Now his vision was so close to coming to fruition that he could taste it. He smiled as he thought of how it tasted even sweeter than the caramel-flavored coffee.

The killer's mind drifted to thoughts of everything he had done since finalizing his plans six months ago. It was remarkable when he added it all up. Of course, he wasn't finished yet. There was still so much more to do, but if things worked out later that afternoon, tomorrow his masterpiece would be unveiled. People wouldn't see it in its entirety at once since it would take ten days to play out, but once completed it would be absolutely stunning. Breathtaking. The world would never forget it. Nor would the city of Los Angeles ever be the same.

Art of this magnitude didn't come cheap. You had to bleed for it, or in this case, have others bleed. So far the killer had had to take four lives. He didn't enjoy killing these people, but it was necessary and he had murdered them quietly without anyone noticing. Soon thousands more lives were going to be taken, and those deaths weren't going to be so quiet. He stood spellbound as he thought about how all these people were going to die, and how Morris Brick was going to be thrust into the center of the carnage.

A sensation below his waist caused him to glance downward, and he realized that these thoughts had given him an erection.

Chapter 2

Parker spotted Natalie first as she waited alone at the outdoor table. The bull terrier let out several excited pig grunts and bulled his way forward, dragging Morris along. The dog scooted under the thick velvet rope that the restaurant used to mark off its outdoor café area, while Morris had to step over it and at the same time switch the leash to his other hand to keep from getting tangled up. Natalie watched with amusement. As always, she looked gorgeous. A petite, slender, dark-haired beauty who still made Morris feel weak in the knees with a smile, even after twenty-four years of marriage.

"Parker caught me off guard," Morris explained.

"He's good at that," Natalie admitted.

Natalie readied herself for the bull terrier's onslaught, grabbing Parker by his thick neck while the dog's rear end wiggled like crazy, his tail wagging at two hundred beats a minute, as he fought to lick Natalie's face. While this went on Morris snuck in a kiss of his own and took a seat adjacent to his wife. After a minute Parker calmed down enough to sit panting.

"He's happy to see you," Morris said.

"Nah, he's just trying to soften me up for some heavy-duty mooching."

Morris laughed at that. The dog could certainly mooch food with the best of them.

A waitress came over with menus. She was new here, otherwise she would've known better than to bring Morris a menu. He was a creature of habit. Ever since the actor Philip Stonehedge had turned him on to this Beverly Hills restaurant he had ordered only their fish tacos, and he did so again. Natalie took a menu and gave it a quick look before asking for an arugula and tomato salad. Morris asked the waitress to bring a roast beef and cheddar sandwich for Parker. "You can skip the bread, horseradish, lettuce and tomato. Just put the meat and cheese on a paper plate."

The waitress gave Parker a cautious look before asking whether the dog was friendly.

"He's a sweetheart," Natalie volunteered.

Morris concurred. "A bit of a clown, but a gentle soul."

This was mostly true, even though over the last year Parker had attacked two serial killers and bitten the arm of a hardened criminal who had pointed a gun at Morris during a jewelry store robbery. But as long as you weren't trying to kill Morris or others, the odds were good you wouldn't see that side of him.

The waitress patted the short, bristly fur that covered Parker's cement-hard head, and the dog's tail thumped against the terracotta-tiled patio. "I'll make sure to add some extra roast beef," she said with a wink. Morris waited until the waitress left before asking Natalie how her day was going.

"Busy." Natalie worked as a therapist and had her private office in downtown Los Angeles. "Before breaking for lunch I barely had time to catch my breath. But I have the luxury of not having to be back for another hour. Yourself? No new serial killer cases, hon?"

She said this mostly as a joke since Morris had sworn off those types of cases for his investigative firm, MBI, but some worry still showed in her eyes. Deep down inside she was afraid Morris would take on another of those cases, and she had good reason for this concern. The last serial killer case had left Morris battered and bruised, the one before that had brought a deranged killer to their door, and the very last one Morris had worked on while he was still an LAPD homicide detective almost killed him.

Her question also didn't come completely out of the blue. Natalie had serial killers on her mind because that night they were going to the Hollywood premiere of *The Carver*, a movie that was based loosely on a notorious serial killer Heath Dodd. Since Dodd's killing ground had been Miami, Morris wasn't involved in the investigation, but he had still been hired by the movie producers to consult on the film. Even with Morris's involvement in the movie, they probably would've skipped the premiere if Philip Stonehedge hadn't invited them to a private dinner party afterward.

"As far as I know Los Angeles is still serial killer free," Morris said. "If that changes, the LAPD will have to handle it without my help. Anyway, as you well know, MBI has gone almost a hundred percent corporate."

This was true. After the Malibu Butcher business, Morris had made a concerted effort for his firm to take on only corporate cases, most of which were either company fraud or employee background investigations, although they were currently knee-deep in a corporate espionage case that they were hoping to break soon.

"*Almost* a hundred percent?" Natalie asked. Parker, who had plopped down on the ground and was now lying on his side by Natalie's feet, let out one of his grunts to show that he also found the matter suspicious.

"We took on an unusual missing person investigation this morning," Morris said. "A guy up and vanished four months ago. No sign of him or his car since. His wife brought us the case. She's desperate."

"She needs closure."

"Nope. She needs the insurance money."

Natalie gave him a reproachful look. "Hon, dear, don't you think you're being a tad cynical?"

"Not at all. She's convinced her husband is dead, and she needs a death certificate before she can collect on his life insurance policy." Morris grimaced at the water spot on his fork as he held it up for a quick inspection. "I felt sorry for her. She really is in desperate straits and genuinely seems to have been mourning him. We're not quite taking it on as pro bono work, but close. MBI will only bill her if we find him or his body, and we'll be capping the bill off at five thousand."

Natalie bit her thumbnail. "Do you think she's right?"

"I don't know. She's convinced that they were happy enough together and he was content with his life. She's also adamant that if he were alive he'd be home with her now. Maybe that's true. Or maybe he decided to start over someplace else. We'll see."

The waitress appeared with their food. Parker got to his feet, his eyes fixed on the tray she carried. The paper plate she had brought held what looked like twice as much roast beef as would normally be used for a sandwich. Parker let out a few excited grunts as he waited for it to be placed on the patio surface. As soon as Morris let up on the leash, Parker attacked the food as if he hadn't eaten in days even though he'd had half a can of his food that morning.

Natalie patted Parker's side. "Our little guy is getting pudgy," she said.

"Nah, it's all muscle."

She gave Morris a funny look but didn't argue. As she ate her salad, she seemed to lose herself in her private thoughts. When she shivered, he asked her what was wrong.

Natalie looked at him as if she didn't understand what he was asking, then offered a wistful smile.

"I don't know. Just something in the air, I guess."

Morris glanced upward. Not a cloud in the sky. If a storm was coming, he couldn't see it.

Chapter 3

Heather Brandley was fuming before she started her five-mile run, and whatever meditative value exercise was supposed to have was wasted on her. In fact, she was even angrier by the time she sprinted past her imaginary finish line, and had spent most of the thirty-six minutes and eighteen seconds that it took her to run a loop around West Hollywood fantasizing about gory and painful ways she could kill all of them. The objects of her ire? The producers, director, and casting agent for *The Bumbleford Affair*. The reason? Yesterday she had been brought in to read for the part of Tom Bumbleford's mother. The producers had already announced that Peter Shays, with his washboard abs and dreamy boyish looks, would be playing the lead, and since he was only a few years younger than her, Heather assumed she'd be playing the mother in flashback scenes. When they asked her to read with Peter, Heather was stunned.

"Peter, darling, how old are you?" she sputtered out, her ears burning a bright red.

"Well, luv, all of thirty-two years," he said in his trademark sheepish manner, an impish smile twisting his lips.

"This is a prank, right?" she asked the director. "You've got a hidden camera back there, right?"

"Why would you ask that?" the director said, pursing his lips as if he couldn't fathom her reason for asking him that question.

"Why? Because Peter is only six years younger than me! And you seriously want me to play his mom?"

"We want you to play his *hot* mom," one of the producers quipped.

Although she couldn't believe this was happening, Heather read her lines like a true professional, and under the circumstances, thought she gave a good reading. As humiliating as the experience was, a job was a job in this godforsaken business. But then to add insult to injury, her agent had called this morning to tell her that while everybody loved her, they'd decided to go in a different direction.

"Who got the part?"

"Sweetie, another call's coming in. I've got to go—"

"Nick, no you don't! If you don't tell me, we're through, I swear it!"

Her agent gave the same heavy sigh he always did whenever he was being forced to spell out bad news. "Stephanie Morrison."

Morrison was two years younger than her, a shade hotter, and two shades blonder. So this was how it was now going to be. When Heather broke into movies at age twenty, her first role was as the hot girlfriend. At twenty-six she started being cast as the "cute" friend. At thirty-two, all she could get were *mom* roles. Now at thirty-eight, she was too *old* to play the part of a thirty-two-year-old guy's mom, even if Peter Shays did look young for his age. *Bastards*!

As she always did, Heather ended her run two blocks from her condo, and after stumbling to a stop, she bent forward and held her knees so she could catch her breath.

Thanks to the anger that had been fueling her, she had pushed herself harder than usual, and a thin sheen of sweat covered her body. There hadn't been a day since she had turned thirty that she hadn't run five miles—even those days when she had to be on set at five a.m. All that running and Pilates and yoga in the hopes of keeping her body slender and toned, and now she'd probably only get grandmother roles! She decided then that she was going to bump her running up to seven miles daily and add an extra Pilates workout each week.

A block away was The Grassy Knoll, and as was her routine, she stopped in for a juice. Rico was working the counter. A pretty gay man with diamond stud earrings, a tight T-shirt and jeans that could've been painted on, and long eyelashes that were to die for. He gave her a long appreciative look up and down before leering at her wolfishly.

"You're looking so fine, girl. You make me almost want to be straight."

"Rico, darling, you're just too kind."

"Simply being honest, that's all, sweetie. The usual?"

"What else?"

As Rico fed kale, carrots, beets, fennel, celery, and jalapeno peppers into a juicer, he asked her about some of the Hollywood gossip he'd been hearing and told her how much prettier he found her than the other starlets in town. "None of them can make me hard like you do, sweetie."

By the time Heather left the store with a juice in hand, her mood had perked up. Rico, bless him, was always good for that.

At the end of the block was a small park across the street from her condo, and as part of her routine, Heather would always sit on the lone bench in the park and enjoy her juice. Today, though, there was someone already sitting there. A man, maybe the same age as Peter Shays. Nicely dressed in a Versace suit and wearing an attractive pair of Italian loafers. Good-looking also, with his sandy-brown hair and neatly trimmed goatee. She caught a glimpse of the Hublot watch on his wrist and had a good idea of how much it cost. So he had money also. She smiled as she thought of how he was the right age for her to play a different kind of mommy to, and besides, the bench was big enough for two. He was good-looking in a cute sort of way and presented himself well. She sat to his right and watched with amusement as he tried to act as if he were too absorbed with what he was reading on his cell phone to notice that she was there. As she finished up her juice, she slurped to get his attention. He looked up then with an exaggeratedly startled expression.

"Oh, hi," he said, blushing. "I didn't realize I had company." He held out a hand. "Jason," he said.

So cute. "Heather," she said as she took his hand.

He opened his eyes wide. "You're Heather Brandley! Wow! I'm such a huge fan. I love everything you've been in, especially *The Day After Yesterday.*"

"You mean today," she said with a thin smile.

He blushed some more, and Heather thought again that he was cute. She also thought about how much she needed this type of an ego boost.

"I guess I was just being dense, but I never made that connection before with that movie title. I hope this doesn't look like I was stalking you, because this is really just an amazing coincidence, but I'm looking to make an independent film that you'd be so perfect for."

Her own smile faded fast. "You were stalking me," she said.

He began to give her a startled look as if he couldn't understand why she would accuse him of something like that, but then cut it off and instead grinned.

"You caught me red-handed," he admitted. "I know you live over there" —he nodded toward the condo complex across the street— "and I was hoping to catch you when you left home. I certainly didn't expect you to sit down next to me on this bench. It must be kismet."

Heather's eyes narrowed as she gave him a dubious look. "Tell me about this movie."

"Pure action. One kick-ass sequence leading into the next. And I want you to star."

"Nudity?"

"None. I do want you in a spandex outfit, though, to show off your ridiculously gorgeous body."

She was flattered, but she kept her tone purely business as she asked, "Budget?"

"Six million." He made an apologetic gesture with his hands. "I know that's not a lot, but this is an independent film, not a studio picture."

"I've worked on smaller budgeted films," she admitted. "How do you plan on raising the money?"

"I don't. I've already got it."

"How is that?"

"I've been successful with my business." He fiddled with his phone and then handed it to her. He had brought up on the screen his company's website, and as Heather scrolled through it he told her that his business was mostly corporate sponsorships and events, but that it had been very lucrative.

"I've seen some of your videos on YouTube," she admitted.

"Not surprising. They've gotten millions of hits."

"How come your website has your name but not your photo?"

"I like to have an air of mystery."

When Heather first started questioning him about his movie, it was mostly as a lark and partly because he was cute, but now this was starting to get serious.

"How much would you pay me?" she asked.

"One hundred thousand plus ten percent of the gross."

Heather had had to work for scale on her last three movies. She concentrated to sound nonchalant as she told him that he could send her a script.

"That's terrific! I'll get a copy in the mail later today." He froze for a moment and made a face as if he were trying to decide how bold he could be, and Heather smiled to herself. He was cute after all, and she was beginning to fancy the idea of getting naked with him for an intensive cardiovascular workout, and so she waited for him to work up the courage to proposition her.

"I've also got the movie storyboarded," he said. "If you have the time, I could take you to my workshop and go over it with you. And maybe dinner at Luzana's afterward."

Luzana's was the hottest spot in Los Angeles. A-listers only. Heather had been dying to get in there—more so she could be seen than even to try the food, which was supposed to be exquisite.

"Do you have reservations?" she asked, a tad too anxiously.

He waved off the question as if he were carelessly swatting at a fly. "Not needed. I have an understanding with the maître d'. If I call him for a table for tonight, it won't be an issue. Especially if I tell him who my guest is."

That settled it. Everybody thinks they can make a movie, and it was more likely than not the script he had was putrid, even if he was willing to sink six million of his own money into it. But being seen at Luzana's tonight would make up for spending time looking over his storyboards. And who knew? His movie idea might actually be decent. She'd seen his videos, and even if making them required a very different skillset than making a movie, he was certainly talented at what he did. Besides, after dinner they could have their tumble in the sack, and she could really use that right now.

"Sold," she said. "I need to obviously shower and dress first—"

"I'll wait here for you." Somewhat magnanimously, he offered, "If for whatever reason you change your mind, I'll understand completely, but if that happens could you send out your doorman to let me know so I don't sit here for hours?"

He is just so cute. "I'll be back in twenty minutes," she promised.

The killer watched as she walked away. He had to admit that she looked nice from behind in her running shorts and tank top. Beautiful legs, too. Long and slender and toned. She turned to look back at him and wave, and he smiled and waved also. Once she disappeared inside her building, his genial smile became something different.

He had done his research and so he knew she'd be sitting on this bench after her run, just as he knew how she'd react to everything he had said. He had read enough interviews with her to know that she'd come back with that idiotic comment regarding the movie *The Day After Yesterday* (a movie he had no intention of ever seeing), which would make her feel oh-so-clever. He further knew that she had never made it onto the A-list and was only being paid scale, and that the idea of being paid a hundred grand and a healthy percentage of the gross would leave her salivating. And of course, like all B-list actors and actresses in this city, she would kill to be seen at Luzana's.

The killer was proud of himself and the performance that he gave. He had been convincingly self-effacing, as if he were actually in awe of her. He'd even been able to blush on command—at least he thought he had. It would be hard to know for certain without a mirror, but he had felt a hotness flushing his cheeks that seemed to indicate that he had succeeded. The book he had read about method acting had helped. It had allowed him to slip into character and stay there until she had left. He had her fooled completely, no doubt about it.

When thirty minutes passed without her returning, the killer wasn't so sure anymore about how much he had fooled her. After forty minutes, he started wondering if he had made a mistake. An uneasiness began working its way into his chest. She was an important piece in his plans. He needed her. Was it possible that he had overplayed his hand? Could he have blown it by mentioning a doorman? Did that make her start wondering how he knew her building had one?

Damn. Damn. Damn.

Why'd he have to mention anything about her doorman! What the hell was wrong with him? He'd had her sold hook, line, and sinker, so why'd he have to shoot off his mouth like that?

He sat frozen, not quite sure what to do. The only way to reach her condo was to first get past the doorman and the building's security system. Because of his disguise he didn't care whether he left the police a video recording of himself on the building's surveillance system, but the doorman was an entirely different matter since he hadn't brought a weapon, at least not a conventional one. He could theoretically use the hypodermic needle that was meant for Brandley, but then what? If he were to kill the doorman now it would disrupt his later plans!

His uneasiness had turned into a full-blown panic, but then he spotted Brandley leaving her building. Her hair was done up, and she wore a sheer green dress that showed off her legs and black stiletto pumps that accentuated her calves. She was certainly dressed to be noticed with a strand of pearls around her neck and long, dangling gold earrings. Or some might say dressed to kill. He snickered inwardly as he thought about the truth. *Dressed to be killed.*

"I'm sorry if I kept you waiting," she said with a mischievous smile. "I hope you didn't think I was standing you up?"

"You had me worried for a bit," the killer admitted.

"I'm so sorry, but I wanted to look decent for tonight."

"Mission accomplished," he said. More inward snickering as he added, "You'll be turning heads later, no question about it."

"You're just too kind." She batted her eyes at him. "Were you able to make reservations for Luzana's?"

"Yep. I've got us a table for seven-thirty. That should give us more than enough time to go over the storyboards and script."

The killer stood, and Heather took his arm. The killer pointed out his Mercedes sedan parked on the street, the trunk of which was more than large enough to hold Heather Brandley's body.

"You'll be driving me in style," Heather said, pleased with how her day was turning out.

The killer didn't bother to correct her. As they made their way to the Mercedes, he deftly removed the hypodermic needle from his inside suit jacket pocket. Heather didn't notice it until it was too late for her to even scream.

Chapter 4

Charlie Bogle entered the Long Beach police station on West Broadway and informed the desk sergeant he was there to see Detective Vernon Howard. The sergeant sized Bogle up quickly.

"You used to be on the force?" he asked.

"Sixteen years with the LAPD."

The sergeant's expression showed he had guessed that. "Name?"

Bogle told him his name, and the sergeant got on the phone, had a quick conversation, then told him Howard was waiting for him. "Squad room's upstairs. Take the first door on your right."

Bogle thanked him, went up the stairs, entered the squad room, and spotted Howard sitting at a desk. When they had worked together years earlier, Howard had looked like he could've been an NFL linebacker. Now he was even bigger—not fat, but much wider, almost as if he had doubled in size. As Bogle approached him, Howard sat motionless with his thick, heavy arms crossed over his chest, his face locked into a deadpan expression. It wasn't until Bogle reached the desk that Howard at last broke out in a wide grin and offered his meaty hand, which was nearly the size of a baseball glove. Bogle's own hand disappeared inside it.

"Damn, Charlie, how long's it been?" Howard asked.

"How long have you been working in Long Beach?"

"Ten years."

"That's how long it's been."

Howard's expression drifted into something wistful. "How's Jenny and the kids?"

"We divorced five years ago. Her idea. Tom and Eileen are both in college, and even though they're local it's still costing me an arm and a leg."

"Ah, man, sorry to hear about the split."

Bogle shrugged. "I can't blame her. I wasn't the easiest guy to be married to. How about you and Marcie and your brood?"

"She's still busting my balls every day, and will be until the day they lower me into the ground. Boys are behaving themselves. Last fall, Vernon Jr. started his freshman year at UCLA. Got himself a football scholarship. Defensive end."

"Wow. That's terrific."

Howard beamed, showing his pride. Then his expression turned serious and he asked, "So you're here to talk about Karl Crawford's disappearance. The wife hire you?"

"Yeah."

Howard's eyelids lowered a bit, but whatever he was thinking he kept to himself. He grabbed a folder from his desk, and told Bogle they'd talk in one of the interrogation rooms. "You want some coffee?" he offered.

"Is it any better than what we used to have on Wilcox Ave.?"

"Some."

"Sure, I'll have a cup."

On the way to the interrogation room they stopped to pour themselves coffee, and Bogle, remembering what the Wilcox Ave. precinct coffee had tasted like, grabbed himself four packets of sugar. Once they were seated in the ten-by-eight-foot windowless interrogation room, Howard peered at Bogle through half-lidded eyes as he sipped his drink. He asked, "Your take on Lauren Crawford?"

"I think she's legit. You don't, huh?"

Howard took another sip before shaking his head. "Not necessarily. But it's one of two things: someone killed Crawford and buried his body, or he took off to parts unknown. If it's the first, she's the only one I could find who would profit from his death, but that would only be if there was a death certificate issued so that she could collect on the life insurance."

"You're thinking she might not want to have to wait seven years to have him declared legally dead, and that we were hired to help speed things along?"

Howard shrugged. "I'm just saying it's possible. Especially if she gave you any hints where you might find his body."

"She didn't give us anything. She seems in the dark about what happened. But if that changes and she calls us with some sort of epiphany, I'll let you know."

Howard appeared satisfied with Bogle's remark. He took out a map of the greater Los Angeles area from the folder he had brought and spread it out on the table.

"Karl Crawford worked for Samson Oil & Gas maintaining the oil wells we've got dotting the Los Angeles landscape," Howard said. "He's been doing that for twenty-two years, and according to his company, he's been a conscientious and reliable employee with a spotless record. On November fourth of last year, he serviced this well over here." Howard pointed a thick index finger to a spot on the map near the outskirts of Long Beach that had been marked with a red x. "According to the maintenance log kept at the well, Crawford signed in at eight thirty-seven a.m. and signed out at ten forty-nine a.m. He was next scheduled to go to this well over here, but he never showed up. Or at least he didn't sign in on the log, and according to Samson there was no sign that maintenance had been done that day."

Howard pointed to another red x drawn on the map, this one north of the first, and near Lakewood.

"Hmm. It looks like the two wells are about seven miles apart," Bogle commented.

"Yeah, that's about right."

"Did anyone see him leave the Long Beach well?"

"Not that I could find. The wells are unmanned, and in isolated locations. Nobody else from Samson was there."

Bogle frowned at that. "So he just disappeared somewhere between the two wells?"

"Yeah, seemingly both him and his car."

"What have you done to try to find him?"

"The usual. Checked hospitals, monitored his credit cards, activated his car theft retrieval system, did a spot check of the area around both wells, looked into his home life. I got nothing with any of that."

"Why didn't you bring in bloodhounds to search for him?"

Howard made a *get real* face at that question. "Are you serious, Charlie? I wouldn't have gotten anywhere requesting that. Maybe if I'd found the car abandoned, or better yet, with his blood, it would've been different. But as it is, what it looks like is he got in his car and decided to drive to a new life somewhere else."

"Why would he do that? Were there any signs he was planning to leave? Marital discord?"

Howard gave Bogle a look as if he couldn't believe Bogle was asking him that.

"Come on, man, the guy's forty-five and doing the same lonely, tedious job for twenty-two years. He was a perfect candidate for a midlife crisis. He could've been putting money aside for months planning for this. Are you seriously going to tell me you've never daydreamed about getting in your car and driving someplace far away and starting your life all over?"

Straight-faced, Bogle said, "Me? I'm living the dream. Why would I ever think of something like that?"

"Yeah, well, I've had those daydreams." Howard seemed surprised that he had admitted that out loud. "Not that I ever thought about it seriously, mind you."

"If that's what happened, why'd he spend two hours working on that first well before taking off?"

"Maybe he finally reached his limit. Who knows?"

"You think that's what happened?"

Howard drank more of his coffee, his eyes narrowing into slits. "For now," he admitted. "But let's see what you come up with."

"Anything else you can think of that might help?"

"Not a thing." Howard crumpled his cardboard coffee cup into a ball and tossed it into a trash can, banking it off the wall.

"Let me walk you out of here."

The two men got up and left the interrogation room.

Chapter 5

They'd left Parker at home during the Hollywood premiere of *The Carver*, but at Philip Stonehedge's insistence, Morris and Natalie swung by their West Hollywood home and picked up the bull terrier before driving to Stonehedge's Malibu estate for his after-the-premiere dinner party.

Natalie hadn't yet met Stonehedge (although she had caught a glimpse of the actor while they were waiting in line to get into the theater) and she raised an eyebrow as they drove through the security gate and continued along the private road that led to the sprawling contemporary-style home. Parker, who had accompanied Morris several times to the property and had learned to associate it with extraordinarily delicious bacon, began making pig-like grunts as he realized where he was.

"Why's our little guy getting so excited?" Natalie asked.

"I'll give you one guess what he was given the last two times I brought him here."

"B-a-c-o-n," she said.

"Correct."

Morris parked behind a long line of other cars and made sure to keep a tight grip on Parker's leash when he opened the door, otherwise the dog would've raced out of the car in pursuit of more of that sublime bacon. Parker was a loyal dog, but bacon was his one weakness. As they made their way to the front door, Parker strained against his leash as he tried to bull his way forward.

"Somebody's overly excited," Natalie observed.

Morris grunted back his acknowledgement.

A waiter in black tie met them at the door with a tray of blue-colored cocktails. Morris knew Stonehedge well enough to know that the drinks would be tasty, so he took one and suggested Natalie do the same. He was right. It was a concoction of blueberries, muddled mint, rum, lime juice, and honey. Natalie also took a sip and concurred that it was delicious.

The waiter informed them that the dinner was being held by Stonehedge's pool in back. He glanced reproachfully at Parker, most likely wondering whether he should allow a dog into Stonehedge's home, but held back any comment and instead proceeded to escort them through the house.

"Nice," Natalie remarked as they went from room to room. "Interesting to see how Los Angeles's royalty lives." As they walked through Stonehedge's designer kitchen, she looked around in awe and commented, "I feel like I'm in an episode of that old show *Lifestyles of the Rich and Famous*."

Morris was too busy keeping Parker in check to respond.

The dinner party out back wasn't quite the small, intimate affair Stonehedge had hinted at. There were approximately eighty people milling about, and a half dozen or so waiters and waitresses walking through the crowd with trays of drinks and food. Morris spotted *The Carver*'s director and several of the actors from the film, and then heard his name. He looked over to see Stonehedge on the other side of the pool beaming at him, the actress Brie Evans by his side. Stonehedge signaled for Morris to join them.

"Our host," Morris said, nodding toward Stonehedge.

"He certainly knows how to throw a shindig," Natalie acknowledged.

It took some time to work their way through the crowd since one of *The Carver*'s producers stopped Morris to chat with him, and other partygoers wanted to make a fuss over Parker. If there wasn't so much food around, the dog might've been spoiled by the attention, but as it was he hardly noticed it. When they finally reached Stonehedge, Morris introduced Natalie to the actor and his stunningly gorgeous girlfriend.

"At last we meet," Stonehedge said, smiling good-naturedly.

"About time, huh?" Natalie said.

"I'd say so. I've only seen the picture of you Morris keeps in his office, but you're even more beautiful in person."

"Aren't you too kind," Natalie said, blushing in spite of herself. She was someone comfortable in her own skin, and compliments of any kind usually didn't faze her, but this was a Hollywood star who had made *People*'s hundred sexiest list, and whose girlfriend topped that same list! Mostly to change the subject so she wouldn't blush any further, she said, "Movies like *The Carver* aren't necessarily my cup of tea—"

"Let me guess, they strike too close to home."

"Exactly. But I thought you stole the movie as The Carver's final victim."

Stonehedge's smile turned enigmatic. "I was supposed to star in it, but I was shot in the leg during a jewelry store robbery. Morris saved my life that day. That was why I played the part in a wheelchair. I still couldn't walk when they filmed my scenes. It's also how I got this."

Stonehedge ran a thumb over the thick scar that was left behind when one of the robbers slashed his cheek open with a gun barrel.

"It gives you a rakish look, luv," Brie Evans said. "Don't you agree?" she asked Natalie.

"It certainly gives him character."

Parker, who'd been standing impatiently, had had enough. With his tail wagging a slow beat, he let out a bark, which was unusual for him, and jumped on Stonehedge so that his front paws leaned against the actor's thighs.

"I haven't forgotten about you," Stonehedge told the bull terrier as he rubbed Parker vigorously behind his ears. Then to Natalie: "This little brute was also responsible for saving my life that day."

Natalie was well aware of the story, and simply nodded.

Stonehedge caught the eye of a waitress he was searching for and signaled for her to come over. "I ordered this specifically for Parker. Wood-grilled lobster wrapped in bacon."

The mention of bacon elicited excited grunts from the dog.

"And of course, you used the world's best bacon," Morris said, using Stonehedge's own words to describe the specialty bacon the actor bought from a small butcher shop in Venice.

"Of course."

The waitress had made her way over and tried unsuccessfully to hide her nervousness about being near Stonehedge and Evans.

"Don't give him too many," Natalie said. "He'll burst."

"A couple will be okay," Morris said, and he tossed Parker one of the appetizers, which he gobbled up and seemed to placate him.

"Can I borrow Morris for a few minutes?" Stonehedge asked. "I'd like to talk shop with him."

Natalie pursed her lips, obviously curious about what that could be about, but she smiled and told Stonehedge that of course he could borrow her husband. "It will give me a chance to ask Brie where she bought her lovely outfit."

Morris, with Parker in tow, followed Stonehedge toward the back of his property where they could talk in private. They stopped a few yards from the edge of the cliff overlooking the beach below.

"They're making a movie about the Malibu Butcher," Stonehedge said. "Well, really about that whack job who dealt himself into the game—"

"Allen Perlmutter."

"Yeah. But even though Perlmutter is the focus of the movie, the Malibu Butcher is a major role, and the producers are offering it to me."

"You'll finally get to play a serial killer."

"If I take the part."

"Are you considering it?"

"I am. The script's got a lot of craziness in it, but it's also crazy good. As long as you're okay with it."

"Why wouldn't I be?"

"You were knee-deep in that swamp, after all."

Stonehedge was right. Morris wasn't thrilled to hear that a movie was being made about that Malibu Butcher psycho, or really three psychos if you included Perlmutter and Sheila Proops, but he had known from the beginning it was inevitable that Hollywood would want to do something with it.

"Someone's going to take the part," Morris said, shaking his head. A harsh chuckle escaped from his lips. "Very meta of them wanting you to play the Butcher since you were one of his intended victims."

"Yeah, but that's one of the reasons they want me. Having me play him would be a wet dream for their publicist."

"No doubt. You know that at least half the witnesses we talked to thought he looked like you?"

"I read about that," Stonehedge admitted. "I don't know. From pictures I saw of him, I don't see the resemblance."

"That's only because the photos they ran in the papers were taken after Perlmutter mutilated him." Morris's lips tightened into a thin smile. "What's my character's name in the movie?"

"Mort Slate."

"I guess that's somewhat imaginative. How much is it like me?"

"Surprisingly close. Last I heard they're talking to Woody Harrelson to play your character. As far as I'm concerned, that would be pitch-perfect casting."

Morris Brick was under no illusions about his physical appearance, and how mismatched he and Natalie were—Nat being a slender, dark-haired beauty, while he was at best comical looking. He also knew that with his short, compact body, spindly legs, big ears, thick, long nose, and thinning hair he proved the old adage of a dog owner resembling his pet. Even if they dyed Woody Harrelson's hair dark brown, the only way the actor would resemble Morris would be if someone squinted extra hard. And even then that person would need poor eyesight. But he chose not to argue the matter.

"You've got my blessing," Morris said. "Mazel tov."

"Thanks, Morris. I appreciate it. Do you want to consult on the film? Nobody knows the real story better than you, at least nobody alive—"

"Other than Sheila Proops."

"Maybe, but they'd have to find her first. What do you say? I could make it a condition on my taking the role, but I'm sure they'd be on board regardless."

Movie consulting jobs were good money, but Morris wanted to change MBI's image from a firm that tracked down perverse serial killers to one that handled more staid corporate work.

"Let me think about it," Morris said.

Parker, who'd been quiet up until then, let out a couple of impatient grunts.

"Somebody wants to get back to the food," Stonehedge observed.

The three of them returned to the party.

Chapter 6

Morris reached blindly to turn off the clock radio, then collapsed back onto the bed. His mouth and throat tasted as if he had gargled with sawdust, and his head throbbed as if it were being squeezed in a vise. *Too many of those blueberry mojitos,* he thought. *Too much rich food also. But damn, those charbroiled oysters were good!*

He lay on his back, listening to Natalie's rhythmic breathing as she continued to sleep, and then struggled to open his eyes against the morning light. When he heard a rustling noise from the hallway, followed by a soft whimper, he remembered that because Nat didn't have to be in her office until eleven, he had decided he'd leave later himself, and so had set the alarm for eight instead of the usual six a.m. If he had planned things better he would've arranged for Parker's twenty-four-year-old occasional dog walker, Kat McKinty, to have shown up earlier that morning. But he hadn't, so he had better get out of bed pronto to take Parker outside.

Morris tried to be quiet so he wouldn't wake Natalie as he stumbled out of bed and slipped on a pair of old jeans and a T-shirt. He grabbed his cell phone and keys, and when he opened the bedroom door he fought to keep Parker from charging into the room. The dog let out an impatient yelp and jumped up and tried to lick him in the face.

"I know, buddy, I'm late this morning. No excuses. Let's get you outside."

The word *outside* elicited several excited grunts from the bull terrier, who proceeded to race down the stairs. Morris badly wanted coffee right then, but that would have to wait. He made a quick pit stop for himself, then continued on to the front door where he found Parker waiting with his leash in his mouth. This was their morning ritual: a tug-of-war before Parker would let go. This time Parker gave up the leash right away.

They were a block away from home before Morris turned on his cell phone. When he checked the text messages, a coolness filled his head as he saw that there was a long string of them from Doug Gilman at the mayor's office. The first message had been sent an hour ago, and read "Call me right away. It's important." The next three were similar, except that "important" had become "critical." Before Morris could read any more of them, his phone rang. The caller ID showed *Los Angeles Mayor's Office*.

This had to be about a horrific murder. That was the only reason Gilman would be this anxious to get ahold of him. Morris considered not answering the call and simply sending Gilman a text reminding him that MBI was no longer taking on homicide investigations. Instead, though, Morris tapped on the answer button. Before he could say anything more than, "I'm sorry, Doug—", the mayor's deputy assistant interrupted him, asking if Morris had seen his text messages.

"I was just going through them when you called."

"You haven't seen my last text?"

"No, not yet."

"Before you say another word, take a look at it."

The world around him grew uncomfortably quiet as Morris scrolled through the messages. He stopped walking and ignored Parker's impatient tugging on the leash as he found the message that read: *this is what was found pinned to the victim.* A photo attached to the message showed a business card dotted with two drops of blood. The card read: *To Morris Brick: I'm just beginning—R. G. Berg, Serial Killer Extraordinaire.*

"You said there was a victim?" Morris asked, his voice sounding tinny and unnatural to his own ears.

"Half of one, anyways."

Gilman gave Morris the details he had, and Morris agreed to meet him where they had found the victim. Or at least where they had found a part of the victim.

Chapter 7

Charlie Bogle handed Mark Sangonese, Karl Crawford's boss at Samson Oil & Gas, a paper bag holding a large coffee and a cinnamon roll, both of which Bogle had bought at a local bakery ten minutes earlier after calling Sangonese to ask what he would like. Sangonese grunted out his thanks. He showed a guilty smile as he said, "If my wife knew I was eating this, she'd kill me."

Sangonese was a chunk of a man in his late fifties with iron-gray hair that had been cut short so that it resembled a bristle brush. Bogle pulled a chair up to Sangonese's cluttered desk and took a coffee and a blueberry muffin for himself from a second bag.

"What do you think happened to Karl Crawford?" Bogle asked.

Sangonese's smile fell flat from his face. "No idea," he said.

"Did his disappearing surprise you?"

"Yeah, I'd say so. Karl had been a model employee. In all the time he worked here, I don't think he called in sick even once."

"How well did you know him?"

"Not well," Sangonese admitted with a shrug. "Karl worked exclusively in the field servicing wells. I'd see him in the office every blue moon, not much outside the office, and he wasn't a talkative type."

"So you don't know whether he held extremist views?"

Sangonese looked surprised by the question. "You suspect he did?"

"No. I'm only trying to figure out what happened to him. If he was a survivalist or white nationalist or something along those lines, it would give me a few ideas of where to start looking for him."

"I never heard anyone mention something like that about Karl," Sangonese muttered. "Never heard that about anyone working here."

Bogle took another bite of his muffin and chewed it before sipping more coffee. Sangonese fidgeted in his chair, but that was because of the tone of the questioning, not because he was lying. At least Bogle was pretty sure of that.

"Anyone here he might've confided in if he was having marital or financial problems?"

"I can't think of anyone," Sangonese said, frowning. "Field maintenance technicians, like Karl, might come into the office half a dozen times a year. It's a good job if you like solitude, but it's not one that encourages camaraderie."

"Would Crawford always be alone at these wells?"

"Usually. I'm on the road one week every month doing spot checks, but I've got seven other field service technicians, so every month I might've been at two of the wells Karl was servicing. During those times Karl and I wouldn't be gabbing all that much."

Bogle consulted his notes before remarking that the police report stated that Crawford went to the first well he was scheduled to service that day, but didn't show up at the second.

"That's not a hundred percent right," Sangonese said. He finished the last bite of cinnamon bun and used the paper bag to wipe his hands clean, then crumpled and tossed the bag into a trash can. "Karl could've shown up at the second well. All I know for a fact is he didn't service the well."

"What you really know is that he didn't sign the log," Bogle said.

"No, I know more than that. If he had opened the well's casing, it would've sent our computer tracking system a signal. That didn't happen. So Karl could've shown up there, but something might've happened to him before he could do any work."

That perked Bogle's interest. "What about security video?"

Sangonese said, "We don't outfit wells with cameras. There hasn't been a need. If the wells are tampered with, we'll get a signal and we then send out a security team."

"How often does that happen?"

"It hasn't yet."

Bogle sighed as he considered all this. It would've been helpful if the wells had security cameras. He asked, "Who knew Crawford's schedule that day?"

"I did. My secretary. I can't say about anyone else."

"How do you decide which wells get serviced?"

"A combination of routine scheduling and remote monitoring." Sangonese cleared his throat and added, "Over the last six months we've been upgrading our wells with more sophisticated software to better detect when maintenance is needed."

Bogle stared at his notes again. He was running out of things to ask, and none of Sangonese's answers were helping him come up with any new ideas. "Can I look at Crawford's company email account?"

Sangonese's thick lips curled into a frown. "I'm not sure Karl's email is still active. Let me check on that, and I'll get back to you." He gave his watch an impatient glance. "We've been at this for fifteen minutes now. I need to get back to work."

Bogle pushed his chair back and got to his feet. When he reached the door, he turned back to Sangonese and gave him a hard look, trying to determine how truthful he'd been. If Sangonese felt any unease at this, he didn't show it.

Bogle said, "If you think of anything that could help, please call me."

Sangonese's expression turned dour. "I can't imagine what that would be," he said.

Chapter 8

Star Wax was a two-year-old wax museum on Sunset Boulevard in Hollywood that competed with the Hollywood Wax Museum, their gimmick being replicas of scenes from newer Hollywood movies. Morris had to circle the area before finding a parking spot three blocks away. It was only ten minutes to nine, but the sun was already bright in the sky, and he shielded his eyes from it as he made his way to the wax museum. He had picked up coffee on the drive over, but it had done little to stop the dull throbbing behind his eyes. The heat from the sun, though, felt good on the back of his neck.

Word hadn't spread yet about a dead body being found inside the museum, but with the official city and police vehicles parked out front, as well as the uniformed officers barricading the front entrance, a crowd of curious onlookers had gathered. Morris squeezed his way through them. He knew one of the patrolmen standing guard, and after a quick few words, he was let in.

Doug Gilman was waiting for him inside. His normally tanned face had grown so pale and unnaturally waxen that he could almost have been mistaken for a wax figure, at least until he stepped forward and offered Morris his hand. His skin felt clammy to the touch. Gilman was a political bureaucrat who had been smart enough to get Morris involved in two previous high-profile serial killer investigations in order to get the heat off the mayor's office, and Morris knew from experience that Gilman tended to get queasy when near dead bodies.

"Thanks for coming," Gilman said, his expression glum. "You made yourself clear before that MBI wasn't going to work on any more murder investigations, but you can see why I had to call you about taking on this one."

"I haven't decided anything yet," Morris said.

"Let's see how you feel after you see the body."

The Star Wax sign out front had been made to look like a Star Wars movie poster, and as Gilman led Morris though the museum, Morris realized why. Even though only the red emergency lights were on, leaving the exhibits in a gloomy darkness, it was still enough for him to see that the first dozen of them were from Star Wars movies. He had seen the first three movies back when he was a teenager, but hadn't seen any of the recent ones, and he didn't recognize the characters in the exhibits until they came across one for *Return of the Jedi*, which showed Princess Leia in her slave girl outfit sidled up against Jabba the Hutt. That one caught his attention. As a teenager, he had a huge crush on Carrie Fisher as Princess Leia.

As they walked through the building, they passed more replicated scenes from recent Hollywood franchises: Harry Potter, Batman and the Dark Knight, and Marvel comic book superheroes. Toward the back of the museum was a Classic Film section, and there Morris passed scenes from *The Godfather*, *Scarface*, *A Clockwork Orange*, *Bonnie and Clyde*, and *On the Waterfront*. As they continued on, he first spotted several crime scene specialists using flashlights to search the area, and then homicide detective Annie Walsh talking with Los Angeles's medical examiner, Roger Smichen. The exhibit they stood near had a thin, dapper man in top hat and tails dancing with a woman in a long flowing gown. Both the figure of the man and the woman looked like they had been sculpted out of wax, but as Morris got closer to the exhibit, he noticed something was very wrong about the woman. Her back was turned to him, so he couldn't see her face, but the way the body drooped appeared unnatural, even for wax.

"It's supposed to be Fred Astaire and Ginger Rogers from *Top Hat*," Roger Smichen said. Morris looked away from the dancing couple in the exhibit to see that Smichen and Walsh had noticed his arrival, and both stood grim-faced as they looked at him. Smichen, a cadaverously thin man in his late fifties, had grown a goatee the last time Morris had seen him, but the ME had since shaved it off, leaving his head hairless except for his sparse eyebrows. Morris had had drinks with Annie Walsh two weeks earlier, but given her severe expression and the dimness of the museum, she looked like she had aged a decade since then.

"You didn't bring your four-legged assistant," Walsh said, straight-faced.

"Nat's got Parker today. Why's it so dark in here?" Morris also noticed for the first time how much hotter and stuffier it was inside the building than it should've been, but he didn't ask about that.

"Only the emergency lights are running. The perp cut the electricity to kill the security system, so right now the building is running off a generator until the electric company reconnects the outside power line. It should happen soon."

"Do they know what time the power was cut?"

"Edison couldn't tell us that, but from the stopped clocks in the building, power was cut shortly after three fifteen a.m."

"Less than six hours ago," Morris said.

"She's been dead longer than that," Smichen volunteered. "From the body's lividity and temperature, I'd say at least fourteen hours."

Gilman had already told Morris that the dead woman replacing Ginger Rogers in the exhibit was the actress Heather Brandley. He moved so he could see the death mask the corpse wore. He remembered the actress from a decade-old TV show, and had thought then that she was attractive and had a perkiness about her. Her eyes were closed and her mouth was drawn as if she were in agony, and her face just seemed so shrunken. Death had a way of diminishing a person, and the rosy-colored blush coating her cheeks and the ruby-red lipstick slathered over her mouth made her appearance all that more grotesque and unnatural. The killer had propped her up so that it would appear as if she were dancing with the Fred Astaire wax figure.

"She was cut in half?" Morris asked.

"Not half," Smichen said. "We were left with the top third of her body. She was cut around six inches above her belly button. I'll be able to tell you with more certainty after I examine her in my lab, but it looks like a circular saw was used."

"Was it done postmortem?"

"I can't tell you that yet. There are no other apparent wounds or trauma, but let's wait and see what the toxicology report reveals."

Morris made out the outline of a thin pole that ran the full length of what was left of the corpse's back.

"A telescopic support pole made of galvanized steel," Smichen explained. "If I lifted up the gown you'd see the scaffolding that was built to support her. Screws were used to attach her hands to the wax figure's." He pointed to the raised round platform that the Astaire wax figure and the corpse were on. "The platform is built to spin around to make it look like Fred Astaire and Ginger Rogers are dancing. If a museum worker hadn't discovered that this exhibit had been tampered with, once power was restored and the museum had opened their doors, our victim would've been spinning in circles in front of customers."

"Jesus," Gilman said.

Morris ignored him and asked Walsh about this museum employee.

"Greg is interviewing him now," she said.

Greg was Greg Malevich, another homicide detective. Morris asked, "Has the lower part of her body been found yet?"

"Not that I know of."

The gown the corpse wore not only reached the floor but puddled by where her feet would've been. Morris lifted it up. He saw the scaffolding, but didn't see any blood.

"Was she drained of blood?" Morris asked.

Smichen said, "I doubt there's much left in her, but no. He encased her wound with plastic sheeting to keep her from bleeding."

Morris considered that. "Probably so he wouldn't make a mess transporting her."

"Possibly."

"Interesting that he was so careful yet his business card had drops of blood on it."

Walsh fished through an evidence bag, and took from it a plastic bag that held the standard-sized business card.

"There are no fingerprints," she said. "And my guess, the blood drops were added intentionally."

Morris wondered about that. "For what reason? Just to get our attention?"

Walsh gestured with a shrug to show that she had no idea.

Morris read the business card again, and felt an uneasiness in his chest as he did so. There was no doubt that R. G. Berg was planning to kill more people, and that he was challenging Morris to stop him. But that didn't mean he had to play this killer's game.

"How'd he get in here?" he asked.

"He dismantled one of the back doors after he had cut power," Walsh said.

"What happened to the Ginger Rogers wax figure?"

"We haven't found it yet," Walsh said. "He could've taken it as a souvenir."

The lights turned on and a noticeable whirring noise from the central air conditioning interrupted the stillness in the building. Fred Astaire's wax twin and Heather Brandley's corpse began to spin in a ghoulish waltz.

Smichen noted, "It looks like the power's been restored."

"I'll get that turned off," Walsh volunteered, referring to the spinning platform.

With the additional light shining on the exhibit, what was left of Heather Brandley's corpse looked even sadder and more diminished each time it spun so that it faced Morris.

"What do you say, Morris?" Gilman asked, his voice tighter than earlier. "Are you going to help us catch this psycho?"

Morris stood staring at the grotesque spinning spectacle. He shook his head, but that was only to try to clear away the anger rising up inside him.

"I haven't decided yet," he said.

Chapter 9

Dennis Polk, one of MBI's investigators, breezed into the conference room, gave Doug Gilman a smirk, Greg Malevich a nod, and Annie Walsh a wink before taking a seat next to Morris. Gilman showed no response, Malevich nodded back, and Walsh glowered at Polk.

"What, no doughnuts or nothin'?" Polk asked.

Morris sat slumped in his chair with his arms crossed over his chest and his eyelids drooping as if he wanted to take a nap. He turned his half-lidded eyes toward Polk for a ten-count before making sense of what Polk had asked.

"Greta's ordering food," he muttered.

Polk raised an eyebrow as he looked at his boss. "Late night?" he asked.

"The night would've been fine if this hadn't happened."

Polk looked around the room at the morose expressions on everyone's faces. "Driving over there was nothing on the radio about a woman being found at Star Wax who'd been cut in half—"

"A third," Walsh corrected.

Polk made a face as if she were unnecessarily nitpicking him. "Okay, a third." He turned back to Morris. "So are you going to keep me in suspense any longer? You hinted earlier this was someone famous. Who was the unlucky lady?"

Gilman had dug through a briefcase, and now reached across the table to hand Polk the legal document that he had pulled out of it.

"I need you to sign an NDA before you can be told anything further," Gilman said.

Polk gave him an incredulous look before raising another eyebrow at Morris.

"Is he serious?" he asked.

"Just sign it," Morris said.

Polk signed it.

"Heather Brandley," Morris told him.

It took Polk a few seconds before the name registered, and then he let out a long, low whistle.

"I haven't seen her in anything in years, but I used to watch that show she was in. *Hot Times in Miami*. Damn, she looked good in a bikini." He rubbed his chin, appearing deep in thought, which was unusual for Polk. "This is going to hit hard, especially given what happened to her. Are we waiting for Charlie and Fred?" he asked.

"Charlie's tied up with the Crawford missing person investigation, Fred's still undercover in San Diego. I'll be filling them in later."

"That's too bad." Polk looked disappointed. Needling Fred Lemmon was one of his favorite hobbies. "So who are we waiting for?"

"Gloria Finston."

"The FBI profiler? The one who worked with us on the Malibu Butcher?"

"Yeah."

"I like her. A smart cookie."

"She's certainly that," Morris agreed. "Doug didn't want me showing you this until you signed the NDA, but the killer left this message behind."

He had a manila folder in front of him, and he took out a copy of the business card that had been pinned to Heather Brandley's gown and handed it to Polk. As Polk looked at it, a hard, angry grin etched his face.

"You gotta to be kidding me," Polk said.

"I'm afraid not."

"This sonofabitch is challenging us. So we're taking on the investigation, huh?"

"Still undecided."

Walsh gave Morris an exasperated look. "What more do you need to make up your mind?" she asked.

"Let's see how this meeting goes."

There was a knock on the door, and MBI's office manager, Greta Lindstrom, brought in a platter with bagels, lox, tomato, Bermuda onion slices, and cream cheese. Everyone but Gilman, who was still looking green around the gills, helped themselves to the food. Polk wolfed down a sandwich and was working on a second when there was another knock on the door, and Gloria Finston entered.

"Sorry if I've been holding you up," she announced, her thin lips forming a tiny *v*. "I was in San Francisco when I got the call about this murder, and took the first plane I could."

Finston was a slight, dark-haired woman in her forties. With her narrow face, longish, thin nose and small pale eyes, she reminded Morris of a sparrow. Smart as hell, though. Finston took the empty seat between Gilman and Walsh so that she sat across from Morris. She'd already been emailed the crime scene photos and knew about the business card that had been pinned to the victim's body.

"Polk hasn't finished off the bagels yet," Morris said. "If you want one, I'd advise you to dig in now before he does."

"I get hungry when I'm pissed," Polk said. "And the card that sonofabitch left for us is doing the job."

Morris understood Polk's anger because the killer's message had the same effect on him. He asked Finston if she wanted anything to drink.

"Tea would be lovely. Chamomile if you have any."

Morris called Greta on his cell phone and asked if she could bring in a cup of chamomile tea. When he got off the phone, Finston asked him if the ME would be joining them.

Walsh spoke up. "It was tricky disengaging the victim from the crime scene." She checked her watch. "Roger only got the body in for a postmortem examination an hour ago. He'll be calling with his findings."

"That shouldn't take long," Polk wisecracked. "It's not like he's got that much to work with."

Morris ignored him and asked Finston whether she'd had a chance to look over the materials that had been emailed to her.

"Yes, of course."

"So you know everything we do. What's your take on the killer?"

Finston showed another of her tiny *v* smiles, this one with a sharper edge. "We're dealing with a narcissistic personality, and one who is extremely detail oriented," she said. "The precision involved in this murder is quite extraordinary. I would guess that he's been planning this for months, if not longer, and he certainly has other murders planned. He picked Ms. Brandley for a reason. She wasn't a random victim."

"It wasn't that well planned out," Walsh argued. "If he had repaired the power line before leaving, it's possible customers would've seen Brandley's corpse spinning around in that exhibit."

"I don't think that was important to him. He left Ms. Brandley the way he did for the police, not for the public. And of course, for you, Morris."

"What about that message?" Morris asked.

"He wants you involved."

"For what purpose? As a challenge?"

Finston shrugged her thin shoulders. "I don't know. The killer has worked out some sort of overarching, grandiose story that he wants to impress the world with, and for some reason he's included you to be part of it."

Greg Malevich cleared his throat loudly enough to get everyone's attention. "What if it's not a serial killer," he said. "Why couldn't it be someone who wanted Heather Brandley dead, and came up with this to have us chasing after a serial killer who doesn't exist?"

"It's not impossible, and it should be looked into," Finston conceded. "But given the elaborate measures that went into this killing, the other scenario is far more likely. I'm confident that we'll be hearing from the ME that Ms. Brandley was drugged and unconscious when she was murdered, and that will also support that we're dealing with a serial killer who will be killing again soon."

"Why is that?" Malevich asked, unconvinced.

"Because I believe our killer is only interested in telling his story, and not in the pain he inflicts on his victims."

Malevich mumbled something under his breath indicating that he still wasn't convinced. Morris asked Finston, "Assuming you're right and this is what it looks like, what happens if I don't get involved?"

"He'll make you get involved."

"How?"

"He'll start targeting people close to you."

That was the answer Morris both expected and dreaded. Before he could say anything else, Walsh's cell phone vibrated as it sat on the conference table. After a quick glance at the phone, Walsh informed the room that it was Roger Smichen. She answered the call, putting the phone on speaker. Walsh told the ME who was in the room.

Finston spoke up. "Hi Roger," she said. "It's me, Gloria Finston from the FBI. We worked together six months ago. Was the victim drugged?"

"Yes. There was enough pentobarbital in her system to have induced a coma. It might even have been the cause of death."

"So in your opinion she was unconscious when she was killed?"

"Yes, without a doubt."

"How easy is it to obtain pentobarbital?" Morris asked.

"It's a schedule two drug. The FBI can answer that better than I can."

"Anything else you can tell us?" Walsh asked.

"The best I can do is a three-hour window for time of death, putting it between five p.m. and eight p.m. yesterday. I started having thoughts after all of you left that a guillotine-type device might've been used, but on closer examination I was right the first time. A circular saw was used.

Twenty-four-inch blade. No other indications of trauma or injury. I was unable to find a needle mark, so she was injected on a part of her body that we don't possess." Smichen's voice dropped off before he added almost apologetically, "Her stomach was shorn open by the saw, and the contents must've been lost then, so I can't tell you what she ate last. That's about it, other than the plastic sheeting glued to her body. This was done meticulously. Almost surgically. I found no other foreign substance on her."

Walsh said, "The perp must've cleaned her off after killing her."

"Most likely. Look folks, I've got other bodies piling up here, so I've got to beg off this call."

A click could be heard as Smichen disconnected the call from his end. Finston showed Morris another of her *v* smiles and asked what it was that was weighing so heavily on him.

"I can't fool a profiler, can I?" Morris said.

"None that I know who work for the FBI."

"I'll take your word on it. I'm also guessing you already know what I want to ask you."

"I think I do. Whether we have a better chance of catching the killer if you join the investigation and keep him on script, or if you don't so that he attempts to improvise other murders to draw you in."

"Very good," Morris said.

Finston looked pleased with herself. "Even if we ignore the value that you and your team would bring to the investigation, we would be better keeping him on script. He would be more predictable that way, and I'm sure the other murders he has planned are as complex and risky as this one, which makes it more likely that he'll make a mistake and give himself away. Also, no matter what we might say in a press release, he's going to want to verify for himself that you're involved, which means he'll be watching for you at one of his future murder sites."

"We need to have someone shadowing me and looking for him."

"Exactly."

Morris mulled this over. He wasn't sure whether Finston was leveling with him or telling him only what he wanted to hear as a way to ease his conscience. If he forced this killer off script by refusing to play his game, and the killer chose someone close to Morris to force his hand, the police could be watching for that and would have a reasonably good chance of trapping this psycho. After the Malibu Butcher case, Morris had promised Natalie that MBI wouldn't take on any more murder investigations, and for his own well-being he didn't want to get near another serial killer, but he wasn't going to allow his wife or his daughter Rachel to be used as staked goats no matter how much police protection they were given. He knew the moment he read Gilman's text message that he was going to have to take this assignment no matter how much he had tried kidding himself otherwise.

His voice flat, Morris asked, "Let's say MBI gets involved and we keep this killer on script. Couldn't he still target someone close to me?"

"I don't believe so. If he were planning to do that, I think he would've done it with his first murder. He has a specific story he wants to tell with these murders, and I'm confident that as long as you cooperate and play nice, he'll stick to only telling his story."

Morris took a deep, long breath through his nose and told Doug Gilman, "MBI's available if you want to hire us."

Chapter 10

The meeting lasted another half hour as Morris and the rest of the team worked out a game plan. The LAPD would continue to pull whatever traffic and surveillance video recordings they could locate within a five-mile radius of Star Wax in the hopes of finding vehicle license plates that were captured between three and three fifteen a.m. While no one thought it was likely that the killer was named R. G. Berg, that lead still had to be investigated, and Polk, with help from several LAPD detectives, would take that on. Morris agreed with Malevich that it was worth investigating the crime as a murder that was dressed up to look like something else, and so Malevich would go after it from that angle and would look for suspects who might've had a motive for killing Heather Brandley. The FBI would attempt to identify stores that sold the scaffolding materials the killer used to support Brandley's body. Finally, Morris and Walsh would try to piece together Brandley's movements from the day before in an attempt to discover where and how Brandley met her killer.

As the meeting was breaking up, Morris found himself drumming his fingers against the conference room table as he thought more about the name the killer had chosen. *R. G. Berg.* Something about it was tickling the back of his mind.

"Why'd he pick that name?" he asked Finston.

The FBI profiler made a *who knows* gesture. "Impossible to say right now other than it fits the narrative that he wants to tell. But the name might still lead us somewhere."

"Bull," Polk groused. "He picked that name only to send us on a wild-goose chase. Or me, anyway, since I'm the unlucky putz who'll be chasing after that wild goose."

Morris didn't argue with Polk. But still, there was something vaguely familiar about *R. G. Berg*, although he was sure that he had never met anyone by that name. Something else gnawing at him were those two drops of blood left on the business card. He asked Finston about that also. "What was the point of that? Could it be this psycho's own blood? A way to taunt us?"

She showed another of her tiny *v* smiles, this one apologetic. "I wish I could tell you, but all I can say is it wasn't an accident."

Morris pulled his cell phone out from his suit jacket pocket and called Roger Smichen.

"Ah, Morris," the ME said on answering the call, his voice sounding sincerely disappointed. "So you decided to break your pledge. I was rooting for you not to, and am sorry to hear that you're letting yourself get mired in the mud with yet another serial killer."

"I could just be calling to say hello."

"But you're not."

"You're right. But Roger, what choice did I have? You saw the card he left for me."

"True, but just because this unhinged individual is dangling bait in front of your nose doesn't mean you have to take it."

"In this case it does. I'll explain why at a later time. I wanted to ask whether the blood on the business card matches the victim."

"I don't know yet. The victim's blood and both drops left on the card are A-positive."

"That's a common one," Morris noted.

"The second most. Thirty-four percent of the population has it. I've sent samples to the lab for a DNA test, which I've marked as urgent, and I'll let you know as soon as I hear back."

"Okay, thanks."

Morris got off the phone, and told Walsh, Malevich, and Polk what Smichen had told him about the blood. Walsh and Malevich were going to head over to the dead woman's condo, and Morris told them he'd meet them there, that he had an errand he needed to run beforehand. As he left MBI's offices, he found himself distracted. Once again, the name *R. G. Berg* nagged at the back of his mind. This continued as he left the building and headed to his car. He stopped and squinted off into the distance, trying to dredge out from his subconscious whatever it was about the name that seemed familiar. After several minutes of standing as still as one of those wax figures in the Star Wax museum, he gave up. Whatever it was he thought he knew, the only way it was going to rise to the surface was if he stopped thinking about it completely.

Morris first drove to the Hollywood station on Wilcox Ave. Doug Gilman had called ahead for him, so they had what he needed waiting at the front desk. After that he called Rachel, swung over to UCLA's campus, and met his daughter as she sat waiting for him on the front steps of the law library. He handed her one of the GPS tracking bracelets he'd picked up from the Wilcox Avenue station house. Rachel stared at it with disdain.

"I need you to wear this, honey," Morris said, his voice choking seeing Rachel's face mottling with anger. "If anyone suspicious threatens you, press the button, and the police will find you within minutes."

"I thought you weren't going to take on any more investigations that would put me or mom at risk," she stated in a low, icy tone.

"It wasn't so much that I took it on as I had it thrust upon me."

Morris explained the situation to his daughter as she stared at him, her face becoming an inscrutable mask. Rachel fortunately took after Natalie instead of himself, and was a slender, dark-haired beautiful twenty-three-year-old. The one thing that she inherited from Morris, besides his stubbornness, were his flinty gray eyes, and they remained unmoved as she listened to him. At the end, she relented and promised him she'd be careful and would wear the bracelet until he told her otherwise.

"Did you tell mom yet?"

"Not yet. I need to give her one of these bracelets, and I figured it would be better if I told her in person."

Rachel agreed that made sense. "If I can, I'll stop by for dinner either tonight or tomorrow. Maybe even sleep over."

"That would be nice." He cleared his throat and added, "It would give your mom more peace of mind if you did that."

Rachel's eyes softened more as she smiled at him, knowing full well that he was speaking as much for himself as for Natalie. She gave him a quick kiss on the cheek, and then turned and headed back into the library. Morris watched as she disappeared into the building.

Chapter 11

Charlie Bogle dropped a fifty-dollar bill on the table. Sitting across from him in the dimly lit and mostly empty Koreatown restaurant was Lionel Simmons, who had been one of Bogle's confidential informants when Bogle was on the force. Simmons, who had been rail thin the last time Bogle had seen him three years earlier, looked like he had lost even more weight, and from the nervous way he grabbed the fifty dollars from the table, had to still be smoking meth.

"If you were a car thief, and you were going to steal a 2004 Chevy Tahoe with a GPS recovery system installed, how'd you make the car disappear?"

Even though Simmons looked like he was trying hard to maintain a badass, empty stare, he broke out grinning from the question, revealing brownish, ruined teeth. Bogle knew that his former CI had at times worked as a car thief.

"What type of system?" Simmons asked.

Bogle told him.

A waitress came over to take their lunch order. Bogle ordered the bibimbap with chicken and Simmons told her he was just going to have tea. During the seven minutes they'd been there, Simmons had drunk three cups of the stuff, each loaded with three sugar packets. The waitress picked up the pile of torn empty packets that Simmons had left on the table before walking off. Once she was out of earshot, Simmons asked how long it took to report the Tahoe missing.

"Around twelve hours."

Simmons made several twitchy movements as he adjusted the way he was sitting and crossed his legs.

"Twelve hours?" Simmons made a noise somewhere between a whistle and an exhalation to express his incredulity. "That gives someone who knows what they're doing all the time they need to rip apart that Tahoe's dashboard and find the device, then smash it to pieces. Or drop it into a garbage disposal. Or hell, you have that much time, you can drive that Tahoe deep into Mexico. Ain't no tracking done there. How long ago did it disappear?"

"Four months."

"You got an exact date? Color and VIN?"

Bogle checked through his notepad, ripped out a blank sheet, and copied the information for Simmons.

"Two bills I'll ask around at chop shops I'm friendly with, and see if they helped make this car disappear."

Bogle gave Simmons a hard look and tried to decide if he would only be throwing two hundred dollars away since there was no telling if Simmons would actually do anything for that money. Karl Crawford's Tahoe could've ended up in a chop shop in Los Angeles, but it could've also ended up in a chop shop somewhere else. Other things also could've been done with it once the GPS recovery device was removed, including shipping it out of the country. Bogle wouldn't put it past Simmons to be playing him for a quick two hundred dollars, but he made up his mind and took a hundred out of his wallet and held it within reach. When Simmons reached for it, Bogle was faster as he pulled it back.

"I'm going to want names of who you talk to at these shops. Dates also. Lionel, I'll be checking up on you, and if you deliver you get the other hundred. If you don't put in the effort, we'll have words later. We understand each other, right?"

Bogle moved the bill closer so that his former CI could take it out of his grasp.

"We understand each other," Simmons agreed. "But that don't mean the Tahoe ended up at any chop shop. As I said, it could be in Mexico, or even all the way down to Chile by now. *She-it*, these signals ain't that strong. No more than eight miles. You find a remote enough spot, you park the car and cover it with a tarp, and police ain't going to find it. But I'll earn this bill, and the other, even if I turn up nothin'." He sat back, and tried to act nonchalant as he asked, "Why's this one Tahoe so important?"

"The guy who was driving it disappeared the same day."

"This guy's who you're really trying to find?"

"That's right."

"A bad dude?"

"Not that I can tell."

Simmons considered that. "I'll see what I can dig up," he promised.

Chapter 12

Nice building, Morris thought as he parked in front of the West Hollywood condo complex where Heather Brandley had lived. "Nice neighborhood, too," he told Parker.

The reason Morris had Parker in the car with him was because Natalie had insisted when they met at her office that he take the bull terrier. "You're the one this killer is obsessed with, not me," she had said. "Besides, I've now got this shiny new bracelet to protect me."

Morris had tried arguing with her about which of them needed Parker's protection more, but Natalie was adamant. She'd also put on a brave face over the fact that he was being sucked into yet another serial killer investigation. "Sometimes the stars just align a certain way," she said, her large, brown eyes melting into Morris's. "This maniac's not leaving you any choice. You're only doing what you have to do."

Morris felt a lump in his throat as he pictured the way Natalie had looked at him. No matter what else was going on in his life, he was a lucky man, no doubt about it.

He got out of the car, and made sure to hold tightly onto Parker's leash as the dog scooted out past him. Instead of heading to the condo complex, Morris walked across the street to the small park that was outlined with bushes, flowering coral trees, and another variety of flowering tree that Morris didn't recognize, this one having paper-thin yellow flowers. Morris used his phone to take a photo of one of the trees. He texted this to Natalie and asked if she knew what type it was. After that, he walked Parker around the park, letting the dog sniff at each bush.

Once the loop was completed, Morris sat on the lone bench in the park. Parker contentedly plopped down by his feet. Five minutes later Walsh emerged from where she'd been hiding across the street and headed toward him. Minutes before Morris had arrived at the condo complex, he called Walsh and they came up with this plan in case the killer was watching for Morris's arrival. It made sense that the killer might be doing so if he wanted to make sure Morris was involved with the investigation, but Morris hadn't spotted anyone suspicious while he did his loop of the park, and if anyone had been hiding in the bushes the bull terrier would've alerted him.

Walsh approached the bench and first greeted Parker, who made his excited pig grunts as he wagged his tail, and then sat next to Morris. "I didn't see anyone waiting here watching for you," she said.

"It was worth the shot," Morris said.

From Walsh's expression, she didn't seem to agree, but she didn't belabor the point. "According to the doorman, Brandley came back from a run around two-thirty yesterday, then an hour later she left by herself with her face made up, hair done, wearing a sexy green dress and black stiletto pumps. Quoting him, *she was dressed to kill.*"

"He had that backwards." Morris peered toward the building's entrance. "How come I don't see him?"

"He doesn't stand by the door. He sits inside by a security desk."

"Hmm. She certainly made an impression on him. Remembering exactly what she wore. Must be a pretty observant guy. Although I bet if I went over there now and talked to him, he wouldn't be able to tell me what you're wearing."

"Maybe not, but Brandley was the big celebrity in the building. And she was beautiful. It's not hard to believe he'd pay special attention to her."

"That could be it," Morris agreed, "but I don't like it when a witness uses a phrase like 'dressed to kill' as a way to describe a murder victim. Makes me wonder if he's playing some sort of mind game."

Walsh was about to argue with him, maybe even tell him he was being paranoid, but he knew Walsh almost as well as he knew anyone, with the exception of Natalie, and he could see the spark in her eyes the moment she agreed he had a valid point.

"Let's go talk to him," she said.

Chapter 13

They found the vestibule door locked. Morris stuck his nose against the glass and saw that there was no one sitting behind the security desk.

He asked Walsh, "How long ago did you leave the building?"

"No more than a minute after you called."

Morris checked his watch. "About fifteen minutes then. Was the doorman still in the lobby?"

She nodded, her face tense. With little conviction, she said, "He could be helping someone with a package. Or taking a break."

There wasn't much chance a doorman would be helping a tenant with a package. Morris had been watching the building's front entrance from the moment he sat on the park bench, and nobody had entered or left the building since then.

He asked, "What's Heather Brandley's apartment number?"

"Forty-eight."

Morris buzzed forty-eight on the intercom. Malevich answered with a brusque, "Who's this?"

"Greg, this is Morris. Annie's with me. Come down to the lobby right away, and if you see the doorman, hold him. And be careful."

"Why, what's up?"

"I'm not sure yet. Just get down here."

Walsh was biting her bottom lip. This was something she did only when she was anxious, and Morris couldn't remember the last time he'd seen her do it. Maybe when he was still on the force and they were working the Vincent Robusto case together.

"He couldn't have been the killer," she said almost as if she were in a daze.

"Describe him."

"Early thirties. Average height, weight. Short red hair. Well-groomed beard and mustache. Square-shaped face. Glasses. Blue eyes." Her expression weakened. "He was wearing white gloves, like you see in those old movies. I noticed them when he handed me the keys to Brandley's unit, and thought it was odd, but assumed it was a policy for the doormen working here. Jesus, it couldn't have been him, could it?"

Morris shrugged helplessly. Finston thought the killer would be watching for Morris, and what better way than to pose as the doorman? And what better way than to shove their noses in it? For the moment, though, all they could do was wait.

When Malevich showed up, a puzzled look creased his face as he opened the door for them. He waved a thumb in the direction of the empty security desk.

"What happened to him?" he asked.

"The million-dollar question," Morris said as he breezed past the homicide detective with Parker leading the way.

It didn't take them long to find a body. This happened after Parker nearly dragged Morris to a bathroom off the lobby and stood growling in front of the locked door, which had an 'Out of Order' sign attached to it. Morris rapped his knuckles against the door and got no answer. After Malevich identified himself and also got no answer, he kicked in the door on his third try. A large man lay crumpled facedown on the tiled floor, a puddle of blood and gore pooling under his head, his color a grayish-white. He was wearing a brown blazer and tan slacks, the type of clothes you'd expect on a doorman. Morris stood outside the room and forced Parker to sit, and clamped his hand over the dog's snout and ordered him to be quiet. Parker's growling dampened to a soft rumble. While this was going on, Walsh kneeled by the body and checked for a pulse.

"The skin's cold," she said through clenched teeth. "He's been dead at least a couple of hours." She pulled latex gloves from her pocket and slipped them on. After a few seconds of feeling around the back of the man's skull, she announced that she'd found the entry wound. She lifted the man's head up and grimaced as she reported that a hollow-point bullet must've been used, and that most of his face was gone.

Greg Malevich had called for backup units after he kicked open the door, and he was now back on the phone calling in the homicide. While he was on the phone, he indicated to Morris and Walsh that he was going to secure the back of the building, and he hurried off.

Morris's phone alerted him that he had just received a text message. He half expected to see a taunt from the killer, but instead it was Natalie, and it simply read "Gold Medallion". He stared at it confused for several seconds before realizing that his wife was giving him the name of the tree he had asked her about minutes earlier.

An excited yapping noise came from behind. Morris turned to see a woman in her late fifties holding a yapping Shih Tzu. The woman was trying to look past Morris to see what all the fuss was about in the bathroom.

"Ma'am, please stand back," Morris ordered.

The woman looked almost as if he had yelled *boo* at her as she took several steps backward. She seemed oblivious to the noise her dog was making. Parker likewise ignored the small dog, his attention focused on what was going on in the bathroom.

"Did something happen?" she asked.

"I'm afraid so. You live here, right?"

"Yes. For seven years."

Morris held an index finger up. "Could you wait here for one moment?"

He turned back toward Walsh. She had taken the dead man's wallet from his pocket, and was looking through it. Morris asked her if there was a driver's license. Her face had a white-hot intensity to it as she nodded. Morris knew she was seething with fury over having the killer in her grasp and letting him go. When she approached the woman holding the Shih Tzu, the woman looked startled and even the dog stopped its yapping.

"Do you know him?" Walsh demanded as she showed the driver's license of the man lying dead in the bathroom, her voice lashing out like a whip.

The woman now looked fearful, her eyes darting first to Morris and then back to Walsh. "Y-Yes," she stammered out. "T-That's Javier. One of our doormen."

"How many do you have?"

"Three."

"Any of them in their thirties with red hair, a short-cropped beard, and mustache?"

"No." Her eyes widened, and now there was only dread in her face. "Are you a police officer?"

"Yes. Detective Walsh. LAPD robbery-homicide division. When was the last time you were in the lobby?"

"I just came down minutes ago so I could take Rascal outside."

"Before then."

"That would be a little before eleven o'clock. Why, what has happened? Is Javier in trouble?"

Walsh ignored the question. "Was Javier Lopez working as the doorman when you came down then?"

"Yes."

"Have you noticed anyone suspicious hanging around the building lately?"

"I don't think so."

The woman was beginning to look unsteady on her feet, and Morris signaled to Walsh to cut her loose.

"Are you okay, ma'am?" Morris asked.

The woman looked grateful for the interruption. "I think I just need some fresh air," she said.

"Why don't you take Rascal outside," he said.

The woman looked like she could've kissed Morris, and she turned and fled toward the lobby. Walsh watched with disgust. She was still seething over the way the killer had fooled her.

"You and your soft spot for dog owners," she said as if she were spitting out vulgarities.

"Is that what she was holding?" Morris asked with a straight face.

The high-pitched wail of sirens could be heard descending on the building.

"The cavalry has arrived," Morris said.

"A lot of good it will do," Walsh complained. "That sonofabitch psycho is long gone."

"Maybe not. He could be hiding somewhere in the building. We're going to have to call the management company and get keys."

She muttered something under her breath that Morris couldn't quite make out, but she didn't argue with him. Of course, he agreed with her. The odds were the killer had left while Walsh was outside hiding so she could shadow Morris, but they were still going to have to search the building.

"Why don't you keep watch over the crime scene. I better get to the door so I can let the reinforcements in," Morris offered.

"Let me show you something first."

Walsh took a plastic evidence bag out of her jacket pocket and handed it to Morris.

"I found this stuck in the victim's wallet."

Inside the evidence bag was another business card, similar to what was left on Heather Brandley's body.

Written on it was: *To Morris Brick: I can only imagine how frustrating this must be—R. G. Berg, Serial Killer Extraordinaire.*

Chapter 14

The killer sat in front of the lighted makeup mirror admiring the job he had done earlier that morning. It had taken him more than two hours of painstaking work, as well as many hours of practicing over the last six months, but the transformation he had achieved was quite remarkable. While the disguise he had put together for Heather Brandley was adequate enough to do the job, this was at a whole different level. He proved this by seeing that Lopez had no clue who he was. The man had blubbered like a baby when the killer marched him into the bathroom, and even when he promised to let Lopez live if the doorman could only tell him his name (which was an inane lie—Lopez's brains were going to be blown out no matter what he had said) Lopez in his panic still couldn't give him an answer. The killer couldn't be too unkind to him; after all, the face now staring back at him in the mirror would've fooled his own mother.

But enough of patting himself on the back. It was time to get to work.

The killer popped out the cosmetic contact lenses, changing his eye color back from blue to brown. Next, he removed the hairpiece. After that he poured solvent into a bowl, picked the right brush to use, and removed the red-colored eyebrows that he had glued on. With those taken care of, he lifted the edge of the latex foam prosthetic that he had attached to the bottom half of his face just enough so that he could work the brush in and dab the tiny bit of exposed adhesive with solvent. This was a slow, methodical process as he worked his way down the jawline, across the neck, and then up the other side of the jaw. After twenty minutes, he was able to peel away the prosthetic, and he went from having chubby chipmunk cheeks to a lean, angular-shaped face. He also lost the beard and mustache that had been glued onto the prosthetic.

He continued the same process with the latex foam prosthetic nose he'd been wearing, and less than eight minutes later he was able to peel it from his face, revealing a smaller, straighter nose. With the prosthetics removed, he got up from the table and headed to the washroom, and there he soaked a towel in hot water, which he used to loosen the dried epoxy sticking to his face. With that done he scrubbed his face clean, and then applied moisturizer to his skin. He studied himself in the mirror over the sink until he was satisfied that he couldn't see a single sign that anything had been glued to his face.

Just like dominos falling. His mouth curved upward into an amused grin.

Even though he didn't get a chance to meet Morris Brick in the flesh as he had expected, he was still quite pleased with how the events of the day were turning out, although he wouldn't have been able to say that earlier. The truth was, he was furious when those two cops had entered the building's lobby without Brick in tow. That had stunned him. How could Brick not understand the warning the killer had left him? It should've been obvious. Was the guy that thick (as a brick!) that he was going to force the killer to make his wife one of the victims before he'd play along? While that lady cop had questioned him, the killer was too numb at first to feel much of anything, but after she had left to go to Heather Brandley's condo, he simmered in rage and imagined all the things he was going to do to Brick's wife to teach the guy a lesson.

The killer was still smoldering in evil thoughts when that same tough lady cop stepped out of the elevator, stormed through the lobby and left the building, but curiously, she veered away from the walkway and disappeared from sight. Well, that left him no choice but to investigate, and he snuck up to the vestibule door and spotted her hiding behind shrubbery with a pair of field glasses. He wondered about that until he saw Brick sitting in the park across the street. The killer then realized what was happening. They were convinced he'd be there watching for Brick to make sure that Brick had taken the killer's challenge. All the killer could do then was whisper to himself, *wow.* The dominos were falling exactly as he had planned. Exactly! The first domino being Heather Brandley, the second having Morris Brick come to Brandley's condo complex to investigate.

But then the killer remembered something he had said to the lady cop in his irritability. This was when he had described Heather Brandley leaving the building yesterday looking as if she were *dressed to kill.* The lady cop might not have picked up on the killer's snarkiness, but Brick just might if it was repeated to him. He also realized that if he waited around for Brick to come into the building, there was a chance one of the building's residents could come by and ask about the doorman who was supposed to be on duty. The killer accepted that it was best to leave. And so he carried out the delivery box that he had brought and left through the back door, which led to the parking lot. He had Brandley's car keys with him, and by clicking on the remote so that her car would beep, he found her Audi and drove off in it.

The killer dumped the Audi three blocks from the alley where he had left his car. In the box were the clothes he had worn to masquerade as a deliveryman, and before leaving the Audi he took off the glasses, blazer, and tie, and put on the shirt with the delivery company logo emblazoned on the front and matching cap to once again appear as a deliveryman. If he were honest about it, he felt exposed and had moments of nervousness as he walked those three blocks to his car, especially when two police cars with sirens blasting drove past him, but they didn't seem to pay any attention to him. Once he was back in his car, it was clear sailing.

* * * *

The killer left the washroom and walked to the kitchen area. He chose the *Capriccio* flavor, and after the coffee finished brewing he brought it to the modeling area where he had miniaturized replicas of the carnage he had planned. Most of it was dark, but two of the models had been lit up—one that showed the Star Wax museum with the back and top removed so that a six-inch version of Fred Astaire and Ginger Rogers dancing could be seen, and another that showed a detailed three-foot-high replica of Heather Brandley's condo building.

The killer felt a sense of pride as he looked over the area. Soon more lights would be turned on. He checked his watch. Fifty-eight minutes and forty-one seconds before the next domino would be falling and he'd be turning on another light.

The killer suppressed a yawn. It was time to get going.

He had brought the clothing he needed for this next part of his plan and, as he dressed, he reflected on how busy he'd been over the last forty hours and how much more still needed to be done before he'd be able to get any sleep. Besides the yawn fighting to come loose, he was still feeling wide awake. Energetic even. Like he could do backflips. He was sure at some point exhaustion would hit him like a truck, but that wasn't going to happen now, not with all the adrenaline pumping hard through his veins. All those months of planning, and he was finally seeing his vision unfolding as he had imagined it would. Of course, it was still very early, and there were so many more deaths to follow, but so far everything was working out perfectly.

The killer drank the rest of his coffee, chose an LA Dodgers baseball cap to wear over his shaved head, grabbed a laptop computer and a pair of headphones, and was about to head out when he remembered that he hadn't glued on any fake eyebrows. Well, that would've been a mistake, maybe even a fatal one! He decided to glue on the blond ones. He also decided to wear the matching bushy mustache and the shaggy dirty blond hairpiece. That would save him time later. It only took him a minute to add the fake hair to his face and head, and then he was off to watch the next domino fall.

Chapter 15

Morris showed Gloria Finston video from the lobby surveillance camera, pausing it the moment the killer dressed as a deliveryman entered the building. The time of day was displayed in the bottom-right corner of the video, and it showed that this happened at eleven eighteen a.m.

Morris said, "He either thought it would take us longer than it did to discover Heather Brandley's body, or he somehow knew it would take several hours after that before we'd come here to search her condo."

LAPD had provided the laptop computer, and Morris and the FBI profiler were sitting behind the lobby security desk with Parker lying quietly by Morris's feet. Finston looked away from the computer screen to search the wall behind them.

"I don't see the surveillance camera," she said.

Morris pointed out the small hole in the back wall that was somewhat camouflaged by a framed painting.

"It's well hidden," Finston observed. "He might not have known he was being recorded?"

"He didn't care. He expected me to get a good look at him. Instead Annie spent ten minutes face to face with him. I think the only thing we can assume about his identity is that he's Caucasian, in his thirties, and that he doesn't have red hair, wear glasses, or have a beard or mustache. And that he's five feet eleven inches tall."

"How did you get his height?"

"We have a point of reference with how he's standing next to the door. The crime scene folks insist that's how tall he is, assuming he's not wearing lifts in his shoes."

Morris continued the video. The killer came to life carrying a box across the lobby and placing it on top of the security desk. While the doorman couldn't be seen in the video, the clipboard that he handed over to the killer could be. As the killer took the clipboard with his left hand, he reached behind his back with his right and pulled out a gun, which he pointed straight ahead. Morris again paused the video.

"The gun barrel looks unnaturally long," Finston noted. "A suppressor?"

"Yep. A 9 mm with a suppressor attached. The gun will still make a noticeable popping sound when fired, but if the bathroom walls are constructed solidly enough, it's likely no one outside of the lobby would've heard it. Forensics will be figuring that out. The blazer and tie he wore when Annie spoke to him must've been inside the box."

Morris continued the video, and it showed the killer transferring the gun to his right hand, sliding the box under his left arm, and disappearing out of the frame. Morris again stopped the video.

"At this point he must have taken the victim to the bathroom. The crime scene folks were able to determine from the blood splatter and the angle of the bullet wound that the victim was on his knees when he was shot in the back of the head. The killer then changed his clothes and masqueraded as the doorman."

"After putting an 'Out of Order' sign on the bathroom door."

Morris said, "Correct. There's also a surveillance camera covering the back door, and it shows him leaving the building at one thirty-seven, again carrying that same box. That was about the time Annie and I were sitting together in the park across the street."

Finston got up so she could walk over to the vestibule door. "He would've been able to see you from here," she said.

"That's right."

Finston appeared deep in thought as she stroked her pointed chin and made her way back to her chair behind the security desk. She looked up at Morris with thoughtful eyes.

"Those inscribed business cards weren't left simply to get you involved in these murders," she said. "While his plan might need you to be involved, he also wants to taunt you. This is personal with him. Very much so. We know he's in disguise, and he could even be wearing prosthetics, but is it possible that you know him?"

"No, not possible. I don't care how much he might've disguised himself, I've never seen him before."

"His animus toward you could be because of a relative you arrested, or even something unrelated to your time as an LAPD detective. Morris, you need to explore that avenue."

Morris felt the same dull throbbing behind his eyes that he had experienced earlier that morning. This was turning into a mess. While he knew Finston was right, he still asked whether it was possible that the killer simply wanted to prove his superiority to the *famed* serial killer hunter. "After all, you said the guy's a narcissist. Isn't that what an extreme narcissist would do?"

"There's more to it than that. He didn't come here just to gloat. He wanted you to be tormented by the fact that you had him and let him slip away."

"If that's true, why did he flee instead of sticking around so he could face me?"

"Because he realized he had made a mistake with Detective Walsh, and he was afraid you'd pick up on it."

Morris started massaging his temples, hoping to soothe the throbbing that had spread from behind his eyes to the back of his skull.

"Possibly," he admitted. "He stuck around after executing Javier Lopez for some sort of demented thrill, but I think he might've had another reason for killing Lopez. You know the story he told Annie about Heather Brandley yesterday returning from a run, and then an hour later coming back down to the lobby *dressed to kill*, as if she had a hot date? I'd bet money that's true—that this was yet another way for the killer to smirk at us, in this case by telling us what actually happened. I'd also bet money that her hot date was with the killer. That he had met her at the end of her run. And I'd also bet that somebody let him know when she had left the building to go running and how long she usually ran for, so that the killer could *accidentally* meet her."

"A doorman working here would know that."

Morris said, "My thoughts exactly."

Chapter 16

"A soft guy like you won't fare well in prison. If I were you, I'd use the time you got left on the outside to toughen yourself up."

Dalton Fowler's reaction gave him away. He should've either acted confused or angry; instead he froze for a heartbeat before forcing a big horselaugh.

"You're a funny guy, Brenner," he said, his laughter giving way to red-faced chortling.

The reason Fowler called Fred Lemmon by the name Brenner was because when Lemmon was brought in three weeks ago to fill Eckhardt Engineering's newly created position of vice president of corporate compensation, he was introduced as Mark Brenner. This was a bogus position, and only the company's CEO knew who Lemmon really was.

"That might be true," Lemmon said, "but ten years in prison is no laughing matter, even if you're lucky enough to serve it out in a federal country club instead of in the California correction system."

Fowler decided to change tack. The amusement dried up instantly, leaving his face chalky white with indignation. He should've gone with indignation first, but he had badly miscalculated. His hands balled into fists as he got up from his chair and took a step toward Lemmon.

"I don't know what you're talking about," he said in a soft, menacing tone.

"Of course you do," Lemmon said. "But let's not waste any more time. Just sit down, okay?"

"Stand up!"

Lemmon sighed and stood up. Fowler took another quick step forward and threw a punch at Lemmon's jaw. Lemmon could've just stepped away from it, but he instead ducked the punch while at the same time driving his right fist into Fowler's stomach. That took the air out of Eckhardt

Engineering's vice president of public relations. Lemmon took hold of his elbow and guided Fowler back to his chair, and then retook his own seat.

"Let me explain the situation to you so you don't keep acting stupid," Lemmon said. "My name's not Mark Brenner and I have no idea what a vice president of corporate compensation would even do. I'm an investigator with MBI, and I was brought in here to find out who's been selling Eckhardt's bids to Thompson Solutions. And you're the guy."

Fowler sucked in just enough air to force out, "That's insane. I don't have access to the bids."

"You might not, but Alice Gleason does, and I followed the two of you to the Sunspot Motel three nights ago. I even snapped a couple of photos of you while you got on her laptop. This was when she was in the shower."

Alice Gleason was the administrative assistant to the vice president of new business development. As far as Lemmon was concerned, the company had too many vice presidents. Lemmon had also fibbed about what he told Fowler. The part about following them to the motel was true. It was also true that Gleason had brought her laptop with her. But the blinds had been closed so Lemmon was unable to see what went on inside the motel room, although he knew Gleason had taken a shower after she and Fowler had had their tumble in the sack, and he also was pretty sure around fifty minutes after they had entered the room he heard through the flimsy motel door not only the shower turn on, but also the sound that laptop computers make when they're powered on.

Lemmon could see the calculating look in Fowler's eyes as he remembered that the blinds had been closed that night.

"One of the slats didn't fit right and it created just enough of an opening through the blinds for me to take photos," Lemmon said. "But that's only part of what I have against you. You're done, Fowler. At least if I show anyone what I have."

Fowler reacted as if he'd been slapped. He bit his lip and asked, "What do you mean?"

"I might want to burn what I've collected," Lemmon said with a guilty smile. "I've got expenses with two kids in college, and I've had my eye on a sailboat. A Corsair. Forty-eight grand used. So I'm offering you a one-time deal. A hundred and fifty thousand and I tell Eckhardt that it's just bad luck that they keep getting underbid by Thompson."

"So you're a greedy swindler," Fowler said.

"Fortunately for you, not that greedy. Otherwise I'd be asking for everything Thompson gave you. You're still going to make out."

Fowler laughed bitterly. "Not after you grab seventy percent." There was more of that calculating look, then, "I'll give you forty grand. That's it."

Lemmon breathed in deeply as he manufactured a pained look. "Make it forty-eight grand so I can buy the sailboat."

"I ought to kick the crap out of you for sucker punching me earlier," Fowler said, his mouth forming a soft pout. "But fine, I'll pay you. It will be worth it to never have to see your cheap, swindling face again."

Lemmon smiled at that. "I don't know, forty-eight grand doesn't make me all that cheap, but whatever makes you feel better about this. I want the money wired to my account today."

Lemmon handed Fowler a folded sheet of paper, who took it as if it were something diseased.

"You'll get it. Now get out of my office before your stench makes me lose my lunch."

Lemmon shook his head sadly at Fowler as he got up from his chair. "If you're going to be a thief you should learn to treat your fellow thieves with more respect."

Lemmon whistled the tune "We're in the Money" as he left Fowler's office. Waiting for him in the office he'd been given was Chester Eckhardt, the founder and CEO of Eckhardt Engineering. Eckhardt's round, jowly face was livid with rage.

"Did you get all that?" Lemmon asked, because he had kept an open cell phone connection with Chester Eckhardt while he had been in Fowler's office.

"Every word," Eckhardt said, his voice shaking with anger. "I'd like to go in there now and break his jaw."

"I don't blame you. If it will make you feel any better, I gave him a good shot right in the breadbasket." Lemmon tapped his own stomach. "The way the color drained out of his face, I'm lucky he didn't puke on my shoes. The good news is you have enough now for an arrest, but I'd suggest waiting for him to wire the forty-eight thousand into the account you set up. It will make the case against him that much stronger."

Eckhardt was still seething. "You don't think Alice Gleason was involved?" he asked.

"I don't think so. I grilled her pretty good. If she fooled me, she's a damned good liar. And a sociopath."

"I don't believe she's that," Eckhardt said with a decisive nod of his head. "Just someone who got taken advantage of. But I'll be talking to her. And I'll be wanting to look at her banking records." He held his hand out to Lemmon. Lemmon took it, and fought to keep from wincing. It was almost like a python had wrapped itself around his hand.

"I'd been hoping that being underbid like we were was a fluke. That sonofabitch Fowler might've cost my company eighteen million dollars." Ekhardt cleared his throat, and added, "This incident has made me realize I need to open a new position. Vice president of corporate security. It's yours if you want it."

Lemmon thanked him for the thought, but told Eckhardt he was afraid the position would become too boring once the other employees saw what happened to Fowler. After a few more words with Eckhardt, Lemmon bid adieu. He waited until he was outside before shaking his hand crushed by Eckhardt's beefy paw. He further waited until he was in his car before calling Morris.

"I rolled the dice like we talked about and got a useable confession, and am available to help with this serial killer case."

"That's good," Morris said, his voice sounding weary over the phone. "We got another body. A doorman by the name of Javier Lopez who was working at Heather Brandley's condo building."

"That was fast."

"Yeah, it was, although I think it was partly a murder of necessity. That the killer needed Lopez dead. We should be able to confirm this after we get a look at some phone records. But I also suspect this psycho wants to keep us from catching our breath. Anyway, I can certainly use you on this. Are you still in San Diego?"

"Yep, I just got in my car. I'll call you when I get to LA."

Chapter 17

"Excuse me, Miss, do you have this in teal?"

For several minutes, Hannah Welker intentionally ignored the skinny man with the scraggly beard as he performed an assortment of pantomimes to get her attention. One of the perks of working for Hipster Dipster was that the sales personnel were required to be rude. It was considered part of the ironic charm of the store. But she also had an English Lit paper due tomorrow on *Wise Blood* by Flannery O'Connor, and she still had over a hundred pages that she needed to read before her shift ended, so she was planning to be more than just *ironically* rude to this guy. If she could get away with it, she was going to flat out act as if he didn't exist.

"*Wise Blood.* Cool book," the guy said. "Must be hard reading it with customers like me bugging you, huh, Miss?"

"It's Ms.," Hannah hissed under her breath.

"Ah ha! I got your attention. Finally. So will you see if you have this in teal? Twenty-eight waist, thirty-six length."

Hannah had made the mistake of acknowledging his presence. He wasn't going to leave now. She looked up from her book to see the skinny guy grinning widely. After all, treating him like dog poop was all part of the fun. Sighing and giving him her best put-upon look, she said, "If that's the only way I can get you to leave me alone, fine, I'll go check."

She got up and flashed him an exasperated look. He giggled, thinking it was part of the act. It wasn't. On her way to the stockroom, she gave an extra-long look at a mannequin she passed in the women's section. This one was dressed in tan leather boots, plaid green and yellow pants, a gray blouse, and a flowery cotton sweater. It wasn't the outfit that made her stare. She kind of liked it. But each time she had passed the mannequin that day something about it seemed off, and she couldn't quite figure out what it was.

She found the teal-colored pants that the skinny guy was asking for. She almost went back empty-handed, because now she was going to have to spend time ringing up the sale. But doing something like telling that guy the store didn't have an item that it did could get her fired, and this was a sweet gig, especially with all the time it gave her for her college work.

She stopped to look again at the mannequin. Something was definitely wrong about it. She decided after she finished *Wise Blood* she'd satisfy her curiosity and figure out what it was that bugged her.

"Your lucky day," she told the skinny guy in her best bored voice as she handed him the pants.

"I'm sorry if I interfered with your reading pleasure," he said, still grinning.

"English Lit assignment," she said.

"Paper due?"

"Tomorrow."

"Ah ha. You figure out yet what your paper's going to be about?"

"I'm not sure yet. I still have over a hundred pages to read. But something about sin and faith."

A loud popping noise, like what a large firecracker might make, got both of them turning in the direction of the stockroom. This was followed almost immediately by a crashing noise.

"What was that?" the skinny man asked.

Hannah had no idea.

"I better go see," she said.

"I'll join you."

She wasn't going to turn down his offer of chivalry. What really spooked her was where the crashing sound came from. It might've only been her imagination, but she could've sworn it was where that creepy mannequin had been set up—the one that had something off-putting about it.

The skinny guy, who told Hannah his name was Josef, led the way toward the stockroom, and sure enough it was the mannequin that had crashed to the floor and now lay in two pieces—the upper torso and the lower half. The lower half was by far the bigger piece, and it didn't look right to Hannah. Whatever the popping noise was, it had split the pants revealing not plastic, but instead what looked like bloodless, way-too-white flesh.

"That's not blood, is it?" Josef asked.

He was pointing at a small puddle leaking out of the lower half. Hannah all at once felt woozy, and she would've collapsed to the floor if Josef hadn't caught her.

Chapter 18

The killer had wanted an outdoor table at the café directly across the street from the Hipster Dipster, but they were all taken. "I could seat you inside," offered the hostess, a petite redhead with a face dotted by freckles.

"Any by the window?"

"Let me check."

When the hostess came back, she smiled apologetically. "Nothing right now. But if you want I could sit you at the bar until either a window or outdoor table opens up."

The killer only had seven minutes before the device he had planted in his mannequin-corpse creation was set to go off, and waiting around for a table wouldn't do, so he instead hurried over to the bakery half a block away and got seated outside there. It wasn't ideal, but he'd still have a view of the show, albeit an obstructed one. But that would be for what went on outside. For the real show, he'd have a front-row seat.

The killer had planted a spy camera inside the store, and by using the store's Wi-Fi connection, he was directing the video feed to a dark and untraceable corner of the Internet. By the time the waitress took his order, he had the feed running on his cell phone and his earbuds plugged in so he could watch and listen to what went on inside Hipster Dipster.

The killer felt a thrill run down his spine when the small explosive device triggered and his Frankenstein-monster mannequin broke apart as he had planned and crashed to the floor. As he had also worked out, the seam of the pants split open, revealing what was underneath. He couldn't help giggling as he watched the young pretty salesclerk faint and the skinny hipster dude catch her, and thought of how he might even be playing cupid with this falling domino. A voice close by startled him. He looked up to see the waitress grinning as she placed his cappuccino and éclair on the table. He removed the earbuds.

"That must be some video you're watching the way it's cracking you up," she said.

He wondered for a moment if she had caught a glimpse of it, because if she had he'd have to kill her.

"It's a real sidesplitter," he said.

She smirked as if she found his choice of words odd but quaint. "Does it have cats in it?" she asked. "I wouldn't mind seeing a funny cat video right now."

"Sadly, no cats. I'm allergic to them."

That brought a puzzled look, as if she couldn't understand the non-sequitur he had thrown at her. In any case, it stopped her from doing any further flirting. He watched as she walked back into the bakery, and he decided that she couldn't have seen any of the video. That was just as well. He was going to be busy enough as it was. He put the earbuds back in.

The killer lay the phone down on the table, and leisurely drank his cappuccino and ate his dessert, and watched as the first police cruiser arrived at Hipster Dipster, then as several more police cruisers and an ambulance joined the party. Soon after that more cars came. A buzz started among the customers sitting at the other tables as they wondered what was happening. The killer, as he listened to the commotion inside Hipster Dipster, kept his focus on the cars that were arriving. It was after Morris Brick left one of them with his dog that the killer picked up his cell phone again so he could watch the video feed.

He wanted to see Brick's reaction to his handiwork, but the sense of someone standing next to him caused him to look up. Once again it was the pain-in-the-ass waitress, and this time she was trying to get a peek! The killer shifted the phone to make sure the screen was hidden from her, and he once more took out his earbuds.

"You look like you're enjoying that," she said with a big grin.

"A special video my girlfriend made for my eyes only," he explained.

That worked as well as if he had thrown a bucket of cold water on her, and in a heartbeat her grin deflated. Instead of walking away like she should have, she asked what he thought was happening inside that store.

"Whatever it is, I'm sure we'll see it on the news tonight."

She nodded as if that made sense, and finally walked away. He'd been smiling pleasantly from the moment she had interrupted him, but it was all he could do to keep from grabbing her by the throat and throttling her. Because of that meddlesome woman he had missed what was going on inside Hipster Dipster. He took a deep breath as he tried to calm his anger, but his hands still shook as he fitted the earbuds once again into his ears.

The video showed Brick standing near the body, talking to a tall, bony bald man, who the killer knew from his research was Roger Smichen, LA's medical examiner. The quality of the audio wasn't as clear as he would've hoped, and the killer had to strain to hear what was being said. Even so, he ended up missing snatches of their conversation. From what he was able to make out, Brick wanted to know about the time of death, whether this was the rest of Heather Brandley's body, and whether the killer had left him another business card. A thin, brutal smile tightened the killer's lips when he heard Brick asking whether the body had been sexually violated.

Really, Brick? You have to take this into the gutter? You can't simply appreciate the brilliance of what I've done?

Brick's phone must've rung. The killer watched as Brick struggled to remove it from his pocket, and then as he stood like stone listening to whatever someone was telling him. After a minute of this, Brick walked out of frame. The killer sat intently waiting for him to return. Others were gathering around the body, but not Brick. The killer kept looking from his phone to Hipster Dipster's front door, but wherever Brick was, he couldn't spot him.

Something caused the killer to look toward the café where he had tried to get a table when he first arrived; the one directly across the street from Hipster Dipster. A strangely familiar-looking man wearing a suit and dark sunglasses stood outside the restaurant. Late forties, short iron-gray hair. This man wasn't much bigger than the killer, but he had a wiry toughness about him that was apparent from half a block away. From what the killer could tell, the man seemed to be searching for someone sitting in the café's outdoor area. The killer's cell phone rang. Not the one he was watching the video feed over, but a burner phone that he also carried. That didn't make any sense. With Lopez dead, there was only one other person who had the number for it, and he shouldn't have been calling him.

The killer took the burner phone out and his blood froze when he saw the caller ID. Morris Brick. He realized then that Brick must've figured out that Lopez had called the killer yesterday to let him know that Heather Brandley was going on her run. He looked in the direction of the man standing outside the café and remembered where he'd seen him before. It was when the killer was researching Morris Brick and his firm. The man was one of Brick's investigators. Ted Lemmon or Fred Lemmon, something along those lines.

The killer broke out of his trance and turned off the burner phone. He looked up to see Lemmon walking toward the bakery. *Jesus*. Brick somehow knew the killer would be watching the store. That was why he called when he did. Because the investigator expected to hear a phone ringing where he stood outside the café. If the killer had gotten a seat there like he had wanted, it would have been over for him. Droplets of cold sweat snaked down his back. He had two choices: stay seated where he was and act as if he were just another customer enjoying a cappuccino and dessert, or leave. Whichever it was, he had to make a decision now!

Lemmon was three storefronts away and moving at a fast clip. The killer's mind locked on him as a fight-or-flight panic took hold. He fumbled with his wallet and dropped a twenty-dollar bill on the table. At least he had enough presence of mind to do that; otherwise the waitress might've made a scene.

As casually as the killer could manage, he got up and headed into the bakery, his heart beating wildly. As he did this, he made sure not to look in Lemmon's direction. Fortunately, he soon discovered the place had a back door for customers. He continued on through the bakery until he was out the door, and then he ran as if his life depended on it.

Chapter 19

From a quarter of a mile away Brad Pettibone thought he saw a car parked near the oil well that he needed to service. As he bounced along the private dirt road, his brow furrowed as he realized that not only was he right about a car being there, but that a man was leaning against it. His first thought was that Mark Sangonese might've gotten rid of his pickup truck for a sedan, but as he got closer he saw the man was taller than Sangonese and had a leaner body type than his boss's squat, bull-like frame. The lines furrowing his brow deepened as he wondered who this guy could be.

Pettibone pulled up next to the stranger and lowered his window. "This is private property, owned by Samson Oil & Gas. You got a reason for being here?"

"I do. My name's Charles Bogle. I'm investigating the disappearance of one of your co-workers, Karl Crawford."

Pettibone made a face at that. "I don't think I ever spoke more than ten words to the man. I can't help you."

"That might be so," Bogle said. "But your boss, Mark Sangonese, told me I could talk to you. He even told me I could find you here."

"Why'd you pick me to talk to?"

"Not just you. I'm talking to all the maintenance technicians."

Brad Pettibone was a large, rawboned man. As he stared at Bogle, his fleshy face folded into a scowl that would've made any bloodhound proud. "You can waste your time and ask me whatever you want. Just don't get in my way. I need to get this well updated and calibrated by five."

Pettibone got out of his Ford Explorer, and moving in a slow, careful pace, opened the back and took out a toolbox, then what looked like a large metal suitcase. He handed Bogle the toolbox, and told him that he could be useful by carrying it over to the well. Bogle did as he was asked while Pettibone followed with the metal suitcase. When they got to the well, Pettibone took a socket wrench out of the toolbox, and went to work opening up the well's casing.

"Go ahead," he said, grunting. "Ask me your questions, not that it's going to do you any good."

"You never had any drinks or spent time with him?"

"I told you I didn't."

Bogle shrugged. "You could've been exaggerating."

"I wasn't."

"Okay, I know that now. Was he friendly with any of the other maintenance technicians?"

Pettibone turned and gave Bogle an openmouthed look as if he couldn't believe how dense he was. "You drove all the way out here to ask me questions like those? I told you, I didn't know the man. I have no idea who he was friendly with."

"You ever hear any rumors about him?"

"I don't hear rumors about anyone. Take a look around." Pettibone clamped his mouth closed as he used the socket wrench to remove one of the bolts, then added, "This is my office every day. That brush and those cactuses are my only daily companions. Besides, I'm not the gossipy type."

"You must have some idea what happened to him."

Pettibone's jaw muscles clenched as he muscled the last bolt. "I don't have any," he said. "It's not something I've spent even a minute thinking about."

"That's a bit callous."

"I told you, I don't know him. What I worry about is servicing the wells I need to each day." He wiped his brow, then said, "Besides, for all I know nothing bad happened to him. He could be somewhere in Mexico smoking weed all day and drinking tequila and whoring around all night."

Pettibone finally budged the bolt. After a half dozen turns of the socket wrench, he removed the bolt, then opened up the casing revealing the guts of the well. Bogle watched as the technician pulled out what looked like a computer motherboard from the machinery.

"We're replacing these on all the wells," Pettibone explained.

"Your boss told me about that. Something about advanced diagnostics."

A hint of bitterness reflected in Pettibone's eyes. "That's right. This way they can service more wells without paying us another dime. Look, I got to get the new board out of my Explorer. You can keep following me around and asking me questions, but I don't see how it's going to do you any good."

Bogle said, "You're right. It was a wasted trip. Thanks for your time."

Both men walked to their respective vehicles. Pettibone busied himself with storing away the old motherboard, and while he did this, Bogle got in his car and drove off. After a minute or so, Pettibone pulled his head out from the back of his Explorer. He watched as Bogle drove over the dirt road that would lead to the highway. Once the car disappeared from sight, Pettibone stuck his head back into his Explorer, this time so he could use a screwdriver on the sidewall. After a few minutes, he had the sidewall opened up, revealing several square, white packages, each weighing approximately twelve pounds. While Pettibone knew the package couldn't explode if he dropped it, he was still careful as he brought it and the new motherboard to the well. After hiding the package far behind one of the compressors so it couldn't be seen if someone opened up the casing, he attached the new motherboard, and then went to work calibrating one of the high-pressure pumps, for all the good it would do.

Chapter 20

Morris's phone rang. Fred Lemmon.

"You were right," Lemmon said. "He was outside watching. Just not from the café across the street. He was at a bakery half a block away. I saw him walking into it before I got there, but he must've taken off like a bat out of hell through the back door. Something else. I think he hid a camera inside Hipster Dipster. His waitress told me he took a table ten minutes before the police arrived and was glued to a video he was watching on his cell phone. I'm bringing her over now to the West Hollywood station to get a sketch done."

Morris waved Annie Walsh over. In a low, guarded voice, he told her that Lemmon believed the killer had hidden a spy camera in the store. She indicated that she'd get on it. Morris returned to his phone call with Lemmon.

"Could she identify him from the video?"

"No. She said his face was shaped differently. More angular. Also, long blond hair that was tied into a ponytail, a thick, bushy mustache, and a smaller, straighter nose. But the shape of his eyes was the same. I'll call you as soon as the sketch is ready. You should get someone to search the back alley behind the bakery. Odds are he ditched his phone back there."

"Will do."

Morris disconnected the call and swore to himself. It had been impulsive on his part to call the killer's phone. He knew that at the time, but when the LAPD got the records for the lobby phone in Heather Brandley's condo building and found a number that was called yesterday that they couldn't identify, he decided to play his hunch that the killer was watching the Hipster Dipster from someplace close by. If he had noticed a bakery on the same block with outdoor tables, he would've sent someone there also. But since the café across the street was the only place he could remember having outdoor seating, he coordinated with Lemmon to position Lemmon there and had three LAPD patrolmen waiting by the café's back door in case the killer tried running. Then he made the phone call.

Dammit! He should've handled it better. But he thought if the killer was watching from nearby, he wouldn't be doing so for much longer. Morris had already been at the crime scene for over fifteen minutes before he got the call about the unidentifiable phone number. If his thinking had been clearer, it might have occurred to him earlier that the killer could be watching the store.

Dammit!

Walsh and one of the crime scene specialists approached him. The specialist told Morris in a whisper that they had found a covert pinhole camera planted inside a mannequin near the one that had been rigged up.

"Odds are it's using the store's Wi-Fi to send out the video feed. We'll bring in a computer forensics specialist and see if he can identify where the feed's going. Maybe we'll catch this maniac that way."

"He was watching the feed on his phone," Morris said.

"Which means he was first sending it somewhere on the Internet. Which further means he could be leaving behind digital fingerprints."

Morris didn't think there was much chance of that. The killer had been too meticulous with his planning to make that type of mistake. From the intensity burning on Walsh's face, she thought differently.

"Okay, leave the camera where it is. Annie, in the event this guy is still watching the feed, what do you say we try to raise his blood pressure?"

"Sounds good to me. The higher the better."

Roger Smichen was standing near the body. Morris sent him a text about what was going to be happening, and what Smichen needed to say, and then he and Walsh joined him.

Chapter 21

An hour later the killer still couldn't believe he had panicked the way he had. The investigator, Ted Lemmon or whatever his name was, would've been looking for a man with short red hair, a carefully groomed beard and mustache, and a square-shaped face. If the killer had just kept his wits about him and sat calmly at the outdoor table nothing would've happened. But in the end, no harm, no foul. He had been at the bakery long enough, and there had been no point staying even a second longer. Actually, there was no reason for him to be there at all, although he knew what had drawn him to the spot—there was something viscerally thrilling about being that close to Brick and all those other cops as they bore witness to his handiwork. In the larger scheme of things, it was only one domino, and there were so many more to fall, but still, he had been especially proud of this one. But that didn't change the fact that he could've watched the video feed from anywhere. He still could.

The killer checked the time. He had a few minutes before he was to meet the movie actress Faye Riverstone inside the swank Hollywood bar he was parked behind. No reason not to watch more of the video while in the safety of his car, especially since he was dying to see Brick's reaction to his latest message.

The signal from the bar's Wi-Fi was strong enough for the killer to piggyback off of, and the killer navigated to the dark corner of the Internet where he was storing the video feed. He fast-forwarded through it until he reached video he hadn't seen yet, and then he continued to speed through this also until Morris and that tough lady cop came into the frame and joined the skeleton-thin ME.

Tell him about the message I left for him, the killer whispered to himself because he knew the ME had found the business card. He had watched when the ME removed the boots from the corpse and the card fluttered to the floor. The ME noticed it also because he picked it up with a tweezer-like tool and deposited it into an evidence bag (as if the killer would be careless enough to leave fingerprints!).

Brick spoke first. The audio faded in and out, and the killer had to turn the volume up and replay it before he could understand what Brick had said.

> *Brick: I rolled the dice and came up snake eyes. Fred found nothing. This sicko wasn't across the street like I had hoped.*

Fred, the killer thought. *Fred Lemmon. I knew it was something like that.* He chided himself once again for how he had overreacted. He should've known Brick and the rest of those cops weren't bright enough to have figured out that he had been there. Yeah, they might've gotten lucky and discovered that Lopez had called him yesterday, and they might even have the number for the untraceable phone he had dumped, but a whole lot of good it was going to do them.

> *Tough Lady Cop (ignoring Brick): You find anything that can help us?*
> *Medical Examiner: The body was sexually violated. Vaginally and anally. This occurred postmortem.*
> *Brick: So we're dealing with a sexual deviant.*
> *Medical Examiner: Yes. To say the least.*

At first the killer couldn't make sense of what was being said. As the meaning of the ME's words seeped in, the killer found himself trembling. None of what was being said was true! Not a single word! Was the ME that incompetent? A thought jolted him. Was it possible his victim had sex before he grabbed her? Maybe even rough sex? Could the ME be mistaking when the sex had occurred?

> *Brick: This deviant cut up Heather Brandley's body so he could hide that he engages in necrophilia.*
> *Tough Lady Cop: Sick bastard.*
> *Medical Examiner: True on both counts.*
> *Brick (showing a pained grimace): We'll have to give this to the media. Let them know what kind of sicko we're dealing with.*
> *Tough Lady Cop: What (garbled) do you think they'll give him?*

Brick: Something simple. My bet, the Pervert.

The killer at first felt sick to his stomach. Soon he could barely see straight he was so enraged. He couldn't watch another second of the travesty unfolding on the video. The last thing he had expected was this level of incompetence. It damn well bordered on malpractice!

Damn it, this wasn't what he had counted on. Because that ME couldn't do his job right, they were going to muddy up his name and try to sully what he was accomplishing? Instead of his work being held in the awe that it deserved, they were going to make it look like the work of a psychologically unhinged deviant. Someone who engaged in sex with dead bodies!

The killer at first sat stewing, but then a simple thought occurred to him. The medical examiner was only talking about a preliminary examination made at the crime scene.

He'll be changing his conclusion once he brings the remains back to his lab for a more thorough examination, the killer told himself. *He can't be this incompetent!*

But what if he is?

The killer decided that couldn't be the case. The guy had reached the level of medical examiner for a major US city. He'll recognize his mistake. He'll have to. The killer was sure of it…but the thought still nagged at him that there was a one in a million chance they could end up spreading those outrageous lies about him. He decided it wouldn't matter if that happened. As more dominos fell the true nature of what he was doing would become apparent to everyone. Brick, the ME, and the rest of them could malign him now all they want, but in a few short days all the dominos will have fallen, and the city of Los Angeles will recognize what he had done. The true meaning of it.

Forget Los Angeles, the world will see it.

A ping from his cell phone broke him out of his trance. He checked his phone to see that the alarm he had set earlier had gone off. It was time for him to have his second date with Faye Riverstone. His last one as well.

The killer checked himself in the driver's side vanity mirror. The blond wig and mustache looked fine, and there were no clear signs of his recent agitation. He got out of the car and took a deep breath. Let them spread their lies. It didn't matter. Brick and the rest of them would be the ones looking like fools once his masterpiece was fully revealed.

Slowly, the killer found himself relaxing, his shakiness from a few minutes earlier mostly gone. He practiced the devil-may-care smile that his research showed Faye Riverstone was a sucker for—the same smile he had used on her when they met three days earlier. The killer had done extensive research on her, reading every available interview in print and watching clips of her talk show appearances on YouTube. He knew where she liked to hang out, and that she was attracted to men with dirty blond hair tied into a ponytail. Bushy mustaches, too, just like the one he had glued on earlier. He also knew how to dress for her, and what to say.

The poor woman never had a chance.

That thought brought a smile to the killer's face. A genuine one. The distress he had felt was forgotten. He headed into the bar where he knew Riverstone would be waiting.

Chapter 22

Charlie Bogle was the last one to arrive, which made sense since he had the longest drive coming from Long Beach. He didn't look happy.

Morris gave him a sympathetic look. "Sorry I had to pull you off your missing persons case."

Bogle shrugged diplomatically. "This has to take priority. Besides, it shouldn't matter if I put the case down for a week or longer. I doubt Karl Crawford's going anywhere."

"You think he's dead?"

"I haven't found anything to make me think otherwise."

Morris waited until Bogle squeezed into the last empty chair at the table before asking Greg Malevich to start things off by reporting what he had found regarding the hipster clothing store.

"Sure thing." Malevich struggled for a moment to work a notepad out of his back pants pocket. He squinted at it as if he were deciphering a foreign language he wasn't fluent in, and then cleared his throat and began.

"There were no signs of a break-in. The store has a low-end keypad security system, and the damn thing doesn't record when it's used. No surveillance camera either, and none in the general vicinity. Right now we need to assume the killer was given access to a key and the security code. When we're done here, I'll be interviewing store personnel to find out who gave it to him."

"What about the woman working there when the remains were found?"

Malevich consulted his notepad. "A young college kid by the name of Hannah Welker. We talked already. She's clean."

Morris took a long drink of his eighth cup of coffee that day as he tried to combat the weariness weighing on him. MBI's lone conference room was as full as he had ever seen it and they'd had to bring in extra chairs to accommodate everyone. In addition to himself, Malevich, and Bogle, also sitting at the table were Gloria Finston, Doug Gilman, Walsh, Polk, Lemmon, MBI computer and hacking specialist Adam Felger, LA Police Commissioner Martin Hadley, and four other police detectives who'd been assigned to the investigation. Lying under the table by Morris's feet was Parker, who was snoring in starts and stops, exhausted from the day's activity.

"So no progress then," Hadley grumbled as he gave Morris an accusatory stare, his arms folded across his chest, his face locked into a frown that would make any bulldog proud. Hadley and Morris were like oil and water. They hadn't mixed well when Morris was on the force, and their relationship only became more strained once Morris founded MBI and took three LAPD detectives with him. Morris knew it killed Hadley to involve him and MBI in the investigation, and even more so that he had to let Morris take the lead on it. But Hadley, first and foremost, was a political animal, and he was smart enough to realize that he needed the public relations cover MBI would bring. Fortunately, Hadley still didn't know about Morris's earlier gambit of calling the killer's phone. If he had, he would've gone ballistic.

"We have a police sketch of the suspect," Morris said.

"Yeah? What makes you so sure about that?" Hadley's thick, rubbery lips clamped shut as his frown deepened, then in a disgusted tone, he complained, "The sketch doesn't look anything like the suspect in the videotape. Which you claim is useless because he disguised himself. Even if that's our perp, what makes you think the drawing is worth a damn? If it's him, he's still in disguise."

"I'm sure that's true," Morris said, his voice reflecting every bit of the weariness he was feeling. "No doubt he's wearing a wig and a fake mustache. We'll be giving the media two sketches. The one showing how the witness described him, another with him bald and clean shaven."

"Not on my watch you won't!"

Doug Gilman spoke up then, suggesting to the police commissioner that they talk privately. Hadley looked like he wanted to offer the mayor's deputy assistant a few choice expletives, but he acquiesced and followed Gilman out of the room, closing the door behind him.

"The man's holding a significant amount of resentment toward you," Gloria Finston noted, her thin lips curved into a smile to reflect her curiosity.

"It goes back a ways," Morris said.

"All the way back to when he was born a pain-in-the-ass," Polk deadpanned.

"Hadley's always been the life of the party," Bogle added.

Annie Walsh bit her tongue to keep from laughing.

The conference room was soundproofed, but whatever conversation Gilman and Hadley had was brief since the mayor's deputy assistant quickly returned. He announced that Hadley had been called away on other urgent matters and wouldn't be joining them any further. "Martin did want me to tell you that he's in full agreement with the mayor's decision that you are to run this investigation as you see fit, and with the full support of the LAPD," Gilman added with a straight face.

"What a mensch," Polk said.

Morris's cell phone rang.

Chapter 23

Roger Smichen was calling about his findings. Morris put the phone on speaker.

"Quite a day so far," the medical examiner said.

"Quite an understatement," Morris corrected.

"Yes it is, and I'm about to make your day even more interesting. We've got a third victim. The remains found in that hipster clothing store are not from Heather Brandley."

What Smichen said didn't surprise Morris. Although this other victim and Brandley had nearly identical body types and the killer painstakingly severed both of them at the same anatomical point so they'd appear to be two pieces of the same whole, Morris had suspected that the killer was playing some sort of game with them.

"A couple of jigsaw pieces that don't quite fit, huh?" Polk asked.

"Our killer tried hard to make it look like they did," Smichen said. "The same blood types, the body lividities identical—"

Morris asked, "Are you saying they were both killed around the same time?"

"Within an hour of each other. My guess less than that. As I was saying before being so rudely interrupted—"

"Which is usually my job," Polk interrupted without noticeably showing his tongue in his cheek.

"Is that Dennis Polk?" Smichen asked.

"None other."

"Of course it would be," Smichen said. "Let me try one more time. Given the damage that the explosive device caused, our killer might've fooled me into thinking this was the missing lower part of Ms. Brandley, at least until the DNA results came back. But I was able to test the bone densities, and they don't match."

"Interesting," Finston said as she nibbled on her small thumbnail, her dark eyes bright with thought.

Walsh asked, "Anything that can help us identify this new victim?"

Smichen said, "As with Heather Brandley, she was blond, between five feet five and five feet eight, and from calluses on her feet and her muscle tone, most likely a runner. Age, between thirty-five and forty. Something else. She has a tattoo below her right ankle. The Chinese symbols for "unbreakable.'"

"A bit ironic," Bogle noted.

Morris told the ME that they needed to see if this new victim's DNA matched the blood found on the first business card.

"We're thinking along the same lines. A sample has been sent to the lab, marked urgent. One other thing I have is there are no signs of additional trauma, and the body was scrubbed clean. I've ordered a full toxicology report, and I'll let you know the results when I get them. Odds are we'll find pentobarbital, as with the other victim."

"Sounds likely," Morris agreed.

"I've got nothing else to report, so let me bid adieu. Even to you, Polk."

Smichen disconnected from his end before Polk could offer a comment. The ME's news that the killer had so far taken three lives, and not two as some in the room might've assumed, had its effect, and the conference room became eerily quiet. Even Parker's snoring had subsided. Morris broke the silence by tasking two of the LAPD detectives who had joined the investigation, Ray Vestra and Franklin Strong, with identifying the new victim. "While it's likely he picked her because she physically resembled Heather Brandley, I'd like you to follow through with all missing person reports. Cast a wide net. There's no telling how long ago he grabbed our Jane Doe."

Vesta and Strong left the room to start their search. Morris picked up the plastic evidence bag that held the killer's latest message to him. Scrawled on the business card was 'Having fun yet?' It was juvenile, but still a taunt. Morris put the evidence bag back on the table.

"Are you still convinced the killer has a personal grudge against me?" he asked Finston.

"Yes. Most certainly. He could've watched the video feed from anywhere, but he needed the satisfaction of being there and seeing you enter the store. He needed the physical proximity to you."

"Any chance the guy sitting outside the bakery isn't our perp?"

"None."

Morris had come to that same conclusion. Even with the disguises the killer had worn, he could see the similarities between the man in the video and the police sketch, especially the shape of the eyes.

"Fred, I need you to dig into my old cases and see if I put anyone away with a son or nephew or what have you who could be this psycho." Morris turned to one of the remaining LAPD detectives, a large redheaded man who looked like he could stand to lose forty pounds. "Gunderson, you'll work with Fred and provide whatever assistance is needed."

Morris next asked Walsh what she had found out about Heather Brandley. He knew what she was going to say since they had already privately discussed it, but he wanted the rest of the room to hear it also.

"A worker at a juice store called Grassy Knoll served her around two thirty yesterday afternoon. He stated she was wearing a running outfit and was shiny wet with perspiration. He also claimed she went running nearly every day, always stopping at the store, and that they kept a tab for her." Her expression soured as she commented that what the killer told her when he was disguised as the doorman was probably true. "Sweat-stained tank top, sports bra, and running shorts were found at the top of her hamper. The lobby surveillance tapes confirmed that she left the building at two o'clock dressed in that same running outfit, returned at two forty-three, and left again at three forty-one dressed the way the killer had described. In each instance, she was alone. This also fits with the doorman, Javier Lopez, calling the killer at two minutes past two to let him know that Brandley was going on her run."

"So he could arrange to meet her."

"Presumably. I haven't found anyone who saw Brandley after she left the juice shop, but I'll keep canvassing. It will help if I can find a witness who saw her getting into a car."

"She probably met him on the same bench we sat on," Morris said. "That must've been a ritual of hers. Go running, get a juice, sit on the bench and enjoy her drink."

"The guy must be a smooth operator," Lemmon observed. "He meets a semi-famous actress on a bench, and minutes later has her running back to her apartment so she can get dressed up and go on a date with him."

"It could be that he was able to offer Ms. Brandley something she wanted," Finston said.

"Like what?"

Another of her tiny v smiles, this one with a sharpness to it. "She was an actress. I'm guessing he offered her a starring role in a movie."

A dull throbbing once again started in the back of Morris's skull. It was as if his hangover from earlier that morning wouldn't go away. Or maybe it was all the coffee he drank that day. In any case, he knew what the FBI profiler said made sense.

He told Bogle, "Charlie, I need you to look into movie producers."

Bogle showed his best poker face as he said, "There are a lot of them. Probably more producers in this town than baristas. Or at least more people who call themselves producers."

"I know. Adam, help Charlie get a list together, and screen out the ones you can."

"Will do," Felger acknowledged.

"That leaves the search for R. G. Berg," Morris said, glancing over at Polk.

"This joker's not named R. G. Berg," Polk argued.

"Most likely not, but the search will still lead somewhere," Finston said. "This killer has been meticulous in his planning, even if he at times has shown a certain rashness. He didn't choose the name randomly. He chose it because it fits into the narrative he's telling us."

Polk didn't look convinced. "If you say so. Me, I think he's having us run around like idiots because it's how he gets his jollies." He turned to Morris. "To answer your question, computer nerd over there"—a nod to Felger—"came up with a list of five hundred and twenty-eight R. G. Bergs, with nine in the Los Angeles area."

"Thirty-one within two hours of Los Angeles," Felger interjected. "The FBI will come up with a more complete list, but it was the best I could do under the constraints I had."

"I've crossed three of the local Bergs off the list, for all the good it will do," Polk said.

"We need an FBI field agent to coordinate this with," Morris said to Doug Gilman.

"Agreed. I'll get on it after the meeting."

"Okay. We've still got a lot more Bergs to look into. Stan, how about you work with Dennis on this?"

Stan Wolowicz was another of the LAPD detectives who'd been assigned to the investigation. A chunk of a man. Five feet eight, and almost as wide as he was tall. He gave Polk a sideways glance. The two of them had worked together when Polk was on the force, so Wolowicz knew what he was getting himself into. "Nobody ever said this job would be easy," he said, keeping his expression inscrutable.

"I feel for you," Lemmon said.

"Ah, Freddy, my boy," Polk said. "Admit it, you missed me the last three weeks while you were living it up in San Diego playing junior executive—"

"Senior executive. Vice president of corporate compensation, to be exact. And all the perks that came with it, including time with their in-house massage therapist and catered lunches."

"In-house massages, huh? I bet your masseuse was a heavyset Russian broad with arms like a gorilla."

"Yoshi? Uh uh. Beautiful slender Japanese woman with hands like a dream."

"You still missed me," Polk argued.

"Like a migraine."

Morris held up his hand to stop their squabbling. "That's enough," he said. "How about instead you get busy trying to catch this psycho before he cuts up any more women?"

The meeting ended. Doug Gilman and Gloria Finston stayed behind with Morris, as they still had business to discuss. Once it was just the three of them, Gilman glanced at his stainless-steel Raymond Weil watch and muttered, "Oh Jesus."

"What?"

"It's already seven thirty-five. We've got an eight o'clock press conference scheduled to inform the good citizens about what's been going on."

"You'll have to do it without me, Doug. I've been dragging all day. So has this little guy." Morris reached down to thump Parker's stomach. The bull terrier's eyes were open. He stretched his legs but otherwise remained lying on his side. Morris straightened back up, saying, "As soon as we finish here, I'm heading home to get some sleep. I've got an eight-ten appearance tomorrow morning with Margot Denoir. Let's see if I can get under this psycho's skin."

Denoir hosted a popular and sensationalized Los Angeles morning show called *The Hollywood Peeper*. Gilman gave Morris a questioning look. "Do you think that's wise?" he asked.

"That's what I'll be discussing with Gloria."

"Whatever you two think is best. If you need anything, let me know."

"I might need round-the-clock protection for my wife and daughter."

"If it comes to that, call me and I'll arrange it." Gilman glanced again at his $1,900 watch. "I need to leave now to make the press conference. What should I say?"

"Just the bare facts. Names of the two known victims, description of the third, and that we're seeking the public's help in identifying her. Don't go into any of the gory details. That's what the killer wants. Make sure the two sketches we have of him get plenty of play. The tip line also. What do you think, Gloria?"

"Exactly how it should be handled."

Gilman adjusted his tie. He seemed to brighten over the prospect of soon being in the spotlight. He gave Morris an assured nod, and told him once more to call if he needed anything, and then he was hustling out of the conference room.

Finston asked Morris, "How do you plan to get under the killer's skin?"

Morris smiled guiltily. "I should've told you this earlier, but with Hadley in earshot, I thought it would be best to wait." He rubbed the back of his neck, his smile turning sheepish. "When we discovered the covert camera hidden inside the clothing store, we put on a little show for him."

Finston asked, "Did you now?"

"Oh yeah."

Morris proceeded to give her a blow-by-blow description of what was said. "If the killer watches this part of the video, how do you think he'll react?"

"Oh, I'm sure he'll see it, if he hasn't already. And I'm sure he'll be furious."

"Is that good for us?"

"Yes, I believe so. There's been a good deal of precision in what he's been doing. I think of him almost like a demented craftsman working in extremely fine detail, and it's not a bad idea to knock him off his game. Are you planning tomorrow to publicly call him out as a deviant who sexually abuses the corpses of his victims?"

"That's the plan."

"It's a good one," she said. "He believes he's an artist, and he's unveiling a great work of art, and that the world will recognize his genius. I'm sure he has already convinced himself that Roger will realize he made a mistake with his medical examination, and it will be devastating for him when you denounce him as little more than a deviant. There's a good chance he'll contact the media to attempt to clear up the record. He might even initiate contact with you."

"Am I putting my family at risk by doing this?"

Finston nibbled again on her thumbnail as she considered Morris's question.

"I don't believe so," she said. "The narrative he's telling has been carefully constructed so far. He might've left room initially for some improvisation to make sure you became involved, but at this point I don't see him veering from his plans, no matter how much you might enrage him."

"And he's going to be enraged."

"Most definitely."

Morris's face weakened as he thought about Natalie and Rachel. "I better call Doug anyways," he said.

"It can't hurt to be prudent."

Chapter 24

"Welcome to my lair," the killer said.

He unlocked the steel door and held it open for Faye Riverstone, who appeared unsteady on her four-inch heels as she stepped into the building. She had to be somewhat tipsy. The actress couldn't have weighed more than a hundred pounds, and during the time they were at the Noire Bar, she drank four tequila cocktails while the killer nursed two beers.

"I've been here before," she said with one of her trademark squinty pouts.

"No kidding?"

"Years ago. When I was a teenager. It was a movie studio then. It looks very different now."

"Before then it was an airplane hangar," the killer acknowledged. "They converted it into a movie studio in the sixties and it went belly up about ten years ago. I've since renovated it to its current condition."

"Very nicely done," she said, impressed. "So this is where the magic happens?"

You damn well should be impressed after all the money I've poured into the place, the killer thought.

Faye Riverstone did a slow three-sixty, gazing around the massive room. This was normally the staging area for corporate projects, and one of the machines the killer had been working on lay zigzagged through half of the room. An elaborate machine, but in its current state quite harmless. A few alterations would change that, but that would be for later. A different staging area for his current lethal dream project could be found in a back room of the building, and Faye Riverstone would soon be joining Heather Brandley and others as a key participant.

"Not really," the killer said with forced modesty. "It's all just lining up the dominos."

"I don't see any dominos."

"Metaphorically speaking. I used dominos when I was first starting out, but they've gotten boring and I now incorporate more clever substitutes." He fingered his fake mustache. It felt as if it had started slipping, and he didn't want to give away his disguise quite yet. "I do have real magic brewing in one of my back rooms," he added. "A pet project I've been working on for several years that will be leaving the world in awe. I'll show you that soon enough. For now, I have a bottle of Krug chilling and a jar of exceptional beluga caviar waiting for us."

Riverstone opened her eyes wide, which was unusual for her since she was famous for her trademark squinty look in movies, which for some reason the critics considered sexy. Maybe it was because of the way she'd also purse her lips as if she were on the verge of pouting.

"That wouldn't be a bottle of 1998 Clos d'Ambonnay?" she asked.

The killer had made special note from an interview she had done three years ago in which she gushed about that vintage of champagne and how sublime it was. It damn well should be sublime at $2,200 a bottle. But, as the killer kept reminding himself, the kind of art he was creating didn't come cheap.

"That's exactly what I have," he said.

The actress squealed and took a step forward, stumbling awkwardly in her heels. The killer caught her arm to keep her from falling to the floor.

"You're trying to get me drunk so you can take advantage of me," she said with an exaggerated pout.

"I'd be a fool not to."

That got her laughing, and the killer joined her.

The actress kicked off her heels, deciding it would be better to go barefoot. "Lead the way, sire," she said, giggling.

As he led her to the kitchen area, she wrapped a slender arm around his waist, and her slight, toned body bumped against his. The killer smiled inwardly as he thought how easy these Hollywood actresses were because of their vanity and sense of entitlement. As long as you were willing to put in the work, as he had done, they were little more than putty.

"Madame, you're sending me certain signals," he said, exaggerating a note of shock in his voice.

"I should hope so!"

Once they were in the kitchen area, she admired the Nespresso machine while he got the champagne and caviar from the refrigerator. While Faye Riverstone busied herself with the caviar, the killer popped the cork off the champagne bottle and poured glasses for both of them, handing one to her.

"*Grazie*," she said.

"Cheers," the killer returned.

He watched as Riverstone took the smallest possible sip imaginable. She barely wet her lips with the champagne.

"Drink up," he said. "We've got this whole bottle to finish."

"My dear sir, this is nectar of the gods," she explained. "It must be savored."

"In that case, spoils go to the victor."

The killer guzzled down his champagne. He smiled thinly as he refilled his glass.

"Bastard," she said, laughing. She took a healthier swallow of her cherished nectar. The killer waited until she emptied her flute also, and then refilled her glass. Of course, he kept his back turned to her as he did so.

"Are you going to let me see your magic?" Her eyes sparkled mischievously as she sipped her champagne and then slowly licked her famously pouty lips. "After all, there's so little of it in the world."

"That's the plan. A small taste of it, anyway."

The killer brought along the rest of the champagne as he took the actress to the back room. That was where he had the modeling area for his masterpiece. He switched on the light for the two-foot-tall replica of the Hipster Dipster clothing store. If someone were to bend down to look through the front window, he would see a broken-apart miniaturized mannequin lying on the store floor. If that same person studied it closely enough, he'd also see what looked like a small pool of blood collecting under this busted mannequin. Faye Riverstone didn't bother doing this, but her face still scrunched up into a look of confusion as she tried to make sense of what she was seeing.

"I don't get it," she said.

"Conceptually it's similar to my other machines," the killer said. "The ones you've seen on YouTube and the ones I build for corporate events. Each event triggering the next. Like dominos falling. Although in this case, the triggering doesn't happen right away. It might take hours. In some cases, even days."

"I still don't follow what you're trying to do here."

"Quite understandable since I've got most of the modeling blacked out, and you haven't seen the news yet to understand the significance of what's been lighted up."

"You're not making any sense at all," Riverstone said, her lips twisting downward, forming something between a pout and a frown.

The killer laughed. "Probably not," he agreed. "Let me show you an animation that shows all the events playing out in sequence. It will make sense then."

"You promised there would be magic."

"There will be," the killer promised.

The killer directed the actress to take a seat on a plush sofa facing a large-screen TV. He remained standing so he could better watch her. The animation was created with computer software and was detailed and realistic. It started when the killer replaced the Ginger Rogers wax figure at the Star Wax museum with Heather Brandley's corpse. Faye Riverstone's confusion became revulsion, and by the time the animation showed what would be happening to her, her skin had become a sickly white and her face was rigid with terror.

"This isn't funny," she said.

The killer smiled hearing how slurred her voice had become. The Rohypnol he had slipped into her champagne was doing its job.

"No, it's not funny," he said. "I told you before, it's magical. You should be honored that I chose you to play a starring role."

That was a lie, of course. She was only going to be a supporting player, but why not at least make her feel more important than that? After all, the killer didn't consider himself a sadist. He didn't show her the terrible things that were going to be done to her as a way to torture her, or to cause her distress. He did it because he wanted to fully share his vision with at least one other person. The world would be seeing the entirety of it soon enough, but he'd been dying to have someone, really anyone, bear witness to the full magnitude of his genius. But this had gone on long enough. She wasn't appreciating what she was seeing. No doubt because of the Rohypnol.

He reached down with the thought of scooping her under the legs with one arm and slipping the other behind her back so he could carry her to his private workshop, but her hand clenched into a tiny fist and struck him in the throat. Her quickness surprised him, and the blow immobilized him, sending him collapsing to the floor unable to breathe. It shouldn't have been possible for her to have moved that fast given the Rohypnol he had slipped her.

In the killer's mind's eye, he imagined his face becoming as purple as a grape. He needed to breathe, and as he struggled to do so, he also fought to get back to his feet.

Oomph.

The noise was forced out of him by a hard blow that struck him in the ribs, the force of which knocked him back to the floor. She must've kicked him hard enough to break a wood plank. It hurt like hell, but the blow also unlocked whatever it was that had kept him from breathing, and he greedily sucked air back into his lungs. Tears welled up in his eyes as he realized that she had saved his life. It was unintentional on her part, but if she hadn't kicked him he would've died of asphyxiation.

He worked himself back to his hands and knees, and then to his feet. He gingerly felt his ribs as he staggered off in search of Faye Riverstone. It was remarkable how hard she had both punched and kicked him. She must've studied some form of martial arts, although the killer hadn't found any references to that in his research.

The killer moved through the building as quickly as his injured ribs allowed. An icy panic squeezed his chest as he worried that he'd been sold a bogus batch of Rohypnol, because it would be the end of everything if Faye Riverstone escaped. He should've used the pentobarbital on her like he had with the others, but he had to be cute about it.

The killer found her outside the building. She had fallen three feet away from the killer's Mercedes, his car keys still clutched in her hand. The Rohypnol had worked after all. His ribs hurt as he picked her up and carried her back inside so he could prepare her for what would be happening next.

As he carried her to his private workshop, she made soft mewling noises, but otherwise the sedative left her helpless.

Chapter 25

Almost every night Brad Pettibone would heat up a can of beef stew or baked beans and a chopped-up hotdog for dinner, all of which he bought cheap at the local Costco. The divorce had left him so financially strapped that he could barely afford his squalid three-hundred-and-sixty-square-foot studio apartment, let alone any decent food, so he had to watch every penny, or at least he did before he made arrangements with "Reuben." Tonight was different. He had splurged on takeout from his long-ago favorite Italian restaurant. Lasagna with a side of meatballs, and another side of sausage. Also, a big slice of their chocolate cake that he used to like so much. And instead of drinking his usual swill, he had splurged there as well, picking up a six-pack of Heineken. Why not live it up a little during his last few days in the States? He would be flying to Thailand on Sunday, never to return…that is unless the authorities caught up to him, which he didn't think was likely, at least not with the fake passport he'd be using, and not with him disappearing into a small Vietnamese coastal village. He'd read about others doing it. He was pretty sure he'd be safe where he was going. He also doubted he'd be able to get Italian food there. Maybe not Heineken either.

Pettibone chewed slowly as he savored a bite of sausage, and then took a long pull on the Heineken and savored that as well. If he was still married to that nag Janice, she would've made him drink it from a glass. He stared absently at nothing in particular, and reflected on the thought that if he'd had the money to spare these last three years, he wouldn't have eaten much differently. He had never learned to cook, at least not much more than making toast and heating up a can of food. Cooking was Janice's job, not that he ever cared for the crud she'd put on the table each night. But the last year of their marriage…he shivered just thinking about it. That was when she had gotten on her health kick and started making dinners with kale and quinoa. Jesus, he hated her. He didn't much care for his bratty kids either. If it was up to him they wouldn't have gotten a dime of alimony or child support, but the bitch had surprised him by going to court and garnishing his wages. That just wasn't right. This was America, goddamn it! The thought of Janice and his kids burning with the rest of LA didn't bother him at all. In fact, he liked the idea of it.

Pettibone knew that was just wishful thinking. There wasn't much chance Janice and his kids would get as much as a scratch when those wells blew up. Reuben claimed a lot of people in Los Angeles were going to die when it happened, but Pettibone wasn't convinced. More likely, not much more was going to happen other than starting dozens of raging well fires and gushing tons of black smoke into the atmosphere. Not that that was anything to sneer at. It was going to be costly to Samson Oil & Gas, and it might even put them out of business. Pettibone liked the idea of that. He felt no loyalty at all toward his employer. Why should he? They'd always treated him shabbily, giving him insulting raises over the years, some years stiffing him altogether.

Pettibone's eyes darkened as he took another long pull on his beer, draining it. He reached for another beer and cracked it open using the edge of the table. It was more than that they had always treated him poorly. Almost from the first day Sangonese was made his boss, the fat turd had had it in for him. Pettibone also knew a little over four months ago Sangonese had planned to fire him. The other maintenance techs thought it was only a rumor that one of them was about to be cut, but Pettibone knew better. He had always been good with a lock pick, and it wasn't hard for him late one night to break into Sangonese's secretary's desk. It didn't take long after that to find the evidence he was looking for: a memo giving Sangonese permission to fire his lowest-performing maintenance tech, which according to the memo was him. He had called Reuben after that to tell him why he wasn't going to be able to plant bombs for him like they had arranged. Reuben asked for the name of the top-performing maintenance tech, which was Karl Crawford, and promised Pettibone he'd take care of it, which he must've done since Crawford disappeared three days later. But that was then. Pettibone knew their new initiative of installing advanced diagnostic boards at each well was so they could fire most of their maintenance technicians, and Sangonese would make sure he'd be the first to go. Another three months tops, and he'd be out of a job, thrown away like so much used garbage. At least that's what would've happened if he hadn't met Reuben.

Pettibone doubted Reuben was his real name. The way the guy had smirked when he had introduced himself to Pettibone, it seemed more like an inside joke. The guy had also seemed unstable, but Pettibone didn't much care. The money he was being paid to plant those bombs would allow him to escape his indentured servitude. Twenty-five grand had already been transferred to an offshore account, and a final payment of fifty grand was scheduled to be made Saturday. It wasn't a lot of money—not as much as Pettibone would've liked, but it would do. He had spent months working out the numbers in his head, and the seventy-five grand, plus another twenty-two he was able to scrape together with loans and selling his car, should be enough for him to live out his days drinking whiskey and cold beer, eating barbecued pork, and screwing young Vietnamese whores.

Pettibone finished the lasagna, then the last of the meatballs, and finally what was left of the sausage. He finished off his second beer, and unleashed a hellacious belch. A shame Janice wasn't there to appreciate it. That uptight prude would've been giving him an earful. He still had the chocolate cake, but decided to save it for later. He grabbed a fresh bottle of Heineken, cracked it open, got up from the small card table he had set up next to the bare-bones galley kitchen, and moved all of four feet so he could plop down on the ratty sofa he had picked up off the street when he first moved in.

What a way to live, he grumbled to himself. *Won't be much longer. Then I'll be living the way a man's supposed to when he's not carrying an ungrateful harpy and three snot-nosed brats on his back.*

He gave a quick look at his surroundings, and first felt only disgust, and then the slow burn of anger. He still had six bombs left to plant before he'd be done, and he thought about using one of them to blow up the apartment building. He was sure he'd be able to figure out how to do that. He could replace the trigger Reuben was using with a timer, and he could fill up his apartment with enough accelerant so the whole building would burn to ashes. Somehow that seemed fitting. The more he thought about it, the more he liked the idea, especially the idea of burning alive the inconsiderate jerks who lived above him. Always making a racket when he was trying to sleep.

Pettibone turned on the TV. He didn't pay attention to it for several minutes as he found himself thinking more seriously about rigging up one of the bombs. It was no longer just a fanciful thought, but something that made too much sense not to do. If the building burned to the ground, the police would assume that he died in the fire also, and there'd be no reason for anyone to look for him in Asia or anywhere else. He could even leave a dead body in the apartment just to make sure they came to the obvious conclusion that one of his bombs went off unexpectedly.

An image flickering on the TV caught his attention. He stared blankly at the two sketches they were showing—one of a man with a bushy mustache and long blond hair tied up in a ponytail, the other presumably of the same man, except he was bald and clean-shaven, and looked a bit like a turtle out of its shell. Pettibone whistled to himself as he realized why the sketches looked familiar. Because they were both of Reuben. When that oddball had sidled up to him in a dive bar on Beach Boulevard five months ago, he didn't have blond hair, and he wasn't bald either. He had short, brown hair, wore glasses, and had a goatee. But Pettibone was sure those police sketches were of Reuben. He paid rapt attention to the rest of the news story, and learned that the man in the sketches was wanted for the murder of the actress Heather Brandley, a doorman working in Brandley's condo building, and an unidentified woman. They didn't say much about the murders other than Brandley's body was found in that new wax museum on Sunset Boulevard and the woman's body was found in a downtown LA clothing store. Pettibone, though, could read enough between the lines to know that both deaths had been grisly.

Pettibone soon found himself wondering if the police were offering a reward, and if they were, whether it would be more than the fifty grand Reuben still owed him.

He badly wanted to know that.

Chapter 26

Morris called Natalie on his way home to see if he should pick up dinner. "I could stop off at Seven Star," he suggested.

"Let me guess, you've got a craving for kung pao chicken and Peking ravioli," Natalie said in an amused voice.

"Well, yeah, but I'd also be picking up your favorite, scallops in black pepper sauce."

"No need, hon. I've got dinner covered. This is a nice surprise, though. I didn't think you'd be making an appearance until at least midnight."

"The better part of valor is recognizing when it's time to give up," Morris said.

"A tough day?"

"Putting it mildly. Have you watched the news yet?"

"I've been avoiding it."

"Just as well. I'll see you in ten minutes."

Nine minutes later, Morris pulled into the driveway. When he brought Parker to the front door and the bull terrier began making excited pig grunts, Morris thought that Natalie must've seen him drive up and was waiting right behind the door. Except when he opened the door, it wasn't Natalie but Rachel grinning at him. She dropped to one knee so she could wrestle with Parker.

"This is a nice surprise," Morris said.

"It shouldn't be," Rachel gasped between laughs as she fought to keep an excitable Parker from licking her face. "I told you I might come by for dinner."

"You did," Morris acknowledged. "Wow. It seems like a week ago since I saw you earlier today."

Rachel extricated herself from Parker and gave Morris a kiss on the cheek. Concern wrinkled her brow as she stepped back and appraised her dad. "You look worn out," she said.

"I am," Morris admitted. "But it's nothing a good night's sleep won't cure."

Rachel scratched Parker behind the ear as the dog leaned against her. Her eyes narrowed as she continued to study Morris.

"Do I still need to worry about the police alert bracelet you gave me?"

"Unfortunately, yes. Things have only gotten worse. Have you eaten yet?"

"Not yet."

"Okay. I'll explain more after dinner."

"So you don't ruin my appetite?" she asked, her eyes like hard slivers of flint as she challenged him.

Morris said, "Uh uh. I know what a tough cookie you are. It's so I don't ruin my own."

Natalie appeared from the hallway, beaming. She handed Morris a glass of beer.

"I thought you could use it," she said.

"One of the many reasons I married your mom," Morris told Rachel.

After leaning in and kissing Morris on the lips, Natalie had to contend with Parker, who greeted her every bit as enthusiastically as he did Rachel. When she could, she took hold of Morris by the arm.

"Our lovely daughter has brought us a veritable feast. Dinner awaits."

She walked arm in arm with Morris while Parker made sure to keep close physical contact with Rachel, his thick, ropy tail wagging at a fast beat. Before they reached the kitchen, Morris sniffed in the air and thought he smelled kung pao chicken.

"Seven Star?" he asked.

"Where else?" Rachel said.

Takeout containers of kung pao chicken, Peking ravioli, scallops in black pepper sauce, pork fried rice, Szechuan string beans, broccoli in garlic sauce, and tofu lo mein lay on the kitchen table.

"Daughter, you know how to make an old man very happy."

"Old man?" Natalie remarked. "Where's that coming from? You're only forty-seven!"

"This day has made me feel old."

"That's because you started it hungover."

"Probably," Morris agreed.

They sat at the table and dug in, with Morris loading up on the kung pao chicken, Peking ravioli, and pork fried rice, Natalie having a little bit of everything, and Rachel sticking with the vegetarian dishes. Parker, who was doing some serious mooching, got handouts from everyone.

As Morris used chopsticks to snatch his third Peking ravioli, he asked Natalie why the name R. G. Berg sounded so familiar to him. A weariness flashed over his wife's face, and he realized then how hard she'd been struggling to hide her worry from him.

"I thought we weren't going to talk about any serial killer business during dinner?" she said.

"I know. I'm sorry. That name's been bugging me all day. I feel like I should know it, but I can't think from where."

"Why's the name important?"

"It's what the killer is calling himself."

Natalie gave it some thought. "I can't remember you ever mentioning anyone named Berg. I don't know anyone by that name, and none of my patients are named Berg if that's what you're worrying about."

"I have a Professor Anthony Berg in contract law," Rachel said.

"How old is he?"

"Sixties. African American. Tall. Distinguished looking."

"Not our man," Morris said.

Natalie put her knife and fork down. While Morris and Rachel used chopsticks religiously when they ate Chinese food, she had never gotten the hang of it.

"How bad is it?" she asked.

"It's bad," Morris said. "And it's going to get worse, especially after tomorrow morning when I shake the hornet's nest."

He told them about the three murders without going into any of the gory details regarding what was done to the bodies, and about his planned appearance with Margot Denoir on *The Hollywood Peeper*.

"We need to rattle him. This maniac is different than your garden-variety serial killer. He's not driven by compulsion or a deep-seated neurosis or anger to kill. Instead, it's all ego. He's trying to impress the world with the way he's orchestrating these killings. In his warped mind, he's creating a great piece of art. If I can strike him where it hurts the most, he'll make a mistake, and we'll catch him faster than we would otherwise."

"Before he takes more victims," Rachel noted.

"That's what I'm hoping."

"You're going to be really pissing him off," Natalie said.

"I know."

"So we need to hold on to those bracelets," Rachel said, her voice falling flat.

Morris hated the threat this maniac posed to his wife and daughter. He hated that they were both trying so hard right then to look brave for his sake. He especially hated the helplessness he was feeling. Parker must've sensed his discomfort because he jumped up, resting his paws on Morris's thigh, and let out an agitated grunt. Morris absently offered him what was left of the Peking ravioli he'd been eating, and the king of the moochers seemed almost reluctant to take it.

"Starting tomorrow morning both of you will have police protection until we catch him," he said. "Twenty-four seven. And we're going to be catching him. This joker's not as clever as he thinks he is."

Natalie asked Rachel, "What classes do you have tomorrow?"

"Only a constitutional law lecture, and I can it watch it online."

"Good. You'll stay here with me." She turned to Morris and said, "For tomorrow anyway we'll make it easy for the police to protect us. Does that help put your mind at ease?"

Morris was grateful that Natalie didn't see clients on Fridays, because if she did he doubted she'd be so amenable. Or maybe she would've been regardless because of Rachel.

"Somewhat," Morris admitted.

* * * *

The next morning, Morris was up by six, and ready by seven to head out for his appearance on *The Hollywood Peeper*. Natalie adjusted his tie and took a step back to give him a more thorough examination.

"Do I pass inspection?" Morris asked with his poker face firmly intact.

Natalie bit her tongue and once again held back a comment on how she wished he had a more stylish suit. Morris owned three suits, all of which he'd bought off the rack twenty-one years ago when he made detective. While snug on him, they still fit, and Natalie knew it was hopeless to get him to replace them. It wasn't that her husband was being frugal, but that his dad, who had also been an LAPD police officer, had bought three suits off the rack when he made detective, and those were the only suits he owned up until the day he passed away. While Morris never talked much about it, Natalie knew it helped him feel closer to his dad doing the same.

"Barely," she said. "Fortunately, you've got Parker to help distract the TV audience from that threadbare suit you insist on wearing. The little guy is very photogenic."

"The suit's fine," Morris insisted. "And I want Parker staying with you and Rachel."

"Absolutely not. We've got the police protecting us. We're going to be just fine staying holed up here all day. You're the one who this serial killer has a serious grudge against—"

"According to the FBI profiler."

"Do you disagree with her?"

Morris made a face as he shook his head.

"Not only does this person have it in for you, but in a little over an hour you're going to be attacking him at his core. So that's why you're going to take Parker. Rachel and I will have the police, you're going to have this ferocious little guy."

"Ferocious? He's a marshmallow!"

Parker, who was lying on the floor nearby, sensed he had been maligned and let out an insulted grunt.

"Not when you're being attacked he isn't."

Morris walked over to the front window and moved the blinds aside. An unmarked police car was parked across the street half a block away and two plainclothes officers were sitting inside. Just as Natalie knew she had lost the battle long ago regarding him replacing his suits, Morris accepted he had lost this battle.

"I'll take Parker," he conceded.

The bull terrier, almost as if on command, pushed himself to his feet, stretched, yawned, and walked briskly over to Morris. Natalie joined them at the front door so she could kiss her husband goodbye. Her hand touched his cheek and lingered there.

"Be careful with this killer. He has nothing but ill intent toward you."

"I will. I promise."

"I get the sense that he's out to manipulate you. It's like he's trying to move you around as if you're a piece on a chessboard."

Morris agreed with her, although he knew this was far more than a game to the killer. He made a quick stop across the street with Parker in tow so he could have a word with the two officers in the unmarked car, letting them know if they needed coffee or a bathroom break to knock on the door, and then he was heading to his TV appearance on *The Hollywood Peeper*.

Chapter 27

Brad Pettibone thought there were pay phones at the bus station, and it turned out he was right. His problem as he stood in front of one of them with a pocketful of change was that they only took credit cards. He couldn't very well use one of those to anonymously call the number for that ex-cop who was in charge of Heather Brandley's murder investigation. If he did, they'd be able to figure out who was calling.

His cell phone rang. He worked it out of his pants pocket and scowled seeing that it was his boss, Sangonese. His first impulse was to turn off the phone, but if he did that it might make Sangonese suspicious, and Pettibone couldn't afford for Sangonese to send another tech to check up on his work. While he had hidden the bombs as well as he could within the oil well's machinery, it was impossible to hide them well *enough*. Any competent tech who dug in deep would find the small square package Pettibone had placed behind the compressors, and the tech would know it didn't belong there.

Pettibone answered his phone. "Mark, is that you?" he said, trying hard to sound friendly.

Sangonese's voice was curt. "You bet it's me. I'm spot checking you this morning. You were supposed to be at oil well number 93 at eight forty-five this morning. It's now nine-eighteen and you're still not there."

"Something came up this morning. I'll be servicing all the wells you put on my schedule. Don't worry about that."

Sangonese's voice took on a petulant note as he demanded, "What time are you going to be at the well?"

"No more than forty minutes."

There was a long silence where Sangonese must've been figuring out how much grief to give him. "Make sure you are," he finally said. "Think of it as your job depending on it."

Sangonese hung up on him.

What Pettibone had said about something coming up was the truth. An understatement, really. At quarter past eight, he had the TV on and was eating the chocolate cake he had saved from last night. After flipping through several stations, he stumbled on the sensationalized local tabloid show, *The Hollywood Peeper*, the one with that flesh and blood Barbie doll. She had on an ex-cop that Pettibone now wanted to call—a guy who was talking about the murders they were convinced Reuben had done. Of course the ex-cop, a guy named Brick who looked remarkably like the bull terrier he had brought with him onto the show, didn't know the identity of the killer since all he had were those two police sketches, but Pettibone knew it had to be Reuben, and he found himself glued to the set. When Brick talked about how Heather Brandley and the still unidentified woman were both sexually violated after they were killed, and that their bodies were mutilated to hide what was done to them, Pettibone understood that Reuben was a sicko freak.

Pettibone had learned months ago Reuben was a cold-blooded murderer after Crawford disappeared. He had also believed Reuben was an idealist who wanted to see the world burn. None of that had bothered him. In fact, he could wholeheartedly get behind burning down companies like Samson Oil & Gas. But this was different. It made his skin crawl knowing Reuben was killing these women to hide his sexual perversions. He couldn't understand how blowing up the oil wells was connected with it, but he accepted that the guy had to be looney tunes. He also knew he could no longer count on Reuben paying the fifty grand he owed him.

Pettibone had doubts earlier about getting the rest of his money, but not like now. These were nearly paralyzing. Before leaving his apartment, he had looked up the phone number for the business that ex-cop ran, and then headed out to find a pay phone so he could make an anonymous call. He could still call the tip hotline number that was given since that one was toll-free, but Pettibone had long ago learned that if you wanted something done you had to speak to the guy in charge.

He made a decision and called MBI collect. When the operator asked him for a name, he said, "Tell them I'm the guy who knows who the killer is."

"That's not a name, sir."

"It will be good enough for them."

He heard her sighing as if she were talking to an insane person, but after being put on hold the call was accepted and a guy asked if he was calling about Heather Brandley's murder.

"What do you think?"

"Okay, how about you give me your name and a phone number in case we get cut off?"

"Never mind that. Let me talk to Brick."

"He's not in the office. My name's Charles Bogle. I'm one of the investigators here. Whatever you were going to say to Morris you can say to me."

"Are you offering a reward for catching this killer?"

"What sort of reward are you looking for?"

"A hundred grand. Not a penny less. You get that offer reported on the news later today, and I'll give you the killer tomorrow wrapped up with a bow. Guaranteed."

"How about you tell me something to show you know who the killer is?"

Pettibone hated giving anything away for free, but he accepted that this was one of those times it would be to his benefit. "The guy's name is Reuben. At least that's what he calls himself."

He hung up the receiver. Seconds later the phone rang back. No kidding. He expected it, just as he also knew the cops were on their way. Pettibone used his jacket sleeve to wipe off any fingerprints he might've left, and then he was speed walking back to his car.

* * * *

Before Bogle had accepted the collect call, the operator was able to tell him the call was being made at a pay phone outside the Buena Park bus station. Bogle knew the guy wasn't going to be picking up when he called back, but he let it ring anyway in case someone in the area picked up and was able to give him a description of the caller.

When Greta walked into his office to tell him about the peculiar collect call that had come in, Bogle was working with Adam Felger to whittle down the massive list of movie producers. He hadn't been kidding the other day when he made the crack about there being more producers in LA than coffeehouse baristas. The list Felger had originally come up with had at least a thousand names on it. The only saving grace was that the LAPD had given them access to the DMV database, so after pulling an all-nighter and looking at driver's license photos (as well as finding other photos online when the licenses proved inconclusive), they were able to cross most of the names off the list, and had been spending that morning making phone calls to eliminate all but eleven possible suspects, none of whom were named Reuben.

Bogle had kept the collect caller on speaker, and he asked Felger what he thought.

"Beyond my pay grade," MBI's computer and hacking specialist said.

Bogle made a face at him. "Did the guy sound crazy?"

"I don't think so."

A minute later he got a call from a detective with the Buena Park Police Department to let him know that the caller had slipped away unseen, but they were going to canvass the area to see if they could come up with a description. "I'll call you if we get anything," the detective promised. Bogle next called Morris and told him what happened.

"A hundred thousand dollars," Morris said, whistling. "You think this guy's legit?"

"No idea. He told me the killer's name is Reuben, which fits with R. G. Berg."

"It does. Any producers on your list named Reuben?"

The phone was still on speaker, and Felger entered a few keystrokes to search the database he had compiled.

"Three," Felger said. "But we've eliminated them."

They could hear Morris over the phone impatiently tapping his fingers against a table. The tapping stopped. Morris said, "Odds are this maniac is using an alias, but give those three a closer look."

"Sure," Bogle said. "What if the guy calls back asking about a hundred-thousand-dollar reward?"

"Tell him it's been arranged. I'll make sure the media starts reporting about it."

Bogle smiled thinly as he fully caught Morris's meaning. "He's not going to be too happy if he delivers up the killer like he's promising, and finds out afterward he's being stiffed."

"Let him sue."

Bogle's cell phone buzzed. Bleary-eyed from working through the night, he had to stare at his phone for a ten-count before he could read the caller ID. No name, only a number he didn't recognize. He begged off the phone with Morris and answered the call with a gruff, "Yeah?"

On the other end, an excitable voice talking in a rapid-fire fashion said, "Your lucky day, Bogle. The miracle I pulled off for you is bigger than any in the Bible. Bigger than Jesus walking on water. *Man*, I earned the other C-note you owe me."

It took Bogle several seconds to realize who was calling. His former CI, Lionel Simmons. "How's that?" he asked.

"That Tahoe you were so hot for? I found out what happened to it."

"No kidding."

Simmons sounded incredulous, almost hurt even, as he asked, "You think I'd kid about something like that?"

Chapter 28

Morris sat at a booth in his favorite LA diner, which had become his favorite because they were fine with him bringing Parker along.

"Hon, he's a service dog, right?" the hostess had asked with a wink the first time Morris had gone there with Parker.

"In a way."

"Good enough."

This was five years ago, and since then Morris went out of his way to eat there, even when he didn't have Parker tagging along.

When Charlie Bogle called, Morris was working on a plate of scrambled eggs with corned beef hash and a sesame seed bagel, while Parker had just finished off a plate of meatloaf with a couple of strips of bacon thrown on, and was beginning his mooching act to get some of Morris's breakfast. After hearing about an anonymous caller promising to deliver them the killer for a hundred grand, Morris began to feel the way he always did when he knew things were getting close. It wasn't because he believed the anonymous caller would follow through. It would be too easy for that to happen, and this killer just didn't seem like he was going to be easy. Morris knew it was going to take a lot more blood, sweat, and tears (and hopefully not too much blood) before it would be over. But if one person knew the killer's identity, there was a good chance others did too. It also meant the killer was making mistakes. Usually sooner than later, mistakes caught up with them.

The name Reuben struck him as odd. While he had eaten plenty of Reuben sandwiches at Bernie's Deli over the years, Morris was sure he'd never actually known a Reuben. *R. G. Berg* had seemed vaguely familiar; Reuben G. Berg didn't. It had to be an alias. Morris was sure of it. He called Annie Walsh.

"Amazing," Walsh said before Morris could get a word out. "I was just about to call you. Seriously. My finger was touching the call button."

"Why's that?"

"We know who the third victim is. Another actress. Drea Kane."

Drea Kane. The name made Morris sit up straighter. Kane was a far bigger name in Hollywood than Heather Brandley. A star, not a supporting player. She also wasn't just beautiful, but glamorous. Like Brandley, she was in her thirties, maybe a few years younger than the other actress. Just last week Natalie had brought home a magazine with a glossy photo of Drea Kane adorning the cover, and it had caught Morris's attention. In his mind's eye, he could picture the way Kane's lips were turned up into an impish smile and how dazzling her green eyes were, as if they were shining brightly with amusement. It was the look of someone who was the only one in the room to get the joke.

"How'd you find that out?" he asked.

"From her agent. Kane disappeared a week ago, which her agent said wasn't that unusual, and when she did that she's usually in Cabo. According to her agent Kane has the same tattoo on her right ankle as the body we found in Hipster Dipster, you know, the Chinese symbol for *unbreakable.* So that and the news reports from last night and your appearance today on *The Hollywood Peeper* made him nervous. When he couldn't reach her, he called us. BHPD found one of R.G. Berg's calling cards in her home. Also, photos. I was just heading over there."

"What do the photos show?"

"Her body being severed with a handheld circular saw."

The image of Drea Kane looking the way she did on that magazine cover being cut in half stuck in Morris's mind, and he found that he'd lost his appetite. He put the plate holding what was left of his scrambled eggs and corned beef on the floor for Parker, and the bull terrier let out a few happy grunts to show his appreciation.

"Give me the address and I'll meet you there," Morris said.

* * * *

"Reuben, right? We'd like to talk to you about your old man, Lyle."

Fifteen years ago, Lyle Ford had butchered four women, using hacksaws to cut off their limbs. His thirty-one-year-old son, who'd been named Toby but was now going by the name Andrew Wayne, showed little reaction to being called Reuben other than staring at Lemmon with a mix of annoyance and confusion. Morris had called a few minutes earlier to inform Lemmon that the killer might be using the alias *Reuben*, but if that name meant anything to Lyle Ford's son, he didn't show it by his reaction.

Andrew Wayne, formerly Toby Ford, said, "You've got the wrong guy."

"My mistake. You're now going by the name Andy Wayne, right?"

Wayne sneered at the hand Lemmon offered and dismissed it with a shake of his head. "This is about that actress and the other woman who were killed?"

Lemmon pulled his hand back. "Why'd you ask that?"

Wayne laughed bitterly. "You think you're the first cop looking at me as a potential serial killer?"

"It's more than that, Andy."

Wayne let out another bitter laugh. "Yeah, well, I don't care what it is. I don't have to talk to you, and guess what, I'm not going to."

Fred Lemmon and Detective Craig Gunderson had cornered Wayne in a back area of a movie set. While Lyle Ford's son wasn't a movie producer, he worked in the film industry building sets for Starlight Pictures, which made Lemmon think that the guy would have the expertise and means to build the scaffolding used to support Heather Brandley's corpse at the wax museum, and also have access to the kind of explosives used in rigging up the mannequin-corpse nightmare found inside the clothing store.

Wayne tried to sidestep past Lemmon, but the MBI investigator stepped in his way and gave Wayne a hard look. The police sketches resembled a thirty-one-year-old Lyle Ford more than it did his son, but Lemmon could still see a resemblance. It wasn't definitive, but the drawing could be him. Given the glint in Craig Gunderson's eyes and the way his blubbery flesh had seemed to harden like rubber, he must've thought it was a possibility also.

"Let me explain the situation," Lemmon said. "Heather Brandley and the other victim weren't just killed. They were cut up. Your old man used to like to dismember women, didn't he?"

Wayne blanched. "A hacksaw was used?" he asked.

"No, this time it was a circular saw. Something that would be perfect for cutting almost anything. I'm guessing you'd have access to one in your line of work."

"This just isn't right." A panic was beginning to show in Wayne's eyes as he looked past Lemmon to see if anyone else might've wandered into the area. His voice breathless, he said, "You can't just come to my place of work about something like this. I've never hurt anyone. It's not my fault Lyle was a psychotic madman."

Gunderson's eyes had narrowed to angry slits, giving him the look of an oversized attack dog who was just dying to go for the jugular. "We're being nice here," he said, his voice a soft growl. "We waited until you stepped back here so we could approach you nice and friendly-like with nobody else around. If you want instead, we can drag your supervisor into this and make sure he understands who your daddy was. Or I can cuff you, and take you in for questioning. If you make me do that, I'll be holding you for the full twenty-four hours. Your call, chief."

Wayne's eyes had become liquid with fear. Or maybe he was about to start bawling. Lemmon wasn't sure which. He put a hand on Wayne's shoulder. A friendly gesture. The way Wayne flinched, he didn't take it as such.

"Help us clear this up," Lemmon said. "You do that and we'll leave you alone. As I said, it's more than we're dealing with a serial killer. More even than he's cutting women up the way Lyle liked to do."

"What is it then?"

There was only one way Lemmon saw of playing this, so he played it straight. "Tell me how you feel about Morris Brick."

Wayne blinked several times as he stared confused at Lemmon. "That's the cop who caught Lyle," he said.

"That's right. Because of Morris your dad was sent to Pelican Bay."

"Lyle," Wayne corrected. "I don't think of him as my father. And your question about Morris Brick, if I could, I'd buy him a beer. Dinner also. Arresting that monster was the best thing that ever happened to me and my mom."

Wayne seemed sincere. Heartfelt even. Lemmon said, "Six months ago Lyle had his head bashed in at Pelican Bay. Are you telling me you don't blame Morris for his death?"

"Why would I?"

Lemmon breathed in deeply and a heavy sigh eased out of him. The guy would have to be a damn good actor to pull off a performance this convincing. Or a psychopath. And that was the rub. The experts still don't know what causes someone to become a psychopath. They have their theories, and there are some who believe genetics is a factor.

"Where were you yesterday from two to three?"

"Thursday?" Wayne asked. He seemed almost too rattled to answer the question.

"Yeah."

"I don't know. I had an errand I had to run yesterday afternoon. It might've been then."

"So no one can vouch for you," Gunderson said. He gave Lemmon a sideways glance, his smirk showing that he found Wayne's answer too convenient.

"I don't think so. No, I don't think anyone would be able to."

"Wednesday then," Lemmon said. "Also between two and three."

Wayne's eyes took on a faraway look as if he were deep in thought. "I must've been here," he said at last. "I was doing carpentry for a set. I know I spent all morning working on it. I might've gone out late for lunch, but I'm pretty sure I was here."

Gunderson gave Lemmon a quick look for his opinion. He shook his head, but the LAPD detective decided to ignore it, and told an increasingly despondent Wayne they were going to take him in for questioning until they could clear up the matter.

Chapter 29

"Sympathy for the Devil" woke the killer. As his mind became more alert, he recognized the song playing over his clock radio and mouthed the word *wow*. The synchronicity of that particular Rolling Stones song being played at that precise moment left him awestruck. It was more than a coincidence. It had to be. It was as if the universe was whispering a dark, unknown secret to him.

The killer had had a busy night. After taking care of Faye Riverstone, he was kept busy with other necessary tasks for his masterpiece until three-thirty in the morning, and it was only then that he was able to crawl into bed. After being up for almost three straight days and nights, he knew he'd sleep for a full twenty-four hours if he didn't set the alarm, and so he set it for nine-thirty. Less than six hours of sleep wasn't going to be enough, but there was still so much he needed to do. For now, he just needed to tough it out. One more week, and this would all be over, his masterpiece fully revealed to the world. He'd then be able to take a bow and bask in his glory, and sleep for as long as he wanted.

As the killer lay in bed, the near religious experience he'd earlier felt had dissipated, and was replaced by a sense of disquiet. Before too long he understood why as he remembered the local TV news broadcast from last night.

The two sketches they showed didn't matter. While it had surprised him that they figured out he'd been sitting outside the bakery (the waitress must've helped them come up with the sketch of him wearing a blond wig and bushy mustache), he didn't think either sketch looked much like him. The one of him hairless was laughable, and made him look almost like a snake. Still, to be on the safe side, he would disguise himself whenever he went out, and when this was all over, he planned to disappear to another continent. No, it wasn't those police sketches that bothered him, but that they intentionally withheld the details of what he had done to his victims. He knew that was Brick's doing; the ex-cop was trying to deny him his due. The killer had ways of rectifying that, and he would do so later that day by leaving an envelope outside the building of one of the local TV stations, maybe the one that broadcasts *The Hollywood Peeper* show.

Even though the police had withheld all the gory details, the story still dominated the news last night. A new serial killer was on the loose and one of the victims was a well-known actress, albeit a fading one who had slipped to making second-rate movies.

Of course, they didn't have a clue about what was really going on. The police still probably believed what they found in Hipster Dipster was the rest of Heather Brandley. That bit of misdirection had been intentional; partly because the killer had found the idea of it amusing, but more importantly it would've ruined his plans if they had learned yesterday that the remains had come from Drea Kane. That domino wasn't ready to fall yesterday. Now it was. In fact, it was imperative for Brick and the police to learn that nugget of information.

The killer stretched lazily, and with a concerted effort, forced himself out of bed. Another lazy stretch, and the killer staggered on stiff legs to the kitchen and started a pot of coffee. As he waited for the coffee to brew, he turned on his laptop, and navigated to an untraceable spot on the dark net. Just as he had hidden a covert spy camera inside Hipster Dipster so he could watch a video feed, he had done the same at Drea Kane's home, and he was surprised to see cops milling around the kitchen where he had left them his message. He wondered how they had discovered that Kane was his Hipster Dipster victim, and decided it didn't matter. It was just as well that they had. It saved him from having to make an anonymous call.

The killer watched the video for several more minutes before forcing himself to turn it off. He had wanted to see Brick at the scene, but so what if he didn't? He had too much to do to let himself compulsively waste time watching for that. For now, he would just have to satisfy himself by imagining Brick's reaction when he showed up at Kane's house. Or he could watch the video later.

The killer closed his eyes and took a calming breath. His latest domino had fallen, but he still had work to do to prepare for the next one.

* * * *

Morris called Annie Walsh on his way to Drea Kane's home in Beverly Hills to tell her about the anonymous caller claiming the killer was named Reuben.

"I can't believe I didn't tell you that before since it was the reason I called."

"I distracted you."

"You did."

"*Drea Kane*," Walsh said. "The heat is going to be coming down on us like a thousand burning suns."

What Annie Walsh said was of course true. Morris had already received a call from Gilman, and another from Hadley, and neither of them were particularly happy. Still, even though it was true, it was out of character for her to say something like that. Morris couldn't remember her ever doing so, and he guessed she had read the line in a book, or heard it in a movie.

He said, "You getting poetic on me?"

She laughed. A sardonic, harsh laugh. "There's got to be a first time for everything," she said. "Or maybe this damn case is getting me punch drunk."

"I guarantee you right now it's making your boss, Hadley, sick to his stomach."

"I imagine so." There were several seconds of static on the line, then Walsh commented about how Reuben was an odd alias. "I don't think I've ever known anyone with that name. The only person I've ever heard of named Reuben was the actor who played Pee Wee Herman."

"That actor's name is Paul Reubens."

"Close enough."

After he got off the phone with Walsh, Morris called Polk, first to tell him about Drea Kane, and then to tell him the *R* in *R. G. Berg* might stand for Reuben.

"So you're telling me to concentrate only on Reuben G. Bergs?"

"Are there any on your list?"

"Not a one."

"Then stick with what you're doing."

"You mean wasting my time? Like I did driving to Lakewood this morning so I could interview eighty-two-year-old Ronald Gilchrist Berg, even though I knew there was no point to it?"

"Gilchrist?"

"That's his name."

"You need to talk to all of them," Morris said. "We need to find out why this guy is calling himself R. G. Berg. There's got to be a reason for it."

"You're sure?"

"No, I'm not," Morris admitted. "But we've got to try to find one. Even if it's a needle in a haystack."

"More like a needle in a hay silo. Anyway, you're the boss, and I'm on my way to Bell Gardens as we speak to talk with Rosalind Gertrude Berg. She might be a lady, but she's still an R. G. Berg. How much do you want to bet I'll be wasting my time with her? I'll give you a thousand to one odds."

"Put me down for ten bucks."

There was a noticeable silence, because Polk hadn't been serious about the bet. Then, "You got it, Morris. That's how sure I am."

He no longer sounded so sure. Risking ten thousand dollars, even on a sucker's bet, has a way of humbling you. Morris was going to get his money's worth out of that ten dollars.

Drea Kane's address was three blocks from Rodeo Drive, and as Morris drove down the heavily tree-lined street, it seemed as if each house was trying to outdo the next. Kane's won hands down. Morris didn't know how to describe it other than as a palatial estate that could've been airdropped from Italy. It took real star power to have a house like that.

He pulled into the last spot in the circular driveway, which had to have been large enough to hold a dozen cars, and took Parker along with him. He kept the bull terrier on a short leash as he had a brief conversation with a uniformed officer standing guard out front, and he found Doug Gilman inside pacing in what looked like a sitting room past the marble foyer. Parker let out a short bark to get Gilman's attention. The mayor's deputy assistant's eyes had a darkened look, almost as if they'd been ringed with soot. He first stared blankly at Parker, and then at Morris.

Even though Gilman had warned them in the past that he was a cat person, Parker had developed an affinity for him, and he jumped on Gilman, resting his front paws on him, his tail wagging steadily. Gilman seemed to pay little attention to this assault by the bull terrier, although he absently rubbed Parker's snout. Morris ordered Parker down.

"This isn't good," Gilman said as he patted the top of the bull terrier's cement-hard skull. "When the media gets wind of this, the heat is going to be unreal."

"Like from a thousand burning suns," Morris said.

Gilman stared at him as if he were crazy.

"Have you been drinking?"

Morris chuckled sourly. "No, although I'm feeling like I could use one."

"Join the club. Kane's agent, Thomas Mildew, is being interviewed by Detective Malevich. He seems legitimately distraught. I don't think he knows anything."

"Mildew?"

Gilman shrugged. "That's his name."

"I'll talk to Greg later. Mildew also." Morris heard a soft murmur from all sides—front, left, and right. It sounded like a storm brewing. He guessed the crime scene team was going through the house looking for any signs of violence or a forced abduction. "Where did the maniac leave his calling card?"

"Kitchen. Straight ahead in the back of the house. Or mansion. Whatever you call this." His color paled, and he added, "The photos are beyond awful. I'll join you."

Parker seemed to sense they were heading to the kitchen, and he huffed as he tried to pull Morris after him, likely thinking there would be bacon involved. Given that the owner of the house, Drea Kane, had been brutally murdered, Morris tried to show the proper decorum and not stare as they made their way to the kitchen, but the house was spectacular, and while he didn't know much about artwork, he guessed the paintings they passed on the walls must've been worth millions. Forget that his West Hollywood home was a shack in comparison—this house made Philip Stonehedge's Malibu estate look like a starter home. *Twenty million at least,* he thought.

The kitchen was similar to what you'd find in a top restaurant. Large enough to fit the entire first floor of Morris's home, it overlooked an intricately landscaped patio and a swimming pool that would've made many luxury resorts envious. Morris absorbed this at a glance, then joined Walsh and two BHPD detectives at the granite countertop. Gilman hung back so he wouldn't catch another glimpse of the photos.

Walsh introduced Morris to the two detectives, and one of them filled him in on what they knew so far. No sign of a forced entry and no blood or other indications of an abduction. Also, the home security system had been turned off, and the front door had been left unlocked.

"The killer wanted to make it easy for us to gain access," Morris said. "That's what he left behind for us?"

The detective nodded. On the countertop was one of R. G. Berg's business cards sitting on a stack of photos. None of it had been bagged yet. Walsh handed Morris a pair of latex gloves. Written on the card was: *What must be puzzling you is the nature of my game. Morris, have you guessed my name?*

"This hack is now ripping off the Rolling Stones," Morris noted.

One of the BHPD detectives grunted in agreement.

Morris picked up the stack of photos and saw that Doug Gilman had been right. They were awful. Each one featured either Heather Brandley or Drea Kane, and showed different stages of their bodies being severed by a handheld circular saw. The killer's gloved hand and part of his arm were visible in the photos. Morris had seen more than his share of dead bodies and the aftermath of horrific violent acts during his years as an LAPD homicide detective, but these photos were something else altogether, and they left him filled with dread and loathing. Logically, he understood why that was. In the first half dozen photos, the actresses were still alive, and their eyes and expressions reflected their horror. As much as he hated looking at them, he felt compelled to study each one in case it held a hidden clue. He was halfway through them when Parker suddenly tried to bull his way past Walsh and one of the BHPD detectives, and get under the granite countertop. Morris took a tighter hold on the leash, and ordered his dog to heel. The bull terrier did so, although not without letting out a couple of frustrated grunts.

"Is there something under there?" Morris asked.

Walsh checked. When she came back up from under the countertop, she was holding an olive-colored flash drive.

"It blended in with the marble floor," she said.

One of the BHPD detectives retrieved a laptop computer. They attached the flash drive and found that it held a single video file. All of them seemed to be holding their breath as the file was clicked on. The video started playing and showed a blond woman naked and lying on what looked like a workshop table that had been covered with plastic sheeting, her arms and legs in restraints. She was still alive, but it wasn't Heather Brandley or Drea Kane. She appeared drugged, her head rolling from side to side. The killer hadn't bothered to gag her, and she made soft moaning noises.

She looked familiar to Morris. He could swear he knew her from somewhere.

"That's Faye Riverstone," one of the BHPD detectives said.

He was right. Faye Riverstone was petite and slender, but she had always played feisty characters in her movies, and that had given her a bigger-than-life quality. The woman tied up on the table looked so diminished. The poor lighting also helped to disguise her.

"The killer likes his blond actresses," Walsh remarked.

They fell into a hushed silence after that. Gilman wandered over and joined them watching the video.

For several minutes, the video only showed Riverstone as she lay helpless on the table, then the killer came into view. He was dressed fully in black, and wore gloves and a black ski mask. At first, he stood sideways to the camera and caressed Riverstone's jaw with his gloved hand. This went on for what seemed like an unbearable amount of time. Even though the actress was out of it, it looked like she was shrinking from his touch. It must've been something subconscious. Abruptly, the killer faced the camera.

"This is meant for Brick's eyes only," he said, his voice a deep base and unnatural, as if a voice changer were being used. "Although I'm sure other police and FBI will be examining this too. I suppose that can't be helped. Brick, I'm not at all happy with how you're trying to deny me my due, and your pettiness is tempting me to cut Faye in half right now. But I'm going to be the bigger man, at least for now, and I'll be sporting and give you a chance to save her life."

He walked out of the frame. Morris timed it and it took him thirty-two seconds to return. When he did, he carried a circular saw in one hand and what looked like a small butane torch in the other; the type of torch a chef would use in making crème brûlée. He lay the circular saw on the actress's naked belly so that the blade faced the camera. It looked huge and ragged, like it could tear through a rhinoceros. The killer then ignited the torch, and a blue flame came out of it. He placed the torch outside the video frame; then he picked up the circular saw. A loud and abrasive whirring noise filled the room as the killer powered the saw on. He moved quickly after that, and seconds later he had cut off the actress's left hand. Her head lolled to the side, her eyes closed, and there was no longer any movement from her. The killer powered off the circular saw and retrieved the butane torch from where he had left it. He used this to cauterize the stump on her arm. When he was done he picked up the severed hand and showed it to the camera. The kitchen where Morris and the rest stood had gone deathly silent; even Parker stood motionless. The only noise was the hissing of the torch. Then the killer spoke.

"Noon Saturday I'll be leaving this somewhere in LA with a clue attached," he said, his voice still mechanically altered. "Noon Sunday it will be Faye's right hand with another clue. Noon Monday, her left foot. Noon Tuesday, her right foot. Brick, if you haven't found her by noon Wednesday, she gets cut in half. Whether she lives or dies, or how many appendages she loses, will now be determined by how clever you are."

The video ended.

"Bastard," Walsh whispered under her breath.

Morris gritted his teeth, his mind busy processing what he had seen. His voice sounded like it was echoing from somewhere outside his head as he said, "We need to get this to the FBI for analysis. These photos also. Maybe there's something in them that can pinpoint where this video was made."

"It looked like he put sheets up in the background," Walsh said.

"Maybe they'll get something when they analyze the audio," Morris argued.

Gilman's voice didn't sound well when he said, "I don't think he had seen your appearance this morning with Margot Denoir when he made this."

That hit Morris like a punch to the gut, because he knew Gilman was right, and he dreaded what the killer would be doing when he did see it. He glanced back and noticed how unwell Gilman was looking.

"Are you okay?" he asked.

"I think I need some water."

Gilman headed to the sink, his legs wobbly. He made it without collapsing, and he tried cupping water with his hand so he could drink it. Morris got a bottle of something called Bling H2O out of the refrigerator, and then helped Gilman to a chair. He cracked open the bottle and handed it to Gilman, who drank it as if his life depended on it. Once he was sure Gilman would be okay, he told Walsh they needed to find out where Faye Riverstone met the killer.

"First step, let's get her recent credit card charges," he said.

Walsh, who was on her cell phone, told him it was being done.

Chapter 30

"I was invited to steal the Tahoe," Clark Clarke said.

"Is that really your name?" Bogle asked.

The car thief rolled his eyes. "Does it matter?" he asked.

"Yeah, it matters. I paid you two hundred dollars. I want to know what you're telling me is on the level."

"Assume it is."

Bogle didn't like the answer, but he let it drop. He was sitting with the car thief, who claimed his name was Clark Clarke, in a booth at a trendy bar in downtown Glendale. It seemed an unlikely spot to meet a car thief, but it was where Clarke wanted to meet. Then again, the guy looked more like a college student than any car thief he'd ever known. Reed thin, shoulder-length curly hair, scruffy beard, T-shirt, jeans, boots, no visible tattoos.

"How'd you get invited?" Bogle asked.

"A website. Think of it as a clearing house for people who want their cars stolen for insurance purposes. Let's say you want your car to disappear. You give the location of when and where the car will be left, and where you're hiding the key. People like me will take the car, with the agreement that we make it vanish within twenty-four hours."

"Why aren't the police monitoring this site?" Bogle asked, dubiously.

Clarke smiled at Bogle as if he were some old dude who was too unhip to know anything. That smile made Bogle want to knock the guy's teeth out.

"I'm sure they would if they knew about it. But the site is in a dark, secretive part of the web, and only people like me are invited."

"You're saying the Tahoe was advertised on this dark, secretive website?" Bogle said, his voice brusque as he challenged the young car thief.

"Exactly."

"What day was that?"

"November seventeenth."

That was the day Karl Crawford had gone missing. His wife didn't call the police until the next morning, and they didn't try locating Crawford's car until later that day. Bogle started taking Clark Clarke more seriously.

"What time did the Tahoe show up on this top-secret website?"

Clarke made a "who knows" gesture with his hands. "I can't tell you when it was first listed, but I noticed it around eight that night."

"You reserved it?"

"That's not how it works. Whoever gets there first, gets the car."

"And you were first?"

"I was. The Tahoe was left in an alley in Long Beach. That's a long hike for me, but it would make a nice score. Around ten I made the trip, and the Tahoe was where it was supposed to be, the key also."

"What happened next?"

All at once Clarke seemed unsure about what to do with his hands, and he started rolling an empty beer bottle between them. His gaze shifted from Bogle to the bottle.

"I drove the Tahoe to a garage I use, stripped it down, and had the body carted off for scrap metal. I was done by three in the morning."

"What about the GPS recovery device?"

Clarke made a face as if Bogle was asking something too trivial to bother answering. "I found it in the dashboard when I tore it apart. I smashed it to pieces with a hammer."

Bogle sat silently for a ten-count as he watched the young car thief rolling the empty bottle between his hands. Something didn't add up.

"Something doesn't add up," Bogle said. "Why'd you agree to tell me this for two hundred dollars?"

Clarke stopped the bottle rolling. His expression weakened, and his gaze drifted back to meet Bogle's eyes.

"There was something wrong about the Tahoe that's been bothering me," he said. "The alley where it was left was dark, and a blanket had been draped over the driver's seat, so I didn't know any of this until I got the Tahoe back to the garage." His voice lowered as he said, "There was a bullet hole in the driver's side window."

"You're sure it was a bullet hole?"

"I'm pretty sure. Yeah. There were no spider web cracks, like if a rock had hit it."

"Where was it on the window?"

"Like it would've hit me here if I was sitting in the driver's seat."

Clarke tapped above his eye.

"What was under the blanket?"

Clarke's expression weakened more. "The seat was sticky with blood."

"You didn't think of calling the police?"

"Come on, man," he said. "In my line of work? And what would I have told them so they'd believe all I did was steal it for what I thought was an insurance scam? No, man, once I took the SUV I had to get rid of it. I couldn't even dump it if I wanted to. I didn't wear gloves that night, and my fingerprints were all over it. But it's been bothering me. That's why I agreed to tell you about it."

Bogle mostly believed him. He was also convinced Karl Crawford was shot once in the face on November 17 as he sat in his Chevy Tahoe, and that his killer used this dark, secretive website to make Crawford's SUV disappear.

"I need the website address," Bogle said.

"You're not getting it from me, but it wouldn't help you if you did. That part of the web doesn't keep traces of anything. That's why people like me use it."

He pushed himself out of the booth. He was taller than he had looked sitting down, at least six and a half feet. With his body fully unwound, he also appeared lankier than thin. He wasn't a lightweight, that was for sure, but Bogle had no doubt he could overpower him if needed.

"I could hold you until the police came," Bogle said.

The car thief appraised Bogle. "I'm sure you could. My story would be I was telling you a tall tale so I could rip you off for two bills. You're not getting anything more from me, because there's nothing more I can tell you."

Bogle didn't like it, but he accepted it. Besides, a deal was a deal.

"Your name's not really Clark Clarke," he said stubbornly.

The car thief smiled fully, revealing a mouth that seemed to have too many teeth crammed into it. "No, it's not. But everything else I've said has been the truth."

Bogle let the car thief, whatever his name was, walk out of the place.

Chapter 31

"Sean Doyle?"

The bartender, who looked a lot like Tom Selleck from the old *Magnum, P.I.* show, had just started his shift. He looked over at Walsh and the badge she was showing him, and a wolfish grin spread over his face. When he noticed Morris next to her, his grin dimmed a bit.

"That's my name," he said. "What have I done to have such a lovely member of Los Angeles's finest looking for me?"

"Nothing you've done. We just have some questions."

Parker let out a grunt, impatient that there was food around he wasn't mooching. Doyle got up on his toes so he could look over the bar, and he noticed the bull terrier for the first time.

"You can't bring a dog in here," he said.

"He's only half dog," Morris said. "Other half, garbage disposal."

"Same rule."

"Don't worry about it."

Doyle shrugged. *Whatever.*

"You were working here at nine twenty-three last night," Walsh said, getting his attention back to her.

"That's right," he acknowledged. "I worked until one." He flashed her another grin, this one somewhere between naughty and an out-and-out leer. "I'm here again until one tonight, in case you'd like to stop by at that time and question me privately. The rest of the night if you want."

"Can it. It's been a long day."

If his feelings were hurt, he didn't show it. "You can't blame a guy for trying," he said, still grinning, now more with good humor than lust.

"Another time maybe."

"Any time you'd like." His lips pursed into a more thoughtful look. "Nine twenty-three. That's an awfully specific time. What was happening then?"

"Faye Riverstone was paying her bill with a credit card. Did you see her with anyone?"

Doyle's grin disappeared, his expression becoming something somber. "We're not supposed to talk about our clientele," he said in a softer, more serious voice. "It's a privacy matter. Celebrities come here because they know we won't talk about them."

Morris placed on the bar both sketches they had of the killer. "This time you can make an exception," he said. "Did you see this man with her?"

Doyle was staring at Morris as if he thought he knew him. All at once it occurred to him from where. "I thought you looked familiar," he said with another grin. "I saw you just this morning on TV." He remembered then what the show had been about, and his face fell flat. "Jesus," he whispered.

"Take a look at these sketches," Morris said.

Doyle did as he was asked. "Ms. Riverstone met someone here," he said, his voice brittle. "I try not to pay attention. That's one of the rules here. But, yeah, Ms. Riverstone came in alone. I think around seven-thirty, and took a seat over there." He pointed at one of the barstools. "I barely had time to make her a drink when she was leaving for that table over there, meeting up with her date." He nodded toward a table in the bar area where the lighting was kept dim for mood and privacy. Then he was back to studying the two sketches. "I think that could be him," he murmured, pointing to the sketch of the killer with a blond ponytail and bushy mustache. "I never got a good look at him, and Ms. Riverstone was the one who kept coming back to the bar to buy drinks. A dear woman. She comes here frequently. Jesus, I hope nothing has happened to her."

"He left with her?" Morris asked.

"I think so." His eyes took on a distant look as he gave the matter more thought, and then he told Morris he was sure of it.

"Did Ms. Riverstone say anything to you about him?" Walsh asked.

"No, but she seemed in good spirits. I had the sense that she was hitting it off with him."

Morris asked, "Did you see the guy here before last night?"

Doyle looked back at the sketches, worry at that moment putting a dent in his good looks.

"They're both the same guy, right?" he said. "Maybe he came in another night wearing a different disguise. I don't know. If he did come in, I don't remember it, or whether he was with Ms. Riverstone. But I don't work Sundays or Mondays. He might've been in one of those nights."

Walsh handed Doyle a card. "If you think of anything else, call me."

He studied the card, an awkward smile on his lips. "I promise I'll do that," he said. He hemmed and hawed for a moment, then added, "I know what you're working on is serious, and I don't want to appear inappropriate saying this, but I don't want you thinking I hit on every lovely lady that comes in here. Almost never happens. But I felt a spark when I saw you. Maybe when you finish this business, you come back here, and I'll buy you a drink or two, and we can chat?"

"There's a chance," Walsh said.

As they walked away from the bar to talk more with the manager, Morris commented that the bartender had fed her a well-practiced line of BS.

"Doesn't matter to me."

"I just wanted to point it out."

"Noted."

Morris didn't bother pointing out what was even more obvious: that the killer had Faye Riverstone buy the drinks so the bartender wouldn't get a close-up look of him.

The bar manager gave them the name and contact information for the bartender who had filled in the last several Sundays and Mondays for Doyle. Even with that information, it took them two hours to track down the part-time bartender. When they did, she told them she remembered a dude approaching Faye Riverstone at the bar, and that the guy smooth-talked her into moving to one of the tables. "He had her laughing within minutes, like he knew exactly what buttons to push."

"Almost as if he had studied up on her?" Morris asked.

"That thought had crossed my mind. The guy came off like a helpless lamb, but I saw him for what he was. A wolf. I almost warned Ms. Riverstone about him, and if she had tried leaving with him, I just might've."

Morris showed her the two sketches, and she pointed to the one of the killer wearing a blond wig and bushy mustache.

"That's him," she said, "I'm sure of it."

"Take a good look at the sketch. Any changes you'd make to it?"

She did as Morris asked, and after a minute of concentrated effort, she told him no. "This was five days ago, and I only saw him sitting down, and I tried not to stare or eavesdrop. But I think that's a good likeness. I hope Ms. Riverstone is okay."

She said the last part as if she didn't think there was any chance of it being true.

Morris didn't say anything comforting in response, such as that he was sure the actress would be fine. He wasn't up to lying to her. Instead he thanked her for her help, and watched as Walsh handed her a business card and asked her to call if she thought of anything else. Morris knew there was nothing else the part-time bartender could tell them that could help Faye Riverstone. But then again, so did Walsh.

Chapter 32

Philip Stonehedge and Brie Evans had reached a rarified place in their budding relationship where they could sit quietly together and feel at ease, and that was what they were doing as they sat on the patio of one of Malibu's trendiest restaurants and enjoyed the view of the ocean, their cocktails, and each other's company. Their solitude was broken by Stonehedge's cell phone buzzing. He gave it a cursory look with the intention of dismissing the call unless it was from his agent. It wasn't his agent, but when he saw who it was, he answered immediately. All of his cheerfulness bled out within seconds. It was a quick one-sided conversation. Stonehedge didn't speak until the end.

"Morris, I can't thank you enough for this," Stonehedge said, his voice unusually somber. He put the phone away and told Brie that the same maniac who had killed Heather Brandley also had killed Drea Kane and abducted Faye Riverstone.

Brie blinked several times as she stared at Stonehedge, her frozen expression looking like a cross between a sick smile and being gobsmacked.

"If you're trying to be funny, you're doing an awful job of it," she said.

"I'm not trying to be funny. That was Morris Brick calling." Stonehedge ran his fingers through his hair. A nervous gesture. "The police will be having a press conference later tonight about Drea and Faye, but he wanted to warn me that the killer seems to be targeting blond actresses who look like you."

Simultaneously, Brie's eyes opened wide, her skin color dropped a shade, her mouth hung open, and she brought her hand to her mouth so that the knuckle on her index finger touched her bottom lip.

"Oh my God," she said.

Anyone witnessing her would've thought she was experiencing shock and dismay, and she was to a degree, but her reaction was also theatrical. She wasn't sure exactly what she was feeling. The idea of this madman targeting her seemed too abstract for her to worry about, but she had mixed emotions hearing about Drea and Faye. She had worked with both of them, and had considered Drea a cold fish who thought way too highly of herself. She was also Brie's fiercest rival and at least a half dozen times over the years had won roles that Brie badly wanted. There was professional jealousy also with Faye, but far more on Faye's part than her own. A bit flighty, and her squint/pouty act had gotten old. After a few moments of reflection, Brie decided that she genuinely felt an affection for Faye, and soon found herself worrying about the actress's safety.

Philip, though, was more of an open book with his emotions, and he didn't have a clue about these conflicting feelings Brie was undergoing, and that was one of the things she found so endearing about him.

"It's terrible, I know," Stonehedge said, his face drawn. He reached for her hand and covered it with his own. She bit down on her bottom lip as if she were struggling to keep from crying. Maybe she was. It was terrible what happened, but she also wouldn't be losing any more roles to Drea Kane.

"Poor Drea. Poor dear Faye," Brie said, her mouth crumbling. She wasn't faking this time, at least not exactly. Right then she was racked with guilt for how she had felt moments earlier hearing that Drea had been murdered by a madman.

"Fly to Seattle with me tonight," Stonehedge suggested.

"I can't. My publicist will kill me if I'm not in LA tomorrow morning."

"This bloodthirsty lunatic might kill you if you stay in town."

"I'll take my chances."

Stonehedge made up his mind. "I'm cancelling my trip," he said, his jaw set. "I'm not letting anything happen to you."

Philip Stonehedge's hand still covered her own. Brie brought his hand to her lips and kissed it. This time there was no overdramatization of the emotion flooding her eyes. What was there was very real, and it made Stonehedge blush.

Get a room already, the killer thought as he watched this from two tables away. He had disguised himself earlier with a prosthetic nose and fake teeth that changed the shape of his mouth and even his jawline. He was also wearing a long-sleeve dark olive polo shirt, sandstone-colored khakis, loafers, dark sunglasses, and a neatly trimmed sandy-brown-colored wig. All quite preppy. Nobody would recognize him from either of the police sketches they had showed on TV.

The killer had angled his chair so it appeared that he was looking out at the ocean while he munched on wood-grilled calamari and sipped a locally brewed pale lager, his sunglasses hiding that he was surreptitiously spying on the Hollywood power couple. While he concentrated to keep his facial muscles relaxed, he had to strain to hear what Stonehedge and Evans were saying because of the bickering couple sitting at the table between him and his target. They were in their sixties and were arguing back and forth over longstanding grievances, and although they did this in low, snippy voices, they caused the killer to lose snatches of the conversation between Stonehedge and Evans. That was unacceptable, especially since the couple was trying to decide where to stay that night: Stonehedge's Malibu estate, Evans's Freemont Place home, or even a luxury hotel for the night. The killer hoped it would be Stonehedge's estate. While the actor had quite a bit of security there, the killer had already found a way in. Evans's Freemont Place residence, on the other hand, was in a gated community. It wouldn't be impossible for the killer to break in, but it would be much trickier. Just as it would be if they chose a hotel.

As the older couple's back-and-forth sniping continued to grate on the killer's nerves, he found himself fantasizing about making them dominoes in his machine. The problem with that was his plans had been so intricately worked out, it would be nearly impossible to make a major change to them now—even if he had the available time to do so—and it would be utterly ridiculous for him to put his masterpiece at risk over pettiness. Still, as he heard the husband complaining for the fourth time about his wife not taking his side over some idiotic argument he had with her sister, the killer considered more seriously getting their license plate information so he could track them down at a later date. He was still making up his mind about this when the burner phone that he carried rang. Only one person had this number, the maintenance tech from Samson Oil & Gas. The killer frowned as he looked at the caller ID and saw that it was indeed Brad Pettibone calling him.

He answered the phone without saying a word. One could never be too cautious. For all he knew the police had caught Pettibone planting a bomb and were now contacting him with Pettibone's phone.

"Is this Reuben?"

The killer recognized Pettibone's voice, and he should've felt relief, but he had picked up the disdain in the maintenance tech's tone. Also, there was no reason that he should've been calling. The killer knew something was wrong.

"Yes," he said.

"We're changing our deal," Pettibone said. "You're going to be at oil well number 18 tonight at midnight, and you'll bring a hundred and fifty thousand dollars in cash. Pack it in a suitcase."

"I don't think this is wise. It would be much better for us to stick to our original arrangement, and for us not to meet again."

"You do, huh? Guess what, I don't care what a freak like you thinks. You be there with the money or I'll call the police from somewhere in Mexico and let them know where all the bombs are planted."

"A hundred and fifty thousand dollars is a lot of money. You're not leaving me much time—"

Pettibone hung up. The killer could've called him back, but he didn't see any point in doing so. It was a troubling call, to say the least.

The killer chewed on his thumbnail as he played back the conversation in his mind and tried to make sense of it. He had called Pettibone yesterday after he had ditched the burner phone Brick had called so he could give him the number for his new one, and at the time Pettibone had seemed his previously submissive self. Something must've happened afterward.

Of course, the killer knew what it was. Pettibone must've recognized him from the police sketches shown on TV last night. Which meant he knew the killer had murdered Heather Brandley and another woman. But why would that upset him so much that he'd call the killer a *freak*? Pettibone had known what he was after the killer had taken care of that other oil well maintenance tech, Karl Crawford, so Pettibone wouldn't lose his job. Besides, he had to know people were going to die when those bombs exploded. So why this sudden change? The killer was sure he had sized up Pettibone correctly before. A weak, but also angry, bitter man who wanted to see the world burn. Five months ago he had fully supported the killer's plans—at least the ones he'd been privy to.

This was bad. The killer had picked up not only disdain, but outright disgust in Pettibone's voice. Why? Because an actress was killed? The police didn't even give out any of the gory details! And even if they had, why would something like that bother a man like Pettibone?

Something was wrong.

Even though he would've had no reason for doing so, the killer had planned on living up to his end of the deal (and what recourse would Pettibone have if he didn't? Sue him? Ha!) and transferring fifty thousand dollars to Pettibone's offshore bank account once all the bombs had been planted. This changed everything. While the killer couldn't understand what caused this change in Pettibone, he knew the threat was real, and it had to be dealt with. Stonehedge and Evans would have to wait. While not ideal, he still had two more days before he'd absolutely have to grab what would be one of his next dominos, no matter how difficult or dangerous it was.

The killer accepted that Pettibone left him no choice. He had to leave Stonehedge and Evans for another day so he could deal with this new crisis. He had ideas of how he would do this, and he'd get some satisfaction, but the thought of Pettibone calling him a freak brought the taste of bile to his throat.

He stood up and dropped fifty dollars on the table—more than enough to cover his bill. He was about to leave, but instead did an about-face and walked over to the older couple, interrupting their bickering. Both of them looked surprised to see him approach them.

"Excuse me," the killer said. "Did I see you drive up in a Mercedes coupe? A beautiful car. I wanted to ask how it drove."

"I'm afraid you're mistaken," the husband said. "We have the Porsche."

"My apologies," the killer said, nodding politely to them.

On his way out, the killer asked the hostess if he could borrow a pen and paper. He wanted to make sure to copy down the license plate for the lone Porsche in the parking lot.

Chapter 33

Short Hills, New Jersey, 1999

"Duh-sage!"

Jason Dorsage's ears burned red hearing his archnemesis, Simon Witt, yell out the insult from across the ninth-grade classroom. For the last three weeks, he thought they'd had an unspoken truce, but Witt must've only been trying to catch him off guard. Jason's jaw clenched so tightly that the muscles surrounding his mouth began aching. He was determined not to give Witt any satisfaction, and so he continued to scribble plans in his notebook for the contraption he was working on in his father's basement.

"Duh-duh-sage!"

Jason's jaw clenched even tighter, making his lips press into thin bloodless lines. He despised Witt with a passion he would never have believed possible even last summer. It was almost comical now that they had been friends two years ago when they were in seventh grade. Back then they liked the same superhero comic books, the same cartoons, the same TV shows, and had a similar outlook on life. In eighth grade, all that changed when Witt out of the blue started making fun of him. At first it had seemed like playful teasing, but soon it became vicious. And then there was the day Jason had fallen asleep in class and woke up gagging, thinking he was going to choke to death on the most bitter, foul tasting stuff imaginable. It turned out Witt had gotten his hands on used coffee grounds and put them in Jason's mouth. He could've killed Witt that day, and from that moment they'd been mortal enemies.

Witt yelled out, "Duh-duh-duh-sage!" This time several other kids in the classroom laughed, which caused Jason's ears to burn brighter. This insult was new. For a long time now, Witt had been using some variation on *Dosage*. Such as *Dosage of Dumbness*. Or *Dosage of Ugly*. For his part, he would respond with *Simon the Zit*. That worked well since Witt had a big red one on his rat-faced cheek. But he wouldn't be able to use that now since he had broken out himself. He wanted to ignore Witt and just keep working on sketches for his contraption while the class waited for their teacher to arrive, but he just couldn't swallow down the hate he was feeling for Witt right then.

"Simon the twit," he spoke out without looking up from his notebook.

That brought some snickering from his fellow classmates, but no real sense of pleasure from Jason. He knew Witt enough to know that the first insult was to lure him into whatever game he had in mind. Sure enough, it didn't take long for Witt to retaliate.

"Bravo," Witt said as he clapped his hands. "So clever. Such a brilliant retort. And it only took you a minute and a half to come up with it. One can only wonder at how much brainpower was required for you to think of adding a *T* to my name. I believe we've found our next Mensa candidate."

More of their fellow students laughed. It wasn't just Jason's ears burning now. His cheeks felt like they were on fire. He looked up from his notebook and stared across the room at where Simon Witt was sitting. His archnemesis had a bemused expression as he looked back, his eyebrows arched, his overly ripe red lips twitching.

"Simon the twat then," he said.

There was a gasp from the doorway, and the class broke into nervous laughter. Jason's insides turned into an icy mush. He didn't have to look toward the door to know that their teacher, Ms. Gilligan, had just walked into the room. The victimized look Witt now showed would've told him that even if he hadn't heard her gasp.

"What did I hear you just say, Mr. Dorsage?" she demanded.

"He's been calling me all sorts of vulgar, hurtful names while we've been waiting for you," Witt said, his way-too-red lips now trembling as if he were fighting to keep from crying.

There was a stony silence, and all Jason could think of was punching Witt in the mouth and bursting those lips open. But he didn't move. Ms. Gilligan broke the silence by ordering him to the headmaster's office.

He didn't bother arguing. It wouldn't have done any good. Witt had several friends in the class, and they were the only ones who would've been willing to speak up; the rest of them smartly didn't want to get involved. Even if Noah were in the class, he would've been too afraid of attracting Witt's ire to say anything.

Without speaking a word, Jason packed away the notebook in his backpack and left the classroom. He didn't even bother to acknowledge Ms. Gilligan with a look.

Avery Academy was an elite private school in tony Short Hills, New Jersey. Their graduates often went on to Oxford or Cambridge or one of the Ivy League schools, and eventually became captains of industry or powerbrokers in the financial sector. No presidents yet, but Avery counted several US senators and congressmen among its former students.

Jason had little doubt this was what Witt was after: to manipulate him into yelling something offensive the moment Ms. Gilligan entered the room. He knew this latest infraction might get him suspended, but wasn't going to get him expelled. But it was one more mark on his record because of Witt, and if Witt successfully kept pushing his buttons, he'd get enough marks so he would be expelled regardless of how much money his father donated to the school. In a way, that would be a relief. Any school, private or public or even a military academy, would be preferable as long as he'd never have to see Witt again. The problem was his father had made it clear that if he were to be expelled from Avery, he would lose his trust fund, and so Jason was stuck. He would just have to find a way not to let Witt keep pushing his buttons. Easier said than done.

What he'd like to do was beat the snot out of him. Actually, he'd like to do far worse than that, but knocking Witt on his ass would be a good start. They were both skinny kids, neither of them athletic, Witt maybe an inch taller. But he had heard that Witt had been taking tae kwon do classes since the start of the school year, and Noah claimed he'd seen Witt performing an exotic kick. Jason had no idea what that would be, and Noah was useless in describing it in more detail, but the thought of some sort of exotic kick connecting with his head terrified him. The thought of losing in a fight with Witt terrified him even more. If that were to happen, it would be too humiliating for him to ever show his face at Avery again, even if it meant giving up his trust fund.

Jason knocked once on the door and walked into the headmaster's office. Headmaster Allan Rector (the happenstance of the man having that last name was remarkable) was leaning back in his chair, his heavily-lidded eyes closed, his thick, sausage-like fingers interlaced as his hands rested on his massive belly. Whenever Jason would walk into the headmaster's office and find Rector like this, he'd always wonder for a moment if Rector might be dead. A huge man, both in height and girth, with snow-white hair and an unhealthy grayish complexion. He had to be in his sixties, maybe even older, and given all the weight he carried he was a massive heart attack waiting to happen.

Jason took heavier steps as he approached the headmaster's desk, and Rector's eyes cracked open.

"Ah, Mr. Dorsage. It has been over three weeks. As much as I enjoy your company, I was hoping I wouldn't be seeing you again under these circumstances."

Jason took the chair opposite Rector and slumped in it. "I was hoping the same," he admitted with a shrug. "But it couldn't be helped."

"The offense?"

"I called Witt *Simon the Twat*."

"I'm sure you had your reason?"

Jason nodded glumly.

"Which class did this occur in?"

"Algebra."

Rector grimaced. "So you said this in front of Ms. Gilligan?"

"She had just walked into the classroom. I didn't know she was there."

"Mr. Dorsage, it appears that you are the victim of unfortunate timing. I'm not going to suspend you, but I'm sure Ms. Gilligan is not particularly fond of you right now. Why don't we give her a chance to cool off?"

With a heavy grunt, Rector bent forward and opened his bottom desk drawer and pulled out a chess set. After placing the board between himself and Jason, he grabbed a white and black pawn, put his large, doughy hands below the desk so he could switch the pawns around, and then held out his hands for Jason to choose one. He chose the hand holding the white pawn.

Over the course of the school year, they had played chess a number of times, even when a teacher hadn't sent Jason to Rector's office. All of their games were close, but Jason was smart enough to know when to make a critical mistake so that he would lose.

Witt might be clever in knowing how to push his buttons, but Jason had more than his own share of cleverness.

Chapter 34

Jason was able to avoid any further contact with Simon Witt, and at the end of the school day he and Noah English eschewed the school vans that would have dropped them off at their homes, and chose instead to walk the mile and a half to Jason's dad's sprawling Georgian colonial. It was a crisp, cold February day, but it was a cloudless sky and the sun was bright, and by walking they'd avoid Witt.

When Jason was playing chess with Headmaster Rector (and he had to make back-to-back blunders before the headmaster saw the winning move), he'd come up with a vague and complicated idea of how he could deal with Witt. It was all very preliminary, and needed a lot more thought and planning before it could take shape, and it might never even come to fruition for the simple reason that Jason was unwilling to put his current project on hold to concentrate on this other plan. But it gave him a small degree of comfort knowing that he had a rather ingenious way of dealing with Witt if he ever decided to invest the time.

Jason's mind was elsewhere as they walked, and he didn't catch what Noah had asked him. He glanced over his right shoulder and saw that Noah was struggling to keep pace, his cheeks mottled pink and white from physical exertion. Noah English was a short, pudgy kid, who wasn't good at either academics or chess. Jason wasn't sure how they'd become friends, except over the last two years Noah had become a hanger-on, a kid who always seemed interested in whatever project Jason had in the works. Maybe he was more a lackey than a friend. It was something Jason had never given any thought to before. He looked back again, and saw that

Noah was falling farther behind. Although he was anxious to get home, he slowed down several steps so the boy could keep up with him.

"I can't wait to see what you've been working on," Noah said in an out-of-breath voice.

"My Rube Goldberg machine."

"Why is it called that?"

That was a good question, and yet another thing Jason hadn't thought about before. Sometimes Noah could surprise him. He was going to have to research it, because he was sure his father would be asking him the same question at some point, although more to trap him than out of curiosity.

"It just is," Jason bluffed. "The contraption isn't done yet, but it's far enough along so you'll have an idea of how it's going to work. I've decided to let you help me finish it. Assuming you want to."

"You bet I do!"

"You'll have to keep it secret."

"Don't worry, my lips are sealed."

Noah made a lip-sealing gesture, complete with tossing the imaginary key over his shoulder. Neither boy spoke after that until they got inside Jason's home. Well, one of his homes. His parents divorced six years ago, and his mother also had a mansion of sorts in Short Hills, but he was rarely there. For the last three years his mother had been traveling abroad in Europe with her young stud boyfriend, and he had only seen her twice during that time, which as far as he was concerned was two times too many.

Noah had taken off his mittens and was blowing on his fingers to warm them up. "I could really use some coffee," he said. A gleam showed in his eyes as he added, "With maybe this much Irish whiskey added."

He separated his index finger and thumb so that they were an inch apart.

"I'll get us coffee, but no whiskey," Jason said. "The work we're doing needs precision. I can't afford any mistakes."

Noah's silly grin weakened, but otherwise he hid his disappointment. While he waited, Jason went off to find the Dorsage family live-in housekeeper, Maritza, so he could ask her to make coffee for him and his guest, and to bring it to the basement. With that done, he took Noah downstairs to show him the winding domino and playing card formations that were interconnected with racing car tracks, trip wires, pulleys, ping pong paddles, electric fans, and other components for the contraption that he had built, and he explained how toppling the first domino would trigger each subsequent event. While he did this Maritza brought them a tray holding two mugs of coffee, cream, sugar, and a plate of freshly baked chocolate chip cookies. She was from El Salvador, twenty-eight, a petite and pretty dark-haired woman. As she left them to go back upstairs, Noah stared after her. Once she was gone, he asked Jason whether he had special privileges with the help.

"Quit being a pig."

Noah seemed to take that as a challenge to leer in an especially ugly way. "You need to tell me she at least gives you hand jobs." He closed his pudgy right hand into a fist and pantomimed giving a hand job.

"You want me to tell her you're asking about that?"

The shit-eating grin Noah showed disappeared in a heartbeat, and was replaced by a look of alarm.

"I was just kidding around," he insisted.

"Forget it. Drink your coffee and I'll show you my plans."

Jason took his notebook out of his backpack and went over his sketches with Noah while the other boy drank coffee and wolfed down several of the homemade cookies. After that they went to work.

* * * *

One of Mr. Dorsage's rules was that the family ate dinner together, and so at seven-thirty that night Jason, his father, his two older sisters, and his stepmother, Vivian, were seated at the dining room table. All of them except Vivian were served a prime rib dinner that their private chef, Maurice, had prepared. Vivian, a neurotic thirty-one-year-old blonde who had already undergone numerous cosmetic surgeries and in Jason's mind looked like a second-rate anorexic porn starlet, claimed to suffer from a number of different stomach ailments, and she was served her usual poached sole, brown rice, and steamed vegetables.

Jason would've liked to have invited Noah to dinner, but he knew his father looked down his nose at his friend, thinking the boy was slow-witted, crude, and a poor influence, and Jason couldn't afford to alienate his father any further. As it was, he had no friends sitting at the table. Both his sisters had always looked at him as if he were some strange alien creature, and neither of them had any interest in him, nor did he have any in them. At seventeen, Lila was closer in age, but even though only two years separated them, it could just as well have been twenty. There was no connection whatsoever. Barbara, five years older, was supposed to be a sophomore at Yale, but claimed she suffered a breakdown of some sort, and was home convalescing. Jason couldn't remember the last time the two of them had exchanged words. And then there was Vivian. While his sisters mostly acted as if he didn't exist, they still tolerated him. Vivian, on the other hand, seemed incensed by his presence. Recently she had gotten on a kick that he shouldn't be allowed to build his Rube Goldberg machine in the basement. She claimed she wanted the space to build a private gym, but Jason understood it was really because she knew building the contraption was important to him.

Jason didn't have much of an appetite that night; partly because the stunt Witt had pulled still bothered him, partly that he was anxious to get back to building his machine, and partly due to the oppressiveness of the room. As he picked at his food, he felt a prickly sensation, as if eyes were on him. He looked up to see Vivian seething as she glared in his direction. She averted her eyes and turned to his father.

"Richard, I am not happy with you."

Mr. Dorsage finished chewing a mouthful of food and patted his lips with a silk napkin before acknowledging his wife with a patient smile.

"Now why would that be, my dear?" he asked.

Her voice was like ice as she said, "Because I've been telling you for weeks that I have plans for the basement, and you persist in allowing your son to use the space for his foolishness."

"What I'm doing down there isn't foolish," Jason insisted more forcefully than he would've liked. Just as Simon Witt could push his buttons, so could Vivian.

Lila and Barbara simultaneously rolled their eyes, both of them bored by the conversation. Mr. Dorsage raised an eyebrow.

"Son, what you're doing down there might be clever and inventive, but it's also certainly foolish."

"I disagree!" Jason could feel the heat rising up his neck, and he forced himself to lower his voice. He said, "Vivian's already had you convert one of the rooms into a private yoga studio, and another into a Pilates studio. Does she really need every bit of space in this house for herself?"

"You're going to let him talk about me that way?"

Without turning to her, Mr. Dorsage made several up-and-down motions with his hand for his wife to calm down.

"What's your fascination with this?" he asked his son.

Jason could've told him the full truth. That he was drawn to the predictability of these contraptions. One event triggering the next, with him acting as God. There was an intrinsic beauty to it that took his breath away. But instead he told his father a different side of the truth.

"This is going to be my life's work," he said.

Lila broke out laughing, and muttered, "What a moron," under her breath. Barbara snickered. Mr. Dorsage frowned.

"If you want your trust fund, you have to first go to a college I approve of, and get a job making a substantial income."

"Because you don't want us to be loafers?" Lila interjected with a smirk.

"Exactly." Mr. Dorsage took a swallow of his wine and patted his lips again. He kept his eyes on Jason as he said, "You need to earn your way through life, and not be given everything."

"I expect to make a substantial income with these machines."

"How do you expect to do that?"

"I have ideas. How about this for a proposition? If by the time I'm twenty-five I'm not making a hundred thousand dollars a year building these machines, you can keep my trust fund."

Lila asked Mr. Dorsage if she could have the moron's trust fund when he failed. He ignored her and instead cut off a small piece of prime rib and chewed it slowly, taking his time studying his son. Even Vivian became unusually still as if she were calculating which would be preferable: the instant gratification of wrecking Jason's current plans, or being patient and seeing him ruin his life in ten years.

Mr. Dorsage said, "If you're serious about this then you should be able to tell me right now why these contraptions are called Rube Goldberg machines. If you can't do that, I want you to clean up what you've been doing in the basement, and I never want to hear about this nonsense again."

Jason smiled because after Noah had left he'd looked up Rube Goldberg in the encyclopedia and he knew the answer.

"Rube Goldberg was a Pulitzer Prize-winning cartoonist. He drew cartoons of zany inventions where a series of events are triggered which eventually accomplish a task, such as his famous *self-operating napkin* machine. In this cartoon, the action of a man lifting a soupspoon to his mouth causes a ladle to toss a cracker in the air, which causes a parrot to fly off his perch to grab the cracker, which causes a further sequence of events until a pendulum with a napkin attached is released, and the man's mouth is wiped clean."

If Mr. Dorsage was impressed with his son's presentation, he didn't show it. His expression remained muted as he chewed and swallowed another piece of the prime rib.

"You'll go to college and earn a degree," he declared at last. "By the time you finish your bachelor's degree you'll be twenty-two, old enough to make your own decisions, and old enough to suffer the consequences of acting stupidly. Hopefully long before then you will have outgrown this nonsense. In the meantime, you can use the basement to build these contraptions."

"So we have a deal? I'll get my trust fund if I prove you wrong?"

Mr. Dorsage's expression turned exceptionally stern. "If after college you persist in this foolishness, that's your choice. If you meet your goal, you'll get your trust fund; otherwise it will be forfeited."

Jason smiled inwardly, quite pleased with the deal he had just struck. This wasn't something he'd ever outgrow. Nor was it foolishness. Building the most amazing Rube Goldberg machine was going to be his life's mission. One that would leave the world breathless.

Chapter 35

Short Hills, New Jersey, 1999, six days later

Jason and Noah were sitting in Avery's cafeteria engaged in hushed discussions when Simon Witt approached them carrying a lunch tray loaded with split pea and ham soup, a grilled cheese sandwich, and an ice cream sundae. Noah noticed Witt first, and signaled by drawing an imaginary line across his throat that they needed to stop talking. Witt didn't join them at their table; instead, he leaned in close to Dorsage and whispered, "I know what you're doing."

Jason had a near irresistible impulse to upend Witt's tray so he'd be wearing the soup and sundae on his school jacket. Somehow he controlled himself and told Witt to get lost.

"You're building one of those mousetrap machines," Witt said, his overly red lips forming an ugly smirk. "Like that old game. Where one event triggers the next."

"You don't know what you're talking about."

Jason tried to stare down Witt, but he was betrayed when he felt a muscle twitch near his right eye. From Witt's self-satisfied look, he had noticed the twitch also. It shouldn't matter to him that his archnemesis had found out about his plans, but it did. What was he so worried about? That Witt would try to outdo him by building a more elaborate contraption? Good luck with that! Jason already had a four-month head start. Still, though, he felt a sense of unease knowing that Witt was aware of his project.

"But I do, *Duh-sage*. Over the last week two of my minions saw you sketching plans for your mousetrap thingamajig. You need to guard your notebook more carefully if you want to keep secrets from me."

"That doesn't mean anything," Jason insisted, knowing full well that he only sounded pathetic.

"Maybe so, but someone close to you ratted you out. I know you've been spending months building it in your basement."

Noah flashed Jason a pleading, desperate look that it wasn't him. Jason returned that with a quick nod. He knew Witt was telling the truth, and he knew who must've betrayed him. Lila. She was a junior at Avery, and if Witt asked her about what her brother was doing in their basement each day, Lila wouldn't think twice about spilling the beans.

"Funny that a rat-faced creep like you would use the term *ratted* out," Jason said. "So you know what I've been working on. So what?"

"So let me see it."

"Why?"

"I'm curious."

There wasn't a chance in the world Jason would share his pet project with Simon Witt. The idea of it was preposterous. He didn't bother telling Witt that, and instead turned away to eat his lunch. Seconds later a loud crashing noise startled him. He looked behind to see that Simon Witt had fallen into a neighboring table, his soup and sundae all over himself and Melissa Goldfarb. Melissa's mouth hung open in shock as Witt worked to disentangle himself from her.

"Dorsage tripped Simon into her!"

Jason stared dumbly at Peter Covington, who had just leveled the accusation against him. Covington was one of Witt's loyal minions. Jason hadn't realized Covington had positioned himself nearby. An iciness filled his head as he thought about how far Witt was willing to go to frame him.

Two of Avery's teachers, Mr. Tremblay and Mr. Langan, came rushing over, demanding to know what had happened. Jason tried insisting that he didn't do anything, but Covington again accused him. Melissa began crying as she sat covered in Witt's lunch. Witt successfully disentangled himself and was back on his feet, pea soup dripping from his face and his jacket. His lips trembled as if he were on the verge of bawling, and he told the two teachers that he had stopped to talk to Dorsage, and when he turned to walk away, Dorsage shoved him from behind.

"It was like he bodychecked me," Witt said, somehow managing several tears to snake down both cheeks. He indicated on his lower back where he'd been pushed. "I don't know why Jason did it. I only stopped to ask him if we could be friends again. I just want him to leave me alone. I'm so sorry Melissa had to get hurt also because of Jason's irrational hatred toward me."

Jason was too flabbergasted to defend himself. One look at Tremblay and Langan was enough to know it wouldn't have mattered whatever he tried saying. Without waiting for either of them to give the order, he got up and informed them he was off to the headmaster's office.

* * * *

The cafeteria incident was a big to-do. The upshot was that Jason received a week's detention, which required him to spend an hour after school each day in the headmaster's office. As he played the headmaster in chess later that afternoon, Rector acknowledged that he believed Jason's side of the story.

"If I didn't you would have been suspended," Rector said as his half-lidded eyes studied the chessboard. "But I was left no choice. I had to give you some punishment, or there'd be hell to pay given that Ms. Goldfarb is also an injured party, and Master Witt was able to produce a vociferous witness, while your witness, Master English, was less than compelling."

"Noah's afraid Witt might start attacking him."

Rector made a grunting noise that he agreed with Jason. His eyes lit up when he saw what he thought was a three-move combination resulting in winning a knight. What he failed to see was three moves later Jason would be able to take his queen. A thin smile quivered over Rector's lips as he made what he thought would be a winning move. Jason tried to decide whether this would be the game in which he beat the headmaster. While he understood the dilemma Rector had been put in, he wasn't happy with the detention.

"Yes, it's a shame Master English couldn't have been more forceful in his defense of you, but even if he had it wouldn't have mattered. Once Ms. Goldfarb got included, I'm afraid the matter was sealed. Let us hope that her parents don't make too big a stink. If they do, I might have to appease them by adding a suspension to your punishment."

Jason made up his mind. This wasn't going to be the day he beat the headmaster. He needed the man's good will. After the three-move combination completed and he lost his knight, he proceeded to make a losing move. The game ended quickly after that. Rector looked pleased with himself as he checked the time and saw that they'd be able to fit in another game.

Once detention ended, Jason could've arranged for a ride home, but he decided to walk so he could clear his head and try to calm down some of the anger that had been choking him since Witt had pulled his latest stunt.

While he had remained calm and composed in front of Rector, inside he was seething, and he wanted nothing more than to hurt Witt. But, as he kept trying to tell himself, he couldn't let himself be distracted. He needed to focus his energies on his Rube Goldberg machine. That was what mattered. He would deal with Witt at another time.

When he got home and saw Lila in the front parlor reading a fashion magazine, he was tempted to chew her out for what she must've told Witt, but he knew she'd be clueless about what she had done. Nor would she care about anything he had to say.

She must've heard him enter the room, because she lowered her magazine and gave him a blank stare, as if she didn't recognize him.

"One of your moronic friends was over earlier," she said.

That didn't make any sense. Noah knew he had detention so he wouldn't have come over. Baffled, Jason asked, "Noah English?"

"I don't know their names. One of those loser morons is the same as the next as far as I'm concerned."

"Shorter than me, chunky?"

"No. This one's your height, skinny like you, kind of gross red lips."

It had to be Witt. Jason found himself trembling. His voice shook as he asked what Witt wanted.

"What's your problem? You look like you're about to go ballistic!"

"What did he want?"

Lila regarded him more cautiously then, like she was dealing with an insane person. "He said that you wanted him to work on your moronic contraption—"

Jason didn't wait for her to finish, her voice becoming little more than a buzz in his ears. He ran past her to the basement door, and then flew down the stairs three steps at a time. He was panting as he turned the corner and saw that his machine had been torn apart. Witt had used the race car tracks, dominos, playing cards, and other pieces of it to spell out "Duh-Dorsage."

Murderous rage consumed him. A loud roaring filled his ears, and for several minutes he was incapable of movement as he stood frozen staring at the carnage done to his beautiful machine. When he left the basement, he could barely see through a red haze that filled his vision. He headed straight to his bedroom and sat at the computer and tried to look up how he could buy a gun, because all he could think of was blasting a full clip of bullets into Simon Witt's face.

He remembered then his vague plan from a week ago, and he decided instead to focus on that.

Chapter 36

Los Angeles, the present

The unmarked car with two plainclothes LAPD detectives inside was still parked half a block away when Morris returned home. He had stopped off for pizza, and he bought an extra one for the detectives who'd been watching his wife and daughter all day. The officers saw him approaching and rolled down the driver's side window. Morris handed over a pizza and a six-pack of beer and told the detectives they could call it a night.

"Things been quiet?" he asked.

"As a mouse. We'll be back first thing tomorrow morning. Six a.m. okay?"

"You can make it seven."

"Both parties going to stay inside the house again?"

"I'm going to try to convince them to do so."

The detective thanked him for the pizza and beer, and drove off. Morris walked back to his car, got Parker out of the front seat and the pizza out of the trunk, and then headed inside. Natalie met him at the front door. While Parker demonstrated by wagging his tail and making several grunts that he was happy to see her, his greeting was more muted than usual as he was distracted by the pizza.

"Only eight o'clock," Natalie said. "I was surprised when you called and told me you were coming home this early. I thought you'd be pulling an all-nighter."

"It wouldn't do me any good," Morris said.

Kissing her, he took hold of her hand, and the two of them headed to the kitchen.

"I'm impressed," she said. "You're learning in your old age."

Morris chuckled, some of his weariness leaking through. "It only took me twenty-some-odd years. Nat, we've got a lot on this psycho, but we're going to need something more before we catch him. Unless the FBI is able to pinpoint him from his purchases, all we can do for now is have the media keep showing those sketches and try to goad him into making a mistake, and wait for our next break."

He put the pizza down on the kitchen countertop while Natalie selected a bottle of wine.

"Pinot noir or Chianti?" she asked.

"Your choice." He opened the pizza box so he could fully breathe in the wonderful aroma and get a look at the half sausage, quarter shrimp, and quarter broccoli pie. The sausage was for him and Parker, the shrimp for Nat, and the broccoli for Rachel. Parker jumped up with his front paws resting on the cabinet door so he could get a look also. Morris let him do so. He figured after the day they both had, the bull terrier deserved that much.

Natalie handed him a bottle of Chianti and a corkscrew. As Morris struggled to pull out what was turning into a very stubborn cork, he asked his wife about her day in captivity.

"It was fine. We've got nice prison accommodations here. I spent it doing yoga and catching up on some reading."

There was a loud popping noise as Morris was able to yank the cork out without spilling any wine.

"How about our daughter?"

"She has all her law books on her tablet, so she was able to spend the day studying. A little, but not too much grousing from her." Natalie showed a conspiratorial smile. "Rachel's holed up in her bedroom now, and I believe she's talking to her new boyfriend."

Morris frowned at that. "I didn't know she was seeing anyone after breaking up with *whatshisname*."

"You mean Paul?"

"That's what I said. *Whatshisname*. What do you know about this new guy?"

"Nothing. It's only a guess on my part, but from the expression on her face when the call came and the way she hurried to her bedroom, I think it's a pretty good one."

"Hmm."

"What?"

Morris said, "Nothing. I'll let Rachel know pizza's waiting."

He didn't want to tell Natalie what he was thinking. He left the kitchen quickly so she wouldn't be able to read anything further from his expression. When he got to his daughter's bedroom, he stood and listened as Rachel talked in a hushed voice over the phone. He knocked, and Rachel came to the door, her face flushed.

"I brought home pizza," Morris said. "You ready to come down and join us?"

"Sure."

Morris lowered his voice. "Your mom told me you have a new boyfriend?"

Rachel smiled thinly, her eyes as hard as stone. "Your wife is very intuitive. I've got to be more careful around her."

"True, but still, tell me about him."

Rachel's thin smile became strained, and her flinty eyes dulled. "Sorry, Dad, but no. We've only been seeing each other for a month. My life, you know?"

Rachel had always been fiercely protective of her privacy, and even more so after a rough breakup with *whatshisname*. That was partly over having a dad who was a cop, and the third degree he gave the boys she dated back in high school, and partly her makeup. Morris expected this response, and he hated what he had to tell her next.

"This maniac we're after has been planning these murders for months. I wouldn't put anything past him."

He didn't know what type of reaction to expect from his daughter, but having her snort out with laughter, then bite down hard on her bottom lip to keep from laughing further was near the bottom of his list.

"I'm sorry, Dad, really. I know you're not being ridiculous, and under normal circumstances this would be worth investigating. But not in this case. The man I've been seeing is not your psycho killer. Even if I hadn't seen those police sketches, I would be able to guarantee it."

"Sweetheart, this maniac is devious, and he's good at using prosthetics to disguise himself."

Rachel made a decision. "You don't have anything to worry about. He's someone you know. That's all I'm going to say about it. And it's not Dennis Polk, if that's what you're worrying about."

"Well, that's good. If it was Polk, I'd have to disown you."

"If it was Polk, I'd have to disown myself."

"It's not Adam Felger?"

She gave him a stern look. "We're not making this a guessing game. I'm hungry, let's go have some pizza."

Morris nodded, properly chastised, but also relieved as well as curious. But he knew better than to push Rachel any further. As they walked together down the hallway, he whispered to her, asking that she not mention any of this to her mom. Rachel in a soft voice told him not to worry.

When they entered the kitchen, Natalie must've sensed something was up. She looked at them suspiciously, while Parker gave Rachel a lukewarm greeting as he was still distracted by the pizza.

"What have you two been conspiring about?" Natalie asked.

"You were right. Our daughter's seeing someone. I was trying to get her to divulge his name, but all she'd tell me is it's not Polk."

"Well, that's a relief, at least," Natalie said with a straight face.

Rachel's expression let them know as far as she was concerned this discussion was over. They sat down then to salad, pizza, and wine, and Parker was finally rewarded for his Job-like patience. Morris was reaching for a second slice when his phone rang. He frowned seeing that Margot Denoir from *The Hollywood Peeper* was calling.

"I have a feeling I'm not going to like this," Morris said to her when he answered the call.

"Probably not. Your pervert killer left me something."

Morris got up from the kitchen table so he could talk privately. He was absent-mindedly still holding the slice of pizza he had grabbed, and because of that Parker followed him.

"Quit being coy, Margot," he said.

"Sorry. An old habit to make sure my audience sticks around after the commercial break. He left an envelope addressed to me outside the Channel Four building. Inside were photographs of what he did to Heather Brandley and Drea Kane. I thought we were friends. You held out on me."

Morris felt a pulse begin beating in his right temple. "I adore you, Margot, you know that. And what I told you was sensational enough."

"I disagree. If you truly adored me you would've told me about this fiend cutting these unfortunate actresses in half. And you would've told me where he left their bodies. At least where he left Brandley's upper half and Kane's lower half."

"You're being coy again."

"True. He included sickeningly gruesome photos from the Fred Astaire-Ginger Rogers exhibit at the wax museum, and the mannequin he devised for that downtown LA clothing store."

The pulse beating in Morris's temple was gone, replaced by a coolness. "When did he leave you the envelope?"

"I don't know. An intern working here found it outside sometime around four o'clock, and left it buried in a stack of mail on my desk. I've since tried asking her if she could be more specific about the time. She can't. I didn't open the envelope until twenty minutes ago. And of course, you're the first person I called."

"Does your building have outdoor surveillance cameras?"

"Sadly, no. I've already asked security."

"Okay, I'll have LAPD pick all of it up. Don't touch any of it again. And Margot, you can't use it."

She laughed. A soft, tinkling laughter. Normally Morris liked the sound of it, but not then. "I'm fond of you, Morris, but no offense, I'm much fonder of the ratings these photos are going to give me."

"If you use any of it, it will hurt our chances of catching this maniac. I'll also be slamming the door shut on you. You'll never get anything else from me."

"Losing your friendship would sadden me immensely. But Morris, darling, you're no longer a homicide detective, and from what I hear most of your private investigations are cut-and-dry corporate cases. So that's not much of a threat since you might never have anything else to give me."

He knew he wouldn't be able to get a court order in time to stop her, nor would it do any good to threaten an obstruction of justice charge.

"I'll trade," he said. "I'll give you an exclusive tomorrow. Prime time. What I have will blow the roof off your ratings."

"Give me a hint."

"Off the record?"

"Yes. Agreed. Off the record."

Morris had an agreement with the LAPD to keep Faye Riverstone's abduction and maiming under wraps, but he couldn't let Margot make those photos public. This psycho wanted recognition for his murders, and their best chance of leading him into making a crucial mistake was to keep frustrating him.

"He took Faye Riverstone," Morris said. "As long as you behave yourself, I'll tell you and your audience all about it tomorrow night."

"I'll behave myself," Margot promised in an oddly reverent tone, at least for her. "Scout's honor."

Morris couldn't imagine Margot Denoir ever being a Girl Scout, but he kept that thought to himself. They had a quick conversation to discuss what time he needed to be at the station tomorrow night. After he got off the call, he looked down to see that Parker had licked the sausage and cheese off the slice of pizza he had forgotten he was holding. The bull terrier gave him a guilty look that his rather clownish theft had been discovered. Morris couldn't help laughing.

"It's just been one of those days."

He fed the bull terrier the rest of the slice. Parker grunted his appreciation.

Chapter 37

The killer had been kept busy most of the day thanks to the monkey wrench Pettibone had thrown into his plans, but by nine o'clock he had everything ready and tested for his midnight rendezvous. With that taken care of, he turned the TV on, switching it to Channel Four. Margot Denoir must've gotten the envelope he had left for her hours ago, and he'd been anxious all day to see how they were now reporting the story. He would've turned on the TV earlier, but he decided to wait until he was ready to deal with Pettibone before rewarding himself.

He didn't have to wait long before a news flash came on about the *Sex Pervert Maniac Killer*. He was stunned by the name they had given him, and even more so by what they were reporting. They didn't use any of the photos he had left for Denoir. Instead, they were *actually* saying that he was sexually violating the dead bodies of his victims, and that his reason for mutilating their bodies afterward was a pathetic attempt to hide his sexual perversions.

For several minutes, the killer felt as if he'd been smacked in the face with a sledgehammer. None of it made any sense! Once the ME got the bodies back to his lab, he should've recognized his mistake. Unless...

A flash of inspiration struck, and the killer realized what must've happened. They were intentionally telling malicious lies about him so the public would believe he was nothing more than a sicko freak. He also knew who was responsible. Brick.

He tried telling himself it didn't matter. Once his death machine fully played out, the world would know the truth regardless of these lies. As he thought about Brick's duplicity the numbness he felt was replaced by a white-hot fury. It had been years since he had wanted to hurt someone as badly as he wanted to hurt Brick right then. He had to go all the way back to when he was fifteen and he came home from school to discover that the rat-faced little turd Simon Witt had destroyed his first Rube Goldberg machine. But he was patient then. He'd be equally patient with Brick. He wasn't going to let Brick maneuver him into making a mistake. That was what he was after. But when this was over, the killer was going to get his hands on Brick's wife and daughter, and he was going to do sickening things to them. Assuming they survived the coming devastation.

The killer checked the time. Only twenty past nine. He knew where oil well number 18 was located since it was one of the wells on the list he gave Pettibone. He had plenty of time before he needed to head over there, but given how he was feeling he'd be climbing the walls if he stayed where he was. He hadn't eaten anything since snacking on wood-grilled calamari in Malibu. A good dinner and a couple of beers would lift his spirits. He knew just the place. A nice casual spot, and it would be on the way to the oil well.

He checked himself in a mirror. The prosthetic nose he had attached earlier was still holding strong. He'd skip the fake teeth this time—it was tough enough earlier eating calamari with them. But even without them, the disguise he had on would be good enough. The killer packed up what he needed for later and headed out.

* * * *

The killer bypassed the first empty spot so he could park with no car on either side of him. A doughy-looking man wearing a windbreaker who had to be a parking attendant came hustling over to him.

"I need you to park over there," he said, referring to the first empty spot.

The killer looked around. While the restaurant had a small lot that often got cramped during its peak times, at that hour there were plenty of empty spaces.

"It's almost ten o'clock. I don't think it will be a problem if I leave my car where it is."

"Friday night's one of our busiest," the attendant said, unmoved. "I need you to move your car or I'll have it towed."

The killer recognized that the attendant had the mind of a bureaucrat. Worse, he was one of those little people who enjoyed wielding the little power he had. Without arguing any further, he got in his car, backed it up, and parked in the first empty spot. The attendant once again hurried over to him.

"You need to get closer to the other car."

The killer stared at the man in disbelief. Maybe he'd be able to park four inches closer and still be able to open the car door, but the point of the request wasn't so that he'd park his car perfectly. This nitwit was busting his balls just to bust them. But it wasn't worth arguing. He got back behind the wheel, and as he tried to adjust his parking, the nitwit attendant moved to the front of the car and started making hand gestures as if he were trying to aid the killer in his effort. The gestures, though, made no sense. It was as if he were drunkenly turning an imaginary steering wheel in all different directions. It was just too much when he started signaling for the killer to bring the car forward, even though he was standing only inches away from the front bumper.

The killer hit the gas, crushing the attendant's legs and pinning him against the other car. He had earlier moved a tire iron up front so he'd have it ready for later, and he grabbed it, maneuvered himself out of the tight squeeze with the neighboring car that the attendant had forced him into, and then started swinging the tire iron at the man's head as if he were trying to crush a pumpkin with a baseball bat.

The man might've cried early on, he might've even been screaming. If he was, the killer wouldn't have been able to hear him over the roaring pounding in his ears. It was only after he had turned the man's head into a bloody pulp that he realized what he was doing. He also understood then just how much anger toward Brick was still simmering beneath the surface.

The killer stood breathing heavily, his chest heaving, as he processed what had happened. His other killings were completely cold-blooded. They were necessary so he could put the dominos in place for his machine. He took no pleasure in the actual killings, only in how the deaths would later be used. This was different. He enjoyed killing this nitwit. More than he would've ever imagined.

The killer's breathing slowed. He remembered then where he was, and that anyone coming to or leaving the restaurant would be able to see him. He looked around and didn't spot anyone. He then sucked in his stomach and squeezed himself back into his car. He felt hungrier right then than he had felt in ages, but he wouldn't be able to eat there now. That was okay. He knew of another restaurant on the way to the oil well that he'd be able to stop at for some takeout. A thought occurred to him. That annoying-as-hell parking attendant might've left blood on his car. Well, if so, he'd take care of it later.

The killer smiled as he backed up and the body pitched forward so that the man landed on what was left of his face.

He gave one last look to make sure no one was watching, and then drove off.

Chapter 38

"You'll be paying me ten grand, right?"

Todd Hurley had asked Pettibone this four times already, and Pettibone was getting sick of the question.

"If Reuben shows up and you do your job, you'll get paid."

Hurley, a thick-bodied construction worker whom Pettibone had met months ago when the two of them were drinking cheap beer in a dive bar, screwed up his face as if he were going to ask another dumb question, but the look Pettibone gave him shut him up.

Pettibone turned away from Hurley so he could watch for Reuben's arrival. They had gotten to the oil well thirty minutes early and from his vantage point he'd be able to see Reuben driving up the dirt road. When that happened, he'd turn the SUV's high beams on and stand in front of it while Hurley stayed hidden behind the SUV with a baseball bat.

Capturing Reuben and handing him over to the police for the hundred-grand reward they were now offering wouldn't be enough. If Pettibone did that, Reuben would tell them about him planting the bombs. But the police would pay for Reuben's dead body as well as they would for him alive, and Pettibone would collect the reward money and disappear into Vietnam before anyone discovered the bombs hidden inside the oil wells. It was a shame the wells weren't going to be blown up, but you couldn't have everything, and getting the money was what mattered most to him. He didn't think Reuben was going to bring any money, let alone a hundred and fifty grand, but if he did Pettibone would score that as well.

He pulled out his cell phone so he could check the time. Three minutes to midnight. He had the unnerving thought that Reuben might've decided to call his bluff and not show up. If that happened, he would have to follow through with his threat. He'd have no choice. He had to be out of the country before those wells blew, and since he'd no longer be able to count on Reuben transferring another fifty thousand to his offshore account, he would have to flee that night to Mexico. Once he was there, he'd screw Reuben over by calling the authorities and letting them know where the bombs were.

Pettibone ducked as a loud buzzing whirled past his head. Whatever the thing was, it sounded like the loudest, angriest hornet that ever lived. The buzzing noise circled overhead, and he searched the pitch-black night's sky for its source.

"What the hell is that?" Hurley yelled out.

A narrow but startlingly bright search light turned on overhead, first illuminating Pettibone, then encircling the SUV and shining on Hurley's face. Pettibone's throat tightened as he realized what it was. A drone. That meant Reuben must've gotten here before they had. It also meant they'd lost their element of surprise. There had to be a camera attached to the drone, and Reuben now knew about Pettibone bringing muscle along.

The drone remained hovering over Hurley, its spotlight zeroing in on his face. Hurley, for his part, shielded his eyes as he squinted at it and tried to make sense of what it was. Pettibone watched as a red laser-like pinpoint dotted the middle of Hurley's forehead, and then as his accomplice's head exploded. Pettibone stood staring at Hurley's crumpled corpse, too dazed at first to make sense of what had happened. Then as if a lightning bolt struck him, he realized Reuben had outfitted the drone with not only a spotlight, but also a gun and a laser sight. When the spotlight turned back onto him, Pettibone started running.

A blind panic took over. Each time the drone buzzed his head or the spotlight turned on him, he would turn and keep running. If he was thinking clearly, he would've tried to make his way back to the SUV. Or maybe he would've realized he was being herded by the drone. But his lizard brain had taken over, and neither of these thoughts could penetrate it. What stopped him was when he ran straight into the path of a swinging tire iron. The blow struck him across the chest and broke his sternum, shattered several ribs, and sent him hard on his ass.

The pain was so intense he had difficulty breathing. Or maybe one of the broken ribs had punctured a lung. He couldn't move if his life depended on it, and he watched as Reuben stepped into view and kneeled down beside him. He looked different, especially his nose, but it was the same person.

Reuben looked at him with something close to pity. "I warned you that it would be best for us to stick to our original deal," he said.

"I'm sorry," Pettibone forced out, his voice a faint whisper.

"Did you plant all the bombs yet?"

"No."

"How many still need to be planted?"

"Three."

"Which ones?"

"I'll tell you if you help me to a hospital."

Reuben stared sadly at him. "You're in no position to bargain."

He tapped Pettibone across the chest with the tire iron. It probably wasn't a hard blow, but the pain that exploded inside of him was something awful and his consciousness ebbed in and out for several moments. He never wanted to experience pain like that again. When he was capable of speech, he told Reuben in the same faint whisper as earlier which oil wells still needed bombs. Reuben must've had a map of the wells on his cell phone, because he consulted it for several minutes before turning back to Pettibone.

"I know why you felt emboldened to extort me," he said. "You believed those stories they're saying about me. They're lies. I mean, I did kill Heather Brandley and Drea Kane, but there was nothing perverse or sexual about it. Their deaths are tied together with everything else I'm doing."

Pettibone stared up at Reuben with glazed eyes. "I believe you," he forced out, his voice now barely a scratchy whisper. "If you help me, I can still plant those other bombs."

Reuben, appearing calm and reflective, seemed to be considering the offer. Then a sudden savageness twisted his features. Pettibone tried to scream before the tire iron struck him again in the chest. Not much more than a gurgling noise escaped from him.

The killer knew the man was unconscious, but he struck him several more times across the chest before he used the tire iron to demolish Pettibone's skull. By the time he was done he felt as if he'd had a good workout. He also felt more relaxed. While he still badly wanted to make Brick suffer, killing Pettibone in such a brutal way had helped him release more of his anger.

He searched Pettibone's pockets until he found his car keys. The killer walked back to Pettibone's SUV and moved Hurley's body into the back of it. Lifting all that dead weight wasn't easy, and the killer had to do it in stages. After he was done he retrieved the drone, and then drove back to where he had left Pettibone. As with the other corpse, it was hard work getting Pettibone and all of his dead weight into the back of the SUV, but the killer persisted until the task was completed.

The killer had had a busy night, and he stood to catch his breath, his neck and chest damp with perspiration. He still had a lot to do, including burying the two bodies and making sure Pettibone's SUV disappeared for good. But at least he had planned this out carefully. He had brought a pair of towing straps in the trunk of his car, which he had left four miles down the dirt road, so he could use the SUV to tow his car to a place where it would be easy to retrieve. Once he was done taking care of the bodies and the SUV, he hoped he would have time to change the note he had left with his latest domino. He had a new one in mind that would cause Brick some pain, and while it would be a lot of additional work, it would be worth it.

With everything that was piling up on his plate, he'd be lucky if he finished by dawn. It was true what they said. Real artists suffer for their work.

The thought occurred to him that no artist had ever worked in a more honest medium. Or created anything as pure as what he was crafting. After all, his canvas was life and death itself. Well, really mostly death.

The killer stood stunned by the magnitude of it all. He knew in his heart the world would be in awe also. There was nothing Brick could do to change that.

He shook himself out of his stupor and got into Pettibone's SUV.

So much to do, and so little time.

Chapter 39

Jan Hornicek was very much enjoying his Los Angeles adventure. What was not to enjoy with all the sun, food, celebrities, beaches, and glamour? Maybe the beer. With the seemingly endless variety they had, he couldn't find his favorite, Kozel Premium, anywhere. While disappointing, not the end of the world. Pilsner Urquell was plentiful here, and that would suffice until he and Anna returned to Prague.

Anna had wanted to shop for clothes that morning, so he was on his own, but he didn't mind. He had found the perfect spot for people watching: a window seat at a coffee shop right across the street from the Chinese Theatre and the Hollywood Walk of Fame. And so he sat enjoying a bacon and egg sandwich on a toasted brioche and a white chocolate and coffee concoction while he watched a parade of sightseers like himself pointing out the different Hollywood stars embedded in the sidewalk and gawking at the impressive theatre.

That's odd, Jan thought as he spotted a small box that had been left on the sidewalk. It hadn't been there even a minute ago, he was sure of that. A fellow sightseer must've left it as a tribute. He looked around to see who might've done it, but there were just too many people. Interesting also that none of the people milling about had stopped to examine the box. As Jan watched this, he found himself more and more curious, not only wondering about the box's content, but also which star it had been left on. He also couldn't understand why people were walking past it as if it didn't exist. All very curious.

He finished up the last bite of his yummy sandwich, and drank the last sip of his even yummier drink, all the while trying to maintain a watch over the box. At times either cars or people blocked his view, but when they passed he saw that the box had remained undisturbed. Amazingly nobody else seemed to pay any attention to it. Jan had had enough. He wiped his lips clean with a napkin, and then hustled out of the shop. It would be dangerous to jaywalk across the four lanes of traffic, so he sprinted to the crosswalk at the end of the block. As he waited for the light to change, he felt his heart beating rapidly in his chest. It wasn't because of the sprinting he had done, but because he would be sorely disappointed if he got back to the Chinese Theatre and found the box missing.

The light changed, and he stutter-stepped past a young teenage girl, narrowly avoiding running into her when she stepped into his path, the girl too absorbed in whatever was on her cell phone screen to pay attention to where she was walking. Jan smiled, thinking of how the same could've happened back in Prague. Teenage girls were no different here than they were back home. Once again, Jan sprinted the half block to get back to the theater.

The box was still there. As he got closer to it, he could see that it was gift-wrapped with a red bow on top. He tried guessing which star it had been left on, and he felt a sense of satisfaction to see that it was Faye Riverstone's. She was one of his favorites. In fact, when they saw *A Winter's Home* last year, Anna accused him of having a crush on the actress. Jan denied it, of course, but he did find her squinty, pouty look quite fetching.

Jan wondered what could be inside the box. A love letter? A knickknack of some sort? Perhaps even a piece of jewelry, such as a broach? Or perhaps a sentimental object to signify the fan's affection for Faye Riverstone? As tempting as it might be to keep the contents as a souvenir, Jan accepted it wouldn't be right to do so. He would open the box to satisfy his curiosity, but otherwise leave it undisturbed.

The box wasn't cardboard like he had thought, but was solid wood. He carefully peeled off the wrapping paper, revealing a finely crafted box that Jan guessed was made of mahogany.

Very nice, he thought as he undid the latch.

When he opened the box, he stared confused at what was inside, because it appeared to be a severed hand. Not just any hand, but a slender hand from a woman, one that had its nails manicured and painted bright red. A look of horror formed over Jan's face as he accepted that the hand was real, and not some sort of movie prop.

"This is simply terrible," he murmured to no one in particular.

A woman next to him screamed.

* * * *

Annie Walsh called Morris a little after eleven to tell him about the box left on Riverstone's Hollywood star. When she got to the part about the witness not seeing who left it, Morris stopped her.

"Of course he didn't," he growled. "Not that it would've mattered if he did. The psycho would've disguised himself. But even if he left fingerprints, a DNA sample, and a copy of his birth certificate, we'd still be blindly chasing after our own tails."

"Morris, hon, you're in rare form today."

"It's this damn investigation."

"I hear you. He left another card in the box. It might cheer you up to hear what he wrote you. The message reads: 'Brick, one would think this is your first rodeo.'"

"That's supposed to cheer me up?"

"I was being sarcastic."

"Mission accomplished. I bet this joker thinks he's being clever."

"I bet so too."

"We might have to do a door-to-door search of Rodeo Drive."

"Yeah, I was thinking the same."

"But maybe not. Hold on."

Morris got up from his desk, and left Parker snoozing as he walked to Adam Felger's office. MBI's computer and hacking specialist was huddled with Charlie Bogle as they searched for more movie producers to investigate.

Morris said, "Adam, put that on hold for now. I need you to search for any connections between the name R. G. Berg and properties on Rodeo Drive."

"Will do."

"A solid lead?" Bogle asked.

Morris sighed. "Only what this psycho is pointing me to look into."

He left Felger to do his search, then got back on the phone with Walsh. "How long was the box sitting there?"

"The witness claims it was about fifteen minutes from when he spotted it to when he unwrapped and opened the box. He was shook up pretty bad when I talked to him. I have no doubt he was trying to be truthful, but I'm not sure how much of what he said we can trust."

Morris whistled softly. "Fifteen minutes sitting there and no one else bothers to grab or open it. What a bunch of jaded people we got here in LA."

"These were tourists walking past it. Not native Angelenos."

"True." Morris checked his watch. "I'll give Adam a half hour to find something. Otherwise we'll start knocking on some Rodeo Drive doors."

There was nothing else to do then but wait.

Chapter 40

Walsh and Malevich were up front with the SWAT team. Morris and Parker hung back twenty feet from the boarded-up storefront. They were there because Felger was able to find out that the seemingly vacant store, which was two blocks from the heart of Rodeo Drive, had been rented out five months earlier to an R. G. Berg.

One of the SWAT team members held a steel tubular battering ram, and when he was given the signal he swung it back and struck the door, breaching it on the first attempt. Chaos ensued as officers ran into the building and then seconds later ran out after one of them yelled *bomb*. There was no explosion, but Morris watched as a one-foot section of the front wall slid open and a toy car shot out of it.

The toy car zipped past him before he could react, but Parker pounced on it, knocking the car onto its side. Morris picked it up and studied it as its wheels continued to spin rapidly. It wasn't cheap, that was for sure, and it had a good deal of heft to it. He guessed it weighed at least ten pounds. Some sort of remote control device was taped onto the top, maybe a garage door opener. He pulled the tape off and removed the device and saw that his first guess was right.

"What are you holding?"

Morris looked up. The question came from the SWAT team leader.

"A toy car," he said. "The damn thing shot out of the building when you broke open the door. What's going on? I thought there was a bomb?"

The SWAT team leader was scowling. "I thought so too. A whole bunch of pulleys and levers started activating."

The bomb squad was called in, and while they waited Walsh joined Morris and studied the toy car as its wheels continued to spin.

"What do you think's the point of that?" she asked.

Morris made a *who knows* gesture, although he had a pretty good idea.

* * * *

The bomb squad arrived with a bomb-sniffing dog from the K9 unit. Parker paid rapt attention to the Belgian Malinois that was brought to the scene, while the dog was all business and ignored the bull terrier. It didn't take long for the bomb squad to determine there were no explosives inside the boarded-up store.

One of the bomb squad members explained to Morris that the purpose of the pulleys and levers was to open the side panel in the wall and unleash the toy car. "It could've been done a lot easier," he said. "Whoever put it together made it far more complicated than it needed to be."

"You guys should stick around," Morris said. "We're going to be needing you again soon."

The officer raised an eyebrow. "Why?"

"Because of the car."

Morris had earlier put the car down, flipping it over so he wouldn't have to hold it. The officer gave the toy car a puzzled look as it lay on its top, its wheels still spinning furiously.

"There's no bomb in that thing," he insisted.

"True, but we need to see where it would've gone if my dog hadn't pounced on it." Morris showed the officer the garage door opener. "This was taped to its top."

The officer examined the device. "You think this is a detonator for a bomb?"

"I think it's possible. If it is, I'd bet the bomb is somewhere on Rodeo Drive."

The officer groaned at the thought of that. "We'll have to shut down the drive. A lot of store owners and shoppers are not going to be happy."

Morris appreciated that this was a massive understatement. Shutting down Rodeo Drive anytime would be a headache, but shutting it down on a Saturday was going to cause an uproar. He left the officer to worry about the logistics of that and headed into the boarded-up store to join Walsh and Malevich. The SWAT team had left minutes earlier after determining the store was empty.

Morris brought the toy car with him, and when he saw the elaborate system of pulleys and levers that had unleashed the car, he couldn't help letting out a short, bitter laugh.

"What?" Walsh asked.

"That psycho has been cheating," he said. "He doesn't have a middle name. R. G. Berg stands for Rube Goldberg."

Walsh gave him a blank look, not getting it.

"This contraption is what's called a Rube Goldberg machine."

"Is Rube short for Reuben?" she asked.

"It is," Morris said, angry at himself for not making the connection earlier.

Parker began making agitated grunts. He stared up at Morris, then lowered his head and attempted to bull his way forward to the back of the building. Morris let go of the leash and watched as Parker ran to the back wall and started pawing at it. Malevich had joined them, and he commented that the bull terrier's behavior seemed odd.

Morris asked, "Do the dimensions of this room look right to you?"

Walsh pursed her lips. "Now that you mention it, it looks shallower than it should."

They knocked on the back wall. It was only a drywall partition, and there was something behind it.

A call was put in for a sledgehammer. When it arrived, Malevich did the honors. After breaking a hole in the drywall, they saw Faye Riverstone. More of the drywall was knocked down revealing that the actress was sitting naked on a chair. Her eyes were open and they held the same empty look as glass, and it looked as if someone had wrapped a narrow red ribbon around her waist. Nobody had to feel that her skin was ice cold to know that she was dead. On closer examination, she didn't have anything wrapped around her, and the reason her bottom and top halves were slightly askew was because the killer had used the circular saw to cut her in half at the waist. He also had used thin wires to hold her in place so it would appear as if she were sitting. One of the killer's business cards had been pinned to her naked belly.

Scrawled on the card was the message: *Guess what, Brick, I lied, but you've been lying too.*

"He wanted her found," Walsh said. "So why bury the body behind drywall?"

"He knew we'd be calling the bomb squad, and he didn't want them finding the body. He wanted me to be the one."

Morris's voice had sounded heavier than usual for a good reason. The killer's latest message had hit him like a punch to the gut, leaving him wondering whether Faye Riverstone would still be alive if he hadn't said what he did to Margot Denoir on *The Hollywood Peeper*.

"Sick bastard," Malevich spat out. At that moment, he looked like he could've torn the drywall apart with his hands.

In another half hour the building was going to be filled with crime scene techs probing every square inch for evidence that Morris knew didn't exist. He had no intention of sticking around to watch them.

"I've got to see where this toy car would've gone if Parker hadn't attacked it," he said. "Do me a favor. When Roger shows up, ask him to make narrowing down the time of death a priority. I want to be called as soon as he has an answer."

Annie Walsh started to say something along the lines that it didn't matter what Morris had said on TV. Faye Riverstone was as good as dead the moment the killer grabbed her. Morris raised a hand to stop her.

He didn't want to hear it.

Chapter 41

They cleared Rodeo Drive. After that, the toy car was brought back to its original starting point and released. Police officers had been interspersed along Rodeo Drive to spot it, while Morris and Annie attempted to follow it.

The car did what Morris thought it would do as it took a right onto Rodeo Drive and proceeded to race down the bike path.

"It must be following a set of programmed GPS coordinates," he said.

He was suspicious when the toy car passed by a parked van that had the business name *Hollywood Party Favors* painted on it along with three balloons, but when the car passed an identical van half a block away, he was sure they had found what they were looking for. Walsh elbowed him when it zipped past a third identical van on the next block.

"The bombs must be in those vans," she said. "Did you notice the red, green, and blue balloons painted on them? RGB. This joker's initials."

"Jesus," Morris whispered. If Parker hadn't knocked over the toy car, hundreds of people would've been around the vans when whatever was inside of them was activated.

The bomb squad was brought back to investigate. When they broke into the first van, they didn't find a bomb. Instead they found an M60 machine gun attached to a tripod made up of two wrenches pivoting on an automatic garage door opener, all of which was mounted to the bottom part of a swivel chair. The gun was locked and loaded with what turned out to be two hundred live rounds. One of the bomb squad members pointed out the road bike cassette that had been attached to the garage door opener. "That's for gear reduction," the officer explained.

Morris said, "This psycho is now ripping off *Breaking Bad*."

The officer shrugged. "I never watched the show."

"They used the same setup in their last episode. Would this have worked?"

"Only one way to find out."

The ammunition was removed, and when the remote control device came within fifty feet of the van, the garage door opener activated, and the machine gun started moving back and forth in a semicircle. If they hadn't removed the ammunition, the area would've been sprayed with bullets. When they broke into the other two vans, they found identical setups.

A new business card from R. G. Berg was left in one of the vans. The message scrawled on it read: *Brick, this is just a taste of the devastation that's coming.*

* * * *

Surveillance video showed a car being towed away and one of the vans being parked in its place. The van driver wore a baseball cap pulled low over his eyes and kept his face hidden when he left the van. The odds were he was the killer in disguise, and catching him on video wasn't going to help them, but they were able to get the name of the tow truck company, and after showing the video to the company's owner, they had the name of the tow truck operator. When they brought him to MBI's offices, he at first tried to profess innocence, but after he was shown the surveillance video, he broke into a big smart-alecky grin and held up his hands in a mock surrender.

"Okay, you got me," he admitted.

"No kidding," Morris said. "Pretty open and shut case for conspiracy to commit mass murder."

The driver was a wiry sort named Ed McGreevy, and from his thick New Jersey accent he had to be a recent transplant. His grin turned into more of a suspicious smile.

"What are you talking about?" he said. "A guy needed some spots for a company event, so for a little money I moved a few cars for him. No real harm, right?"

"The vans that were moved into the spots were meant to kill hundreds."

"You're making this stuff up," he insisted.

McGreevy was trying to maintain his smile, but it froze into something sickly, and as he looked at the stone-faced expressions from Morris and Walsh, a panic set in. "I swear I knew nothing about it," he said, talking in a rapid-fire way. "I was just trying to help out what I thought was a local businessman and make a little extra cash for myself. That's all I thought I was doing. Do I need to be talking to a lawyer here?"

"Not if you tell us everything you know."

Walsh shot Morris an annoyed look for making that offer, but she didn't contradict him.

"Yeah, sure. I'll tell you everything."

McGreevy proceeded to do just that. A little before noon he was approached by a man in his early thirties who was desperate for three parking spots on Rodeo Drive. The man claimed he'd been hired to provide props for a flash mob dance scene that was scheduled to take place, and that he was royally screwed if he couldn't get those spots. McGreevy was paid two grand, but claimed he really did it out of the goodness of his heart. "The guy told me he'd be going out of business if I didn't help. Any decent soul would've done the same."

A police sketch artist was brought over, and while the sketch showed a clean-shaven man with short brown hair, a larger nose, and a different-shaped mouth, Morris had no doubt that it was their killer. The shape of the head and the eyes were the same, and the mouth probably looked the way it did because of fake teeth.

When they had gotten all they could out of McGreevy, he asked if he was free to go.

Walsh said, "I'm still going to book you for illegally towing those cars."

"Fair enough," McGreevy agreed.

While Morris and Walsh were dealing with McGreevy, Bogle had tracked down R. G. Berg's landlord, but he didn't bother bringing him back to MBI.

"The guy knows nothing," Bogle told Morris. "Everything was done through the mail, and payment was made with cash." Bogle showed a tight-lipped grin, a look that Morris knew reflected anger instead of anything related to mirth. "You're going to hate this part of it," Bogle said.

"Try me."

"The killer used your home address in his correspondence. So that's where the rental agreement was sent."

Morris's home had a mailbox instead of a slot in the door. Most days both he and Natalie were out, and one of them always took Parker with them. It wouldn't have been hard for the killer to check his mail for a rental agreement, nor for him to go unnoticed while he did so.

"You're right. I do hate that part of it."

"I'm psychic that way," Bogle said with that same tight-lipped grin.

"He rented the store five months ago, right? Do you know when the agreement was mailed out?"

Bogle consulted his notepad and gave Morris the date. "I think you were in Italy then," he added.

Morris nodded. He and Natalie were on what was really a belated
honeymoon since it was the first vacation of that type they'd ever taken.
Rachel was house-sitting during that time—really pet-sitting Parker.
Morris involuntarily shivered at the thought of the killer coming to their
home while Rachel was there alone.

Bogle asked, "Are you okay?"

Morris shifted his gaze from Bogle, knowing otherwise his investigator
would be able to tell he was lying.

"Yeah, I'm just thinking how he must've been checking my mailbox
every month for the rental bill."

Bogle said, "He wouldn't need to do that. He paid six months' rent
upfront. So what now? Should I keep looking at movie producers?"

"No. We need to track down those vans. Also, the M60s. Pick one and
I'll give the other to Polk."

"I thought the FBI was looking into the M60s?"

"They are, but I still want one of us involved."

"Okay, I'll take the vans. A guy could get shot looking into stolen guns.
Better to let Polk have that. What about Fred?"

Morris made a halfhearted damned-if-I-do-damned-if-I-don't gesture.
"I still want him to keep doing what he's doing. More and more this is
looking like Gloria's right and this psycho has some sort of grudge against
me. I just can't figure out what it is."

"The guy's a whack job. You'll never figure it out. Is what I heard true?
Faye Riverstone was already dead before he pulled his 'sawing a woman
in half' magic act?"

"That's what Roger claimed. Death was caused by a massive coronary
and not the systemic shock she would've suffered when he used a circular
saw to sever her body. He was able to narrow time of death between late
Thursday night and early Friday morning."

Bogle rubbed his cheek as he considered that. "The coronary must've
happened as a result of him cutting off that poor woman's hand. In any
case, she died before your interview with Margot. If you've got nothing
else for me, I have some vans to look into."

The look Morris gave Bogle had him turning back with a raised eyebrow.

"It's nothing," Morris said. "Just that Rachel mentioned to me she's
seeing a new guy. That it's someone I know."

No crack in Bogle's poker face. If he was who Rachel was seeing, Morris
wouldn't be able to divine it from his expression. While Bogle was smart,
solid, and a good-looking man, he was also forty-five and divorced with

two kids, and Morris had heard stories when he was married about his womanizing. Because of that he was hoping it wasn't his top investigator.

Bogle asked, "She won't tell you who it is?"

"Bingo."

"Do you want me to look into it?"

If Rachel was seeing Bogle, he didn't give any hint of it. If he suspected that Morris was worried he might be seeing Rachel, he likewise gave no hint. He played it as if it were an accepted fact that he wouldn't betray Morris's confidence by dating his daughter. Or maybe that was just the way it was. Morris had learned long ago never to get into a poker game with him, at least not if he didn't want to lose his shirt.

Morris said, "If you happen to hear something."

"Sure. If it's Polk, I'll also put a bullet in his ass. That will sideline him long enough for your daughter to come to her senses."

"Sounds like a plan."

Chapter 42

Parker stretched and plodded over to Gloria Finston, his tail wagging. The FBI profiler, who had just entered Morris's office, favored the bull terrier with a smile and consented to scratch him behind the ear.

"I understand you're a hero," she said to the dog.

"He might've saved hundreds of lives today," Morris volunteered.

Parker grunted contentedly, his tail picking up speed.

"That's what I heard," Finston said. She turned her smile to Morris. "Quite an eventful day, huh?"

"To say the least."

He had already given her the major bullet points over the phone, but he hadn't told her yet the meaning of the killer's *R. G. Berg* alias. He did so now, and it seemed to fascinate her. As she listened, she chewed lightly on her thumbnail, her small dark eyes glistening.

"It adds up," she said. "I was wrong about him trying to tell a narrative. At least in a sense. What he's doing is constructing a kind of Rube Goldberg machine."

"He's killing these actresses so he can use them as dominos?"

"In his own perverse way, yes. Each of these events are designed to lead you to the next, and this latest one was meant to have you trigger the next event where M60 machine guns would've fired hundreds of rounds into pedestrians and shoppers."

"Except it didn't work."

Finston left Parker to take the chair across from Morris's desk. The bull terrier followed along after her and plopped down next to her.

"Thankfully," she said.

"Natalie told me this psycho's trying to move me around like a piece on a chessboard."

"Your wife's a perceptive woman."

"She is that," Morris agreed. "So what happens now that his demented Rube Goldberg machine has gone bust?"

"I'm sure he's spent years dreaming of doing this, and I'm also sure he's wrapped much of his ego and sense of self-worth into it. He expects the world to gasp at his brilliance, and it will be a blow to him now that his masterpiece has been marred. But he's not going to give up."

Morris expected her answer. "Because he's still got his grand finale."

"Correct. Today was only supposed to be a taste of the *devastation that's coming*," she said, quoting the killer's last message.

Morris made a face as if he tasted something bitter and unpleasant. "So this psycho's expecting to kill thousands instead of the hundreds who would've died today if his plans had worked out. Quite a piece of work."

Parker interrupted them by making an excited grunting noise. He flipped himself onto his feet, his tail wagging, and he scampered to the door. A second later a knock came, and Greta opened the door enough to inform them that the food had arrived.

"Do you want me to bring you yours and Parker's?" she asked.

"Not necessary. Why don't you leave it all in the conference room?"

Parker followed Greta out of the office.

With a heavy grunt, Morris pushed himself to his feet, and explained to Finston that he had ordered takeout from the Oak Grill. "An army travels on their stomach, right? Anyway, I ordered plenty, including their Caesar salad with wood-grilled sea scallops, which I remembered you liked last time." Morris checked his watch. "I still have an hour before I need to head off for my prime-time special with Margot Denoir. How about we continue strategizing over some food? See if we can get to the conference room before Polk finds the Caesar salad?"

"An excellent suggestion."

Polk and Adam Felger had beaten them to the conference room. Polk, at least for the time being, had left the Caesar salad alone, and grabbed one of the prime rib sandwiches for himself. Felger, who was the only vegetarian in the office, had snared the grilled asparagus and portabella mushroom wrap. The fact that Rachel was also vegetarian made Morris look at Felger a beat longer than he normally would've, but he otherwise kept his suspicions to himself. He nodded to his two employees. Felger, who had his mouth full, gave him a thumbs-up sign for ordering the grilled veggie wrap and offered Finston a nod. Polk, who also had his mouth full, didn't let that stop him from saying "Hi ya" to Finston, and telling Morris that he already had an answer about the M60s. "I'll tell you what I found after I have a couple more of these."

"I'll be waiting with bated breath."

Morris found the Caesar salad, handed it to the FBI profiler, and then grabbed two of the prime rib sandwiches: one for himself, and one without horseradish for Parker. When he handed the sandwich to an overly excited Parker, Polk let out a disgusted groan.

"You're going to give good food like this to a mutt?" he asked.

"He's a full-bred bull terrier."

"I don't know. I've heard the noises he makes and seen him eat. He's gotta have some American Yorkshire in him."

Morris had no idea what Polk was talking about. He had heard of Yorkshire terriers, but he'd never heard of a dog breed called an American Yorkshire. Polk, for his part, was staring back with a straight face, as if what he said made perfect sense.

"American Yorkshire is a breed of pig," Gloria Finston said. She explained to Morris that she was a fan of the game show *Jeopardy*.

If Parker was insulted, he didn't show it, as he was too busy chewing on a piece of the prime rib sandwich.

Polk broke out laughing. "I've been waiting weeks to use that."

Morris said, "I hope it was worth it."

"Definitely."

Bogle walked into the conference room and asked if anyone was dying in there.

Felger said, "Just Polk cackling,"

"I thought it was someone's death rattle."

Polk made a face. "What are you talking about? I've got a pleasing laugh. Just ask my mom."

Bogle shrugged, looked over the food piled up on the table, and took one of the wrapped sandwiches marked prime rib. They were the favorite among the MBI investigators, and whenever Morris ordered from the Oak Grill, he always made sure to get extras since Polk usually binged on three of them.

For the next ten minutes, they ate in silence. Polk broke the quiet by telling Bogle he screwed up giving him the M60 assignment, that he already had it done.

"That's why I gave it to you," Bogle said. "I wanted to make sure you had an easy enough job."

"Damn nice of you." Polk reached over and grabbed another prime rib sandwich. He unwrapped it, but before taking a bite, he announced that the guns had been stolen five months earlier from a Kansas armory. "FBI hit a dead-end back then in their investigation. But those three M60s weren't the only things stolen. The thieves also took a crate of grenades and six hundred pounds of C-4."

"Shit," Morris said.

"That's for damn sure," Polk said. "At least we know what this prick plans to use for the *devastation that's coming.*"

Chapter 43

The killer feverishly paced the back rooms of his once-upon-a-time airplane hangar turned movie studio turned private workshop. He had too much on his mind to stand still. Namely, he couldn't figure out what had gone wrong.

He had been part of the crowd milling about when the police arrived at the boarded-up vacant store he had rented five months earlier using his alias R. G. Berg. Once the police showed up he knew he didn't have much time until those idiots broke down the door, triggering the next sequence in his death machine, and so he hurried to a safe spot on Rodeo Drive where he'd be able to watch the ensuing carnage. But it never happened. After twenty minutes of standing around and waiting on the side of the street that would be untouched by gunfire, he found a café where they offered him a window seat, but still nothing happened. An hour later the police cleared not only the restaurant, but all of Rodeo Drive.

They must've broken down the door, and that should've triggered the small but complex Rube Goldberg machine he had constructed, which would've slid open the panel in the wall while at the same time disconnecting the toy car from the power cord that was keeping the car fully charged, and finally switching on both the car and the reconfigured garage door opener. After that the car should've been sent on its merry way and hundreds of people should've died as a result. He had thoroughly tested every part of it, and it made no sense that it didn't happen. Even if they had cut power to the building before breaking down the door, everything still should've worked since there was nothing requiring electricity in the series of trip wires, pulleys, and levers.

The killer later watched the local news hoping to learn what went wrong. While the closing of Rodeo Drive dominated the broadcast, no official statement was given about why it happened, and the anchors speculated that it must've been due to a gas leak. There was no mention of the three vans the killer had left on the busiest section of the drive. Nothing about the machine guns. Or about Faye Riverstone's body being discovered. There was nothing about anything, except that Brick would be appearing on a special prime-time episode of *The Hollywood Peeper* later that night. The killer knew Brick was only going to be spreading more lies about him.

Until today his death machine had gone off flawlessly, even if there were a few minor hiccups, such as Pettibone thinking he could extort extra money from him, and Brick lying his ass off on TV simply to discredit him. What Pettibone did was insignificant; if anything, it gave the killer an opportunity to devise a rather clever method of taking care of the issue. What Brick did was far more upsetting, but in the end it shouldn't matter—at least not once the world saw all of it. Today's fiasco was different. It was a blemish that the killer would never be able to remove, and he felt sick to his stomach over it.

But in the end, Los Angeles will be in flames and the world will watch on in wonderment.

That was what the killer had to keep telling himself. Every great work of art must have at least one flaw, even if it's something only the artist can spot. When this was all done, people would be talking about what the killer did to Heather Brandley, Drea Kane, and Faye Riverstone. Also Brie Evans, because he was going to take her that night. And they'd be talking about the final act.

The killer sniffed back several tears fighting to come loose, clenched his jaw, and told himself once again that this was all true. When his death machine was seen in its entirety, this one tiny blemish would be looked upon as insignificant. He'd be the only one seeing it as something as large as the ocean.

The killer's pacing had taken him to the modeling area. Half of the models were lit, half of them still dark. Tears welled up in his eyes as he looked at the model he had expected to light today. He had worked so hard to get all the little details just right. Scaled versions of the same stores on Rodeo Drive, bullet holes in the plate glass windows and walls, tiny corpses and pools of blood covering the sidewalk. If someone were to study it closely, they'd also see more dead bodies and splatters of blood in a dozen of the stores. The model had been so beautiful crafted, and now it sat there mocking him. As a tear broke loose and snaked down his cheek, the killer stomped on the model as if he were Godzilla attacking the actual Rodeo Drive, crushing it into pieces. Afterward he brought over a trashcan, and used a dustpan and brush to remove all evidence of the model's existence.

A heaviness settled in the killer's throat as he looked over the remaining models. His Rube Goldberg Death Machine no longer made any sense. There was nothing that would connect the last event to the next.

Inspiration struck. The killer gasped as he saw a way to do it. He would have to remove most of the remaining unlit models and speed up the timetable of the machine's completion, but he saw how he could fit in a domino so that it would all work. For the next several minutes he busied himself doing exactly that, reconfiguring the modeling area so that his machine would once again be whole.

Yes, yes, yes, he whispered to himself. He had saved his masterpiece. It might be different than what he had originally planned, but it would still be a thing of beauty. All that was needed was for him to grab the last elusive domino.

The feelings of hopelessness and worthlessness that had been crushing him just minutes earlier were replaced by pure elation as he thought about what would be happening tomorrow when the final domino fell.

Hell on earth would be coming to Los Angeles.

Chapter 44

Morris had turned down the makeup artist's offer to add a touch of bronzing color to outline his cheekbones and use some powder to touch up his forehead and nose, even after her warnings that he would look pasty and sweaty on the air without it. He didn't much care how he looked. Margot, however, did not share his sentiments, and had been expertly made up to appear completely natural on TV, as if she weren't wearing any of the foundation, blush, eyeshadow, mascara, or lipstick that covered her face. Her blond poofy hair, though, would look every bit as shellacked on TV as it did in real life.

At the moment, they were sitting cattycornered to each other on the set while Parker lay on the floor next to Morris chewing a rawhide bone, seemingly oblivious to the lights and the show's personnel that were running about. Margot also appeared oblivious to her surroundings as she studied her notes.

The director kneeled in front of them and began silently counting down from five, mouthing each number while simultaneously using the fingers on one hand. Morris had witnessed this a number of times over the years, and it always amazed him how Margot's notes would disappear by the time the director reached one, and the way she would be breathlessly facing the camera the exact moment he mouthed *action*. There had to be something psychic going on.

Tonight was no exception. The notes disappeared on *one*, and when *action* was mouthed, Margot was breathlessly telling her TV audience that the reason for this special prime-time edition of *The Hollywood Peeper* was to break a startling new development in the *Sex Pervert Maniac Killer* case. She then introduced Morris, and welcomed Parker back to the show.

Parker paid no attention to her speaking his name and continued to chomp away on the bone.

"Morris, you confided in me only moments before we went on the air that this monster abducted another of our beloved actresses?"

This was of course a lie, but he played along. "Sadly, yes," he said. "He abducted Faye Riverstone Thursday night, and he murdered her shortly afterward."

Margot recoiled in horror. This wasn't a surprise since they had discussed Riverstone's death over the phone and how it should be handled on the show.

"Oh my God. Faye also? That makes three of our brightest stars taken by this creature!"

Morris was impressed at how her skin color seemingly dropped a shade and the way she squeezed out two tears. If he didn't know better he would've sworn she was genuinely shaken up by the news. Margot was good, he had to give her that.

"With the public's help, we'll catch him," he said.

"Yes, certainly." Margot turned to address the show's director. "Diego, please put in the left corner of the screen the police sketch a witness provided, and the hotline phone number for tips." She then faced the front camera. "Remember, people, there's a hundred-thousand-dollar reward for information leading to this monster's capture." Once again she turned to Morris, her expression earnest as she tugged at the fingers on her right hand. "Did he violate poor Faye like he did Heather Brandley and Drea Kane?"

Morris and Gloria Finston had discussed this before he left for the interview, and they were of the same mindset. He needed to keep sticking in the needle. The killer would be at a low point, desperately trying to revise his plans so his demented Rube Goldberg machine would again make sense, at least in his mind. The more Morris attacked his ego and insulted him, and the more he demeaned him with lies, the more likely it was the killer would make an impulsive mistake.

Morris said, "I can't go into specifics, but yes."

"Afterward he mutilated Faye Riverstone's body?"

"I'm sorry, I can't discuss this in greater detail, but yes. This is a very disturbed individual we're dealing with."

"But he does this in a pathetic attempt to hide his sexual deviancies?"

"That's what we've been able to determine."

Margot shivered, exaggerating the reaction enough so that her TV audience would take notice. "What else do you know about SPMK?"

Morris knew the answer but he feigned confusion and asked what SPMK stood for since it would be sticking another needle into the psycho.

Margot smiled as she knew exactly what he was doing. "Shorthand for the name we've given him. Sex Pervert Maniac Killer."

"Of course." He made a show of shaking his head as if he couldn't believe he hadn't known that. "I hadn't heard him called that yet. I'll tell you the profile we've worked up with the FBI. Early thirties. He's wealthy due to an inheritance. Extreme narcissism. He also can be superficially charming, but he's a loner who has never been in a romantic relationship—"

"Because he only wants to have sex with dead bodies!"

"There's that," he agreed. "But even if he didn't have this unnatural sexual compulsion, he still would never have any interest in a relationship. He's someone who's had few friends in his life, and no close ones. We also know he disguises himself with cosmetic contact lenses, wigs, fake facial hair, and prosthetics, such as fake noses, chins, teeth. He's handy with tools and electronics. And he's clever but not nearly as smart as he believes he is. He also has an unusual obsession with Rube Goldberg machines."

Margot turned again to the director. "Diego, do you know what a Rube Goldberg machine is?"

The director said he thought he did. "Let me see if I can find a video."

This had been prearranged, and he had a clip from YouTube lined up. As they broke away to show the clip, Margot leaned toward Morris, a mischievous grin playing on her lips.

"Your dog's a charmer," she said. "We've gotten over forty calls so far asking either what type he is or whether he's available for adoption. I should rent him for future shows."

"Hmm. Maybe it was a mistake bringing him. First, I don't want him getting a swelled head, and second, I want your audience paying attention to what we're saying."

Parker stopped chewing for a moment to stare up at Morris. He must've decided Morris wasn't serious, because seconds later he was back to gnawing on his bone, a good third of which he'd already ripped to shreds.

"Darling, don't fret. I guarantee you, they're paying attention. I hope you appreciate that I haven't challenged you regarding the killer's sexual proclivities. For example, I could've asked about the forensic evidence you have."

Morris made a face as if he were offended by the accusation. "You think I'd make something like that up?"

She laughed. "I know you would. But catching this bastard is what matters. That and the ratings. So I'll be a good girl and play along. I won't even mention any of the photos that were sent to me, even though I'm dying to."

The director signaled that they'd be back on the air in three. After he counted down to zero, Margot asked, "Given his obsession with such a strange thing, should we be calling him the Rube Goldberg Machine Killer instead?"

"He would love for us to do that."

"Then we'll leave him as the Sex Pervert Maniac Killer. Even though it's quite a mouthful."

"But more appropriate."

Margot flashed Morris a *gotcha* look. It made him think of how a cat might look right before pouncing on a small, helpless critter.

She asked, "Did SPMK have anything to do with Rodeo Drive being shut down today?"

That wasn't something they had talked about. Someone had tipped her off, and he wondered if it could've been the killer himself. She wasn't being such a good girl anymore, but he understood. It was all a matter of ratings. He also knew it wouldn't do any good denying or stonewalling her. She wouldn't have flashed him that look if that was all she had.

"Yes," he admitted, properly chagrined. "We thought people's lives were in danger. I can't go into specifics, but I can tell you SPMK attempted a mass killing, again to hide the true nature of his other murders. Fortunately, his plans were imbecilic and had no chance of working." He flashed Margot his own look. "How about we cut to a commercial break?"

"Morris, darling, it's not time for that."

He leaned in close so he could whisper in her ear, "I think you'd better call for that break. Otherwise you viewers at home will be watching me put you on my knee and paddling your ass raw."

While she maintained her smile, her race reddened, even through all the makeup that had been layered on. She signaled to the director to take them to commercial.

He growled, "Who told you about Rodeo Drive?"

She laughed, trying to bluff him. "Come on, Morris, it was an educated guess. And a pretty obvious one at that."

"Uh uh. I don't buy it. I saw the look in your eyes. You have something."

She dropped her bluff. "Sorry, luv, but I can't betray a source."

"I have to know if the killer contacted you again."

She made a face. "Jesus, Morris, if it was him I would've told you. But if it was someone, say, Commissioner Hadley, I just wouldn't be able to do it."

So it was Hadley. He hadn't agreed with Morris's decision to keep the killer's involvement with the Rodeo Drive incident quiet, and so he decided to get it out this way. Morris stood up and removed the microphone clipped to his suit jacket. He wasn't happy with Margot at that moment, and besides, he had accomplished what he wanted to and saw no reason to stick around.

Margot said, "Luv, don't take it personally."

"You sandbagged me, sweetie."

"Just a teensy bit. Besides, all's fair where ratings are involved!"

Morris waved to her as he walked off the set. Parker grabbed what was left of the bone with his mouth, and trudged along after him.

Chapter 45

The killer had taken off his sneakers so he could sneak more quietly, and he didn't make a sound as he crept over the hardwood floor in Stonehedge's bedroom. While his eyes had acclimated as much as they could to the dark, it was still pitch black in the room. He felt around the wall until he found the controls for one of the window blinds. He cracked the blind open, letting in enough ambient light from the moon so he could see Stonehedge and Brie Evans lying on the bed. The actor was curled up on his side in a fetal position, his back to his girlfriend, while Evans lay on her stomach. The top sheet and blanket had been kicked off so that the killer could see that the lovebirds had gone to bed *au naturel*.

The killer made his way to Brie Evans's side of the bed and stood enjoying her nakedness. She was going to be the shapeliest and loveliest of his dominos. The killer had watched Brick earlier that night on TV, and while Brick had continued to make outlandish lies about the killer engaging in necrophilia, he was right about him never having had a girlfriend. But that didn't mean the killer was a virgin, only that he never wanted anything more than hookups, and the reason he didn't enjoy the other actresses he took was because he'd been too busy with his plans. As he studied Brie Evans's curves and the delightful shape of her ass, he decided this time would be different. Since everything would soon be coming to an end, he was going to enjoy her body before he transformed her into his final domino.

But enough of that.

The killer had brought a dishcloth from Stonehedge's kitchen, and he balled it up in his right hand and then injected Evans in the shoulder with a healthy (or really unhealthy!) dose of pentobarbital. Her eyes cracked open. For a moment, she was too groggy to understand what had happened. But as she realized that there was someone else in the room with her and Stonehedge and made sense of the sharp pain that had bit into her shoulder, her eyes opened wide. Before she could scream, the killer sat on her and took hold of the back of her head while at the same time pushing the dishrag against her mouth. A soft, muffled sound came out, but not enough to wake Stonehedge. Still, she tried to fight him, but the barbiturate was already working and robbing her of her strength, and within minutes she was out cold.

The killer's original plan had been to take her and leave Stonehedge unharmed, but that was before he watched Brick on TV. The lies Brick told were bad enough, but to call his plans today *imbecilic* was more than the killer could bear. He had researched Brick for months, and he knew Stonehedge and Brick were friends. That wasn't why he needed to use Evans as a domino—that was just a lucky coincidence—but because of what Brick had the audacity to say on TV, he was going to do whatever he could to hurt that smug bastard ex-cop. Which meant his plan had changed, and he was no longer going to leave Stonehedge alive. The next message the killer left Brick was going to be painted in blood on Stonehedge's bedroom wall.

The killer removed a hunting knife from its sheath and tiptoed to the other side of the bed. He positioned himself so he could slice open the actor's throat once he pushed him onto his back, but as he was reaching for Stonehedge's shoulder, the actor rolled over onto his other side.

Fine, the killer thought, *you just made it easier for me.* He reached across Stonehedge's body so he could put the edge of the blade against the actor's throat, but a hand wrapped itself around the killer's wrist.

The killer tried to pull his hand free, but he was positioned awkwardly and had no leverage. Stonehedge's grip felt like a vise as it tightened.

"Your breath woke me," Stonehedge murmured as if he was still struggling to fully wake up. "It smells awful. Like cheap cat food."

The actor was twisting the killer's wrist as he rolled himself onto his back. The killer thought his wrist was going to break, and he had to clamp his mouth shut to keep from screaming in pain. He didn't want Stonehedge picking up the knife, so instead of dropping it, he flung it as far as he could and heard it clattering on the wood floor.

The actor was now raising himself as he continued to twist the killer's wrist. Their eyes locked. "You sick freak," Stonehedge swore. With his free hand, he punched the killer in the nose. The killer's eyes began watering, and he tasted his own blood as it streamed out of his nostrils and dripped down his face. When Stonehedge reached back to punch him again, the killer poked him in the eye. The actor released his wrist, and the killer fled from the room.

His wrist felt like it had been broken, and things had not gone as planned, putting it lightly. Surprisingly he had remained calm throughout the ordeal. It was meant for him to take Brie Evans, and because of that he knew he would prevail as long as he didn't panic. But he now needed to lure Stonehedge out of the bedroom and toward the kitchen. When the killer had been there earlier, he saw plenty of sharp knives he could use, and as he heard the actor's footsteps racing behind him, he couldn't help grinning.

That's right, the killer thought, *you're too angry right now to think clearly. Good. In another few seconds, I'll be grabbing a butcher's knife and cutting your heart out.*

A loud explosion made the killer nearly tumble to the floor. Less than a heartbeat later he felt something hot and deadly whizzing by his ear. Stonehedge had a gun and was shooting at him.

The killer's grin froze on his face, becoming something sickly. In a split second, he knew everything had been turned around. He was no longer the predator but the prey. He let out a yelp and dove to the floor, somersaulting forward as another explosion rocked him. Something primal deep inside him told him that he would've been shot dead if he hadn't done that. Momentum sent him rolling back onto his feet, and he was then racing to the front door. He reached it without being shot, and seconds later he was fleeing from the house, his heart thumping wildly in his chest.

He knew Stonehedge wasn't giving up. He could hear the actor behind him. It would be a long run down the private drive to the security gate, and the killer knew if he tried going that way he wouldn't make it. Instead he turned to race around the house. When he felt another bullet whizz by, it only made him run faster.

The killer made it to the back of Stonehedge's property. He heard waves up ahead breaking violently against the beach, and the moon provided enough light for him to see that he was racing toward the ocean. He couldn't see much else, and he had no idea that there was a thirty-five-foot drop to the beach below, at least not until he ran off the cliff.

* * * *

Philip Stonehedge had slowed down to a walk when he saw the freak was going to trap himself at the cliff's edge. While he had raised his gun, he had decided he would give the freak one chance to surrender before shooting him dead. The last thing he expected was for the freak to run off the cliff.

He stood stunned as the freak appeared suspended in midair. Then Stonehedge remembered the gun and got off a shot. He was a good thirty yards away, and in the dark he couldn't tell whether he had hit him. If he hadn't, the drop to the beach below was thirty-five feet, and that might do the job. Or at least break one of the sonofabitch's legs.

The actor jogged to the cliff's edge, being careful not to tumble over himself. It was too dark for Stonehedge to see if the freak was lying sprawled out on the sand below.

Stonehedge had no way of getting down to the beach, other than jumping like the freak had. He needed to call the police. He remembered then that he was naked, that he didn't have his house keys or cell phone, and that when he left through the front door, he had closed it behind him so that it would lock and the freak wouldn't be able to double back and get to Brie.

Shit.

But he still had his gun. He walked to the glass patio doors with the thought of shooting one of them and shattering the glass. He needed to call the police about the freak, but he was also worried about Brie and getting an ambulance for her. Before he had chased after the killer, he had checked on her. She was breathing, but she was out cold, and he knew the freak must've drugged her with something.

He aimed his gun and shot into one of the glass patio doors. It didn't shatter. All he did was put a small bullet hole through it.

Shit.

He had no choice about what he had to do next. The shrubs and trees and other natural fencing between his property and his neighbor's was too dense for him to cut through, even if it was daylight and he was wearing clothes. He'd have to run barefoot and naked an eighth of a mile over the loose gravel surface of his tree-lined private road and hope that the power had been cut off only to his house and not the security gate also. He knew that the freak had cut off the house's power when he had tried turning on lights and nothing happened. If the security gate was still functional, he would be able to alert the police from there. Otherwise, he'd have to hike a half mile to one of his two neighbors, and then knock on their door in his current state of undress.

Shit.

He sprinted off in the direction of the security gate, and tried to ignore the stitch that had developed in his side and the loose gravel biting into the bottom of his feet.

Chapter 46

Morris made it a habit to turn his cell phone off before he went to bed. That night he not only kept his phone on, but he kept it next to his pillow like he had read many teens were doing these days. He didn't expect to have to instantly respond to a text message like these teens did, at least according to the article he had read, but he wanted to know if anything broke with the investigation. It wasn't just MBI and the LAPD working on it anymore. Because of the stolen M60s showing up in those vans, and the threat that the killer also had a crate of hand grenades and six hundred pounds of C-4, teams from the ATF, FBI, and Homeland Security were involved. Morris had also learned that in addition to the FBI hitting a dead end with the Kansas armory theft, their two top suspects had been found dead five days afterward in a Wichita motel room.

Since he'd been expecting a call, he never fell into a deep sleep, and was in a restless state when the phone rang. He was awake instantly although his eyes weren't focusing well enough yet for him to read the caller ID or see what time it was. He answered the phone before it rang a second time, and asked the caller in a raspy whisper to give him a minute. From the light breathing noise Nat made, he knew she was asleep, and he didn't want to disturb her, so he pushed himself out of bed and headed for the hallway, his legs stiff. Once he had the bedroom door closed behind him, he squinted again at the phone and could see that it was Annie calling, and that it was three forty-seven. He felt his pulse quicken. Something had broken. Annie wouldn't be calling at this hour otherwise.

He headed down the stairs so he could start brewing some coffee. He needed his fix of caffeine before heading out. "I'm all ears," he said.

Usually that got a laugh out of her because one of the ways Morris resembled his dog was that he had big ears that also stuck out. Not this time, though.

"The killer broke into Stonehedge's Malibu residence and attacked Stonehedge and his girlfriend, Brie Evans."

Morris had reached the bottom step, but he stopped as a coolness flooded his head. "Are they okay?" he asked, his voice not quite right.

"He tried to cut Stonehedge's throat, but the bastard lost the fight, and your buddy escaped mostly intact with only significant injuries to his dignity. The jury's still out on Evans. He drugged her with something. She was unconscious when the paramedics arrived, and has been taken to Encino Medical Center."

Morris concentrated to recall the drugs the killer had used on his other victims. "I'm betting he drugged her with either pentobarbital or Rohypnol," he said.

"I already called the hospital and mentioned that to her doctor."

"Okay. What about the killer?"

"Stonehedge punched him in the nose and bloodied him up pretty good, leaving us plenty of DNA. He also took several shots at him, but apparently missed. The bastard escaped when he jumped off the cliff in back of Stonehedge's property."

Morris was moving again, and at that moment stepped into the kitchen. He grabbed the coffee pot and brought it to the sink. "That's quite a drop," he noted.

"Thirty-five feet."

"You said he escaped. So the fall didn't kill him?"

"Unfortunately, no. If it injured him, it didn't injure him enough. By the time officers arrived at the scene, he was gone. Tracks led a mile down the beach, and it looks like he then cut through private property to get back to the road. We've got calls to all the emergency rooms in the area to be on the lookout for him."

Morris couldn't help feeling disappointed. If only the sonofabitch had fractured his spine or broken a leg.

"What was that about Philip and his *dignity*?" he asked.

"When he chased the killer out of the house, he did so *sans* clothing. He also locked himself out."

"And of course he didn't have his cell phone."

"Nope. No pockets to put it in."

"His security gate has a police alert code. So he had to hike out to the road."

"Except the killer had cut power to the property, which also disabled the security gate. This left him having to take a stroll along the East Coast Pacific Highway and buzzing one of his neighbors. Except the neighbor didn't answer the buzzer, and with Stonehedge now panicking about Brie Evans, he jumped the gate and ended up pounding on the neighbor's front door."

"Without any clothes."

"Exactly."

"I get the picture. Where are you now?"

"I'm at Stonehedge's residence with the crime scene team."

"Okay, I'll be there as soon as I can."

"How about you going first to the Encino Medical Center? That's where Stonehedge is. You can interview him more thoroughly."

Morris had started the coffee, and when it was done brewing he'd fill up a thermos and take it with him. He kept a change of clothing downstairs just for this contingency.

"I'll be leaving in five," he told Walsh.

"I'll let you get dressed and do whatever else you need to do, and will fill you in more when you're on your way."

Chapter 47

"They weren't answering their buzzer, so I hopped the gate and miraculously didn't damage any of my privates dangling free. When I get to their house I'm freaking out, and not only because that psycho's on the loose, but I'm worried sick about Brie. At least I had the presence of mind to drop the gun before I start pounding on their front door. But you still have to picture it. I'm in the buff, soles of my feet bleeding from running on all that gravel, and wild-eyed with worry. When my neighbor answers the door—a seventy-year-old tigress by the name of Lucinda who's been flirting with me ever since I moved in—I try telling her it's an emergency. She's been eyeing me up and down, and she cuts me off, saying she can see that, but now's not a good time. That her husband's asleep in their bed, and she wouldn't be able to relax knowing he might wake up and catch us, so it would be better for me to come back the next day when he's golfing."

Stonehedge broke out laughing then. He was in much better spirits since Brie's doctor told him they were able to identify that she'd been drugged with pentobarbital, and that they now had her on fluids. While she was groggy and would need to be under observation for the next twelve hours, she was no longer in any danger.

His laughter was short-lived, however, and he shook his head as if he were amazed by the memory. He continued telling Morris what happened.

"I'm in no mood to try to explain to her that I'd been attacked by the psychotic murderous freak who's been terrorizing LA or that Brie could be dying from whatever he injected into her, so I push past her, and head to the kitchen where I find a phone. She follows me and is staring at me as if she's not sure whether she should scream, grab a knife so she can defend herself, or rip off her clothes for me. I guess she realized what was happening when she heard my end of the 9-1-1 call. So after I get off the phone, I ask if she can please bring me something to cover myself with. And she asks, 'Do I have to?'"

"Quite a story," Morris said. If he found the story at all amusing he wasn't showing it. Instead, he was looking somewhat melancholy. "I can't help thinking this was my fault."

"How's that?"

"That I egged him on with my appearance last night with Margot Denoir."

"Why would that matter?"

"This guy researches everything. He knows we're friends, and he wanted to do something to hurt me."

Stonehedge made a motion with his hand brushing away Morris's concerns. "A psycho's going to do what a psycho's going to do. Not your fault, Morris. This freak knew what he was doing. This wasn't something spur of the moment. He must've scoped out my house and been planning this for some time. Besides, you warned me that he was targeting actresses who looked like Brie. If you hadn't I wouldn't have been sleeping with a gun under my pillow. I can't believe I missed him all four times I shot at him."

"It's harder than it looks in the movies to hit a moving target, especially in the dark and when you're running also."

Stonehedge started to make a face as if he were disgusted with himself, but ended up grinning. "That's right, blame us actors. How come you didn't bring the little guy?"

"Rachel's staying at the house until this mess is over, and when she's home Parker sleeps in her room. I didn't have the heart to drag him out of there at four in the morning."

"And this way he's home protecting Nat and Rachel."

Morris smiled, his true motive uncovered. "That also," he admitted. "What can you tell me about this guy?"

Stonehedge grinned savagely. "I tried like hell to break his wrist. I might have succeeded."

"Let's hope so. Anything else?"

"I insulted his breath."

"That's something."

"I gave him a good shot to the nose. I don't know if I broke it, but I bloodied him."

"I heard that. Thanks to you we've got plenty of his DNA."

The actor's grin became more of a grimace. "His face couldn't have been more than two feet from mine, but the lights were off, and all I can tell you for certain is he has a shaved head and he didn't have any facial hair. I don't even think he had eyebrows."

"That's more than we knew before," Morris said. "I should tell you, we found out how he got into your house. Through the skylight above the kitchen. He was able to force it open, and then he climbed down using a rope ladder, which he left in the kitchen. He must've planned to get it on his way out."

Stonehedge frowned thinking about that. "If the skylight is tampered with, it's supposed to send an alarm to the police." Then he remembered about the power to his property being cut.

"That sonofabitch," he swore. "Damn, I wish I had shot him."

Chapter 48

Short Hills, New Jersey, 1999

Jason's second-period English class was interrupted by the school secretary, Mrs. Partridge, entering the classroom and informing the teacher that Master Dorsage was to proceed immediately to the headmaster's office.

Jason got up from his desk and looked apprehensively at his teacher, then at Mrs. Partridge. "Is anything wrong?" he asked.

Mrs. Partridge, in a tone icy enough to leave frostbite, replied, "Headmaster Rector will explain to you what this is about."

As Jason left the room with his head lowered and looking like he was being led to the gallows, Simon Witt broke out laughing and said loudly enough for the whole class to hear, "I bet dumbass Dorsage is getting booted out of Avery."

Jason didn't return to the classroom, but later that day waited in the hallway for Witt, and when he saw him, he rushed his archnemesis and dragged him into the boys' room before Witt could react. Witt stumbled backward and almost fell to the floor before recovering his balance.

Jason stood trembling, his hands clenched, his breathing rapid. "I should kick your ass for what you did," he threatened, his voice strained as if it took every ounce of self-control he possessed to keep from physically attacking the other boy.

At first Witt looked alarmed, but as he watched Jason, a calculating look took over.

"You're a maniac," he said.

"I know what you did, you rat-faced creep!"

"I don't like you calling me that!"

"The name fits more than ever. I know you *narced* on me."

Witt took a small step backward and fingered his chin as he considered the accusation. "What makes you think I did that?" he asked.

Jason burst out with an angry laugh. "Rector showed me the anonymous letter you wrote saying you witnessed Anthony Lepke selling me Adderall."

"I take back calling you a maniac. You're a delusional maniac."

"You don't think I recognized your handwriting?"

Witt continued to finger his chin, a glimmer brightening his eyes. "Let's say I'm guilty as charged," he said, teasingly. "There's nothing you can do about it, except bend over and take it from me one more time."

Jason stood exasperated. He stammered out, "You want to mess with me so badly you're willing to mess with Lepke also?"

"You bet I do. And what do I care about Lepke?" He made a face as if he wanted to spit out something unpleasant. "He's a moron who shouldn't be at Avery. It's embarrassing having someone like him here."

"You're unbelievable. But guess what? Your plan didn't work. Rector told me he's not going to punish a student because of an anonymous letter. So you didn't get anything out of this!"

Witt smiled nastily. "I wouldn't say that's true. Seeing you work yourself into a sputtering tizzy is priceless." He pointed a bony index finger at Jason. "If you ever touch me again, I'll kick you in the face."

For good measure, Witt demonstrated one of his exotic tae kwon do kicks, and he made sure to push his shoulder hard into Jason's chest as he brushed past him and left the bathroom. Jason stood shaking, amazed at not only how well it had gone, but at his performance. Easily Oscar-award caliber, if he said so himself. The secret was channeling all of his hatred for Witt into it.

It had been five weeks since Witt destroyed the Rube Goldberg machine he was building, and it was so rewarding to see the first several steps of his plan work so perfectly. The first step had been taken a week ago when he did in fact buy Adderall from Anthony Lepke. The second was executed earlier that morning when he gave an equally convincing performance for Headmaster Rector. Most of what he had told Witt was true. Rector questioned him about the anonymous letter that accused him of buying prescription drugs from Lepke on school grounds. Rector, while unhappy about the charges made in the letter, did in fact tell him he wasn't going to take action based solely on an anonymous accusation. Jason had even mostly told Witt the truth about the letter being written in Witt's handwriting, although it was really written so it would appear as if Witt had written it.

He smiled thinking about that part. He had plenty of writing samples from when he and Witt were friends and they had spent afternoons working together on a story outline for a graphic novel. It took hours of practice before he could master Witt's handwriting, but he felt confident the anonymous letter he had forged to look like it came from Witt's hand would fool almost anyone, even many handwriting experts.

He moved over to the sink and turned the faucet on, then proceeded to splash water over his face as if he were upset and trying to calm himself down. He kept this up until he heard the toilet flushing in one of the stalls, and then looked up startled as if he thought he'd been alone in the boys' room. This was another part that Witt didn't know about. Jason had seen Lewis Pomerantz earlier enter the bathroom, and he had made sure Pomerantz had gone into a stall before lying in wait for Witt. His plan required a witness for his confrontation with Witt, and Pomerantz would more than do. While he wasn't known as a big gossiper, his girlfriend was, and before the end of the day all of Avery would be hearing about it. Without a doubt. Even Headmaster Rector.

Pomerantz left the stall and made it a point not to make eye contact with Jason. He walked over to the sink two away from Jason's, not to wash his hands, but so he could check himself out in the mirror as he combed his hair.

"You were talking to Simon Witt, right?" he asked.

Jason straightened up and stopped splashing water on his face. He gave a stunned look. "I didn't know anyone else was in here. Come on, man, be decent about this, don't tell anyone what you heard."

Pomerantz smirked as he put his comb away. Without saying anything else, he left the bathroom.

Word would soon be spreading. No question about it. Assuming Witt didn't go running to Rector first, the headmaster would feel compelled to bring Witt to his office to ask whether he was the author of the letter, and Witt would undoubtedly take credit for it. There was little chance the smug little prick would be able to help himself from doing otherwise, or even bother to think about the consequences. And there were going to be consequences. Lepke was two years older than them. He was also bigger, heavier, and a lot meaner in a brutish sort of way.

Jason marveled at how everything was falling so neatly into place. In a way, he had created a living and breathing Rube Goldberg machine.

He squeezed his eyes closed, and in his mind's eye he could see all the events lined up as dominos, each falling into the next.

It gave him goose bumps.

Chapter 49

At first Simon Witt thought Duh-sage had given him a wonderful gift, but as he thought more about it, he realized instead it was a puzzle that needed solving. He couldn't just go to Rector and claim ownership of the anonymous letter Duh-sage had blathered about for the simple reason that he didn't know what details were in it. If Rector started questioning him about when and where the incident in question took place, Witt would be caught in a lie. He could pretty much guess where Duh-sage and Ape Boy did their transaction. The likely spot would have been behind the facilities building. That was on the far side of the campus, and nobody ever went there except for that kind of activity. But the big question still remaining was when it happened. That was what Witt had to figure out because he badly wanted to hurt Duh-sage. He couldn't say exactly why that was, but he did. He also didn't mind the idea of hurting Ape Boy, who as far as he was concerned was a dullard who didn't deserve to be at Avery. It really was disgraceful having someone like him at the school—this simian-like creature with his unibrow and ridged forehead. Witt's lips curled in disgust as he pictured Ape Boy. If anything, he'd be doing the school a great service if he were to cause Ape Boy to be expelled.

Witt wondered briefly who wrote the letter, but he decided it didn't matter. He also doubted that the handwriting looked anything like his own—Duh-sage believed that because he would've seen only what he wanted to see. He would want to believe that only Witt would write a letter like that. Obviously, that wasn't true. Someone else out there also wanted to hurt him. Or maybe that person just wanted to hurt Ape Boy.

Witt found himself hoping it was the latter. He felt strangely possessive about being the one to torment and hurt Jason Dorsage.

He did, though, have an idea of how to get the information he needed. Noah English. He just needed to figure out the right opening so he'd catch English off guard. He'd have plenty of opportunities to engage English in seemingly innocent small talk since English's locker was next to his.

During his next two classes Witt had trouble paying attention as he kept playing out different scenarios in his head of how he could trick English into divulging the information he wanted. He was distracted enough with these thoughts that he missed the whispers of *snitch* from his classmates and the dirty looks he received. It surprised him when his history teacher asked him to remain after class. She waited until they were alone before telling him that Headmaster Rector wanted to see him. "You should be discreet," she suggested.

Witt took her advice and waited until the hallway was clear before knocking on Rector's door. He knew it had to be about the letter. Was it possible that it did look like his handwriting and the headmaster wanted to see him after examining all the students' handwriting? Or maybe Duhsage had blurted out to Rector that he thought Witt wrote it?

He still hadn't made up his mind whether he was going to try bluffing Rector, but the bloated walrus-human hybrid made it easy for him when he handed Witt the letter and asked whether he was the author.

Witt took his time reading it, somewhat amazed that the handwriting did look like his own, but he chalked it up as a bizarre coincidence, and nothing more.

"Yes," he said, nodding earnestly. "I felt it was my responsibility as a student at Avery to report witnessing such dangerous and illegal behavior." He forced a degree of humility as he added, "I regret not having the courage earlier to sign my name."

Rector leaned back in the leather chair, fingers interlaced as his hands rested on his enormous belly, his eyes closing as if he were falling asleep. But they didn't close completely.

"I see," he said. "So your reasons were purely altruistic, and not personally motivated?"

Witt felt his cheeks reddening. "A student selling another student drugs is against the law. As headmaster I thought you'd want to know if this was happening on school grounds? Maybe I was wrong?"

Rector's eyes glazed under his thick eyelids. "No, you're not mistaken," he said bluntly. "That is all."

The headmaster picked up a report from his desk and focused his attention on it. Witt had been dismissed. Still, he sat for a minute staring at the bloated Rector, his cheeks smoldering with humiliation. It made no sense. There was nothing for him to be feeling humiliated about. And there was no reason that Rector should've treated him so contemptuously!

When he finally left, he felt as if he'd won a strategic battle, yet lost the war. It was a funny feeling, and he didn't understand the reason for it.

Chapter 50

Short Hills, New Jersey, 1999, 10 days later

Dorsage and Lepke weren't expelled as Witt had hoped; instead they were only suspended for a week. To make matters worse, Witt learned later the same day he had seen Rector that Pomerantz had overheard his conversation with Dorsage and had spread it all over the school. Soon almost everybody was calling him a snitch, and Lepke's fellow ape-like friends were giving him the evil eye when he passed them in the hallway. Even his own small circle of friends began avoiding him. All of this made Witt start to wonder more about how the handwriting in that letter had looked like his own. Was it possible Dorsage had set him up? Risk expulsion to make Witt a pariah in the school? All he knew for sure was that he needed to keep a low profile and hope the matter would blow over.

Once Lepke returned from his suspension, Witt heard whispers that Lepke was looking for him. He wasn't necessarily scared of that ape—after all, he had his green belt in tae kwon do, and felt he could handle Lepke in a fight if it came to that. Still, he was careful as he moved around Avery, making sure that there were always teachers around. That was why it was such a surprise to him after he had walked into the boys' room that three of Lepke's friends followed him in. He could've sworn there was nobody around when he had darted into the bathroom.

"If you do anything I'll see that you're expelled," Witt threatened. "And I'll get the police after you."

"Because you're a snitch," one of Lepke's friends said.

Witt tried to walk past them, but one of them pushed him back.

"So it's going to be three against one?" Witt asked.

"Uh uh," one of them said. "We're just here to make sure you don't leave."

It didn't take long after that for Lepke to walk into the bathroom. His friends let him pass by.

"Who's the moron now?" Lepke asked.

Witt was nervous. While he had sparred in class, he'd never been in a real fight. Still, he knew that the element of surprise meant everything. Without giving Lepke any warning, he spun around to deliver a tae kwon do kick, but before his foot could make contact with Lepke's jaw, Lepke caught his ankle. For a painful moment, Witt stood helpless on one foot, then Lepke punched him so hard in the chest that Witt thought he was going to die. He didn't die, though. Instead there was a dizzying whirl of motion as Lepke grabbed Witt by the back of his collar and dragged him into one of the stalls, then forced his face into the toilet bowl. Witt tried to hold his breath, but Lepke punched him in the side forcing him to gulp in water. Just as Witt was sure he was going to pass out, Lepke pulled his head out of the toilet bowl.

"I hate rats," Lepke said into Witt's ear, his breath smelling like sour milk. "I think they should all be drowned."

Lepke dunked Witt's face into the toilet bowl again and waited until Witt was on the verge of losing consciousness before pulling him out of the water.

"You're going to come here every morning at seven a.m. on the dot for a private baptism," Lepke said in a soft, menacing voice. "You don't do that, or you tell anyone about what I'm doing to you, and I'm going to hurt you so bad you'll never forget it. I'll break every bone in your face, and that's just for starters. It don't matter whether I go to juvie, or you get me expelled, I'll be working in my dad's company. You can't hurt me. But I'll find you afterward. That's a promise. You believe me, rat?"

Witt was too petrified to do anything but nod.

For what seemed like an eternity, Lepke held him by the scruff of the neck as he studied Witt, a confused look spreading over his face.

"Why'd you want to cause trouble for me?" Lepke demanded.

Witt wouldn't have been able to talk if his life depended on it, even if he had anything to say.

Lepke punched him again, this time in the shoulder.

"You be here tomorrow at seven sharp," Lepke warned. "I'm not kidding about what I told you before."

Lepke and his friends left then. Witt gathered himself and left the stall. He was in a state of shock as he grabbed a handful of paper towels and dried his hair. As he gazed at his reflection in the mirror, he saw red-rimmed eyes staring back at him and skin the color of what you'd see on a corpse.

He understood what Dorsage had done to him. His enemy had not only won whatever war they'd been engaged in, but had completely and utterly obliterated him. It was over, and surrender was no longer a possibility.

He still had no idea what was coming.

Chapter 51

Short Hills, New Jersey, 1999, 15 days later

Jason would've bet none of the other students in the classroom picked up on Headmaster Rector's distress when he interrupted their fourth-period French class to ask Simon Witt to accompany him, but then again, Jason knew Rector better than any of them. Witt, for his part, meekly obliged like a little bitch, not even uttering as much as a peep. When school was abruptly closed at the end of the fourth period with no statement given, rumors started to fly. Some students claimed that the police had been waiting in the hallway for Rector to escort Witt from the classroom, and that the boy was later handcuffed and driven away in a police car. Other students were saying they saw police cars and an ambulance rushing to the facilities building, some with their lights flashing.

Even if Jason hadn't seen the anxious look on Noah's face, he knew better than to get into one of the school vans with him. While Noah wouldn't be stupid enough to intentionally talk about their plan so he could be overheard, when he got overly excited like this he tended to be louder than he realized. Anyway, it was a sunny early spring day, and Jason was feeling absolutely wonderful, so he didn't mind the idea of walking home. Noah realized that Jason wasn't planning to take one of the vans, and he started jogging to catch up to him. By the time he got alongside Jason, he was wheezing like he'd just run a mile instead of a hundred feet.

"The cops must've found the drugs in Simon the Twit's locker?" Noah asked as he struggled to catch his breath.

"I didn't do it yet."

"But that was the plan!"

Jason shot him a look because Noah had said this too loudly. There wasn't anyone within earshot, but if there were they would've heard him. That wasn't the real plan, only what Noah believed it to be—that they were framing Witt, making it look as if he was the one selling Adderall at the school. This was why Noah had spied on Simon Witt for him so he could get him Witt's locker combination. It wasn't a hard thing to do since Witt had a neighboring locker, and Jason had worked with him, showing him how he could use a small hand mirror to get the combination. The trick was not to be too greedy. Just try to get one number at a time so that Witt wouldn't catch him in the act.

Jason said, "I heard that Anthony Lepke was dunking Witt's face in the toilet each morning, and I didn't want to do anything to interfere with that."

Noah's face wrinkled with confusion. "Then why did Rector pull him out of class? And why did they shut down the school?"

Jason shrugged as if he didn't have a clue, but he knew that the police must've searched Witt's locker and found the magazine that he had hidden there. It was the type of magazine that had ads for guns and knives and other weapons, and if you send cash to a PO box, they mail you the weapon, no questions asked. If the police found the magazine, they would've seen an ad circled for a hunting knife with an eight-inch blade. After they pulled Witt from the classroom, they would then find that same knife in his backpack, which was the knife Jason used to kill Anthony Lepke. He had wiped the blade clean after pushing it deep into Lepke's back, but he knew that forensics would find traces of Lepke's blood and determine that the knife was the murder weapon.

He was quite pleased with how all the dominos had fallen exactly as he arranged them. While it was easy to hide the magazine in Witt's locker—he was able to do it before school started and nobody was around—he didn't think he'd have a chance to hide the knife there. But after killing Lepke during their one-hour lunch break, nobody was in the hallway when he got to Witt's locker. Even better, when he opened the locker, he found Witt's backpack. Well, that was just too perfect. If anyone had been near the locker, he would have ditched the knife somewhere else that would still implicate Witt, but hiding it in the backpack was beyond perfect.

Even without the knife, the police would've eventually arrested Witt. Jason had ordered the knife the day after he heard about Witt's toilet bowl baptism, and had it mailed to an address three houses away from Witt's. He knew that an elderly lady lived there, and that her mail piled up each week before someone would bring it into the house. Yeah, it was a gamble that the old lady or someone she knew would get to the knife before he did, but the gamble paid off, and the police would be convinced that Witt had the knife mailed to her house. There was also a good chance that the police would find one or more witnesses who saw Witt during their lunch break either heading to the facilities building or walking away from it. Jason had left Witt an anonymous note sending him behind the facilities building to talk about how they could deal with a mutual enemy, Lepke. Witt would of course be showing this note to the police, but they'd believe he wrote it himself in a clumsy attempt to provide an alibi. Nobody, though, saw Jason walking to or from the facilities building. Avery Academy was over a hundred and sixty years old, but as prestigious as the school was it badly needed modernization. The school still used a network of tunnels from the facilities building to the rest of the campus to provide heating, and Jason used one of the tunnels from the gymnasium's basement to get to and from the facilities building without being seen.

While he had nothing against Lepke, and killed him because it was a necessary part of his plan to destroy Simon Witt's life, Jason had also wondered for a long time how he would feel murdering someone. What he discovered was that he didn't feel much of anything. He didn't get any pleasure from it, but the act also didn't bother him, and he knew he wasn't going to be tortured by it. In the end Lepke turned out to be nothing more than one of the dominos that needed to fall so that his Rube Goldberg–like machine would run without a hitch. If anything, Jason felt a sense of pride that he'd gotten the job done with only a single hard shove of the knife. While he had studied anatomical drawings so he'd know where to stick Lepke, it was still quite a feat.

As they walked together and Noah acted increasingly hyper about the mystery of why Witt was removed from the classroom, Jason wondered whether he was going to become a problem. He'd already worked out a way to get rid of Noah if needed. His plan involved a bottle of Canadian whiskey, a half dozen of Vivian's Valiums, and making it look as if a drunken Noah had fallen asleep on the train tracks.

He still wasn't even sure whether Noah was a friend or simply a lackey. What he did know was that if he had to kill Noah, it wouldn't bother him a bit.

Chapter 52

Los Angeles, the present

Morris was surprised to find Adam Felger in the office.

"What time did you get in?" he asked.

Felger looked up from his computer, bleary-eyed and seemingly startled by Morris's presence.

"I never left last night," he admitted with a lopsided grin. "After all, you did give me that assignment yesterday."

"I thought you finished it last night?"

"I did. Sort of." His grin turned more lopsided. "You never really feel like that kind of list is ever done. That if you keep searching you'll be able to add another name to it."

Morris said, "Dedication, then."

"Really just stubbornness." Felger leaned back in his chair as he rubbed his eyes and stretched, then gave Morris another bleary-eyed look. "I spent part of the night trying to find more names for the list, but I was also looking into another angle. There has to be something connecting Heather Brandley, Drea Kane, and Faye Riverstone, but I can't find it. They didn't act together in any movies or TV shows, or date the same guy, or get nominated for the same award, or anything else I've tried thinking of, but my gut's telling me if I keep digging I'll find a link."

Morris had done his share of Internet searches since these killings started and likewise had come up blank. "It could just be they remind him of someone from his past that he's been obsessing about," he said. "Or maybe they're actresses he's had crushes on. Or his reason might be something that only makes sense within his twisted mind."

"Maybe," Felger conceded. "But unless you ask me to do something else, I'd like to keep looking."

Morris wasn't going to discourage this kind of initiative. Besides, it was six-thirty Sunday morning, and as far as he was concerned Felger could spend it any way he wanted.

"Add Brie Evans to your list," he said. "The psycho tried to abduct her last night, but his plan didn't work."

"Is she okay?"

"Mostly. She's at Encino Medical Center now, but she's expected to fully recover." Morris checked his watch, and tried to remember what time Katz's Bagels opened. "I'll be making a run for bagels and cream cheese in an hour. Anything special you'd like me to pick up?"

Felger said, "Whatever you get will be fine with me."

Morris left MBI's hacking specialist and headed to the kitchen area expecting to find the coffee pot empty since Felger was more of a Red Bull drinker, and he had seen a small collection of empty cans piling up in Felger's office. The pot was empty as he had expected, and he started brewing a fresh one. As he waited, he heard MBI's outer door open, and he left the kitchen area to see Charlie Bogle walking in holding a large bag from Katz's Bagels. Morris glanced at his watch and saw it was twenty minutes to seven.

"I didn't think they opened until seven," he said.

Bogle shrugged. "For most of their customers. For me, they make an exception."

He handed over the bag. Morris opened it and breathed in the smell of freshly baked bagels. "There's got to be at least two dozen," he said.

"Three dozen," Bogle corrected. "And a two-pound tub of cream cheese."

"That's a lot of bagels since it's just you, me, and Adam right now."

"Computer boy's in this early?" he asked. "What for?"

"He's being stubborn."

Bogle nodded as if that made sense to him. "I figured with all the agencies now involved we might get a big crowd dropping in. And if Polk shows up, half the bagels will be gone."

"No one on the federal payroll will be dropping by on a Sunday morning. But you've got a good point about Polk. So why are *you* here before seven on a Sunday?"

Another shrug from Bogle. "I wasn't sleeping well, so I figured I'd just as well be here as anywhere else. But if I was married to someone like Natalie, there's no chance I would've gotten my ass out of bed this early."

"I wasn't planning to either," Morris admitted. "But we had some excitement last night." He told Bogle about the killer breaking into Philip Stonehedge's home, and what he'd been doing since then.

"This joker was able to run away after jumping off a thirty-five-foot cliff?" Bogle asked incredulously.

"At least limped away."

"That's too bad."

"Area emergency rooms will be looking for him."

"Not much chance he'll go to any of them."

"Probably not," Morris agreed. "But you never know. He might think he's disguised well enough to try it. Especially if he has a broken wrist, or busted leg."

"We got his DNA now?"

"Quite a bit of it."

Bogle thought about what had happened and chuckled to himself. "Your actor friend and his main squeeze live charmed lives."

"What are you talking about? They had a psycho trying to kill them last night."

"But they survived with nary a scratch, which is more than you can say for those other actresses. And if I ever ended up naked at a neighbor's door at three in the morning, pounding on it like a crazy man, I'd probably get shot a half dozen times before I'd be able to tell my side of the story."

"You need new neighbors. I'm going to let Adam grab some bagels, and I'll meet you in the kitchen. A fresh pot of coffee should be ready."

"Okay. And I'll tell you about the vans."

Morris wasn't surprised that Bogle had already discovered where the killer got the vans that had been left on Rodeo Drive with the machine gun contraptions. When he offered Felger his choice of bagels, his hacking specialist searched through the bag and grabbed two of the *everything* bagels, and while they didn't have raisins, they had just about everything else: salt, garlic, onion, poppy, caraway, and sesame seeds. Felger bypassed the cream cheese, and nodded thanks as he nibbled absently on one of the bagels. The intense look burning in his eyes made Morris wonder whether his employee's stubbornness had paid off, but he didn't ask Felger about it, figuring Felger would tell him if he found something.

Bogle had two cups of coffee ready, and while they prepared several bagels with cream cheese to bring back to Morris's office, Bogle told him that he had spent the previous evening going through police reports for stolen vehicles and found that Wyman Cable reported three of their vans missing four months ago. "Six days later one of their security guards was found shot to death in his Buena Park apartment. Quite a sorry pattern with this guy. You make a deal with him, and he rewards you by shooting you dead after you deliver. The Buena Park PD is requesting ballistic reports from the Kansas shooting. I would bet a week's pay they're going to match."

"Unless he dumped the gun after the Kansas shooting and used a second one for the security guard."

"He wouldn't do that," Bogle said. "He'd want us to be able to connect the two crimes. He's just so damn full of himself for it to be any other way."

Morris had to agree with the investigator's assessment. Even though it seemed like a dead end, they needed to show the police sketches of the killer to the other security guards working at Wyman Cable in case the killer had tried approaching any of them. He'd give it to one of the LAPD detectives, maybe Ray Vestra.

He and Bogle brought the coffee and bagels to his office and started going through the hotline calls that were received after his TV appearance. Franklin Strong had manned the hotline until midnight, and left a report saying most of the eighty-seven calls that came in were either from shut-ins or mentally unstable individuals, but he circled seven calls that he thought were worth investigating further. Overnight twenty-nine more calls were logged by the LAPD. Morris particularly wanted to know whether there was overlap between the hotline calls and the list Felger put together. He and Bogle were checking on that when Natalie called him.

"Think of my surprise when I woke up and found you gone," she said. "I could've sworn we went to bed together last night, unless I was only dreaming that part of it."

"I know. I'm sorry I pulled my Houdini act, but I got a call at a quarter to four and didn't want to wake you. This maniac went after Philip and Brie last night. They're both okay, but the maniac escaped and I've been tracing loose ends since then."

"Wow," she said.

"I know."

"Are you any closer to catching him?"

"I think so. He's probably injured. Maybe severely. And when we catch him, we'll be able to convict him. Philip bloodied his nose pretty good so we now have plenty of DNA."

"I don't think you're going to be able to catch him," she said, her tone worried. "He'll make you kill him if it comes to that."

"He might try, but it doesn't mean he'll succeed."

"Promise me you'll be careful and won't take any chances. If he can take you down with him, he will."

Morris said, "I'm not going to let him do that."

"Promise me!"

"You've got it."

Natalie asked, "Where are you now?"

"The office. I'm not alone. Charlie and Adam are keeping me company."

"And Parker?"

"I wouldn't have been able to drag him out of Rachel's room at a quarter to four in the morning, so he'll be with you gals today. I made sure before I left that there was an unmarked car half a block away watching the house. Just try to stay inside. And try to keep Rachel home. I've got a feeling it won't be much longer."

Natalie said she'd try her best to keep their daughter corralled one more day, and expressed her concern again about Morris's safety before ending the call. After Morris tucked his cell phone back in his pants pocket, Bogle commented that it sounded like Natalie was worried about him.

"She is," Morris admitted, but otherwise didn't discuss the matter further. They were going through more of the hotline calls when Felger walked into Morris's office with a hard grin etched on his face.

"You're not paying me enough," he said.

"That's probably true," Morris agreed. "Talk to me, boychik."

"They were in a movie together. All four of them. A cheesy, low-budget flick called *The Satan Plan*."

Bogle asked, "A horror film?"

"It's supposed to be a suspense thriller. The title is because this evil genius is planning to bring hell to LA."

Morris felt a catch in this throat when he asked Felger to describe the movie's plot.

"I found a copy on the Internet and fast-forwarded through most of it. The evil genius plants bombs in forty oil wells encircling LA, and when they explode they trigger a massive earthquake that leaves the city looking like a nuclear bomb had exploded. It's pretty bad. The reason I missed it earlier in my searches is that Drea Kane and Faye Riverstone didn't use their real names in the credits. But when I saw that Brandley and Brie Evans were in it, I decided to watch it. The movie was made fourteen years ago, and Brie, Kane, and Riverstone were only teenagers, but I recognized all of them. Something else. A geology professor at UCLA by the name of Andrew Hastings consulted on it."

Morris asked, "You think he could be our guy?"

"No. He'd be sixty-three now. But he's still a professor at UCLA, and I figured you might want to talk to him."

"In case this is how the psycho plans to use the six hundred pounds of stolen C-4."

Morris didn't say this as a question, but Felger told him that was exactly what he was thinking. Morris noticed that Bogle was giving a thousand-yard stare. He asked his investigator what had him so deep in thought.

"I was just wondering," Bogle muttered under his breath before his eyes shifted to meet Morris's. "This could be connected to Karl Crawford's murder four months ago."

"His alleged murder since you can't actually prove it."

"True, but I'm convinced he was shot to death while sitting in his car. What if this psycho approached Crawford about planting bombs in the oil wells, and killed Crawford when he turned him down? Or he could've killed Crawford so he could take his job? He could've planted explosives in dozens of oil wells by now."

"Ah, hell," Morris said.

"My thought exactly," Bogle agreed.

Chapter 53

Todd Blankenford woke up with his head throbbing and his mouth tasting like he had spent the night sucking on a urinal cake. He tried opening his eyes against the morning light, but the effect was like tiny slivers of glass shooting into his brain. He grabbed the pillow from behind his head and held it over his face so it would muffle his screams.

This shit had to stop. At some point, he had to accept that he was fifty-seven, and stop doing this to himself. But for now, he needed to take inventory.

He forced himself to concentrate. He remembered being at Club Dumont in North Hollywood and drinking tequila. He also remembered later digging into his cocaine stash. But tequila and cocaine by itself wouldn't cause this wicked pray-for-death hangover. There must've been something else. He stopped his inventory when he heard someone stirring next to him.

He lifted the pillow from his face and struggled to open his eyes enough so he could see the naked girl lying on his bed. He vaguely remembered her from last night. Very young and pretty. So he had taken Viagra too. He also remembered her giving him molly, and that it made his brain feel fuzzy. He needed to remember that tequila, coke, Viagra, and molly were not a good combination, at least if he didn't want to suffer another morning like this one.

He gingerly rolled onto his side so he could get a better look at the sweet young thing lying next to him, being careful to move his head at a glacial pace. She was lying on her stomach, but he could tell that she was more than just pretty. Simply luscious, no question about it. Dark brown hair, olive complexion, lithe body. How many shots of tequila did he have before he approached her? Eight? More than that? He must've given her his standard spiel. No doubt he told her he'd put her in the latest crap TV show he was directing, although he wouldn't have used the word *crap*. Masterful. Suspenseful. Cutting edge. Some BS along those lines.

He reached out and lightly traced a finger from her hip to her knee, feeling how cool her flesh felt and thinking about how he always liked them young. This one had to be at least twenty-five years his junior, maybe even more.

Oh sweet Jesus, he moaned inwardly. While he liked them young, he needed them legal, and he started having an uneasy feeling this one might not be. He couldn't afford to have another incident. It would be the end of his career in Hollywood. While he might only be directing the crappiest TV imaginable, it paid the bills.

He carefully rolled off the bed, biting his tongue to keep from groaning out loud. He felt a greater sense of urgency than before, and he staggered through the bedroom searching for her pocketbook. When he didn't find it, he slipped on a silk bathrobe and headed downstairs.

He found her pocketbook among their clothing and he groaned when he saw a large red stain and a mostly empty wine glass lying on his one-of-a-kind $18,000 kidney-shaped white satin sofa. He groaned again when he spotted an empty $300 bottle of Burgundy that had been knocked over, leaving an even bigger stain on his cream-colored carpeting. What would have possessed him to open a bottle of wine last night after everything else he'd had? He decided he'd worry about that later. The carpeting could be replaced, and there was a chance the sofa could be either cleaned or reupholstered. For now, he had bigger fish to fry.

Blankenford searched through her pocketbook and found her driver's license. If the license was legit, the naked girl lying asleep (or passed out) in his bed was Mary Anne Callahan, age twenty-two, and with a Van Nuys address. She looked younger than that, but girls were looking younger to him all the time. Certainly a correlation of sorts with him becoming an old man. He could breathe easier now. His sofa and carpeting might've gotten ruined but at least he wouldn't get mired in another scandal and lose his last chance of working in Hollywood.

As he squinted at the license, something about it troubled him, and he soon realized what it was. The name Callahan didn't fit with the olive-skinned girl he saw in his bed, and made him think that the license might be a fake. When he found the diamond engagement ring (no more than an eighth of a carat) and the slim gold wedding band that had been hidden away inside a zippered pouch, he understood why she had that last name. She was married. At least she was legal and he wouldn't have to worry about another scandal like the one that had derailed his career fifteen years ago, but this still wasn't good. He had sworn off married girls after the last one's husband chased him naked out of his house with one of his own golf clubs. The guy would've killed him if he had caught up to him. Blankenford might often feel like an old geezer these days, but he could still run like the wind when he had an insanely jealous husband chasing him.

He put the rings back in the pouch, zipped it up, and slipped her driver's license back into her purse. With her pocketbook put back together, he started a pot of coffee brewing. A year ago he had bought a newer style coffee maker, one where you use prefabbed capsules to make a single cup, but he had too many mornings like this one where he knew he needed a whole pot if he was going to make it out of the house. With the coffee started, he checked that his robe was tied, then headed outside to get the newspaper. He was a dinosaur in that regard—he needed to start the day reading the newspaper while pouring copious amounts of coffee down his gullet.

The sunlight nearly obliterated him, but he made it back into the house in one piece. He chuckled to himself as he thought he should get a dog for precisely this reason—to retrieve the morning paper for him when he was this hungover, which was most mornings. With that task accomplished, he shoved a handful of sugar packets into his bathrobe pocket and brought the newspaper, pot of coffee, and a mug to the breakfast nook he had set up in an area of the kitchen that did not get any direct morning sunlight.

The first cup he drank, which included three sugar packets, helped clear some of the fuzziness from his head, and removed some of the sewer taste in his mouth. After a second cup, he was ready to take a look at the front page of the paper and saw that Faye Riverstone had been murdered by the madman who was terrorizing Los Angeles.

What a bloody shame, he thought.

He had directed her years ago when she was just a teenager. An exceptionally stunning girl even then, especially with those pouty lips, and he might've tried bedding her if he hadn't just had his legal problems. Not only was she a breathtakingly beautiful seventeen-year-old, but she was smart enough to use a stage name for the movie, which was just simply awful.

He settled back in his chair and thought more about the movie. It was the first job he was offered following the brouhaha that transpired when those parents accused him of sleeping with their fifteen-year-old nymphet daughter. While the charges were miraculously withdrawn after a hundred-grand payoff, he nonetheless felt lucky to be hired for any film, even one where the script was a complete mess and the budget a joke. Little did he realize back then that the movie would lead him down a road of awfulness. Well-paying awfulness, but still nothing but one piece of dreck after the next.

For years Blankenford had tried to forget about the movie, but as he drank a third cup of coffee and read the rest of the article about poor, sweet Faye, his mind drifted back to the film. As frightfully bad as it was, it did have a talented cast, including several other budding actresses who, like Faye, were destined for stardom.

"Dear Lord," he whispered as he realized that other actresses from the film had also been killed by that madman. He was considering calling the police and notifying them about that fact when he heard footsteps. He looked up to see Mary Anne Callahan walking into the kitchen wearing one of his T-shirts. While he was skinny, he had a long body. She couldn't be more than five feet two, and the T-shirt came halfway down her thighs. Still, she looked self-conscious in it.

"Hi," Blankenford said with as much of a smile as he could manage. "Grab a mug and pour yourself some coffee before I finish off the pot."

She did just that, getting up on her toes so she could take a mug from the second shelf, her shirt riding up as she did so. Blankenford, being a gentleman, only gave her a quick, admiring look. After she sat down across from him and was sipping her coffee, he asked if she wanted anything to eat.

"There might be some food in the fridge. Possibly even some eggs. If not, I could have breakfast delivered."

"Coffee's all I want," she said in a scratchy, unhappy voice.

Blankenford frowned at her. "I didn't tell you my superpower last night did I?" he asked.

She looked at him as if he were crazy.

"It failed me last night, because tequila is my kryptonite. But I have the uncanny power to look at a pretty young girl and know whether she's married, and as I look at you in the light of day, my superpower is beeping like crazy."

She opened her eyes wide as if she were impressed, and then just as quickly they glazed. "You went through my purse," she said.

He smiled. "Guilty as charged. But it doesn't change the fact that you deceived me."

She smirked. "You wouldn't have brought me back here last night if you knew I was married?"

"I might very well have, because you are gorgeous and, as I mentioned earlier, tequila is my kryptonite. Really one of many, if I were to be honest about it. But it doesn't change the fact that I didn't realize I was committing adultery."

"Don't worry," she said. "I'm not telling my husband anything."

"I'm relieved to hear that. But won't he be curious as to your whereabouts last night?"

"No, he won't be." Anger darkened her face. "He's in Vegas for a bachelor party. I'm sure he spent the night screwing hookers." She choked up, as if thoughts of what her husband might be doing right then was too much for her to bear. Then in an accusatory tone she demanded to know whether he was really going to give her a part in a TV show.

"I would never lie about something like that," he promised her.

Blankenford got up from the nook so he could grab a slip of paper and a pen. He wrote down a phone number and handed her the slip.

"Call me Tuesday," he said. "It won't be a big part, probably no more than ten seconds of screen time, but you'll get a credit."

The part he had in mind was as Dead Girl #2. He was sure the executive producer would let him give it to her if he insisted.

Her mood softened, and Blankenford understood why. Last night, with the help of booze and drugs, she had believed him when he promised her a part, otherwise she would've picked one of the young studs at Club Dumont to get back at hubby, no matter how charming and wealthy he might be. In the cold, sober reality of the day, she had likewise convinced herself that he had fed her a line, like so many people in this town do. Well, Dead Girl #2 might not be much of a part, but you never knew what might catch a casting director's eye and lead to stardom. She might or might not have any talent, but she certainly had the looks.

"My husband's flight home isn't until later this afternoon," she said. "Do you want to go back upstairs?"

"You're a vision of loveliness," Blankenford said. "But I don't think it would be wise for us to tempt fate."

She nodded as if she understood what he was saying.

Chapter 54

Philip Stonehedge waited a fraction of a second too long to pretend he didn't recognize that it was Margot Denoir recording a segment by the ocean's edge. She was waving at him, and then running toward him. Her camera crew stayed where they were.

Margot was wearing a navy blue suit with a skirt that came down just above the knees and, as a concession for being at the beach, she wore flats instead of her usual high heels. Margot was notorious for wearing heels when she was on TV because of how well they showcased her well-toned calves. Still, even in flats, it must've been a struggle running on sand, and she was breathing heavily by the time she reached him. Even though it was windy, her well-coifed blond hair didn't budge. It could've just as well been made of plastic.

"Margot, what a surprise," the actor said with a false smile as if he meant it.

"I know, Philip, darling. How wonderful!" she said, beaming, and barely containing her excitement.

They hugged and air kissed each other on the cheeks.

"Margot Denoir. The hardest-working woman in television," Stonehedge said. "I thought you'd be spending today basking in the glow of your triumph last night."

"A thirty-eight-local share," she said.

The actor whistled. "You killed it."

She smiled wryly. "I had help from your friend, Morris Brick, his adorable brute of a dog, and of course, the actual killer."

"Just terrible what has happened," Stonehedge said, his tone turning solemn. "Drea, Faye, and Heather all gone because of that freak." Putting his acting skills to good use, he asked as if he were clueless about what the answer would be, "What are you and your crew doing here on a Malibu beach?"

"A tip." Her smile turned into something sly. "I heard that SPMK broke into one of the mansions along the East Coast Pacific Highway and escaped using the beach."

"You're kidding?"

"That's what I'm being told. It made me wonder whether it was your mansion. I tried buzzing your gate an hour ago, but nobody answered."

Stonehedge smiled as if she had to be joking. "Why would you think that?"

"It occurred to me given his other victims that Brie might be next on his list. And since she *is* your girlfriend—"

"Friend," Stonehedge corrected.

Margot made a face over his insisting on lying about Hollywood's worst-kept secret. "If you say so. How is Brie?"

"She's well."

"Hmm. I was wondering because she's not answering her cell phone, nor the buzzer at either of her residences."

"I believe she's at Palm Springs this weekend."

Margot gave him a look as if she knew he was lying, but didn't pursue it any further. "Darling, my imagination must've gotten the better of me. It's a relief to know that Brie wasn't harmed by this monster." She took a step closer to him. The way she looked at him right then made him feel like he was an insect she was studying under a magnifying glass. "Did something happen to your right eye?" she asked.

"Why?"

"It looks red. Like you've been poked in it."

"Nothing happened. Must just be allergies."

Her eyes dulled just enough to show she didn't believe him, but she let the matter drop and instead smiled sweetly at him. It really was a nice smile, and if he didn't know her better he might've forgotten that there was little difference between her and a piranha. At least if you gave the piranha a cute ass and stunning legs.

She said, "I was hoping you'd do me an enormous favor. I know that at one time you were romantically linked with SPMK's victims."

"I dated Drea years ago. The stuff about me and Faye were rumors, and nothing else." His brow furrowed as he thought more about it. "I did act with Heather once in a film. A lovely woman."

"Still, I would be so grateful if you'd let me interview you about your remembrances of these three wonderful actresses."

"Right now?"

"Yes, darling, of course. The beach would be a perfect location for it."

Stonehedge knew what she really wanted to do was sandbag him on the air. She'd gotten more than a tip, otherwise she wouldn't have been trying to hunt Brie down. If he agreed to the interview, she'd go from piranha to pit bull and wouldn't give up until she shook the truth out of him.

"Sorry, luv," he said. "But my head's in a funny place after what happened to Drea, and I need some solitude right now. A walk on the beach is about all I can handle. But it's been lovely seeing you. As always."

He turned from her and ignored her protestations as he continued his hike along the beach. While his neighbor swore she didn't have any surveillance video from last night, he wasn't sure he believed her. Even if TMZ didn't air video of him naked and out of his mind with worry as he buzzed the security gate, the story was going to come out soon, and Margot would be furious with him for not giving her an exclusive scoop this morning. But Morris had asked him if he could keep it quiet for now, and so he planned to do exactly that. Besides, Brie would want to be with him when they told their story. Maybe the two of them would reward Margot later with another prime-time special. If you were an actor you did not want Margot unhappy with you. That little blond dynamo held a lot of power in Hollywood.

It was a three-mile hike from the town beach parking lot to the cliff that bordered his property, and Stonehedge was lost in his private thoughts as he continued his trek. The events from last night still didn't seem real. Instead they were like a nightmarish delusion, as if he'd had a bad peyote trip. He still couldn't believe he'd grabbed that freak's wrist when he did. He was mostly asleep when it happened, but he'd still somehow managed that. If he hadn't, he'd be dead. Brie would be dead. Those thoughts made him shiver, even with the strong California sun beating down on him.

After leaving Margot, he had moved to the shoreline, and the waves at times ran up above his knees. He barely noticed. When he recognized the three sycamores that grew on the left side of his property, he walked toward the cliff. The wind hadn't yet erased the imprint in the sand the freak made when he landed. One foot closer to the cliff face, and he would've hit rocks instead and died.

Stonehedge closed his eyes and tried to picture the freak blindly jumping off the cliff in the pitch-black of night and surviving the fall enough so that he could run a mile on the sand and escape through the first property with beach access.

It would make a hell of a movie, he thought.

He began thinking he should hire a screenwriter and produce the movie himself. The more he thought about it, the more he liked the idea. He just wasn't sure which role he'd want to play. Himself or the killer.

Chapter 55

The killer was inside one of the large downtown LA chain drugstores, and he moved like a crippled old man as he hobbled to the pharmacy window located in the back of the store. He placed two knee braces and three elastic bandages that he needed for his wrist and ankles on the counter. The pharmacist asked whether he'd be buying anything else.

"Yeah, I've got a prescription. Just one moment."

The killer unzipped the backpack he brought and took out a hand grenade. "Yep, here it is," the killer said as he held it up so it could be seen.

The pharmacist blinked several times. "I don't understand," he said.

"Seriously? You don't recognize a prescription for a thirty-day supply of OxyContin when you see it?"

While there was a Plexiglas partition that came down almost to the counter, there was still a one-foot gap so that customers could slide over prescriptions, money, and credit cards, and the pharmacist could slide back purchases, change, and credit card slips for signing. The setup would've worked just fine in keeping someone from robbing the pharmacy with a gun since the pharmacist would be able to duck safely behind the counter, but it provided little protection against a hand grenade. As the pharmacist stared at the small deadly device in the killer's hand, he soon understood that fact.

"I'll get your prescription for you right away," he promised, his voice fading into a frightened whisper.

"Act smart," the killer warned. "As if your life depends on it."

The pharmacist looked like he was on the verge of passing out, but he moved to a locked cabinet on the other side of his area. His hands shook as he unlocked the cabinet. The killer caught him glancing at a door twenty feet away, and knew what the man had to be thinking. Could he make it through the door in time? It was a good question. The hand grenade had a five-and-a-half-second fuse, not that the pharmacist knew that. The killer decided the odds of the man escaping were about fifty percent. The pharmacist must've either decided the odds weren't good enough or he didn't have it in him to give it a try, because a look of defeat settled over his features, and instead of glancing again at the door that might've taken him to safety, he began counting out pills.

The drugstore had opened promptly at seven a.m., while the in-store pharmacy didn't open until nine-thirty. The killer had waited until ten minutes before then to hobble into the store and pick up the knee braces and elastic bandages that he badly needed so he could bring them to the pharmacist just as the man had finished unlocking the cash register. At that early hour on a Sunday, the drugstore had few employees, and there were no other pharmacy customers waiting.

The killer had disguised himself with a prosthetic nose and chin, fake teeth, and a wig and facial hair that gave him unruly red hair and a scraggly beard and mustache. Along with several grenades, he had also brought a .38 caliber pistol, which he would use if needed. While it could be argued that it was pure hubris on his part not to have brought the gun with him when he broke into Stonehedge's home, and that he was now paying the price for his arrogance, the killer had his reasons. From the moment he had decided he was going to hurt Brick by slaughtering Stonehedge, he had envisioned so clearly cutting the actor's throat from ear to ear that the thought of bringing a gun just seemed not only unimportant, but sacrilege. He knew he'd be able to sneak through Stonehedge's bedroom without making a peep, just as he knew he'd be able to drug Evans without her stirring enough to wake her boyfriend. It just made no sense that Stonehedge would be able to grab his wrist the way he did.

The killer winced in pain as he watched the pharmacist dispensing the OxyContin. He felt as if he'd been in a bad car crash, with his body aching from head to toe. Along with the overall soreness, he believed he had a broken wrist, torn ligaments in his knees and ankles, and maybe even shin splints. He still couldn't believe he'd been able to run along the beach after jumping off that cliff. It must've been fear and adrenaline pushing him, because he could barely walk now. The fear that had consumed him back on the beach wasn't of being caught, but of his death machine not completing.

Things had not gone well over the last twenty-four hours, to put it bluntly. He had lost his chance to grab Brie Evans. He accepted it. He would now have to go with a different option. A much lesser one. But he could still plunge LA into chaos and destruction. Everything was still in place for that to happen. He'd be cheating with this last domino, but few people other than himself would ever know that. Brick would, and that fact galled him, but when the oil wells blew and LA was swallowed up by earthquakes and fires, it wouldn't much matter what Brick knew or thought. At least the killer had to keep telling himself that.

The pharmacist brought a prescription bottle filled with pills back to the counter. Before he could slide this through the opening, the killer told him to open the bottle and show him one of the pills. The pharmacist did this. The pill was larger than the killer expected it to be and it was blue instead of white.

"I thought it was supposed to be white," the killer said.

"Different potencies are different colors."

That made sense to the killer. And he did see the letters "OC" etched onto the pill. He told the pharmacist to slide the bottle through the opening. While the guy had every right to be scared given that the killer was threatening him with a hand grenade, he had picked something else up from him.

"You must've recognized me," he said.

The pharmacist, alarmed, shook his head, but there was a certain look in his eyes that said otherwise.

"It doesn't matter," the killer said, sighing. "Lie down on your stomach, close your eyes, and a count to a hundred before moving. You do that, and maybe you'll live through this."

The pharmacist did as he was directed. The killer had told the truth. It didn't much matter whether the pharmacist knew that he was who the media was calling by that ridiculous name: *The Sex Pervert Maniac Killer*. By the end of today this would all be finished. The final act of his machine would be unveiled and the killer would be flying to South America to recuperate and rest. By the time the authorities learned his true identity, he'd have bought himself a new identity and altered his appearance with enough cosmetic surgeries that he wouldn't have to worry about using prosthetics again. The killer knew all this was true. He didn't need to kill this pharmacist who was lying on the floor quaking in fear. This wasn't part of his death machine, only something he needed to do so he could see the day through. But when he had thought about Brick moments earlier and how badly his masterpiece had been marred, it put him in an exceptionally rotten mood.

The killer pulled the pin on the hand grenade, counted to two, and dropped it next the pharmacist. He'd leave the pharmacist's life to chance. After all, the man still had three and a half seconds to keep his wits about him and toss the grenade through the opening between the counter and the Plexiglas partition.

As the killer limped his way toward the back door, he took another grenade from the backpack, pulled the pin, and rolled it down the aisle. He was walking out of the store when he heard the first grenade detonate. The explosion was louder than he thought it would be.

Chapter 56

Even though he had joked with Morris about this very thing happening, Bogle could barely believe it when the man stepped out of the house and pointed a 9mm pistol at him.

"Take it easy there, fella," Bogle said. In a slow, fluid movement he started to raise his hands in surrender, but then flicked his right hand into the man's gun wrist, knocking the pistol aside so it no longer pointed at him while also grabbing his wrist. Simultaneously, he stepped forward with his left foot and twisted his body so he was parallel to the gun arm while using his open left palm to strike the elbow. The speed and power of the twisting motion of his body would've delivered enough force to make the man drop his weapon, but Bogle put extra muscle into it so that the man cried out in pain, and he felt well justified in doing so. Morris's actor friend, Stonehedge, could stand in front of someone's door at three a.m. butt naked and pound on it like a wild man, yet here he was at a quarter to ten on a sunny Sunday morning, clean-shaven and wearing a suit, and he's the one someone's going to point a gun at? The thought of it pissed him off.

"You broke my arm," the man complained as he clutched his injured elbow.

"Your elbow is hyperextended, that's all. Otherwise you'd be either passed out or screaming." Bogle picked up the dropped gun, pulled out the magazine, and emptied its bullets into his hand. He ejected the round in the gun's chamber, then dropped the bullets into his suit jacket pocket. "What are you doing pointing a gun at me?" he demanded.

The man showed an aggrieved expression. "What are you doing snooping around my door?"

"You mean knocking on your door?"

"Those are your words, not mine."

"I wanted to ask you about your neighbor, Mark Sangonese."

"How am I supposed to know that?" The man sniffed peevishly as he rubbed his elbow. "For all I know you could be that psycho who's all over the news."

For a long moment Bogle could only gawk at the man who had held a gun on him.

"You jackass," he said. "The police reports have the suspect as five feet ten, a hundred and seventy pounds. I'm six feet one and two hundred and ten pounds. And I don't look anything like him."

"That's who I thought you were when I looked out my window and saw you hanging around my door," the man argued.

"Why in the world would this psycho drive to Long Beach to break into your house? You got any blond starlets stashed away in there?"

The man gave him a confused look, not picking up on Bogle's sarcasm. "I don't understand what you mean."

"Forget it." He handed the man back his now empty gun. "Like I told you before I'm trying to get ahold of your neighbor—"

"That's your problem."

The man tried to scoot back inside his house, but before he could close the door, Bogle stepped forward, blocking him. A dog barked angrily inside. Fortunately, the animal must've been kept in a closed room, because if it was anywhere near as ill-tempered as its owner, the situation would've become even more unpleasant.

"Uh uh," Bogle said. "When you pointed your gun at me without any legal justification, it became your problem also. You're going to do everything you can to help me, or I'm going to drag your ass down to the precinct on West Broadway and have you booked for assault and battery with a deadly weapon."

"What are you talking about? You were the one who assaulted me!"

"My force was justified. What you did wasn't. You can't just point a gun at anyone who knocks on your door."

"It's my property!" the man insisted, his face folding into a perfect picture of belligerence. "You saying I can't use a gun to protect my property? This is America, ain't it?"

Bogle sighed. "You want to argue with me? I was on the LAPD for sixteen years. Right now, I'm deputized by them. If you want we can go down to the West Broadway precinct and see which one of us gets booked. Or you can help me find your neighbor."

The man's face screwed up as if he were going to argue some more, but he must've thought better of it, and instead said he didn't know where Sangonese was. "We're not exactly friends," he said.

"I can give you Maria's cell phone," a woman's voice said.

Bogle looked past the man to see that they'd been joined by a thin and pale woman wearing a ratty cloth robe and pink fuzzy slippers. She was standing by what looked like the kitchen entrance. Her husband shot her an angry look but otherwise held his tongue.

"Maria is Mark Sangonese's wife?" Bogle asked.

"That's right. I think they're in church now. I know Maria goes every Sunday, but I'm afraid I can't tell you which one."

Finally, someone in this house who wasn't a complete jackass!

"Ma'am, her cell phone number will be just fine."

* * * *

Maria Sangonese's cell phone rang to voicemail right away, which meant it was turned off. Instead of driving to every church in the Long Beach area to find Mark Sangonese, Bogle had the LAPD locate the address of the cell phone. Services were still going on when he walked into the church. He spotted Sangonese in the third pew with a woman who must've been his wife, Maria, and four girls ranging from tiny to teenager. Bogle squeezed past several of the churchgoers in the pew behind Sangonese so he could tap the Samson Oil & Gas manager on the shoulder. Sangonese turned and gave him a confused smile as if he were having trouble placing Bogle.

"We talked in your office a few days ago," Bogle said in a whisper that seemed to carry throughout the church. "I was looking for Karl Crawford then. We need to talk. It's urgent."

A glimmer of recognition showed in Sangonese's eyes. His smile stayed frozen on his face, but from the way he looked at Bogle he couldn't fathom what Bogle could possibly want from him.

"I'm sorry, but can't this wait until the service is over?"

"No. We think someone is planning to blow up your oil wells."

What remained of Sangonese's frozen smile turned sickly as if he thought this had to be a bad joke. Once he realized Bogle was serious, he moved quickly, squeezing himself past his family. He followed Bogle out of the church, and once they were alone outside he demanded that Bogle explain himself.

"What the heck is going on here? You first come to me about the disappearance of one of my employees, and now you're stalking me at church to tell me some sort of cockamamie story about oil wells being blown up?"

"Calm down, okay? How about you read this."

Bogle pulled from his inside jacket pocket a copy of the letter the LA mayor's office provided deputizing MBI's employees for investigating Heather Brandley's murder.

Sangonese at first seemed too incensed to understand what he was reading, but as he stared at the letter his expression changed more into a look of bewilderment.

"This is about that madman who's killing those actresses?" he asked.

"Yeah. This psycho's not just killing actresses. We know he's in possession of six hundred pounds of stolen C-4. We also know he wants to blow up oil wells around LA, thinking that will trigger some sort of cataclysmic earthquake. What we suspect is that he killed Karl Crawford so he'd be hired as Crawford's replacement, which would give him the opportunity to hide explosives in the well casings."

"I didn't hire anyone to replace Karl," Sangonese said.

Bogle had been sure that it happened the way he believed it did. The pieces just fit too nicely together for it to be any other way. What Sangonese said left him puzzled.

"How'd you get Crawford's work done if you didn't replace him?"

Sangonese frowned. "Due to the planned revamping of our remote monitoring capabilities, I was going to reduce the headcount by one and fire our lowest performer. After Karl went missing, I had to keep the other service tech onboard."

"Who was that?"

"Brad Pettibone." Sangonese looked away from Bogle and chewed on his thumbnail. When he shifted his gaze back to Bogle, he looked like someone who'd been told a joke a few minutes earlier and was only now getting the punch line. He said, "The funny thing is, Pettibone was supposed to service four wells yesterday, but he didn't show up at any of them. I couldn't reach him either. I tried calling him a dozen times, but he wasn't answering his phone."

Chapter 57

Todd Blankenford arranged for a taxi to whisk Mary Anne Callahan away, and once the coffee did its job and made his head feel like it was no longer going to split apart, he mixed half a quart of top quality tequila with the correct proportions of orange juice, pineapple juice, and grenadine to make a pitcher of his slightly altered version of a tequila sunrise. It wasn't so much to have a hair of the dog as a way to slip comfortably into the day. Still draped in only his robe, he brought the pitcher, a glass, and the Sunday paper to the patio, and settled down on a lounge chair. At some point he must've drifted off, because he was startled awake by the sound of an intruder approaching. When he saw that the man had unruly red hair and a scraggly beard and mustache, he thought this must be the Callahan young Mary Anne had married.

"Let's be civilized," Blankenford suggested, his body tensing as he prepared to make a run for it.

If the intruder was indeed a cuckolded husband hell-bent on revenge, he didn't act the part given the *ah-shucks* apologetic smile he showed.

"Ah, man, I'm sorry," the intruder said. "I tried ringing your bell, but no one answered. I heard someone rustling around back here, and thought I'd check it out."

"You must've heard me snoring," Blankenford said cautiously. He was still preparing to bolt if necessary. He wished he could see the man's eyes so he could tell whether violence was imminent, but the man had them covered with dark shades. "What's this about?"

"I guess it would help if I introduced myself," the intruder said, shaking his head over his indiscretion. "Do you mind?"

The intruder had nodded toward a nearby chair. Blankenford gestured for him to sit, and the intruder shuffled over to the chair, moving with his legs bent in an extremely bowlegged way, as if he were imitating a crab. The director guessed the man must've hurt his knees, maybe his ankles too. He noticed the thick bandage wrapped around the man's right wrist.

"God only knows what you must be thinking having some strange dude walk into your private backyard like this," the intruder said with an amused grin. "My name's Marty Luce. I'm a detective working out of LAPD's homicide division on those crazy killings being done by the guy they're calling SPMK."

"Your name sounds familiar," Blankenford said. "Have we met before?"

"I don't know. I worked vice before homicide. Could I have run into you then?"

Blankenford thought about it, and decided it was just one of those names. On closer inspection, he also realized this wasn't someone sweet Mary Anne would've married. She would've hitched up with a young stud closer to her age. Someone much better looking. Bigger and broader also. This guy was too scrawny for someone like Mary Anne.

"Sex Pervert Maniac Killer," Blankenford said as he remembered what SPMK stood for.

"Yeah, that's the one. Quite a mouthful, huh?" Luce chuckled to himself. "You'd think the media could've come up with something easier on the tongue, like the Star Killer. That name would've made so much more sense, especially since the whole pervert stuff is a lie that us cops are spreading."

"Really? Why would you guys lie about that?"

"A tactic we're using to get under his skin. Between you and me, this guy's too smart to fall for something like that."

Blankenford cleared his throat and sat up straighter in the lounge chair. "What exactly are you here for, detective?"

"It would help if I told you that, huh?" Luce again shook his head, as if he couldn't believe the way he'd been acting. "The media hasn't gotten ahold of this yet, but this guy, the Star Killer—"

"You mean SPMK?"

Luce made a face. "Again, not a good name. But whatever." He seemed to lose his train of thought, and Blankenford prompted him about what the media didn't know.

"Yeah, sorry about that. This guy's absolutely brilliant, and he's got us chasing around in circles so much he's leaving all of us dizzy. But as I was saying, he tried to abduct Brie Evans last night—"

"My God! Brie also? Is she okay?"

"She's fine. Not even a scratch. But it made me think about this funny coincidence. The three actresses he killed, plus Brie Evans, were all in a movie you made."

"*The Satan Plan*," Blankenford said. "Dreadful film."

"I don't know. I saw it when it came out and thought it was pretty good."

"So you're the one."

"Ha ha. Good one. But I'm thinking it might not be so much a coincidence. This guy might be targeting the actresses from your movie."

"I had the same thought earlier when I saw in today's paper that SPMK killed Faye Riverstone," Blankenford said.

"You mean the Star Killer."

"The maniac," Blankenford conceded.

"Did you call the police about that thought?"

"I was going to, but I got distracted," Blankenford admitted.

"No harm done. But I'm thinking he might not be after just the blond bimbo actresses from the film. You might be in danger too."

Blankenford looked alarmed by that prospect. Up until that moment he'd only been worried about enraged husbands chasing after him. Because Mary Anne Callahan wasn't the only married young thing he'd slept with over the past year.

"Should I be getting police protection?" he asked.

"That's something we need to talk about. How about we go inside? I'm sweating like a pig out here."

"Sure. Certainly."

Blankenford didn't need to see the cop's eyes to know the guy was stoned. Not weed, though. If he had to guess, this Luce character had shot up with heroin, and was now floating. Blankenford had learned long ago that the right cops could help you score weed and coke, or if they weren't holding, could point you to someone who was, and because of that he always made it a point to cozy up to the cops working security details or other jobs on the TV shows and movies he directed. Over the years he had gotten blotto drunk more than a few times with cops he had gotten to know, and had even done coke with some of them. Because of this, the thought of a cop being a heroin junkie didn't seem impossible. Or maybe Luce wasn't shooting up, but instead using prescription opioids.

As Blankenford led Luce through the patio doors and into the kitchen, he couldn't help thinking something was wrong. The guy just didn't seem like any cop he'd ever known. More than that, there was something off-putting about him. But if he wasn't a cop, who was he?

Blankenford realized then why the cop's name had sounded so familiar. *Martin Luce* was the name of the madman from *The Satan Plan*. He stumbled in his panic as he understood who this man *really* was.

He gave a little scream as he lunged for the open bottle of tequila sitting on the countertop, and grabbed the bottle by the neck. What slowed him down for a brief half second was worrying about all the tequila that would spill out when he swung the bottle at the psycho masquerading as a cop.

That half second was all the killer needed to stick a hunting knife into Blankenford's kidney.

Chapter 58

Morris had never met a geology professor before so he had no idea what to expect, but if he didn't know better he would've guessed Andrew Hastings was a retired cop instead of a university professor. A large rough-hewn man with a bald head, craggy face, and bushy steel-gray mustache. On second thought, Morris decided it made perfect sense for a geology professor to physically resemble a rock formation.

Hastings's hands were heavily veined, and a twinkle lit up his eyes as he greeted Morris at the door and welcomed him into his house.

"I saw you on TV last night," Hastings said, his voice as craggy and rough as his features. "I'm more than a little curious why you're interested in that movie I consulted on."

"The reason's simple. I'd like to know whether blowing up oil wells around LA could trigger a massive earthquake."

"I figured as much, but why? What does that have to do with this madman you're chasing?"

"What I'm telling you is confidential," Morris said. "And I'd like to ask that you keep it as such."

"Of course."

"The psycho seems to be a fan of *The Satan Plan*."

"Jesus," Hastings mouthed, his eyes taking on a faraway look as if he were remembering something from years ago. "I hadn't thought about it until now, but those young actresses he murdered were all in the film."

"We also believe he's in possession of six hundred pounds of stolen C-4."

"And you think he's planning to use it to blow up oil wells? Six hundred pounds of C-4. Jesus." Hastings didn't need much time to think about it before telling Morris it could be disastrous.

"How many oil wells do you think there are within a thirty-mile radius of Los Angeles?" he asked.

"I've noticed a few," Morris said.

"Thirty-five hundred. Let's go to my study so I can demonstrate with computer simulation what would happen if as few as forty of them were blown up."

As the geology professor led Morris through his home, he asked Morris how many earthquakes he thought Oklahoma had had during the past year.

"Half a dozen?" Morris guessed.

"Over eighteen hundred. Do you want to guess what caused these earthquakes?"

"They were manmade?"

"Yep. And not by blowing up oil wells, but by injecting wastewater into disposal wells. But what they're doing in Oklahoma is child's play compared to what we're talking about here. Blowing up forty oil wells would introduce a significant stress along the San Andreas fault lines, and if my work in the area is correct, it would force the North American tectonic plate under the Pacific tectonic plate."

"That would be bad?"

"I'd say so."

Hastings brought Morris into his study, which was cluttered with papers and stacks of books, and had framed magazine covers and articles hung on the walls. The geology professor took a seat at the computer in a worn but comfortable-looking leather chair, and Morris pulled up a chair alongside him. The computer was already on, and Hastings brought up a map of California. After a few mouse clicks, a thick red line stretching from northern California almost to Brawley in the southernmost part of the state overlaid the map.

"The San Andreas fault line," Hastings explained.

After another couple of mouse clicks, another red line was drawn, this one running over the Salton Sea so that it appeared parallel to the San Andreas Fault.

"The Salton Trough Fault," Hastings said.

After more mouse clicks, more faults lines were drawn on the map.

"As you can see, Southern California has a good deal of seismic activity. Blowing up and, in effect, setting fire to oil wells around LA would create a major geological disturbance. Let me demonstrate."

After more mouse clicks, thousands of tiny dots representing oil wells were drawn on the map.

"I worked with a certain government agency to develop this software, the name of which I'm not at liberty to tell you," Hastings said, his voice heavier and rougher than earlier. "I'm going to select forty wells from Long Beach to LA, and we'll see what the effect will be if, say, eight pounds of C-4 are used on each of them."

"Why eight pounds?"

Hastings grimaced as if he were suffering from a bad case of heartburn. "If I remember right, that was what was used in the movie."

Morris's cell phone rang. Annie Walsh. He excused himself and left the study so he could talk privately. When he answered the phone, Walsh told him that someone had robbed the downtown Ritegreens using a hand grenade.

"He wanted painkillers," Morris guessed.

"That's right. A thirty-day supply of OxyContin. Also a couple of knee braces and elastic bandages."

"Did he kill anyone there?"

"He exploded two grenades. The pharmacist took some shrapnel and is at UCLA Medical. He's shook up pretty bad, but he'll live. Miraculously no one else was hurt."

"When did this happen?"

"Over an hour ago."

"A hand grenade was used and we're just finding out now?"

Walsh let out a pronounced sigh. "What can I say?"

"Okay, forget it. Who's handling it from LAPD's end?"

"I am."

"I'll send over one of my guys. Fred or Polk, your choice?"

"Do I need to tell you?"

"No, you don't. I think I know what this psycho's endgame is. He's planning to blow up oil wells. He thinks it will cause a massive earthquake that will destroy LA."

There was a heavy silence from Walsh's end. Then, "Any chance he's right?"

"I'm talking right now with a UCLA professor who thinks it could happen. I'll call Fred about Ritegreens and will call you back when I know more."

Morris got off the phone with Walsh and called Lemmon, who answered on the first ring.

"I got to MBI a little while ago," Lemmon said. "Adam filled me in on what's going on. You think this lunatic is really trying to cause an earthquake?"

"I don't know," Morris admitted. "Right now I'm working on that assumption. An hour ago, he robbed the downtown Ritegreens using grenades. He wanted OxyContin."

"So he hurt himself when he jumped off the cliff behind your actor buddy's property."

"It appears so."

"And if he's got the stolen grenades he's probably also got the stolen C-4."

"Again, that's the assumption. Annie's working the robbery, and I want you to work it with her."

"Okay, will do. Morris, just as well you're giving me this. I hit a wall looking at guys with grudges against you. I don't think you have any history with this guy. If he has a beef with you, it's in his head only."

"I'm thinking that as well."

Morris put his cell phone away and joined Hastings in the study. The geology professor gave him a quick sideways glance and commented that from Morris's expression, the news he got didn't appear to be good.

"More confirmation that he has the stolen C-4."

"I figured as much. I've got everything set up, but I suspect the results won't cheer you up any."

The UCLA professor used the mouse to press a button labeled "Start." After several seconds, the number 9.2 flashed on the screen.

"I'm guessing that's not good news either," Morris said.

"No. it's not. That's the magnitude earthquake the simulation is predicting. To put that number in perspective, we expect the shifting of the tectonic plates to eventually cause a 7.0 magnitude earthquake, which LA will be able to handle with a minimal amount of damage. An 8.0 magnitude earthquake would release thirty times more energy, and would cause approximately two hundred billion dollars' worth of damage and a death toll estimated at two thousand lives. An event that causes subduction—forcing one tectonic plate below another—is a whole different ball game, and a 9.0 magnitude earthquake would release a thousand times more energy."

"What would the damage be?"

"Catastrophic. Toppled buildings, gas mains and water lines rupturing, fires raging. Death toll in the hundreds of thousands." Hastings showed a pained smile as he rubbed his eyes with his index finger and thumb. When he stopped, his eyes had a reddish look. "But this is only a simulation. Purely theoretical. It might not work out this way."

The look he gave Morris showed he didn't believe that to be the case.

Chapter 59

Charlie Bogle didn't bother getting a search warrant for Pettibone's studio apartment, and instead tracked down the building's live-in superintendent. He flashed the super his old LAPD police badge, and explained to him about Pettibone's suspected involvement with the maniac who was killing Hollywood actresses.

"There was something about that guy I never liked," the super said, nodding to himself over this confirmation. "Always an unfriendly puss on his face. Not once ever saying a kind word."

"It's worse than that. We think he wired up his apartment with explosives to blow up the building."

The super was a short, stocky man in his forties, and he gave Bogle a look as if he had to be kidding. "This ain't some sort of joke?" he asked.

"Unfortunately, no. That's the evidence we got."

The last part was a lie, but only a little one. Bogle remembered Pettibone's churlish disposition when he met the man at the oil well, and he thought it likely that if Pettibone was planting explosives in oil wells, he'd save some for his apartment.

The super started blinking nervously as he realized that Bogle was serious. "Don't you need a search warrant?" he asked.

"Not at all. As a representative of the building's owner, you can let me in."

"Yeah, okay." More rapid blinking. "Should I be knocking on doors and getting people out of here?"

"Not a bad idea. How about you give me the key to the apartment, and I'll bring it back to you when I'm done."

The super's hands shook as he struggled to remove a key from a large chain he kept attached to a belt loop. Once he handed over the key, the super hurried away.

Pettibone had a first-floor apartment, and as Bogle walked up a flight of stairs from the basement where the super lived, he wondered what the odds were that Pettibone had a bomb in his apartment. He decided it was less than fifty percent for the simple reason that Pettibone most likely went missing because the psycho killer got rid of him. It wasn't any accident that the anonymous call about "Reuben" came from Buena Park, the same city where Pettibone lived. If Pettibone was working with Reuben, he must've thought about turning the guy in for a reward after he saw the trumped-up news stories about the killer's sexual deviancies. Maybe he tried squeezing extra money out of Reuben. If that was the case, he could've gotten himself killed before he had a chance to rig his apartment up with C-4. But even if all that was true, there could still be a bomb.

Bogle stood motionless in front of Pettibone's apartment door and wondered if there was a bomb what the likelihood was that it would be rigged up to explode if someone opened the door. That type of trigger would be a lot more work than setting one up to work off a timer or a cell phone call. Bogle decided if there was a bomb it would be triggered by a cell phone, since that would be the easiest trigger to rig up and Pettibone would know for sure when it went off. Even though Bogle knew this made sense, he held his breath after unlocking the door, then stood motionless for a good ten count with his hand on the doorknob.

His cell phone rang suddenly and it nearly gave him a heart attack. He frowned at the caller ID. Mark Sangonese was calling.

"I just searched the last well Pettibone serviced and there was no bomb," Sangonese complained. "This is not how I want to be spending my Sunday."

"That's only one well," Bogle said. "Check more of them, okay?"

Sangonese hung up.

Bogle took another deep breath and carefully turned the doorknob, trying to feel for any resistance. The door clicked open, and no explosion. He opened it a crack, then slid the letter he had showed Sangonese earlier from the top of the door to the bottom trying to find a trip wire. After that he ever-so-gently opened the door, his heart thumping crazily by the time he was done.

"Okay," he whispered to himself to calm down. "No explosives yet."

He had brought a Phillips screwdriver with him, but Pettibone had a small tool chest in his apartment, and Bogle used tools from that to take the closet door off its hinges and the back off the dresser bureau. He worked cautiously, but he didn't find any C-4 that had been rigged to explode. He did, though, find hidden in the sock drawer an authentic-looking passport for Robert Jones with Pettibone's picture. In the same drawer, he also found an airplane ticket to Bangkok, Thailand, that was supposed to leave LAX that morning at seven fifteen.

He turned on Pettibone's laptop computer and was trying different passwords to unlock it when he received another call from Mark Sangonese. This time he barely recognized the Samson Oil & Gas manager's voice. It sounded tinny and unnatural.

"I couldn't hear what you said," Bogle told him.

Sangonese cleared his throat. "One of my guys found a package at another well," he said. "It was hidden behind one of the compressors. It's square, and he doesn't know what's in it, but it weighs about ten pounds."

Chapter 60

Polk thought the metallic black Bentley sedan parked in MBI's lot stuck out like a sore thumb. It didn't surprise him when he found one of the killer's fercockta cards stuck under the windshield wiper. He called Morris.

"Our twisted friend left a Bentley in our parking lot," he said. "He also left you one of his calling cards. Here's what he wrote: *Brick, unless you're a lot smarter than I think you are, the beginning of the end starts today at four p.m.*"

"You said this was left on a Bentley?"

"Yeah, pretty fancy-looking car."

"Hmm. Unfortunately, I have an idea what's in the trunk, but have the bomb squad check it out. I should be back in the office in twenty minutes."

"Will do."

Polk kept his distance from the Bentley in case either some of the missing C-4 or one or more grenades were being used as a booby trap, and made a call to the bomb squad. After they arrived and secured the area, he headed inside to MBI's office suite. A few minutes later he was talking to Adam Felger when Morris arrived.

"Bomb squad still doing their thing?" Polk asked.

Morris told him that when he had pulled into the lot they were drilling a hole in the trunk so they could look inside. "Do we know whose car it is?" he asked.

"Computer boy figured it out," Polk said. "A TV director."

"The one who directed *The Satan Plan*?"

"The same one," Felger said.

Morris heard the outer door for the suite open, and he left Felger and Polk to find one of the bomb squad members looking for him.

"There's no bomb in the trunk," the officer said. "But there is a body. Male, in his fifties."

That was pretty much what Morris was expecting. He called Annie Walsh to let her know, then grabbed Polk and the two of them headed back to the parking lot to meet Todd Blankenford, the director of *The Satan Plan*. The bomb squad had left, but in their place were plenty of LAPD officers and crime scene specialists. Morris had a quick talk with one of the detectives, and he and Polk then had a look at what was inside the Bentley's trunk.

"You'd think a luxury vehicle like this would have more trunk space," Polk noted.

Morris had to agree with him. The trunk did not appear to be very spacious, and Blankenford, who was wearing only a silk robe, looked as if his body had been folded in half so it could be crammed into the space.

"Stabbed in the back," Morris said. "I count seven wounds."

"Not a lot of blood," Polk noted.

"He must've bled out where he was stabbed."

"Four to one odds the killer got this poor sap at his home? Fifty bucks?"

"I'll pass."

Polk looked deep in thought as he rubbed the three-days' worth of stubble growing on his chin. He was either contemplating how the murder must've gone down or trying to come up with a way to tempt Morris into taking what he thought was a sucker's bet. If it was the latter, he gave up on it. "Crime scene guys are going to find a mess there," he said.

Morris slipped on a pair of latex gloves. He had noticed a slight bulge of something small and rectangular inside the bathrobe's pocket, and what he found was a flash drive.

* * * *

Fred Lemmon headed first to the downtown Ritegreens, which was busy with police, ATF agents, and FBI. He spotted Greg Malevich near the front entrance, and the detective escorted him to the back of the drugstore so he could see the damage. First up was the destruction from the grenade that exploded in the aisle. Lemmon was amazed at what he saw. The grenade didn't just blow a hole through the aisle, but obliterated it, and left the carpeting scorched, the metal racks twisted and torn, and cold remedy bottles blown to pieces.

"There's no surveillance video from inside the store," Malevich explained. "When the first grenade went off, it sent the few people in the store ducking for cover, so no one saw the perp throwing the second one."

Lemmon nodded toward the back door. "He left through there?"

"Yeah."

"He must've tossed the grenade behind him when he was leaving so no one would follow him."

"Mission accomplished."

"Any outdoor video?"

"Yeah, but nothing that's going to help much. We got the perp leaving the store and walking with his knees splayed—bowlegged-like. He must've injured himself when he jumped off the cliff behind Philip's property. That's got to be the reason he wanted the opioids. But the video doesn't show him getting into a vehicle."

"Philip, huh? You're on a first name basis with Mr. Hollywood?"

Malevich broke into a grin. "Yeah, you could say so. I spent some time with him six months ago during that Malibu Butcher business. A helluva nice guy who doesn't act like the typical hotshot actor."

Lemmon let out a soft whistle when he saw the pharmacy area. Debris was scattered throughout, and the grenade left a large blackened hole where a sink had been along the back wall.

Although it wasn't necessary, Malevich explained what happened. "The perp dropped the grenade so it landed next to the pharmacist, but he got lucky and was able to toss it into the sink that used to be back there. If he had put too much muscle into the toss, the grenade would've bounced back at him and he'd be dead now. Or at least missing several body pieces."

"Not so lucky. He still picked up shrapnel."

"Better than the alternative."

Lemmon wasn't so sure. It would've been better if the store hadn't gotten robbed. Or if the maniac hadn't dropped the grenade in the first place. Or for the pharmacist's sake, if he had called in sick that morning.

"So what's the plan?"

Malevich made a face as if he didn't have a good answer, or at least one that he liked.

"We've got officers canvassing for anyone who spotted the perp getting into a car," he said.

Lemmon didn't bother pointing out the obvious. That if any witnesses spotted the killer doing this, the odds were good they'd get the make of the car wrong. And even if a witness thought there was something suspicious about the guy and tried to pay attention to the license plate, they'd get that wrong too. It was tough enough for trained police officers to get the license plates right.

After Ritegreens, Lemmon headed to UCLA Medical Center where he found Annie Walsh alone in a waiting area. He took a seat next to her.

"Did you hear from Morris about the latest?" she asked.

"The Bentley? Yeah, he called me."

"This psycho's been busy," she forced out through clenched lips.

"I guess he didn't like the movie," Lemmon observed. "By killing the director and most of the stars, they won't be able to make a sequel."

"Funny," she said, although she didn't appear to be amused. "You've been hanging around Polk too much."

"Ouch. Sadly, that's probably true, although the accusation still wounds deeply."

Her expression weakened. "Did Morris tell you what he thinks this psycho is trying to do?"

"Cause a massive earthquake? Yeah, he told me."

"Do you think it's possible?"

Lemmon shrugged. "The guy's bat-guano crazy. I wouldn't bet on it. How come we're sitting out here?"

"The doctor needed to sedate the victim. She'll let us know when we can talk to him."

For the next seventeen minutes Walsh appeared lost in her private thoughts while Lemmon stared at his hands. He'd been carrying a torch for her from the moment he met her after joining the homicide/robbery department, but he was married then. He still was, at least technically. The last few years things had become shaky between him and Corrine. That didn't matter. Whatever feelings he had toward Walsh, he was determined to keep bottled up.

A doctor entered the waiting area and told them they could talk to the patient. "He's heavily sedated right now, but he's lucid."

They were brought to a private room. The pharmacist was lying in bed with thick bandages wrapped around his arm, middle, and thigh.

"Mr. Singer? My name's Detective Walsh, and this is a private investigator, Fred Lemmon. We're here to talk to you about what happened today at Ritegreens."

The man's eyes opened wide. He was in his thirties, and under normal circumstances might've seemed more robust, but he looked frail lying in the hospital bed.

"I was never so scared in my life," he said in the slow cadence of someone who'd been heavily sedated. "That man dropped a hand grenade right next to me. It could've killed me."

"We know."

"It didn't explode right away. I was able to pick it up and throw it behind me, and I covered my head with my arms. I was told the grenade landed in the sink. That's the only reason I wasn't hurt worse."

It was only a matter of routine since they knew the killer they were chasing was the one who had robbed the drugstore, but Walsh showed him the two police sketches they had.

"He wasn't bald, and didn't have blond hair either." Singer squinted as if he were trying to picture the man's face. "He had red hair and a beard. Also, his nose was much bigger. Crooked too. And his chin was pointy and longer. But he told me who he was."

"He gave you a name?" Walsh asked, surprised.

"No, not that. But he told me he was the one killing those actresses." Singer looked confused and bit down on his thumb as if he were trying to remember something. "No, that's not right. He didn't say it like that. But that's what he meant from the way he looked at me when he told me I must've recognized him."

"Did he have any resemblance to the sketches?"

Singer frowned as he looked again at the sketches. "He was wearing dark sunglasses so I couldn't see his eyes. Maybe the shape of his face if you ignore his chin."

"Anything else you can tell us?"

"He didn't seem to know anything about OxyContin," Singer said. "He asked for a thirty-day supply, but he didn't specify the dosage." He blinked several times. "I gave him the highest one. A hundred and sixty milligrams. That's meant for people with an opioid tolerance."

That interested Lemmon. "What happens when he takes it?"

"If he doesn't have a tolerance?"

"Yeah."

"It depends on how many he takes at one time. If he only takes one, the immediate effects could be feelings of euphoria, drowsiness, lethargy, nausea, and respiratory depression."

"What do you mean respiratory depression? He could stop breathing?"

"It's possible."

"Let's hope that's what happens," Walsh said.

"What happens if he takes more than one?"

"Three hundred and twenty milligrams for someone with no tolerance could be lethal. At the very least, it should knock him out for a good long while. Maybe even put him in a coma. Definitely lethal if he chews on a pill instead of swallowing it."

"One can only wish," Lemmon said.

"Amen," Walsh added.

Chapter 61

"The best-laid plans," the killer murmured under his breath as he worked to alter the Rube Goldberg machine into something deadly. This was the machine he had constructed in the front of his workshop. The harmless one. But it was always meant to be made into a killing machine, so the killer didn't have to make too many changes to it.

As he oh-so-carefully added a special trip wire to the machine, he realized he'd lost his train of thought. This had been happening often since he took the OxyContin. Given how hazy his mind had become, it was a good thing he had only taken one pill instead of the two he'd originally planned. He remembered then that he was going to say something about mice and men, and that got him giggling. Men were soon going to be dying by the thousands, but so were mice. Rats and cats and dogs also. Cockroaches were probably going to be spared. LA would be burning to the ground, but cockroaches would find a way to scuttle to safe places, just as the killer had his plan for escape.

He stopped and tilted his head as he tried to think what any of that had to do with mice and men. He giggled again as he remembered what he was going to say. *The best-laid plans of mice and men.* He'd been giggling a lot since taking that pill. He didn't giggle when he threw the grenades. Later he did when he was alone in the car and remembered the way that pharmacist looked when he showed him the grenade. Eyes bugging out. It was like something from an old Bugs Bunny cartoon. He hadn't seen one of those since he was a little kid, but he used to like them. The way one event would lead to the next. Kind of like a Rube Goldberg machine.

The killer lost his train of thought again. Something about giggling. He remembered that he had giggled when he stuck the knife into that movie director's back. It wasn't exactly funny, but it sort of was. The way the knife just seemed to go in so easily, like he was pushing it into a warmed-up tub of butter. The little yelp the director gave was also kind of funny, at least it struck the killer as such. Also, the way *Blankenfart*, or whatever his name was, just seemed to crumple to the floor. The killer stuck the knife into him more times to see if he'd find that funny also. He didn't, although he still giggled with each thrust.

He knew it was the OxyContin making him silly, because he acted like a goofball with *Blankenfart,* which had to be why the guy realized at the last moment the killer wasn't a cop. He could be excused for his behavior. He'd always been a straight arrow, and had never tried any recreational drugs before, not even as much as a puff of weed. He'd also never taken any prescription painkillers. This was all new to him. The opioid might be muddling up his thoughts, but at least he could move around and squat and kneel and do all the other things he needed to do, even though he was walking awfully funny. There wasn't much chance he would've been able to get *Blankenfart*'s body into the trunk of the Bentley if he hadn't taken the OxyContin. Or climb a ladder like he did minutes ago. His knees and ankles were a mess, and he was going to be in a great deal of pain when the medication wore off, but he'd worry about that later. Because something very big was soon going to be happening.

What was that again about mice and men?

He stopped what he was doing and squeezed his eyes tight, trying hard to cut through the fog in his brain. He was determined to remember. It just seemed important that he do so. He didn't giggle this time as the answer came to him. *Death*. So many of them were going to die. He hoped Morris Brick wasn't going to be one of them. He wanted Brick to witness the devastation. He wanted his nemesis crushed by the knowledge that he had failed to save anyone. Unless Brick was a complete idiot, he must've made the connection with what the killer was doing and the movie *The Satan Plan*, but that wasn't going to help him. By the time Brick realized who the killer was, it would all be over.

If Brick survived what was coming, he'd find this studio eventually, maybe weeks from now, and the killer wanted to make sure everything was ready for when that happened.

The killer broke out giggling over the idea of Brick being killed by his very last Rube Goldberg machine.

Chapter 62

The flash drive the killer had left in Todd Blankenford's robe contained a single video file. Morris played it for the MBI team and Gloria Finston. The video file was a scene from *The Satan Plan*, and it showed LA hit by a massive earthquake.

"Kind of cheesy filmmaking if you ask me," Polk remarked, unimpressed.

"True, but according to UCLA Professor Andrew Hastings, an accurate depiction of what will happen if he blows up as few as forty oil wells. Charlie, what did the bomb squad determine about the package hidden in the well outside of Torrance?"

Bogle had already told Morris about this, but he reported to the rest of the room that it was a bomb made with ten pounds of C-4. "He used a triggering device that's activated by a sequence of radio frequencies."

Finston asked, "Will they be able to search all the oil wells by four o'clock?"

"Not a chance. Since the Kansas armory robbery, Brad Pettibone serviced a hundred and eighty-seven different wells. If the search is limited to only those, the police expect it will take over twenty-four hours to clear them."

"Even if they could do it by four, what are the odds this wackadoodle will play fair and wait until then?" Polk asked.

"Not good," Finston admitted.

Morris looked at the hardened expressions worn by his investigators. These were seasoned ex-cops who'd seen it all and knew they were in a bad situation. Gloria Finston looked more preoccupied than worried. He cleared his throat to get everyone's attention.

"All ATF, Homeland Security, and FBI agents who were added to the investigation yesterday are now being deployed in one of two ways—investigating maintenance techs employed by oil companies with wells in the Los Angeles area, or securing the local airfields since this maniac may be planning to use a small plane to trigger the bombs. Hadley's also not going to be providing us any more personnel. This is leaving us thinner than I had hoped, but we're not going to just sit here and wait until four o'clock."

"What's the plan? For us to hightail it out of LA?" Polk asked with a straight face.

"That's one way to go. But I was thinking instead we try to catch this bastard."

"Isn't that what we've been trying to do?" Lemmon asked.

"Yeah, and he's been doing a good job running us around in circles. But we're now going to take the game to him. This guy has an obsession with Rube Goldberg machines, and I asked Adam yesterday to put together a list of Rube Goldberg aficionados in the area."

"I didn't know there was such a thing," Lemmon said.

"It appears there is." Morris picked up a copy of the list Felger had put together and gave it a quick look. "According to Adam's research there are seven people in the greater LA area who've posted Rube Goldberg machine videos on YouTube or elsewhere on the Internet, four of whom professionally build these machines. He also added thirteen names of area people who are members of different Rube Goldberg interest groups."

"There are people who make money building these crazy things?" Polk asked.

"Supposedly."

"Funny world. Where is computer boy?"

"Adam's busy on another task." Morris handed copies of the list to Bogle, Polk, and Lemmon. "We're going out together in pairs. This maniac is too dangerous for us to tackle alone. Charlie and I will take the names east of Interstate 110. That divides things up evenly. You'll see that some names on the list have an 'N' next to them. That means Adam was able to determine either by photos or age they're not the killer, but we still need to show them the police sketches since they might know him."

"Since they might be traveling in the same circles," Bogle remarked.

"Exactly. So if you get any other names, call Adam and he'll do whatever preliminary research he can and assign the person to the appropriate team."

Polk let out a low groan. "It's after one now. We each have ten of these Rube Goldberg *aficionados* to visit in less than three hours, assuming this psycho plays fair, and we got a good chance of more names being added to our list. Fred and me have to go as far as Ojai, which by itself is an hour-and-a-half drive. The feds or LAPD can't give us any help?"

"I asked and was given a flat no. They all claim they're being stretched too much by today's developments." Morris smiled thinly. "Hadley also called it a *fool's errand* before hanging up on me."

"What do you think?" Lemmon asked the FBI profiler.

"I think we can safely say the killer has invested a great deal of his ego in constructing these types of contraptions," Finston said. "It's reasonable to assume that he has met others in the area who share his interest."

"How come you look so conflicted then?" Lemmon asked, digging in.

She showed one of her tiny *v* smiles, although the effort seemed strained. "It's not over this, but his purpose for leaving the latest victim's body and the flash drive for us to find."

"He's just taunting us," Polk said, his thick forearms folded across his chest. "He wants to let us know what's coming."

"That's part of it," Finston conceded. "But he has other purposes. He left what he did to act as the final domino in his machine. They're supposed to be clues that lead us to the triggering event for his Armageddon."

Morris said, "I called Annie fifteen minutes ago. She's at Blankenford's home now and is tearing it apart looking for any sort of clue the maniac might've left. If there's something there, she'll find it and let me know."

"I don't think this poor unfortunate film director is meant to lead us to the triggering event. Instead it's something about the movie."

Morris grunted noncommittally over that possibility. "I'll ask Adam to look more into that idea. Gloria, will you provide Adam with whatever assistance he needs with his current task?"

"Of course."

The meeting broke up with Polk and Lemmon making a beeline out of the MBI office suite.

On the way out, Morris stopped off to talk with Felger.

Chapter 63

Morris caught up to Bogle in the parking lot. He offered to drive and Bogle didn't argue. They'd barely gotten underway when Bogle commented that he had called his ex earlier.

"I told her to round up the kids and drive out of LA," he said.

"Is she going to do that?"

"Yeah. She's heading out to the desert until this blows over." He chuckled. "She's either going to be eternally grateful, or she's going to want my head on a stick."

"I hate to say this, but I'm hoping for the latter."

"Me too." Bogle gave Morris a sideways glance. "How about Natalie and Rachel? Did you send them packing?"

"I tried, but no dice." Morris made a face. "Nat flatly refused to go. I didn't even bother with Rachel. I would've gotten nowhere with her. Out of the three of them, Parker's the least bullheaded."

"You're thinking then that this could actually happen?"

Before Morris could answer, his cellphone rang. It was Felger. He put the call on speaker.

"I was able to get ahold of a sister of one of the guys on the list," Felger said. "Her name's Lila Farnsworth, and she lives in New Jersey. Her brother is Jason Dorsage. He was one of them that I wasn't able to find any photos from the Internet. You're going to want to hear what she has to say."

A woman's voice came on then. "Hello? Is there someone I'm supposed to be talking to about Jason?"

"Yes, Ms. Farnsworth, my name is Morris Brick. Did my associate Adam Felger tell you what this is about?"

"You think Jason might be killing those actresses in Los Angeles."

"Is that a possibility?"

"I don't know. I haven't seen my brother in years, and I was never close to him. I don't know what he's capable of doing."

"Were you shown the police sketches?"

"Your associate texted them over. It could be him but I can't tell you for sure. I've never seen him with his head shaved, and he's not blond. His hair is dark brown, and he always kept it long and shaggy when he was home."

"Home being New Jersey?"

"Yes, we grew up in Short Hills. I still live there. My brother moved to California after college. He wouldn't have gone to college except Dad made it one of the conditions for him to get his trust fund."

"How much was it?"

"I don't know exactly, but I'm guessing it was the same as mine and Barb's. Fifteen million dollars."

"Barb? A sister? Would she have kept in touch with Jason?"

"No. She had less to do with him than I did. And I had as little to do with him as possible."

"How about your parents?"

"My dad died five years ago, and by the way, Jason didn't go to the funeral, not that I expected him to. If my mom has anything to do with him, I couldn't tell you. My parents divorced when we were kids, and she sold her house in Short Hills and moved permanently to Europe when I was in college. I couldn't even tell you if she's still alive."

"Did you know whether Jason was ever interested in something called a Rube Goldberg machine?"

She let out a short, disgusted laugh. "He was doing that stuff back in high school, and took over our basement with it. Vivian was not happy."

"Vivian?"

"My dad's second wife. And don't ask whether she could be in touch with Jason. They barely tolerated each other. But about those stupid thingamajigs, Jason wanted to skip college and make his life's work building them. I remember him getting into a fight with my dad over it, and the idiot bet his trust fund that he could make a hundred thousand dollars a year doing it. Either through dumb luck or some sort of scam I haven't figured out, he managed to do that. I think the day my dad signed over the trust fund was the last day he ever saw or heard from my brother. Not a big loss, if you ask me."

"Do you have any pictures of Jason? We've been having trouble finding one."

"I'm sorry, I can't help you there. I don't know where you could get one. Maybe from his high school or college yearbooks?"

"Where'd he go to school?"

"All of us went to Avery Academy here in Short Hills for high school. I couldn't tell you where he went to college. That was how much interest I had in him."

"Anything else you can think of that might help?"

"There is something. As far as I could tell he only had two friends throughout high school, both of them geeky losers. One of them was arrested for stabbing to death another kid who was supposedly bullying him. The other got run over by a train a few weeks later, and the story that came out later was he got drunk and passed out on the tracks. This happened when I was a junior, so Jason would've been a freshman. It always seemed a little peculiar to me, but if anyone ever suspected Jason of being involved, nobody ever did anything about it. Does that help you at all?"

"A good deal, actually. If you think of anything else, please call."

Bogle was studying Felger's list. He told Morris that Jason Dorsage had a Long Beach address.

Morris had been driving back roads to get to a Compton address. He reversed course so he could get onto the 405 South heading to Long Beach.

"She might've checked off a few of the boxes in the profile, but she didn't give us anything concrete to prove he's our guy," Bogle said.

"No, she didn't."

"There's certainly no love lost between them, that's for sure. It could also be some wishful thinking on her part. Who knows? She might get a piece of his trust fund if he goes to prison for committing a felony."

"It's possible," Morris admitted.

"But you like him for this."

"I'll reserve judgment until I see what he looks like."

"Let's see if I can speed that up."

Bogle called Vernon Howard. The Long Beach detective answered after the fourth ring, his voice more gravelly than the deep base Bogle had heard recently.

"Charlie? Good to hear from you, man. I'm barbecuing up some sausage and steaks later this afternoon. Always room for one more."

"I'd like to, but no rest for the weary."

"You're working, huh? Is this about Karl Crawford?"

"Yes and no. It's related, I think, but it's much bigger. You'd be doing me a huge favor if you could have one of your Long Beach officers take a photo of a local resident and text it to me at this number. The guy might be dangerous, so probably a good idea to send two officers to see him. And if he looks enough like the police sketches we've put out for the psycho killing those actresses, it wouldn't be a bad idea to hold him."

"You think he could be *that* guy?"

"A chance. Maybe only a small one. So for God's sake don't have them go in with guns blazing."

Howard's voice took on a more formal tone as he asked how SPMK was mixed in with Crawford's disappearance.

"It's complicated. Let me tell you next week. I should have it pieced together by then. I'll text you the guy's name and address."

Howard sounded peeved about not being given more information, but he didn't push it, and promised he'd get Long Beach officers on it right away. After Bogle got off the phone, he texted Howard the information he promised.

For several minutes they drove in silence, broken only by the sporadic thumping of Morris's fingers against the steering wheel.

"We might as well wait until we see the photo before getting anyone else involved," Bogle suggested. "If he looks enough like the killer, Long Beach PD will take him into custody."

"Or they'll be walking into a trap."

"We don't know he's our guy," Bogle argued.

Morris's drumming stopped, and a resolve hardened his flinty gray eyes. He called Doug Gilman. The mayor's deputy assistant sounded harried.

"Tell me you have good news," Gilman said.

"We've got a lead. I should know soon if it's SPMK."

"Jesus, I hope so. Morris, this is a nightmare. We've found four more bombs. Right now we're trying to get the governor to deploy the National Guard so we can search these oil wells faster, while at the same time working on an evacuation plan in case they start blowing up. And on top of that, we're trying to secure the air fields."

"I don't think he's planning to trigger the bombs with a small plane."

"No? Then how?"

"The same way he was going to trigger those machine guns."

"With a toy car?"

"No, but the same idea. With one or more drones that have been preprogrammed with GPS coordinates. If you get the National Guard involved, it wouldn't be a bad idea to have sharpshooters posted to shoot down any drone. The question then would be the reach of the transmitter he's using to activate the bombs."

"Ah hell," Gilman said.

"Yeah, I know," Morris agreed.

Chapter 64

Morris and Bogle were fifteen minutes outside of Long Beach when Bogle got a call back from Vernon Howard. Bogle put it on speaker.

"Sorry to disappoint you. I sent a squad car over to the address you gave me but the guy's not home," Howard said.

"Are they sure?"

"As much as they could be. No one answered, no car in the driveway, and neighbors haven't seen him in days. They showed the sketches around and none of the neighbors were willing to say he's SPMK. But none of them were willing to say he's definitely not. Something strange. I asked to have his license photo from the DMV database, and it's not there. He's got a license, but his photo's missing."

"He must've paid someone to remove it."

"Could be. Should we be putting out an APB on this guy?"

"All we have right now is a hunch and a missing DMV photo. It would've helped if a neighbor could've identified him as SPMK."

"Yeah, it would've. Keep me posted."

Bogle put his phone away and asked Morris what he wanted to do.

"I brought a lock pick along," Morris said. "We'll see what we can find inside of Dorsage's residence. For all we know he might be passed out and in an OxyContin stupor."

"I was hoping you'd say that," Bogle said.

Less than a minute later Morris got a call from Adam Felger. "I found the connection," Felger said.

Confused, Morris asked what he was talking about.

"The reason SPMK left Todd Blankenford's body at MBI. The clue he wanted to leave you. It turns out *The Satan Plan* was filmed right outside of Long Beach at a movie studio that was shuttered twelve years ago. Five years ago the property was bought by Kinetic Productions. It took some digging, and I had to unravel three different shell companies, but any guesses who owns it?"

Morris gave him the obvious answer. "Jason Dorsage."

"Yep. I'll text over the address."

"Text it to Charlie's phone."

"Will do."

Bogle received the text and after some fiddling with his cell phone he told Morris they were two minutes away if he took the next left. Morris floored the gas and took the illegal left turn going eighty and ignoring the horn blasts from the angry drivers he cut off. While this was going on, Bogle tried calling Police Commissioner Martin Hadley, got no answer, and next called Vernon Howard.

"We got something solid," he told Howard. As he explained what they had, Morris pulled over so he could collect a chunk of concrete from the side of the road. Bogle didn't need to ask what the concrete was for, but did suggest they wait for Long Beach PD.

"It's going to take them time to mobilize and get here," Morris said. "We both know this maniac has no plans on waiting until four. As soon as he's ready he's going to be unleashing his drones, or whatever he's planning to use to trigger those bombs. Besides, as private citizens we can do things the police can't."

"We're still being deputized by the mayor's office."

Morris dug his cell phone out of his pocket as he fought the wheel to keep the car from fishtailing. He handed it to Bogle.

"Text a note of resignation to Doug Gilman effective immediately."

Bogle did this, then pulled his pistol from a shoulder harness so he could check that the magazine was loaded and there was a bullet in the chamber. They both saw the sign for Kinetic Productions. The building was on a private drive and sat parallel to the road. While there was no gate, there was a surveillance camera.

"He's going to know we're coming," Bogle pointed out.

"Only if he's watching the monitor. I'm betting he's too busy right now getting things ready."

Morris drove down the private drive and pulled into a parking lot. He angled the car so it was facing the building's entrance and came to a stop when he was a hundred yards from it. "Front or back?" he asked Bogle.

"Back." Bogle glanced at the odometer. "A hundred and eighteen thousand miles. You were going to be needing a new car soon anyway."

"I guess." Morris breathed in deeply and let it out in a loud exhale. "Any chance I could be wrong about this?"

"None. How are you going to keep the steering wheel from moving?"

"I've got a steering wheel lock in the trunk."

They left the car and moved to the back of it. Morris opened the trunk, handed Bogle the lock and the key for it, and then took out the golf clubs he'd bought five months ago. He took lessons then, and was still shanking most of his drives, but was determined after the Malibu Butcher business to take up a hobby that was healthier than chasing serial killers. With the golf clubs out, all he had left in the trunk were jumper cables and a locked gun box. He dialed the lock combination, opened the box, and took out a .40 caliber pistol. He slid out the magazine, checked it, and then checked the two other magazines he kept in the box. He decided twenty-four rounds would be enough.

Bogle had locked the steering wheel in place, and joined Morris by the back of the car. He asked whether he could borrow one of the clubs. "I wouldn't put it past this guy to have trip wires back there," he said.

Morris nodded to take one, and Bogle selected a three wood, and then moved in a fast jog toward the right side of the building.

Morris jammed the concrete slab in place so that it forced the gas pedal to the floor. There was a chance he was wrong about the killer using some of the stolen C-4 to booby-trap the building's entrance, but even if he was, this would still be the fastest way inside.

His cell phone rang. Doug Gilman calling about the resignation text. Morris turned his phone off. He positioned himself so he'd be able to jump out once the car started moving, then shifted from Park to Drive, and rolled out of the car as it sped forward. He landed on his back and was getting onto his knees when the car hit the entrance and an explosion blew open the front of the building and sent the car flying eight feet into the air.

He'd been right about the C-4. The hole blown through the building was engulfed in black smoke, and Morris raced toward it with his gun held up to his right shoulder.

The hundred-yard sprint took a toll on his forty-seven-year-old knees, but adrenaline pushed him, and he ignored the stitch in his side. He narrowed his eyes to a sliver and held his breath as he made his way around the twisted frame of his car and through the thick black smoke and the opening where the front entrance had been.

He dove to the floor and rolled, ending on his stomach with his gun stretched out in front of him.

The maniac wasn't there. Instead there was some sort of complex contraption. A Rube Goldberg machine. He heard a rumbling noise to his right and looked to see a bowling ball rolling down a track. The ball hit a bowling pin, which started a chain reaction of more pins being hit before releasing a spring and sending a knife slicing through a trip wire. This released another spring, causing the pin to be pulled from a hand grenade and the grenade to be sent hurtling through the air toward where Morris was lying.

He scrambled to his feet and dove away from the grenade. It exploded and Morris felt something hot and metallic biting into his lower leg. He didn't look at his wound; instead he turned toward all the new sounds he heard. More objects were being toppled, more balls rolling down tracks, more trip wires and springs being released. The contraption had eight different tentacles, each having its own independent chain of events. Something caused Morris to glance upward, and that was when he saw the lattice of grenades waiting to rain death.

One of these tentacles was going to release the grenades. Morris searched for the mechanism that would cause the pins to be pulled and the grenades dropped. He spotted it, and followed it back until he saw which tentacle would trigger it, and then he started firing at the race car track that was in the middle of it. He hit it with the third shot, breaking up the track into several pieces and stopping the grenades from dropping on him. He emptied his gun as he fired at more of the tentacles, destroying three of them. Within seconds the other tentacles finished harmlessly without tossing any more grenades or deadly objects at him.

Morris looked up again toward the ceiling, and saw that one of the tentacles would've opened a panel in the roof if he hadn't destroyed it. A man who must've been Dorsage was moving frog-like on a catwalk directly underneath the panel. Morris couldn't see what he was picking up, but he knew what it had to be. A drone. If Morris hadn't shot up the Rube Goldberg machine it would've been released to blow up the oil wells.

As he struggled to his feet, he pulled out the empty magazine and slid in a replacement. Dorsage was already running away. Morris fired at him, but struck the catwalk instead, and Dorsage disappeared from view.

Morris tried to run after him, but the wound in his leg slowed him to a hobble. He saw Dorsage racing down a back staircase and carrying what had to be a drone. It was bigger than the commercial ones he'd seen in stores.

Morris was seventy feet from the back door. He slowed to a halt, raised his pistol, held his breath, and aimed. When Dorsage stepped into view, he fired, but some sort of sixth sense caused Dorsage to duck, and the bullet instead struck the glass door. Dorsage was quickly outside with the drone, moving in a severely bowlegged, but surprisingly quick, gait. Morris fired two more shots as he tried to hit Dorsage through the door, but the killer was already out of sight.

Morris gritted his teeth as he chased after him, trying his damnedest to ignore the hot, screaming pain burning through his leg. As he pushed his way through the back door, he first saw Dorsage thirty yards away busying himself with the drone, and then he spotted Charlie Bogle lying in a crumpled heap.

A rush of anguish and outrage filled him. He raised his gun and aimed it at Dorsage as he hobbled toward the killer.

The drone started to make a whirring noise, its propellers spinning.

"Turn that off and lay on the pavement," Morris ordered, his voice catching in his throat and coming out as a raspy croak.

Dorsage looked toward Morris at first as if he didn't recognize him, then his face twisted into something violent and hateful.

"If you shoot me, I'll be letting go of this! You know what will happen then. People will die and it will be your fault!"

Morris continued hobbling toward the killer, his gun aiming dead center at him. He was close enough that he was sure he'd hit Dorsage, but he needed to get closer before he'd be confident about hitting the drone, because that was what he planned to shoot.

Dorsage seemed to sense what he had in mind. His expression shifted to one of intense fury, and as he held the drone with his right hand, he reached behind his back with his left and pulled out a gun that he must've had wedged in his pants. He was swinging this around when Morris shot him in the left eye. Dorsage fell backwards, the drone releasing from his grip. Morris fired at the drone until his gun clicked empty, but it zipped away from him faster than he would've expected. He thought he heard one of the bullets ping off of it, but if he hit the drone, he didn't bring it down.

He moved over to Dorsage and saw that his bullet had torn out the man's eye. Skull fragments and gore littered the pavement, showing that the bullet must've exited the back of the killer's head. He was dead.

Morris heard sirens approaching from several miles away. The Long Beach PD. Bogle remained crumpled on the pavement. A heaviness welling up his throat nearly left Morris choking as he made his way over to him and kneeled by Bogle's body. He'd been shot in the chest, but he was still breathing. Morris pulled out the empty clip, slid in his last one, and fired into the air to alert the approaching police where he was. He could see several police cruisers racing down Kinetic Productions' private drive.

Chapter 65

Charlie Bogle lay in the hospital bed with a thick bandage wrapped around his chest. His skin had an unhealthy grayish pallor, and his face appeared craggier and older than it should've given that he was only forty-five. When his eyes cracked open, it seemed to take a long time before he recognized Morris.

"How long have I been out?" he asked, his voice weak and raspy.

Morris put a straw to Bogle's lips so he could sip some water.

"Eighteen hours. You've been up before, but you were too drugged to realize what was going on."

"Yeah? So I'm going to live?"

"It appears that way. At least that's what the doctors keep saying. I do have some bad news. I didn't know this before but you've got B-negative blood, and there was only one of us at MBI with the same blood type."

Bogle's face turned craggier with the news. "Polk," he said.

"Yep. You've now got three pints of Polk's blood coursing through your veins."

"Lord help me." Bogle's eyes took on a faraway look. "He must've shot me from a window. I never saw the bastard. What happened to him?"

"Dead."

"That's good. So you stopped him."

"Mostly. His plan was to release two drones. That didn't happen, but he still got one of them in the air. Three oil wells blew up."

"No kidding?"

"It could've been a lot worse. The drone was pretty high tech and was powered by both a hydro fuel cell and solar. It could've been flying around for hours. The crime tech guys were able to figure out its flight plan from programmed GPS coordinates, and it would've blown up at least twenty-two wells except four of them were already cleared of bombs, and when I shot at it I damaged its fuel cell enough to send it crashing after passing seven of the wells. As it was, LA felt tremors from the wells that blew up. I heard they measured a 3.1 earthquake."

"What do you know? It would've worked. Maybe Jenny will give me a break," Bogle said.

"She should. So far they've found forty-six bombs. Charlie, we did good."

"We paid a price. I doubt I'll play the saxophone again, and you lost your car."

"Do you even know how to play the sax?"

"No, but now I never will."

"Don't be too sure. I talked with your doctors. They're saying you'll be making a full recovery. One of your ribs took most of the brunt and punctured a lung, but it also redirected the bullet from doing any major damage."

What Morris had said was true, but he was also sugarcoating it. Bogle had lost a tremendous amount of blood and there was a good deal of internal patchwork that needed to be done, and it was touch and go for the first twelve hours. Bogle seemed to sense Morris was sugarcoating it, and his expression showed that he was dubious. He gave Morris a sideways glance, and his face folded into a grimace. "Ah, jeeze, I just noticed you're in a wheelchair."

"I took a piece of shrapnel in the leg. It's a scratch compared to what happened to you, and I'd be walking around now except I need a second surgery to repair some tendon damage. That's why they put me in this chair." Morris chuckled. "Nat thinks my suit's ruined and I'll have to buy a new one. The poor woman will be once again disappointed when Marv does his magic."

"How's Natalie taking this?"

Morris became subdued. "You know. She's tough, and she's trying to be strong for my sake, but it still hit her hard. I've been seeing the cracks when her guard's down. If you know what I mean."

Bogle knew exactly what he meant.

"You're a lucky man, Morris."

Morris agreed. There was little doubt about that.

Chapter 66

Los Angeles, one month later

There was no more magic.

At least that was what Marv claimed. The suit damaged by the shrapnel was beyond repair. While Morris would've liked to replace it with a suit off the discount rack, he wasn't going to deprive Natalie of something she'd been dreaming about for years, namely picking out a new suit for him. And so he didn't complain when she took him to the ritzy men's clothing store on Rodeo Drive that Doug Gilman recommended, nor utter as much as a peep when she had him try on eleven different suits before deciding on the one she wanted for him. He also kept quiet when he saw the suit's price tag. He likewise didn't say anything when she picked out eight dress shirts and four new ties, nor when he saw the final bill.

They had brought Parker along. They didn't have much choice in the matter. The bull terrier had taken it hard when he saw that Morris had been injured, and he acted as if it was his fault for not being there to protect him. Since then the dog had insisted on staying close by. Even when he tried on the suits, the dog camped right outside the dressing room and nothing would've budged him.

Up until a week ago, Morris had been using crutches, but he was now able to get around with a cane. As they were leaving the store with their purchases, he commented that Natalie looked quite pleased with herself.

"You bet I am," Natalie said. "I've been wanting to do this for years." Her smile dimmed and worry creased her forehead. "I just hope the alterations can be done in time. You're not wearing one of your old threadbare suits to the ceremony!"

That Saturday the mayor was going to be awarding the entire MBI team, including Parker, distinguished service awards. Morris agreed only on the condition that Commissioner Hadley be the one to put Parker's medal around the bull terrier's thick neck. He later heard from Annie Walsh that Hadley threw a conniption fit when he found out, but that the mayor insisted he do as he was told.

"Marv promised me he'll have it ready by Friday night, and Marv's word is gold."

As they walked, Parker made sure to keep his thick body between the two of them. Morris glanced over at his wife as she carried the bundles from the clothing store, and he was again stunned at just how beautiful she was.

"I hate to tell you this but you're not going to get another chance to replace my other two suits," he said. "This time I'm done with serial killers, no matter what they do to try to drag me in. MBI's only taking corporate cases from this point on."

"Don't say that."

Morris was surprised by her reaction. "What do you mean?"

"You can't fight it if another one of these cases comes along that you need to take," she said. "You're too good at what you do. If you didn't stop that madman, thousands might have died."

"Nat, Charlie almost died."

The truth was, he'd almost died too, but Natalie didn't know that. Another second, and he would've lost his chance to disrupt Dorsage's final Rube Goldberg machine, and live grenades would've been falling all around him.

"He didn't, though." A wetness showed around her eyes, and her voice choked a bit as she said, "And maybe Rachel might have if all those oil wells exploded."

Morris didn't mention that although Bogle didn't die, something had changed with his investigator and friend. He was gaunter in the face, and a half step slower, but there was something else. A gloom had settled over Charlie Bogle and it seemed like a shadow now darkened his features. But it had only been a month. Maybe that would all pass.

Morris was holding Parker's leash in his right hand but that didn't stop him from reaching over to Natalie. She was holding packages in both hands, but they still managed to lock pinky fingers as they walked to Morris's new car, a Lexus sedan. Natalie had picked it out and the city of Los Angeles picked up the bill, although they expected to recoup the money from Dorsage's estate.

Epilogue

Parker had behaved himself until Hadley tried slipping the medal around the dog's neck. That was when the bull terrier bared his fangs and growled.

The ceremony was being well-covered by local and national media, so Hadley attempted to show he was a good sport by joking that the dog's reaction was because of his aftershave, *eau de salami*. After three more attempts, each ending with bared fangs and growling, the police commissioner lost whatever semblance of good humor he was attempting to project. His jowly face grew chalky white and he growled in a low enough voice for only Morris to hear that he better control his dog.

"Martin, relax. He's only smiling."

"I mean it, Brick. There will be serious consequences if he bites me!"

Morris had had his fun. He held out his hand for Hadley to hand him the medal, and he slipped it around Parker's neck, and in exchange got back an excited grunt from the bull terrier and a lick on the nose.

A few minutes later as the mayor presented medals to each member of the MBI team, Morris caught a look exchanged between Rachel and Doug Gilman, answering the question about who his daughter was dating. He kept this knowledge to himself, not mentioning it to Natalie during the cocktail reception that followed the ceremony. When he had the opportunity, he pulled the mayor's deputy assistant aside.

"You're looking really sharp in the new suit," Gilman remarked, a big grin on his face.

Morris ignored the compliment, and instead asked him if Rachel told him about how he had starred for his high school baseball team. Gilman's grin disappeared and his cheeks reddened.

"Morris, I wanted to tell you I was seeing Rachel, but she insisted we keep it quiet."

"I understand. My daughter's stubborn like you wouldn't believe. She gets that from me, except more so. But I have a reason for mentioning my baseball days. I was good with the glove thanks to my low center of gravity. Nothing got past me. But I was even better with the bat. My pop used to like to say I could hit the ball a mile. My senior year I hit two home runs in the state championship to help us win the title. Yeah, I could always hit the ball hard."

Morris held out his cane as if it were a baseball bat. His eyes grew wistful, but he shook himself out of the past and used the cane again to support himself.

Sighing, he said, "My pop was disappointed that I quit the game. My coach and others thought I had a chance to play pro ball, but my pop was a police detective, and I always had it in my head I'd be one also. So I majored in behavioral science in college with the expectation I'd join the force after graduating. That's how I met Nat. I was a senior when she was a freshman."

"Rachel didn't tell me any of this."

Morris said, "There's no reason she should've. But I have my reason. I kept the bat I used in the state championship game. I thought if I had a son I'd teach him how to play ball with it, and pass it along to him. But when we had Rachel, I found another use for the bat. I showed it to every boy she dated in high school, and I promised them I'd break their legs if they ever did anything to hurt or disrespect my little girl. I meant it, too. I stopped doing this when she got into college. Rachel's a tough cookie, as you know, and she'd be furious with me if she caught me doing that again. Still I wish I had warned the last guy she dated, because if I had, I would've used the bat on him regardless of the consequences."

Gilman met Morris's gaze. "I really like Rachel," he said. "Morris, you've got nothing to worry about."

"Good." Morris clapped Gilman on the shoulder. "Let's grab some cocktail shrimp before Polk finishes them off."

**Don't miss the next page-turning
Morris Brick thriller by Jacob Stone**

CRUEL

Coming soon from Lyrical Underground, an imprint of Kensington
Publishing Corp.

Keep reading to enjoy a sample excerpt . . .

CRUEL by Jacob Stone

Prologue

Downtown Los Angeles alley, 2:18 a.m.

The rat grew frantic in its efforts to escape the trap, its front claws a blur as they scratched against the wire mesh. This one was older than the juveniles already collected, and showed the scars of a lifetime spent skulking through Los Angeles alleyways and sewers. Half of one ear had been torn off, its grayish-black fur was matted, and a dozen wounds had scabbed over. While the rat was larger than the others, it was still emaciated enough to be able to squeeze through a hole the size of a quarter. Rats like this one were crucial for what was coming.

The newspaper stories from 2001 didn't mention rats; neither did the ones from 1984. That had to be because the reporters weren't told about them, or really about any of the specifics. In 1984 the newspaper and TV reporters described the murders only as depraved and sickening. A police officer must have given them that description, and someone with a touch of poetry in his soul gave the killer the name the Nightmare Man. That name stuck—both in 1984 and in 2001—but the name didn't fully do the killer justice. While horrific, monstrous things were done to the victims, they were things that could have only come from the nightmares of a lunatic.

Just as a variety of cicadas awaken every seventeen years, so did the Nightmare Man. October 2nd would mark the seventeen-year anniversary of the start of the last killing spree, and new victims had already been chosen. They were both the least and most fortunate people alive. They would be dying the worst deaths imaginable, but they would also have a kind of immortality, their fates forever entwined with that of the Nightmare Man. Because of that, they would never be forgotten.

The cage was picked up. The rat inside backed up and got on its hind legs, its small black eyes shining with malevolence as it bared its teeth. It was certainly an ugly thing, and would do nicely for what was needed.

A homeless woman lay curled in a fetal position as she slept next to a Dumpster. She stirred as the cage holding the rat was carried past her. Her blood-rimmed eyes cracked open, her round, craggy face turning toward the soft padding of footsteps. In a raspy croak that sounded as if her throat had been scraped raw with sandpaper, she asked for money.

Even from several feet away, the sour smell of cheap gin on her breath assaulted the senses.

A decision now had to be made: whether to kill the old woman or ignore her. A moment of reflection revealed a third option—simply hand the homeless woman a twenty-dollar bill, and that was what was done. The woman mumbled something unintelligible as she accepted the money. She turned away as she hid the bill within one of her layers of clothing, and then she presumably fell back to sleep.

That was how it needed to be. It wasn't time yet for the Nightmare Man to awaken from his slumber. October 2nd was still a full ten days away. That was when the killing would start again. Besides, snuffing out the life of this old woman wasn't necessary. Her alcohol-addled mind wouldn't later connect this late night intrusion of her makeshift home with the Nightmare Man's return.

But the Nightmare Man was coming.

And Los Angeles would soon be weeping tears of blood.

Chapter 1

Morris Brick had not been to Luzana's before, and for good reason. The restaurant on North Cahuenga Boulevard had a reputation for putting a serious dent in their customers' wallets, but even if that wasn't the case, there was little chance he would've been able to get a table there. Luzana's had become Los Angeles's most exclusive hotspot. A place for Hollywood royalty, sports celebrities, and the ultra-rich to be seen and noticed. Morris might've become a minor celebrity after years of catching depraved serial killers, but that still wouldn't have bought him a table reservation at Luzana's, and so it only mildly surprised him when the maître d'hôtel gave him the snootiest look he had ever seen. He was genuinely surprised, however, after the man peered over his stand to see that the pig-like grunt came from Parker, Morris's all-white bull terrier, that he made a shooing gesture with both hands. That was just plain rude!

Morris arched an eyebrow and, keeping his voice amicable, asked, "Am I supposed to guess that means you have no available tables? At twenty past two on a Tuesday?"

If it were possible, the maître d'hôtel would've climbed onto a step ladder so he could look further down his nose at Morris. "Apparently," he mumbled under his breath.

Morris stood his ground and lazily rubbed his jaw. If he were the vindictive type, he could've called in a favor at the mayor's office and had the place shut down for a kitchen violation—imagined or real, it didn't matter. After all, six months ago he and his team at Morris Brick Investigations, commonly known as MBI, very likely saved the lives of hundreds of thousands of fellow Angelenos, and at a heavy cost. Charlie Bogle almost died after being shot in the chest, and hadn't been the same since, even quitting MBI two months ago. Morris himself took shrapnel to the leg from a booby trap, and it was only since last month that he was able to put away his cane. But as tempted as he was to drag the maître d'hôtel out from behind the stand and teach him some manners, he maintained a calm demeanor and told him he was meeting a friend at the restaurant. "Philip Stonehedge. He's already been seated," he said.

The maître d'hôtel gave him an incredulous look. Stonehedge was high up on Hollywood's A-list, and not only that, he was dating the gorgeous Brie Evans, who sat near the top of the list. But since there was a remote chance Morris was telling the truth, he asked for Morris's name and made a phone call, keeping his voice low so Morris couldn't eavesdrop. Shortly afterward a waiter came bustling out of the main dining room and whispered something to the maître d'hôtel, whose attitude quickly changed toward Morris.

It was almost like a magic wand had been waved—in less time than it took to snap one's fingers, his contempt transformed to full-blown obsequiousness. He bowed and asked Morris to follow him, and as he led them through the crowded dining room filled with Hollywood royalty and other studio muckety-mucks and to the bustling outdoor patio, Morris resisted the urge to plant a kick onto the man's well-padded derriere.

Parker had been behaving himself, but he suddenly grunted excitedly and lurched forward as he strained against his leash. The bull terrier must've spotted Stonehedge, who was grinning at them as he watched from his table, the thick, jagged scar running down his cheek giving his grin a sardonic quality. The actor had gotten the scar from being slashed with a gun barrel. This happened after he had arranged with the mayor's office to tag along with Morris on the Skull Cracker Killer investigation, although it wasn't SCK who did the slashing but a vicious criminal by the name of Alex Malfi who didn't appreciate the actor trying to interfere with a Beverly Hills jewelry store robbery. Malfi further showed his displeasure toward Stonehedge by shooting him in the thigh, and the actor would have died if it wasn't for Morris's later heroics.

Stonehedge left the table to tussle with Parker, then shook Morris's hand, and reached over to bring him in for a hug. The maître d'hôtel stood off to the side until Stonehedge slipped him a fifty. Morris and Parker joined Stonehedge at the table, which already had several platters of food waiting for them. When the bull terrier grunted impatiently, the actor fed him a piece of meat from one of the platters.

"Wood-grilled lamb tenderloin wrapped in jamón ibérico," the actor said, beaming. "Absolutely delicious."

Morris knew enough Spanish to guess that jamón ibérico was a kind of expensive imported ham. Given the way Parker wolfed it down and grunted for more, the dog must've concurred with Stonehedge's assessment.

"Don't give him too much," Morris said. "He needs to lose a few pounds."

Stonehedge laughed at that. "Don't we all?" he asked.

That was certainly true for Morris. He needed to drop ten pounds from his waistline, but for someone who enjoyed gourmet food as much as Stonehedge, his friend somehow stayed as lean as a marathon runner. Before he could object, Stonehedge fed Parker another piece of lamb. Morris snared a piece for himself, and had to agree it was exceptional.

A waitress came over to take his drink order. Stonehedge had a bottle of champagne already at the table. When Morris tried ordering a beer, his friend stopped him.

"You're not seeing me off with a beer," he insisted. Then to the waitress, "My buddy will have a *le daiquiri*."

Before Morris could say anything, the waitress was rushing away from the table. "*Le daiquiri* as opposed to a daiquiri?" he asked.

"It's the *le* that makes it so special," the actor said with a straight face. "When you taste it, you'll be glad I changed your order. If not, you can always have her bring you a beer. Besides, this is the last chance I'll have in four months to be so obnoxious with you."

"At least you admit it."

Stonehedge lifted his champagne glass, his eyes narrowing as he gazed at the slightly rose-colored bubbly. "I'm painfully self-aware of my indulgences and faults." He took a sip of his drink, and turned again to Morris, his lips showing a pensive smile. "I'm glad you were able to make it. And I'm glad you were able to bring the little guy also."

"He never would've forgiven me if he knew I'd lost him a mooching opportunity at Luzana's."

As if on command, Parker let out an impatient grunt. Stonehedge fed the dog what looked like a blackened piece of meat from another platter. "Truffle-encrusted Wagyu beef," he said. "It's even better than the lamb."

Morris whistled Parker over and ordered the bull terrier to lie down. The dog grudgingly did as he was commanded, but not without letting out a few unhappy grunts.

"I'm not sure I'll be able to get him to eat his dog food after this," Morris complained.

"Eh, if you put it in front of him, he'll eat it."

That was mostly true. Parker rarely ever walked away from his dog dish when there was still food in it. He was also a champion moocher, and Morris himself had proven over the years to be a soft touch, but he was trying to change his ways since Parker's last visit to the veterinarian. That was three weeks ago, and the veterinarian confirmed what Natalie had been telling him: that Parker needed to lose weight or it could cause health problems later on.

Morris asked, "When are you leaving?"

Stonehedge took another sip of his champagne. "Flying out of LAX at eight this evening, and with losing eight hours I won't be arriving in Dublin until two tomorrow. Then a two-hour drive to Galway." His expression grew wistful. "My last decent food until then."

"This time you're making a romantic comedy?"

Stonehedge had taken what looked like a fancy slider from one of the platters and was munching on that. He waited until he swallowed his food before nodding. "You've got to try one of these, Morris. They're amazing. But yeah, that's right. *Stumbling in the Rain*. Not the best title for a rom-com, but the script's good, and my co-star is the lovely Claire Rose. The film will be a nice change of pace from the thrillers I've been making of late."

Morris took Stonehedge's advice and tried one of the sliders, and it was every bit as good as his friend had claimed. The filling was a thick slab of bacon coated with a sweet bean garlic glaze. He didn't have the heart to deprive Parker of bacon that delicious, and he scraped the garlic glaze off and fed the rest of the slider to his dog. Tomorrow would be another day to get back onto Parker's diet—and his own, for that matter.

Stonehedge watched with an amused grin, but held back any comment as their waitress had returned with *le daiquiri*. Morris took a sip and had to admit it was better than any beer he could've ordered.

"A shame Brie isn't co-starring with you," Morris said.

Stonehedge made a face at that idea. "They wanted her, but Brie's tied up for the next two months. Probably better that we're not acting together. Competition's not the best thing for actors in a relationship. But we'll be seeing each other. Next week she's flying to Munich for a promotional event, and I'll hop over for a visit and take advantage of the beginning of Oktoberfest. But enough about that. How about yourself? Any interesting cases?"

"Mostly run-of-the-mill insurance fraud work." Morris grabbed another piece of wood-grilled lamb and fed it to a grateful Parker. "The most interesting of which was a stolen coin collection I closed last week. The collection was appraised six months ago at one point two million and was supposedly stolen three months later in a home burglary. It turned out that the owner had sold off the collection to several private buyers, and then staged the burglary. What he really bought for himself was a grand larceny charge."

"You're right. Sounds pretty run-of-the-mill."

"You can say what you're really thinking. Boring."

"Well, yeah, compared to hunting serial killers."

"After that psycho Jason Dorsage, I'm fine with boring."

"You say that now, but just wait until you're chasing after your next serial killer. Knowing my luck, it will be when I'm in Ireland, and I'll miss all the fun. And—" The actor abruptly stopped talking and snapped his fingers to get Morris's attention. "Hello? Are you still there? Damn, Morris, you faded on me, like you went away somewhere deep in your head."

"What?" A glint showed in Morris's eyes as they shifted to meet Stonehedge's, a hard grimace tightening his lips into a thin line. "Just a random thought. Nothing worth mentioning."

Stonehedge had been right, and Morris was lying now. It was more than just a random thought that had distracted him. In fact, he was so distracted that he had fed Parker another piece of lamb without realizing he had done so. The bull terrier certainly didn't mind this absentminded lapse.

He hadn't thought about the Nightmare Man murders in years, but something caused a disturbing fact about those killings to resurface in his mind. Maybe it was because of what Stonehedge had been talking about, or maybe something else was responsible. Whatever it was, it occurred to him that October 2nd would be the seventeen-year anniversary of when the last killings started.

The Nightmare Man was never caught. When the first set of killings happened thirty-four years ago, there was a witness who had described the killer as a man in his late forties. Even if the Nightmare Man was still alive, he'd be close to eighty now, if not older than that.

Still, Morris couldn't help feeling a sense of dread knowing what might be coming in only a week.

Acknowledgments

I would first like to thank my editor, Michaela Hamilton, as this book, as well as my Morris Brick thriller series, wouldn't exist without her.

In advance, I'd like to thank the Kensington team who'll be supporting this book and doing their magic to make it shine: Lauren Jernigan, Michelle Forde, and Alexandra Nicolajsen.

A big thanks also to my college buddy Alan Luedeking, who, as with all my books, muddled through my initial draft and helped smooth out the language. Also, my longtime friend (since second grade) Jeff Michaels for also providing feedback.

I owe a special thanks to the great cartoonist Rube Goldberg, whose clever inventions helped inspire *Malicious*. I'd also like to apologize to the producers and writers of *Breaking Bad* on behalf of my bad guy from *Malicious*, Jason Dorsage, for appropriating their nifty "machine gun in a trunk" gadget from their "Felina" episode. What can I say? Dorsage is a world-class jerk!

As always, I'd like to thank Judy, my wife and best friend, for her encouragement and support, and for also helping to make my manuscript more readable.

ABOUT THE AUTHOR

Photo by Judy Zeltserman

Jacob Stone is the pseudonym for Dave Zeltserman, an award-winning author of crime, mystery, and horror fiction. His crime novels *Small Crimes* and *Pariah* were both named by the *Washington Post* as best books of the year, with *Small Crimes* also topping National Public Radio's list of best crime and mystery novels of 2008.

His horror novel, *The Caretaker of the Lorne Field*, was short listed by the American Library Association for best horror novel of 2010, a Black Quill nominee for best dark genre book, and a Library Journal horror gem.

His Frankenstein retelling *Monster* was named by *Booklist* as one of the 10 best horror novels of the year, and by WBUR as one of the best novels of the year.

His mystery fiction is regularly published by *Ellery Queen Mystery Magazine*, has won Shamus and Derringer awards, and twice has won the Ellery Queen's Readers Choice award.

Dave's novels have been translated to German, French, Italian, Dutch, Lithuanian, and Thai. His novel *Small Crimes* has been made into a film starring Nikolaj Coster-Waldau, Molly Parker, Gary Cole, Robert Forster, and Jacki Weaver, and can be seen on Netflix. His novels *Outsourced* and *The Caretaker of Lorne Field* are currently in development.

Printed in the United States
by Baker & Taylor Publisher Services